MOVE THE STARS

JESSICA HAWKINS

© 2017 JESSICA HAWKINS
www.JESSICAHAWKINS.net

Editing by Elizabeth London Editing
Advanced Beta by Underline This Editing &
Becca Mysoor of Evident Ink
Proofreading by Tamara Mataya Editing
Cover Design © R.B.A. Designs
Cover Photo by Perrywinkle Photography
Cover Models: Chase Williams &
Miranda McWhorter

MOVE THE STARS

ISBN: 0998815527
ISBN-13: 978-0998815527

TITLES BY
JESSICA HAWKINS
LEARN MORE AT JESSICAHAWKINS.NET

SLIP OF THE TONGUE
THE FIRST TASTE
YOURS TO BARE

SOMETHING IN THE WAY SERIES
SOMETHING IN THE WAY
SOMEBODY ELSE'S SKY
MOVE THE STARS
LAKE + MANNING

THE CITYSCAPE SERIES
COME UNDONE
COME ALIVE
COME TOGETHER

EXPLICITLY YOURS SERIES
POSSESSION
DOMINATION
PROVOCATION
OBSESSION

PART 1

1

LAKE, 1999

By New York standards, there was nothing all that strange about my outfit. This city had no shortage of strange. It might've been the fashion capital of the world, but pairing Corbin's extra-large gray sweats with a party clutch wasn't worth a second glance. The cab driver didn't care about my sloppy bun or muddy sheepskin boots. He'd surely witnessed enough cab rides of shame to assume that at eleven in the morning, that was what this was.

"You can let me out here," I told him, pointing to a corner so he wouldn't go around the block. I gathered my handbag and stilettos, then passed over the cash Corbin had insisted on giving me. As I exited, my boot caught under the seat, and I nearly stumbled face first into the snow. Apparently, along with a not-so-fresh-off-the-runway look, I was also sporting a hangover from last night's holiday party.

It was early December and fucking freezing, but at the same time, the city's first snow of the season blanketed everything with pure white. Flurries had started the night before and hadn't stopped yet, which was why Corbin had suggested I not do my usual walk home. Even though the snowflakes were light and airy, almost nothing, the sidewalks had become fluffy. I stomped through the slush toward my building, unconcerned that it wetted the edges of the UGG boots my mom had sent last Christmas.

Strung lights adorned the East Village shops. Their windows displayed black and gold party dresses, velvet platforms so high they'd put the Spice Girls to shame, and vintage fur coats. I caught sight of my reflection and almost laughed at the gray-on-gray explosion of sweats and UGGs. I'd looped my hair on top of my head, and a few escaped pieces hung around my face. Mascara darkened my under-eyes, but I didn't care. Not even a little. I looked like shit and held my chin high.

Who did I have to impress anyway? Even if I were to encounter the future love of my life today, I wasn't ready for him. I wouldn't be for a while. I'd had over four years to mourn losing Manning, and it seemed I needed more, because I didn't even feel close to ready for anyone else.

The flakes fell a little heavier, like someone had shaken up a snow globe in my little corner. When I saw a very tall dark-haired man across the street, my heart squeezed in my chest. I was used to that, seeing Manning in the crowds of Union Square or leaning on orange traffic cones to peer into a manhole or paging through the *Times* on a park bench.

Through the snowy haze, this man bore an uncanny resemblance to Manning—except for a tailored coat, dress shoes, and suit and tie. Definitely not Manning. Yet he stared at me the way Manning did. Tightened my stomach the way only Manning could. And as I got closer, it was Manning's molten brown eyes that stopped me dead in my snow-soaked boots.

I hadn't seen him in over four years, but of course I'd know him anywhere. Impossible as it was, Manning stood across the street, watching me.

People passed between us, but we might as well have been alone in the city. Everything else fell away. He looked both ways and stepped off the curb. The sleet would ruin his nice shoes. It was all I could think, such a little thing in such a big moment.

One of my strappy, black stilettos slid out of my hand. By the time I'd picked it up and brushed off the ice, he was there, standing in front of my apartment building—and me.

His eyes traveled from the tangled mess on top of my head, down my oversized sweats, to my boots, and back up. It wasn't my finest moment.

"Lake," he said.

My name from his mouth took me back four years and four months. *One word* had the power to reverse all the work I'd done since the night I'd left California. The countless mornings I'd had to force myself out of bed when I'd wanted to cry myself back to sleep. All the times Val had dragged me out to meet people when I would've preferred to be alone with my pain. Four years' worth of holidays I'd spent without my family. *One word* turned me from an independent college graduate, making her own way, to a stupidly naïve eighteen-year-old girl witnessing the love of her life's wedding to another woman.

I had to swallow before I could speak, my throat dry from shock and the wintry day. "What are you doing here?"

He squinted over my head, toward the fifth floor, directly at my window. "Technically, I'm here for work."

"Work?" I glanced at his tie. "What work?"

"It's been months since anyone's heard from you." He sounded strangled as well. Maybe his knot was too tight. "Years since we've seen you."

"That's on purpose," I said. My heartrate kicked up, leaving me flustered. All the emotions of the night of the wedding rushed over me. My world shattering as Manning had said "I do." My eyes leaking while Val and Corbin hid me in their arms. My shame when wedding guests had rubbed my back, commenting on how sweet it was that I was so emotional over my sister's big day. *Inconsolable* was the word they'd been

4

looking for. *Embarrassed* would've worked, too. I'd had to deliver a maid of honor speech, a passage I'd plagiarized from *Chicken Soup for the Soul*, the only way I could manage wishing my sister and her new husband "all the happiness in the world."

"I didn't say you could come here," I said. What gave him the right to ruin what had been a perfectly good morning? To stir memories I'd fought hard to bury? My jaw ached; I'd been clenching my teeth. "You can't just show up like this."

"I've been worried, Lake."

Worried. *He* was worried. Good. I hoped it kept him up at night, his worrying. That he replayed over and over in his head my silent sobs as I'd stood by the altar and kept my mouth shut.

Manning and I stared at each other, the sky gray, snowflakes falling between us. Val would say it was the perfect setting to film a New York romance.

Manning shifted on his feet, loosening his tie a little. He looked so very out of place, and so uncomfortable. Different. But with his eyes on mine, we were us again, an unlikely pair—the Young Girl smitten with the Worst Possible Man.

He glanced up at the building again and then down the street. I knew what he was going to say before he even opened his mouth. A layer of pretty white innocence couldn't hide the trash lining the curb, graffitied steel doors, or the sleeping homeless man bundled in a storefront.

"This neighborhood isn't safe," he said.

The old me might've blushed at his concern or teased him for his overprotectiveness, but I'd changed that night I'd lost him for good. This neighborhood was all I could afford, but aside from a couple break-ins on the block and a mugging one street over, I'd never personally had a problem. In fact, Frank, the man in the sleeping bag, acted as a sort of lookout for us. I brought him coffee, food, and warm clothes on occasion. But Manning hadn't earned the right for me to put him at ease. I'd suffered, and I wanted the same for him. I lifted a shoulder. "It's not exactly Park Avenue, I admit, but that's not your concern."

"If your dad knew—"

"Stop." I refused to go down that path. Seeing Manning again was enough to reopen wounds for who knew how long. I didn't need him to remind me my dad couldn't be bothered to look out for me anymore. "I can take care of myself, as you can see."

Manning put his hands in his pockets and broke our gaze to look at my seemingly fascinating fifth-floor window. How he knew it was mine, I wasn't sure. "You just . . . disappeared," he said with what sounded like a mix of pain and confusion, maybe even wonder. Well, four years was a long time to wonder. I'd left before he'd even returned from his honeymoon. It'd been the only way forward. I couldn't live in the same state as them a moment longer, much less see them together one last time.

"I had to."

"But why New York?" He scanned the area, shaking his head. "Why *this* city, with the highest crime rate in the nation, with its pushy people and cold, ugly skyscrapers?"

That was Manning's problem. He couldn't recognize beauty where it wasn't obvious. He didn't feel the energy that propelled this city. He'd turned down real love because others would judge it. He refused to accept what he deserved unless it was bad. "Actually, crime has fallen off significantly since Mayor Giuliani took office. You don't know anything about this city or me so maybe you should . . ." *Go.* I needed to say it. I owed it to myself to kick him to the curb. How many times had I imagined seeing him again? Envisioned him falling to his knees, as broken as I was, telling me he'd made a mistake? It was the only thing I wanted to hear, and for that reason, I didn't trust myself.

"I *do* know about this city," he said, his eyes drifting back to mine. "This avenue in particular is known for drugs and prostitution."

Taken aback that Manning had even heard of my tiny corner of the East Village, my guard dropped a little. "How do you know that?"

"Because I looked it up. Does that surprise you?" He ran a hand through his neat hair, his forehead wrinkling. "I've tried to picture you here," he said. "I can't. Not knowing where you live, how you are—it makes me . . ."

I looked away. He didn't have to finish. Had I known when I'd made the decision years ago that leaving suddenly would frustrate Manning? Of course I had. At USC, he could place me. Imagine me doing all the things everyone wanted for me. When he wasn't keeping tabs on me through my parents, he would've seen me on a semi-regular basis. Los Angeles wasn't much of a step beyond Orange County—which was how he'd wanted it. And I relished that I'd been able to take that away from him.

"It makes you what?" I prompted, knowing he wouldn't finish his sentence. If Manning couldn't tell me what I'd wanted to hear back then, he certainly wouldn't now that he was a married man. "Are you *happy* I left?" I asked. "Does having me gone bring *joy* to your life?"

His nostrils flared as I provoked him. "You know it drives me fucking insane, Lake."

My breath caught. Manning didn't swear in front of me, not ever. It was exactly what I wanted to hear—that after all these years, I was still making him crazy—but his confession brought neither relief nor satisfaction. The truth was, it scared me that I wanted him to suffer, because it meant I wanted him to care. I'd come too far to let him unravel me. He was too much, his black hair trimmed, jaw smooth, face bronzed even though the suit made it seem as though he didn't work in the sun anymore. I couldn't tell if he was slightly leaner or slightly taller, but he was as handsome as ever.

I shouldn't have been thinking any of that about him, the man who'd broken my heart—my sister's husband. "Well, you've seen me." I stuck my shoes under my arm to get the key from my purse. "So, bye."

I turned and let myself into my building, trying not to let him see how I fumbled with the lock. Once inside, I let the door shut behind me and hurried up the stairs. I lived on the fifth floor of a pre-war walk-up with intricately carved banisters and crown moldings. Even with Manning's eye for architecture, I knew all he'd see were the dusty corners, sagging doorjambs, and loose steps. My boots pounded the old, creaky wood. It didn't matter how many times I'd made this hike, I was still out of breath by the time I reached my floor. The effort shook me and my confidence. I leaned my forehead against the door of my apartment as Manning grew bigger in my mind. For years, I'd imagined how it would feel to see him again, and now that I had, I realized I hadn't gotten a single thing I'd wanted out of it. No apology, no begging or pleading. It was already over. Not even ten minutes. How could I want to give him any more of my time? He'd had more than he deserved already.

Lost in my thoughts, I didn't hear the footsteps until they reached the landing of my apartment. With a deep inhale to steel myself, I looked back at Manning. I should've known a locked door wouldn't stop him from coming up here. I should've known when it came to me and my safety, he'd push until he got what he wanted. Back then, I'd thought I'd known how to stand up to him. I'd begged him on a breezy beach one night not to marry her. I'd told him I'd wanted him in the truck, no matter the cost. I'd asked him to choose me. He'd always done what he'd wanted, though.

Manning wasn't out of breath, just a little stuffy in his suit.

"You look like you have somewhere to be," I said.

"I came from a breakfast meeting."

"At eleven on a Sunday?" I jammed my key in the lock, jiggled until it gave, and lifted the door by its handle to get it to open.

"Is it broken?" he asked.

"No, just old."

"It's broken. Get the landlord to replace it."

"It's *not* broken," I said, closing the door on him too hard. My heart raced, desperate for a little more time. A few more words, a few more moments to get to know the man in the hall who looked a bit older, a bit more tired, and still everything I dreamed of on a regular basis. I forced myself to lock the door and step away so I wouldn't change my mind. He had no right. None. I shouldn't have even given him the last few minutes.

The handle turned, and with a loud snap, the door creaked opened. Manning filled the doorway. "See?" he said. "Broken."

I frowned. "Well, now it is."

We stared at each other, the air between us growing thick. Manning took over the shadowed hallway of my tiny apartment. If I wanted to leave, I'd have to go through him. Touch him. Smell him. Let the foreign wool of his expensive-looking suit scrape against me as I squeezed by him. I recognized the warmth pooling in his chocolate eyes. He looked me over, too, but the restraint he usually had wasn't there. "It's freezing in here," he said. "Don't you have a heater?"

"It's a crapshoot. Sometimes the radiator works, other times it doesn't."

"I can fix that," he said.

Fix it, I thought. *Fix me. Tape my paper heart back together.* My resolve cracked a little. Letting him in didn't mean I forgave him. Maybe spending time with me would remind him of what he'd given up and of all the pain I'd hopefully stuck him with when he'd returned from his honeymoon to find me almost three thousand miles gone.

"Do you have tools?" he asked.

I was used to the cold. I had blankets and sweatshirts and earmuffs and mittens but the truth was, nothing kept out the chill like the radiator. I moved back a few steps, an invitation. "In the closet."

While Manning jimmied the front door shut, I put my heels and purse in my room. As I stepped out, he came down the gray hall toward me, his shoes echoing on the hardwood floors. I didn't stop him. I didn't say a thing as he removed his coat and folded it over the back of a brown leather loveseat Corbin had found and carried upstairs for Val and me.

Manning took it all in, though there wasn't much to see—a bedroom, bathroom, and a kitchenette separated by a breakfast counter. Pictures of Val, Corbin and me with our friends hung on the fridge next to take-out menus under magnets. His eyes landed on the disheveled futon in the living room. "That's Val's," I said. "She's my roommate."

"Your mom mentioned."

With Corbin and I both on the east coast, my best friend Val had lasted one semester in California by herself before she'd transferred to New York Film Academy. This city suited her best of the three of us—she fit with New York the way I did with Newport Beach. Or used to, anyway. Val had loads of friends, events to attend, and an on-again, off-again boyfriend who gave her nothing but grief. Currently, they were on again, which meant she was at his place most of the time, leaving me the apartment's tiny bedroom.

Manning walked over to the laminate coffee table that held pink bottles of Victoria's Secret lotion and perfume, loose change, and paycheck stubs. On the floor underneath, Val had stacked *Vogue* magazines and videotapes hand-labeled "Buffy" and "Empire Records." None of our furniture matched, but Val and I had gotten every piece on our own, and that was important to me. I knew Manning wouldn't see it that way, though. His eyes stopped on a lighter and half-smoked joint forgotten on the folding table where we sometimes ate.

His examination slid under the surface of things, the way it always had with me, reading not just my body language but my most intimate thoughts. Taking in not just the mess around us, but the details of my seemingly little life.

"What is this?" he asked about all of it and nothing in particular.

"You told me to soar." I opened my arms to indicate the things around me. "That's what I'm doing."

Since the gray day darkened the room, he reached up to switch on an overhead lamp and my eyes went right to the spot his wedding ring should've been. The realization that he wasn't wearing it caught me off guard and I looked away quickly, hoping he wouldn't see that I'd noticed.

His eyebrows met in the middle of his forehead. "It's a fucking dump, Lake."

Even though I knew he'd say it, my face heated. "At least it's *my* dump." The phone rang, piercing the stillness of the room. I ignored it. "I didn't run to Daddy for help. I didn't latch onto the first man who came my way."

"Is that what you think your sister did?"

"Go to hell." How fucking *dare* he bring her into this apartment? This was my home. My dump. My shitty city. I loved it here because it was mine, not theirs. Trying to hide the way I shook, I went to the

13

phone, picked it up, and slammed it back down to stop the ringing.

"Lake—"

"I don't need your pity," I said, turning back to him.

"I wasn't going to give it to you." He rubbed the back of his neck. "I was just going to ask which closet the tools are in."

"Forget the heater," I said. "We can fix it ourselves."

"Then why haven't you?"

Because I *couldn't* do it myself, and Corbin wasn't all that great with handiwork, and the landlord did nothing for us unless Val distracted him into agreeing to help. That usually involved her pulling down her top until her boobs were nearly out.

"Tell me where the tools are for my sake," Manning said. "I spent all of yesterday in airports and on planes, and I need to do something with my hands."

The thought of him doing anything with his enormous bear hands made my stomach tighten, but so what? He had some nerve coming in here like this, telling me what he needed. "Don't fix my heater. Don't check on me. Just go."

"I'm not here to check on you."

"Yes you are. You want me to be exactly what I was, the way you used to know me. Well, I'm not, but I've got all my fingers and toes." I held up my palms. "So what more do you want?"

His chest rose and fell as we stared at each other, his ears reddening. Seeing the way I still got under his skin gave me great pleasure.

"There's nothing for you here," I continued. "You wanted me to move on, so I did, and I no longer need you. You can't have it both ways."

"You *didn't* need me," he said through his teeth. "That was the whole point. Or so I thought." The apartment was so small, he only had to turn around to see into my bedroom. "You had the world at your fingertips." He stared at my unmade bed a few moments too long. "You were supposed to go to USC and excel, meet someone worthy of you, lead a fulfilling life, but this? This is—"

"This is *my life*," I said, my throat thickening. Fuck, who was I kidding? He was the one getting under *my* skin. Fifteen minutes alone with him and this was what he did to me. I was losing my cool. "What makes you think I'm not fulfilled? What makes you think I haven't met someone worthy?"

Working his jaw back and forth, he muttered something.

"What?" I demanded.

"You didn't spend the night here."

"Obviously not. As if that's any of your b—"

"Where were you?" he asked.

"You know where."

"I won't believe it unless—"

"Corbin's. I was with Corbin."

15

The air in the room thinned. Manning had spent so much time hiding his emotions from me that it was unsettling to watch pain cross his face. He looked as though he didn't quite believe what he was hearing, even though my mom must've mentioned Corbin some time over the past few years.

"Whose sweats do you think I'm wearing?" I asked. It wouldn't help anything, but I wanted to inflict the same brand of pain on him that he had on me.

He curled his hands into two fists, as if he was physically holding words inside—the warnings he obviously wanted to give me, the demands he had no right to make. I took satisfaction in his obvious jealousy. "I didn't know it would turn out this way, Lake. Your life, and mine, nothing is how I thought it would be."

Surprised by the rawness in his voice and his confession, my confidence wavered. He wasn't holding back like he normally did, and that was new territory for us. Four years apart had changed me— had it changed him, too? I had to turn away so he wouldn't see my weakness. If he was trying to say he'd made a mistake, I didn't trust how I might respond to that. For all the times I'd fantasized about hearing it, I realized now that it wouldn't matter. I couldn't just forgive him. It wouldn't erase anything. Nothing could be done with an apology. So it was all better left unsaid. "I have somewhere to be, and I'm sure you do, too, so let's leave it at that. You can show yourself out."

The bathroom was five steps forward, and each one away from him was more difficult to take than the last—but it had to be done. Inside, I wrenched the handle to latch the door so it wouldn't swing open. I leaned my hands on the sink and looked at my sloppy hair. Mascara clumped on my lashes, jet-black like a bottomless hole. The hollow of my neck quivered with my pulse. I didn't want him to leave. Not ever. I wanted nothing more than to go to him. To ask him to stay. Sometimes, late at night, I could smell the briny, sawdust sweat I'd come to love on the construction site. I'd convince myself it was on my pillow, as if Manning and I had recently made love. It was one of many demented fantasies I'd had since moving here. Did Manning have a single clue how alone I'd felt since the day I'd met him and couldn't touch him? Did he understand the agony of knowing I'd never call him mine?

He'd never realize how badly he'd hurt me when he'd walked down the aisle with Tiffany. I couldn't move past that betrayal. I couldn't pretend he hadn't chosen her over me.

I took my hair down and brushed it out, then got makeup remover from a shelf behind the mirror. As I erased a night of good times with friends that had now been tarnished by Manning's presence, I heard the *click* of a door outside the bathroom. I paused, concentrating on the rusty ring around the sink drain. I couldn't go after him. I couldn't . . .

It was true that I'd thought of him every day, wished to see him just once, even from afar, wished for a phone call to tell me it'd all been an elaborate nightmare, wished for *him*. Now that he'd come, I'd sent him away. Any way I sliced it, it hurt.

I couldn't let him stay after what he'd done, and I couldn't bear to see him go, so I stayed right where I was, listening to the deafening silence of an empty apartment.

2
LAKE

In my bathroom, a space I could barely do the splits in, the aftershocks of Manning's visit reverberated through me. I was sixteen again, so giddy I was sick to my stomach, unsure of anything but my reaction to him. How could so many years of progress evaporate in under half an hour?

I finished fixing myself up. Corbin and I had breakfast plans, and I'd only come home from his place to change. I was supposed to be at the restaurant already.

I opened the bathroom door to throw on some jeans, but when I stepped out, I nearly tripped over a body. Manning was splayed on his back, a wrench in his hand as he worked under the radiator. "Hall closet," he muttered. "I found the tools."

The floor was as clean as it could get—I'd vacuumed and mopped the day before, all six-hundred square feet of it—but he was still on the ground of a New York City apartment. "You'll get dirty." Why did I care? I didn't. I shouldn't. "Why are you wearing that anyway?"

"What? A suit?" His eyebrows cinched together as he either tightened or loosened something, I couldn't tell. He flicked his tongue over his lower lip. "I work for your dad now, out of the Costa Mesa office, selling pharmaceuticals."

I let the information sink in. I hadn't spoken to my father since I'd told him I wasn't going to USC and he'd exploded with enough force to shift tectonic plates. It was a wonder he hadn't caused the state of California an earthquake. Mom rarely mentioned Manning to me, but then again, that would've been hard to do in conversations that didn't even last ten minutes. Tiffany had called me more in the beginning, but we were always interrupted before things could get too deep. I made sure of that. I'd assumed Manning was still doing some form of construction for my dad. Instead, he was pushing drugs at doctors' offices on behalf of Ainsley-Bushner, a company my father had worked his way to the top of. "You're . . . a salesman?"

"Pretty much." His muscles strained his dress shirt as he worked. "You didn't know?"

"No." A tiny bit of my resentment fizzled. The job was all wrong for him. Manning needed to build things, if not literally, then in the sense that he was creating something to improve lives. He'd wanted to be a cop to help others, but since he could no longer do that with a record, I would've thought he'd have stayed in construction or tried some kind of social work. Even I could admit that despite how Manning had hurt me, his intentions had been good. Maybe I wasn't the only one who'd suffered the past few years.

"Why?" I asked. "That suit . . . it's . . . I hate it."

"Yeah?" he asked. "Doesn't *Corbin* wear one?"

"How do you know that?"

"Your mom." I rarely talked to my mom about Corbin, and because of that, she seemed to have fabricated some vision of our lives here. Or maybe it was Corbin who'd exaggerated things to his parents. He was always trying to convince me to visit home, to call or write, as if it was his duty. Our dads worked together, and although I doubted my father gave much thought to me or Corbin, it occurred to me that Manning might know Mr. Swenson from the office. "You work with Corbin's dad," I said.

"Yeah, but I don't see him much."

"Do you see my dad a lot?"

"Some days of the week. And Sundays for dinner."

So they still had family dinner. Why shouldn't they, just because I wasn't there? "Oh."

"He misses you," Manning added.

Instinctively, I tensed, but I tried to calm my voice before answering. "He said that?"

"No, but I can tell."

Of course Dad hadn't said that. If he missed me, he had a funny way of showing it. He'd never once reached out. He'd probably removed all traces of me from the house. I assumed he'd taken down anything that reminded him of USC and turned my room into a gym or entertainment room or something.

"Do they know you're here?" I asked. By *they*, I really meant Tiffany, but I didn't want to talk about her at all.

"In New York?" Metal clinked against metal. "Yes."

"You know that's not what I mean."

I waited while he continued to do whatever the hell he was doing. His silence said everything. Tiffany didn't know he'd come to my apartment. He wasn't supposed to be here. Neither was I for that matter— now I was *really* late for breakfast—but I had so many more questions for Manning. Why had he come? What would he tell them when he got home? How long was he in town for? Asking meant I cared, and Manning already held enough power over me. I couldn't go back to that time in my life, when I thought I'd never move past him. When I'd spent what should've been my first semester of college trying to pick up the pieces of my life. The times Val had held me on the couch in the middle of the day, *Ricki Lake* in the background, a box of Kleenex clutched in her hand. She'd since banned any mention of Manning's name in this apartment. If she were to walk in and find him here, she'd dropkick him all the way back to California, which was probably what I should've done by now.

"Your mom knows I'm seeing you," he said finally. "But she's the only one. She wanted me to take you to a show."

"A show?" I asked.

"Broadway."

Oh, how I loved my theater. It was a safe topic for conversation and one of the only things my mom knew about my life here—I went to the theater whenever I got the chance. Sometimes that meant skipping a few meals or letting Corbin spend money on me even though I hated to let him. For musicals and bright, flashing lights and once-in-a-lifetime performances, I tended to let my excitement get the best of me.

Not now, though. I made myself stand there not asking which show, waiting for him to finish.

Eventually Manning got up and brushed off his slacks. My eyes rose with him. "The whole unit really needs to be replaced," he said as he fixed his tie in the reflection of the window.

"It's fine," I said. "I'll tell the super." We'd told him plenty of times that our heat was broken, but I needed Manning to leave or I'd revert back to one of two people—the child I was before the wedding, or the shell of myself I'd been right afterward.

"What else—" He turned and stopped as his eyes landed on my hair, which was no longer pulled back.

Aside from a trim and some highlights, I hadn't changed it much since I'd left, even though Val always threatened to shave it off while I was sleeping to get me to shed my beachy image. I blushed a little as Manning followed the length of it, down to my breasts. "I . . ."

I had to tilt my head back to see him. It reminded me of all the times I'd looked up at him, hoping for any sign that he'd noticed me, salivating for breadcrumbs, convincing myself our secret glances and touches meant something. I wasn't that girl anymore, but in only half an hour, that was what he'd turned me into.

He cleared his throat, blinking back up to my face. "What else around here needs repairing?"

"Nothing. Just leave it, Manning. Please."

He flinched as I said his name, then reached behind me to check the lock to the bathroom—which was also busted. "I guess the question is, what *isn't* broken?" he said.

A flush worked its way up my chest. My apartment wasn't much, but it was mine. I'd flown across the country, despite a fear of airplanes, all by myself. I hadn't even had Corbin to hold my hand since he'd returned to New York ahead of me. I'd done everything on my own—gotten jobs, apartments, student loans, and I'd enrolled in NYU with nothing but a couple hundred dollars I'd saved from a part-time summer job back home. I'd become a pro at keeping plants and goldfish alive and sometimes Val, too. "I'm sorry things aren't up to your standards," I said, letting the sarcasm drip.

"*My* standards?" he asked. "This place isn't fit for the mice it definitely has. This neighborhood—no, this *city* isn't you."

"You might find it hard to believe, but I like my life. I'm free now. Nobody tells me how to live. Nobody puts me in a box. I drink, I smoke, I-I have s—" I stopped as his knuckles whitened around the wrench. As much as I wanted to rub sex in his face, I couldn't bring myself to say it. "I'm not the golden child here, and my friends don't expect me to be. Corbin doesn't put me on a fucking pedestal and expect me to stay there to keep him happy."

"That's not fair," Manning said. "All I ever wanted was to see you happy, to see you become everything you were supposed to, even if it meant shutting off my own wants . . . and needs."

"Oh, right," I said wryly, stepping back and nearly stumbling over Val's rollerblades. I kicked them away with the heel of my boot. "*Safe, cared for, happy.* You wanted me to stay the sixteen-year-old girl you knew. You wanted me to go on living the life you thought was right—to stay close to my family. To be the prodigal child and live a sunny life in sunny California, and *huh*, that worked out well for you, didn't it?"

He stared hard at me. "This isn't what was supposed to happen." He ran his hand over his face.

"I didn't . . . the choices I made . . . I never thought you'd end up worse off, that you'd leave home—"

"That isn't my home. It hasn't been for a long time. You made sure of that. You chose her, and you took that life away from me."

"I didn't *choose* her."

"Then you chose yourself," I said, my voice rising. "Either way, you didn't choose me. You've lost any right to care or have an opinion. So don't come in here and judge my life and say I'm worse off. How dare you talk about *wants* and *needs* when you went to someone else to satisfy them."

He set the tool on my windowsill, his movements measured, his response slow, as if he were picking his words carefully. "My wants and needs were taken care of but never *satisfied*."

"And what about mine?" I shot back. "I needed *you*, Manning. I felt like nothing and nobody without you."

The radiator groaned, shuddering to life suddenly before it shut down. Manning also seemed to kick on, his face reddening as the muscles in his jaw ticked. "Does it make me happy to see you living like this? No." He looked around the room for what must've been the tenth time, as if committing all the details to memory. Only now his brown eyes were full of something I couldn't quite place. Pain? Regret? "I worried all the time, and apparently, I was right to."

"It could've all been different. I would've done anything you'd asked." I swallowed the lump in my throat in the silence that followed. "I would've stayed at USC and waited for you and *loved you*. It might've cost me my family, but look around. I lost them anyway. They don't feel like home anymore. I don't have a home. All I have is what you see here. Why did you do it?" I asked. "Why didn't you stop it?"

"You know why," he said.

"No I don't. You kept telling me it was for the best. That it was to protect me from you. But when you married her, you shattered my world." I gestured around at my things. The textbooks I'd worked overtime to afford, which sat on the bottom shelf of an IKEA bookcase I'd built myself. In the sink were wineglasses that'd seen many parties with friends I'd made when I'd just wanted to live under the covers and give up on people altogether. "These are the pieces, and they might not look like much to you, but they're all I have. I've found a way to be happy. You can't come back into my life and tell me it's a mess when you're the one who created it."

"I knew it would hurt you," he said, his posture sagging, "but I thought you'd pick up and move on and experience everything I would've held you back from."

"I did. This *is* everything," I said, shrugging with as much nonchalance as I could muster. "Look around. This is what you wanted for me."

He pursed his lips. "You have to know I never thought you'd leave. That everything I do is because I . . . because—"

"Because *what*?" I got in his face. "If you still can't say it after all these years, then get the fuck out of my life. You treated me like glass, but I'm made of more, Manning. You missed out." My downstairs neighbor's dogs barked, as if cheering me on. "You really missed out."

"I know that." He took a step and ducked to avoid hitting the ceiling lamp, the wood floor creaking under his massive frame. "Why do you think I'm here?"

I hesitated, caught off guard by the question and his nearness. "For work."

"Wrong." He towered over me. The intensity in his eyes bordered on heat, the kind I'd seen before, the kind I'd tried—and failed—to convince myself I'd imagined. "Work was an excuse to get to New York."

No part of me thought Manning would come to New York and not check on me—but was he saying he'd come *just* for me?

I struggled for a deep breath I couldn't seem to get. I'd pushed Manning many times over the years, but only that night on the beach had he ever let his emotions get the best of him. If I asked, would he really tell me what I'd wanted to hear back then? I'd figured out what I was made of over the years, but my heart hadn't turned to stone. Could I even handle it? "You have a wife," I said. "Go home to her, and don't ever come back."

"That's what you want?" he asked.

My heart raced from being close to him again, all my instincts telling me to flee. "Actually, part of me wants you to stay . . . so I can call Corbin and give him the pleasure of kicking your ass."

He winced. "Don't say his name to me."

"Corbin, Corbin, Corbin. You must be thrilled such a *worthy* man was my first kiss, my first love, my first . . ." I chickened out. "Do you get off on it, Manning? Do you fantasize about pushing me right into his arms, about all the ways he touches me, kisses me?"

As Manning's eyes darkened, the room seemed to as well. He took up enough space to make it feel as if the apartment's walls were closing in. "You act like I wanted this for myself," he said. "I wanted it for *you*, but you don't have to rub it in my face—"

"Why not? You forced *me* to stand there and watch *you* with *her*." I pushed past him and started gathering up the assortment of tools, tossing them back in their cardboard box. I grabbed his blazer and coat from the loveseat and held them out to him. "Here."

With his eyes on mine, he came toward me. In what felt like slow motion, he took his things, but I didn't let go. He splayed his hand, and his fingertips accidentally brushed mine—except that he didn't pull away.

Maybe it wasn't an accident.

Goosebumps traveled up my arm. "What are you doing?" I asked.

"I'm leaving, like you told me to."

It wasn't what I'd meant. *Why are you touching me*, I wanted to ask, but I was scared if I acknowledged it, I'd be unable to resist touching him back. "Where will you go?" I asked.

"I don't know." He paused. "My hotel. For now."

I held on—to his things, to his warm presence in the cold room, to the love rising inside me. He was standing in front of me again, as I'd often hoped for, but I didn't know if I was allowed to want him here.

He tried to take his coat again. I clung to it. My chin wobbled. It wasn't fair that she got him, that I had to kick him out when I wanted to get closer to him. After a few tense seconds of tug-of-war, he pulled the coat hard enough to bring me with it. "Lake." The warmth of his presence turned to undeniable body heat. "You don't really want me to go."

"You can't tell me what I want," I said, my voice hitching as I stared up at him. "You can't tell me what to do. I'm not sixteen anymore."

"No, you're not, are you?"

I froze, caught off guard by the way his voice noticeably deepened.

His pulse quickened at the base of his neck. "All the ugliness I tried to spare you was for nothing. You're not safe. You're not loved, not the way you should be. Your family is gone. You're not soaring."

"I am, though." It was a pathetic protest, but it was true. It'd taken me a long time to get to this place, and things were finally going well. A few days earlier, I'd graduated quietly with Corbin and Val and some other friends in the audience. They'd taken me out to an expensive dinner and we'd brought home cheap champagne. "I'm starting my career. I've got good friends, an apartment, and most importantly, a life of my own. I'm happy, Manning."

We were face to face now, just the coat between us. He frowned. "Then tell me there's not one thing in the world that can make you happier," he said, "and I'll go. Tell me you are truly content with all this. With *him*."

I needed to lie. I needed Manning to go and stay gone if I had any chance of making it through this life. There was no point in dragging everything back into the light. What could it serve, except to break me again?

I couldn't lie, though. Not to him. "I'm as happy as I'm capable of being," I said.

"That's not good enough."

"It's all I can do. It's what you left me with. Maybe one day down the line, ten years, twenty, I can be truly happy, but without you . . . I don't think . . ." His expensive shoes touched the tips of my ragged boots. We were closer than we'd been in more time than I could measure. My heart pounded in rhythm with an ache between my legs I hadn't been sure I'd ever feel again. No part of my body wanted him to go.

Now, I could read the emotions in his soda-pop brown eyes—regret, pain, anguish. But under it all, I recognized something else that turned my legs weak. The day Manning had been released from jail and I'd stumbled into the foyer in front of him, the heat in his eyes, the hunger, had haunted me. I hadn't understood it then, but I did now.

He'd wanted to fuck me. Badly.

He'd been locked up a year and a half and seeing me had inspired some kind of carnal reaction in him. It was *the* fantasy, the one that got me off like no other. Imagining he'd put me over his shoulder and carried me right out of that house, past my dad, past Tiffany. He'd take me in the backseat of Tiffany's car because he couldn't make it longer than that. I'd masturbated over and over to that, and to the night I'd found him at his kitchen sink in nothing but his boxer-briefs. That rawness in his face, his terrifying grip on my wrists, the way he'd pinned me to the counter with his hips—it was the stuff my dark fantasies were made of.

My heart raced, lust and memories coursing through me. I moved into him a little, and his hand tightened around the fabric. A horn blared outside, and as if startled, Manning bent his head, coffee and toothpaste on his breath, and lessened the great height disparity between us.

There was so much unsaid. So much that *needed* to be said. Whatever was happening had to be stopped, but only heat existed between us at that moment, unleashed after years of being bridled.

Manning tossed his coat out of the way, scanning my face. When he touched the hem of my sweatshirt, I flinched. He lifted it slowly. Underneath was the little black dress I'd worn out to the bar the night before, bunched around my hips. He ran his hand up the cheap satin, stopping under my breasts. With that one touch, my nipples roused, my skin pebbled, my hairs stood on end.

I was putty in his hands, but I didn't want to be. I didn't know if I could have him, so I didn't want to look at him, much less feel his hands on me. "Why are you here, Manning?"

"I never stopped thinking about you, not for a day. I needed to come here and see with my own eyes if you were better off without me."

I shivered. And if I wasn't better off? Then what? The answer scared me more than his thumb pressing into my rib, setting free a kaleidoscope of butterflies inside me.

"I'm here because you . . . this . . ." His voice lowered and scraped from his throat as he slipped his other hand under my sweatshirt to take my waist. "It keeps me up at night. It makes me insane. And some days I think I'd kill for it."

With the word *kill*, my insides pulled deep. This was it, the carnal side of him I'd seen glimpses of. My focus wavered with his hands on me, but I only just remembered what a mess I was, wearing a dress I'd partied and slept in. I hadn't shaven my legs in days. "Manning . . ."

His hands moved slowly, hidden by the sweatshirt as they explored me. "Want me to stop?" he asked.

Like that night on his kitchen counter, I still couldn't believe Manning was just touching me. I wanted it, but I was older now. Smarter. I knew how dangerous his hands were. "I . . ."

"Just say the word. Say *stop*."

I breathed hard. I quivered. I thought about the times I'd felt him hard against me and hadn't been able to do anything about it.

I didn't tell him to stop.

He cradled both sides of my ribcage, moving his hands upward until I was forced to raise my arms. When he pulled off my sweatshirt, one of my thin dress straps fell over my shoulder. He touched my hair, drawing the long strands through his loose fist and over his palm. He still hadn't kissed me. It'd been over six years since the day we'd met, and he *still* hadn't kissed me. What was he waiting for? He looked anywhere but into my eyes, clearing my hair from my neck, running a thumb along the hollow of my collarbone. He pulled down my other strap and wet his lips, undressing me the same torturous way he'd dismantled my heart, piece by piece, slow and painful. It felt simultaneously natural and unnatural.

I'd spent years telling myself, being told, this wasn't allowed. I gripped his dress shirt. "I *hate* this suit."

"Why?"

Was Manning really here? It had to be him. The man in front of me bore a small scar on his upper lip and the faintest crook to his nose, evidence of his time in prison. But now he looked like he belonged on the front page of the *Wall Street Journal.* "It's not you. It's not the man I knew."

"What if it's who I am now?"

Maybe it'd be better that way. He was different, and so was I, and if anyone needed to be different people in order to continue down this path, it was us. I didn't want polished Manning, though. I wanted his roughness, the man who'd been to hell and back, who had callused hands to match his hardened heart. "It's not you, I know it isn't, please, Manning . . . just—"

He put his arms around me, hovering his lips above mine. "Just what, Lake?"

Take it off. Kiss me. Love me. Choose me.

I couldn't do this. I'd asked him for all of this before, and he'd denied me. It would destroy me to have him and lose him again. My heart raced as much out of fear as desire. "Stop."

He tightened his hold on me, but then, he did as I asked. Manning let me go. "You're right."

My nipples, hardly sheathed by my little dress, hardened with the loss of his heat. I hugged myself. Knowing I was right didn't ease the hurt. "It's better this way," I said quietly.

Without looking at me, he shook his head. "It isn't. I know that now. But I can't expect you to let me in just like that."

"Let you in?" If Manning was here to do more than check on me, he had to know what that meant. He and I could never just be alone in a room. We could never touch and kiss and then walk away unscathed. "You need to go before I make a huge mistake."

"My being here is not a mistake, Lake. I came to see, and I saw, and now I know."

There was only one thing to say to that, to a truth I couldn't accept, despite how desperately I wanted to. "You came too late. You wasted your time."

"Time is never wasted on you," he said. "You told me that once, the day I—"

"Got out of jail," I finished. "Did you think I could forget? You barely looked me in the eye after all that time apart. Why was that, Manning?" I asked, even though I knew.

He blew out a long breath. "Because I wanted you," he admitted. "And I was ashamed."

"You didn't need to be." I picked up his coat and handed it to him. "But you were, and you made decisions you can't take back. So go. Go home to her."

He withdrew as if I'd slapped him. "You think I can return to that life after this?"

I crossed my arms, not to make a point, but because my hands shook. My stomach churned like I was going to be ill. I *wanted* nothing more than for him to break down all the walls between us, but what I *needed* was for him to be sorry he'd ever stepped foot on a plane. To feel the unrelenting sting I had when the one person I didn't think I could live without had rejected me. "After what?" I asked. "What could seeing me have possibly changed for you? You've been here less than an hour."

"I've been here years," he said. "Sick over losing you. Tortured that Corbin might make you happy. Wondering if you might still want me. I've been stuck in this place, unable to move on. It's not my feelings that've changed, but—"

We jumped apart at a knock on the door, as if we'd been caught doing something wrong—because we had.

"Lake?" I heard from the hallway. "Is everything okay?"

Corbin.

Manning set his jaw. "What's he doing here?"

"I'm coming in," Corbin said.

Manning looked from me to the door. "Lake, tell him to go."

I yanked my sweatshirt back over my head. "He has a key."

Corbin breezed into the apartment the way he had hundreds of times before. This was as much his domain as it was Val's. Considering Val spent so much time either with Julian or at work, Corbin was here nearly as often as she was.

He stopped in the hallway as his eyes landed on us. "What's this?" he asked me.

I cleared the grit from my throat. "Manning's in town."

"I see that." Corbin looked between us. "We were supposed meet for brunch half an hour ago, Lake. I called, but . . ."

The tension in the room thickened. It might as well have been Tiffany who'd walked in, because if Corbin suspected anything, he wouldn't let Manning get away with it.

Tiffany. I'd gone this long not thinking of her as a real part of all this. Not letting the reality of her, my sister, into the room. But I couldn't ignore the facts any longer—Corbin made everything real. I had almost kissed my sister's husband.

I wiped the heel of my palm over my warm hairline. "Corbin and I have plans," I said.

Manning shrugged into his suit jacket. "I could eat."

"Didn't you just have breakfast?" I asked.

"I'm hungry again." He glanced at me from under his lashes. "Starved, even."

Starved. Food had been, over the years, one of the only ways I could show Manning I loved him, and he knew that.

I should've told him no, but I knew Manning would find a way. I didn't want to make a scene in front of Corbin anyway. Even though he and I hadn't talked about Manning in years, I was almost certain Corbin had suspected my feelings for Manning before, during, and after the wedding. He had to have known, deep down, that all my suffering when I'd moved here wasn't simply because of the fights I'd had with my dad leading up to my departure.

"Fine," I said. "Let's go."

"Better change," Corbin pointed out. "Can't go having breakfast in what you slept in now that you're no longer a college student."

"*What?*" Manning's face fell. "You dropped out?"

"Graduated." I straightened my shoulders as I glanced from him to Corbin and back. "Last Thursday."

"But it's December. Your Mom was planning on flying out for the ceremony next June."

Since I'd made my decision to leave California right before fall, I'd missed the first semester at NYU and started in the spring instead. I wasn't sure I would've been able to handle school anyway on top of moving to such an overwhelming place with no money and a battered spirit. "I didn't tell Mom," I said. "I knew it would hurt her that I didn't want any of you there. Not even her."

"You had me and Val, though," Corbin said. He came and threw an arm around me, turning to Manning. "Tell Cathy not to worry. I was there every step of the way."

Manning and Corbin exchanged looks that could melt steel, which was my cue to duck out from under Corbin's arm and into my bedroom to change clothes.

3

MANNING

Corbin led us from Lake's apartment to the restaurant where he and Lake had planned to have breakfast. I stayed a few steps behind them. When he put an arm around her shoulders, I had to refrain from stopping him. The urge to separate them hadn't lessened since I'd last seen them together. Even at my own wedding, I'd watched Corbin like a hawk. The difference was he had her attention now, and I didn't. What apparently remained the same was that I wanted her as fiercely today as I had back then.

Seeing how she lived, hearing what I'd missed, touching her, getting a taste of what I'd dreamed about, had nightmares about, had tortured myself over . . . it confirmed that coming to New York was the right decision.

I'd been a patient man. I'd been a good husband. I'd provided for Tiffany, and she'd helped me understand over the years I probably wasn't destined to become my father. But there existed a divide between us that I hadn't been able to cross while I still had feelings for Lake. When my parole had ended, I'd starting planning this trip, but even then, I'd fought myself. After what I'd put Lake through, it wasn't fair to just show up. It'd killed me slowly, though, the not knowing—what she was like now, how she lived, who she loved.

I weaved through crowded city sidewalks, bounced off puffy coats, tripped over dog leashes, and sidestepped trash bags on every curb of Manhattan. The company had flown me out here for a week to work, but for months I'd been preparing myself to face Lake. In that time, I'd begun to realize—if I got here and had even the slightest doubt that Lake was better off without me, I'd be unable to walk away. I needed to let her go or make her mine for good. I couldn't handle the in between anymore. She'd stumbled out of the cab this morning looking anything but perfect, and still, my mouth had watered for her. I'd remembered how hungry I was. No matter how close Tiffany and I had gotten, no matter if I'd been good for her and she for me, she'd never feed my deepest hunger. Not the way Lake could.

And while Tiffany slept in Egyptian cotton and liked to eat out three or four nights a week, Lake had next to nothing. The question was no longer whether

I was good for her. It was how I'd atone for my mistakes, from earning her forgiveness to untangling myself from the life I'd built on the west coast.

Corbin took Lake's hand. She glanced back at me. Lake wasn't the wide-eyed girl I'd once known, begging for me to destroy her. She wasn't pure as watermelon Chapstick on never-been-kissed lips. She wasn't perfect anymore, she wasn't young and naïve, and that meant I could act on all the things I'd fantasized about doing to her. And that was definitely a fucking problem considering I was still a married man.

In the restaurant, Corbin took Lake's coat and scarf and went with the hostess to hang them up. It was a stupid thing to get jealous over, but I did. I leaned in to Lake and said, "Tell him to go. I need time alone with you."

She tucked her hair behind her ear, glancing after Corbin. "I gave you enough time already."

"Look at me," I said.

Hesitantly, she shifted her eyes up as I dropped mine to her lips. I'd almost kissed her and now it was all I could think of. I'd never be this close to her again and not burn for it. To sink into her smell, feel her downy-soft hair against my cheek, then tangled in my fingers and spread over my skin as she slept on my chest . . .

Up until this morning, all that had been an impossible fantasy. Maybe she'd thought our conversation in her apartment was the end of this, that I'd stay in New York this week and not see her again, but it wasn't. All it'd done was make me realize that before I could even think of kissing her, I needed to earn her trust again. I needed to tell her what she still meant to me.

But as long as Corbin was around, I had a problem on my hands.

The hostess led us past a Christmas tree with winking multi-colored lights and tables of crayon-wielding kids to a blue vinyl booth. Corbin gestured for Lake to sit first. I would've had to push him aside to be next to her, so I was forced to take the seat across them.

I'd barely glanced at the menu before a waitress approached. "Morning, you two," she said to them. "Want the usual?"

"Yeah, but bring Lake a Coke and hash browns, too." Corbin passed the waitress his menu and his eyes over me. "She likes that when she's hungover."

"Corbin, don't," she said quickly. "I'm not hungover. I barely drank anything last night."

She didn't want me to think she had, anyway. I didn't like hearing about it, either. I couldn't really pretend she didn't do those things—she had a new life here. She'd grown up. We were both different, but deep down, wasn't she still the Lake I knew? Wasn't I still the same man? Without that, who were we? While I looked forward to learning more about the girl sitting across from me, I wasn't ready to say goodbye to the one I'd known just yet.

"So no hangover remedy?" the waitress asked.

Lake flicked her nail on the edge of her menu, biting her lip. "You can bring the hash browns."

The waitress knew them, and Corbin knew Lake. What she liked to eat, at least, but I could learn that. Knowing mundane details wasn't anything compared to reading her the way I did—it didn't rival how she anticipated what I needed and when. Maybe Corbin thought he knew her, maybe *she* thought he did, but not like me.

I could've sat and watched Lake all day, but the waitress cleared her throat at me. "Do you need another minute?"

Lake took my menu away and gave it to the waitress. "He'll have the number one. Add avocado." As she said it, she avoided my eyes, color high in her cheeks. Well, that was all the evidence I needed. Food was an expression of her love. Ever since the day we'd met and she'd made me a monster sandwich, she'd liked to feed me, to watch me eat, to be the reason I was content.

Corbin leaned back in the booth, stretching his arm behind Lake. "How's Tiffany?" he asked.

Reality cut through my adulation. If I could've, I'd have asked Corbin to leave. I wouldn't put it past him to tell Tiffany he'd found me in Lake's apartment, though. I didn't want her to find out that way. Until I got my shit sorted, I'd have to play nice. "She's fine."

"And the family? Charles? Cathy?"

45

"Everyone's good," I said, trying to keep the irritation from my voice. "You know that. You were over for Thanksgiving."

Lake turned in the seat to gape at him. "*What?*"

"I only stopped by to say hi," he said to her. "They miss you. They want to know about you."

Cathy was the only one who'd admit it. Lake's dad went beet red at the mention of her name, and Tiffany had never been good at expressing her emotions, so she usually clammed up when it came to Lake. That didn't mean they didn't miss her, though. I knew they did.

"How could you not tell me?" Lake asked.

"I knew you'd freak, and I was only there ten minutes."

That was true. Since I'd already booked my trip to New York, and Tiffany had been acting strange about that, I'd disappeared to the backyard during Corbin's visit. I didn't want anyone thinking I cared to hear about Lake or the New York trip would be off for good. But after he'd left, all Cathy could talk about was how she'd had a feeling Lake and Corbin might be getting serious.

And if I hadn't already had my plane ticket, that would've been enough to get me to buy one. How serious was it, though?

The waitress filled our coffee cups. Lake added a splash of cream and Corbin handed her two packets of sugar. The morning after her prom, four and a half years earlier, she'd wanted to drink coffee just because

I did. Now, she looked like a regular caffeinator. While I ached for the old Lake, it was as if I were meeting a new side of her, and that was something I'd never thought I'd get.

"Is it your first time in New York?" Corbin asked, stirring his coffee, the spoon *clink clink clinking* against the sides.

"Yeah."

"How do you like it?" he asked.

Fast-paced wasn't my speed. I wasn't sure how to feel about the city yet. It was dirty, cramped, and noisy. Orange County was paradise by comparison, and even that could sometimes get to be too much for me. Even though my time at Camp Young Cubs had ended in handcuffs, I sometimes wished to be back in Big Bear—that time had stopped the night Lake and I had sat under the stars. Before the arrest. Before any of this.

"He won't like it here," Lake answered for me, dropping her eyes to the buttons of my dress shirt. "I can't picture it." She didn't like the suit. It didn't align with how she saw me, and she looked different to me, too, so I understood. She was a little older, not as put together, and definitely not as trusting. That didn't mean I didn't want her as she was, though.

"I might. I've barely seen it," I said to her, hoping she'd understand that I could accept this new life of hers. That I wanted to be part of it. "I only arrived late last night."

"And Lake's apartment was the first stop you made?" Corbin asked.

"I had something to give her." I shifted my gaze to Lake. "And it's time-sensitive."

Corbin looked between us. "Well, what was it?" he asked her.

"When Cathy found out I was coming," I said, "she asked me to check on Lake." I took the Broadway tickets she'd given me from inside my suit jacket and showed them to Lake. "The show is tonight. *Miss Saigon*—"

She snatched them. "I told my mom I wanted to see this."

"It's too bad you can't go since you work tonight," Corbin said, his arm still behind her as he played with her hair. I'd just gotten that golden silk in my hands for the first time in years, and he'd been running his fingers through it all this time? Fuck him.

"Oh, yeah." Her shoulders slumped as she set the tickets on the table. "I totally forgot."

Corbin shifted against the vinyl, his lips thinning into a line. "You should've told me you wanted to go. I'll take you another night," he said to her while looking at me. "Lake and I have been to lots of shows. Cathy knows that."

I took the tickets back. Lake's disappointment was palpable, but I wasn't going to push it in front of Corbin. I'd get her to the show, even if I had to reschedule for a different night next week. "Not a problem," I said.

She sucked in a breath like she was going to protest, and then seemed to think better of it. "I'll call my mom and thank her. It's been a while since we spoke anyway."

Now Lake wasn't only disappointed, but sad, too. I was close to her family, and the gap between them was great for no good reason. Lake had to have missed her parents, just like they missed their daughter, but until either Charles or Lake swallowed their pride and made the first call, it would stay that way.

"She works so damn hard," Corbin said, pulling her into his side. "This one has *two* jobs on top of her auditions, not to mention she was in class several hours a week up until recently. She loves staying busy, but she deserves a break."

I kept my eyes on Lake. All I heard was Corbin speaking for her the same way her dad had. I'd once wondered if this prick was better for Lake than I would be, but if he treated her anything like Charles had, then I wouldn't feel an ounce of guilt stealing her out from under him.

"I don't work any harder than you," she said to Corbin.

I turned my attention to him, seeing an opening to learn more about the person I'd be going up against. "What do you do?" I asked him.

"Finance."

"What's that mean?" I got bits and pieces about Lake from Cathy, but out of self-preservation, I'd sometimes tuned out specifics when it came to Corbin.

"Since I graduated last year, I've been an investment analyst at a hedge fund. I shadow a portfolio manager—"

"I see." I didn't see. As it turned out, I didn't care. I'd already decided Lake could do better. "What's a hedge fund?"

"Oh, okay." Corbin sighed. "Let me back up. Basically, my boss manages capital—that's money—pooled by these investors who, like, they're big time guys . . ."

Lake noticed me staring at her and blushed. God, it felt good to be back in her presence. To have put my arms around her and been close enough to practically taste her breath. It was like the first lick of what could be a never-ending cone of my favorite ice cream. She might've told me to stop because she was fighting herself—and me. She had every right to. I wanted her to give in, but I needed her to be sure about us before anything happened, because once I started down this path, I wouldn't be able to turn back.

When I realized Corbin had stopped talking, I asked Lake, "And what do *you* do? I know you were enrolled in Tisch, the art school, and that's about it," I said. "Your parents don't even know what line of work you're in."

"Line of work?" she asked, failing to suppress a laugh. "I work part-time at an animal shelter for minimum wage."

That didn't surprise me. Lake had a scar on her arm from trying to extract a scared kitten from a bush, and though I didn't really see the connection between acting and animals, at least it suited her. "That sounds all right," I said.

"And the other part of the time, she works the graveyard at this twenty-four-hour Ukrainian diner," Corbin added.

"Corbin," Lake muttered under her breath.

It took a moment for that to register. I hadn't thought her situation could get any worse, but I was wrong. By the way she looked at her lap, Corbin wasn't kidding, and Lake knew how I'd feel about this. "The *graveyard*?" I asked, my voice bouncing off the booth.

Lake chewed on her thumbnail. "That's what we in the industry call the nightshift . . ."

"I know what the goddamn graveyard means." I took a soothing breath to keep from exploding like her dad, because that had sent her thousands of miles away. "How did this happen?" I asked.

"Well, typically you fill out an application, have an interview with the manager, and—"

"Lake." I leaned my elbows on the table, leveling her with a glare that made her sigh.

"It's not that bad," she said. "It's only a few avenues from my apartment, so I can walk there."

"You *walk*," I deadpanned. "In the middle of the night?"

"I met her after work the first few times," Corbin said, "but it's tough because I'm sometimes pulling twelve-hour days. Good thing I figured out pretty quickly that she's tougher than she looks."

"Stop talking about me like I'm not here," Lake said. "I don't work because it's convenient. I do it to pay my rent and loans. That's all there is to it. End of discussion."

"See what I mean?" Corbin winked at me. "I've got an eye on her, though," he said before leaning in to whisper in her ear.

He had an eye on her. He was staking his claim, and not just with his arm on her shoulder. By the ease of their intimacy, it was clear they'd been together awhile. Maybe since the wedding, even. He'd seen her through the hard times I'd caused, taken her to shows, walked her home from work in the middle of the night . . .

Made love to her.

My stomach churned. I'd never so much as kissed Lake, but I knew one night with her would change everything—it was the reason we'd never had that one night. Was Corbin to Lake what Tiffany was to me? A safe kind of intimacy? Or did he give her more?

Did he give her as much as I could?

The idea of it felt so wrong that my throat closed, and my scalp heated. I wanted to reach across the table and pull him off her. I had to talk myself down before I made a mistake. Maybe she'd needed to get him out of her system to know it wasn't meant to be. I knew Lake would never wonder about another man if she had me, but maybe *she* didn't know that. She didn't think I was coming for her. How could she? I hadn't known I would until recently. As much as I'd fought it, as wrong as I knew it was, I still loved her. As I'd looked around that shitty apartment, I'd seen all the ways I'd fucked up. From day one, I'd wanted the best for her, and if this was it, I knew I could do better. The longer I was in her presence, the more certain I was I had only one option left—tilt the universe until she fell into my arms.

Lake shook her head at her lap in response to whatever Corbin had whispered to her. "No, it's okay. It's fine."

Corbin wanted me out, too. He was right to. Rationalize as I did, I still couldn't help the flush of heat working its way up my chest as Corbin said something else to make her smile. His fingers drummed against her shoulder. Their relationship was my fault. I had no right to get angry, but I was. I wanted to send him packing but not before I knocked him cold for getting parts of Lake I didn't even have the pleasure of knowing about. Yet.

The waitress rescued me, dropping our food at the table and forcing Corbin to remove his arm from Lake.

The "number one" Lake had ordered me was a double-decker egg sandwich with bacon, avocado, and sauce. It came with a side of toast and fruit and was probably enough food for two people. In other words, it was perfect. Two bites in, I groaned with satisfaction, and it was only then that Lake stopped watching me and started eating her oatmeal and hash browns.

I glanced at my watch. I needed to leave soon for another sales meeting or I'd be late. I'd been in New York less than twenty-four hours, and I was ready to blow off everything to spend more time with Lake.

"You here for work?" Corbin asked, noticing I'd checked the time. "Man, my dad would've loved for me to go into pharma. So much money there, but then again, Wall Street's got me doing all right."

"Sure," I said, chewing.

"You knew he worked with your dad?" Lake asked Corbin. "Why didn't you tell me?"

"You're always saying you don't want to know anything about home." He sipped his coffee and shrugged at me. "Where'd they put you up?"

"The W. In Union Square." I washed down my food with some coffee. "I think it's new."

"Oh, yeah. I've seen it. Your schedule must be packed. I doubt you came all this way without lots to do."

I ripped off part of a bacon strip with my teeth, looking between them. Corbin was right, but I was finding it hard to care about work. I couldn't say that in front of him, though. "I've got a busy schedule," I agreed, swallowing. It'd been the only way I could prove to Charles I needed to be in New York. "I wanted to make sure I checked in on things, though. For Cathy."

"For Cathy." Corbin nodded, then glanced at Lake and laughed. "Lake, babe," he said, "you already got ketchup on yourself."

Lake pulled her sweater taut to see the stain. "Damn it."

"At least you have time to go home and change before work . . . unlike the Upper East Side mixer incident."

She rolled her eyes as she patted her top. "Only me."

"I took her to a party hosted by my firm," he said to me. "First time I introduced her to my colleagues, and she spilled champagne all down the front of her Versace dress. The one I'd just spent hundreds of dollars on."

My patience was growing thin. I'd had enough of Corbin's peacocking, his inside jokes and expensive taste, and his fucking hands all over her.

Like old times, Lake seemed to pick up on my irritation. She put down the napkin. "I have to get home and shower if I'm going to get to work on time."

"I'll walk you," I said.

"Where's your next meeting?" she asked.

"Not around here," I said. "It's in Manhasset."

Corbin's eyebrows rose. "That's a drive."

"Yeah, it's not technically a sales call. I'm playing golf with a client of mine from Orange County, because he's going to introduce me to . . ."

Lake looked at me as if she didn't know me. I didn't blame her. I'd had things to take care of the past few years, like a wife and a mortgage, and if golf was the answer to getting more clients, I had to play the game. I'd once told Tiffany I'd never become her dad, but the commission structure Charles had put in place for me made it impossible not to want more and more. Truth be told, I'd never dreamed of living the life I was now—owning my home, having a pool, surprising Tiffany with expensive gifts that she bragged about to her friends. This doctor I was meeting today could set me up with another three or four sales appointments while I was in town, and if I wasn't letting Lake go again, that meant I had a divorce in my future, and knowing Tiff, that would get fucking pricey. "It could be pretty lucrative for me to hit a tiny ball around for a few hours," I explained.

"Oh." Lake frowned. "Well, if it's lucrative."

"Hope you've got a change of clothes," Corbin said.

"I'll pick something up at the club."

Lake and I held each other's gaze as Corbin signaled for the waitress. "Are you coming over tonight?" he asked Lake.

"I won't be done at work until late."

"What about after?"

She finally turned to him, her head tilted. "It'll be close to midnight."

"Yeah." He rubbed the back of his neck. "I guess."

I removed my wallet, but Corbin waved me off. "I've got this," he said, taking the bill up to the cashier.

I didn't need to make a show of paying for the meal. If Corbin wanted to give me time alone with Lake, I wouldn't argue. "The show's at seven tonight," I said to her.

"I already told you I have to work at the diner."

"Then quit." I hoped she'd say yes, but she didn't seem as outraged about her *graveyard* shift as I was. "Or fake a stomachache. I thought you loved Broadway."

"I do, but . . . I don't see the point of spending time together when it's only going to . . ." She swallowed down her words. She'd done that a few times already in the apartment, and all I could do was stand there and watch. It took every ounce of self-restraint not to take her in my arms and promise her the world just to ease the sadness in her eyes.

"Cathy made me promise I'd take you," I said. "She had a whole plan to keep it from Charles and Tiffany, just so I could make sure you were okay—and show you a good time."

Lake looked at the table. I didn't want to make things harder on her, but we needed one-on-one time. If I had to play the Mom card, I would.

"Let me get you a cab, Manning," Corbin said, calling us to the front of the restaurant. "Hailing one is kind of an art."

Lake got up, so I followed. As we made our way outside, I lowered my voice. "I'll pick you up at six. Unless you want dinner before rather than after."

Lake met eyes with Corbin. "Will you get my coat from the check?" she asked him.

"Of course."

As soon as he left, she turned her eyes on me. "I thought it was just a show."

"You need to eat, don't you? It would mean a lot to Cathy. She wonders all the time about how you're eating." I held open the door for Lake, but she only eyed me, skeptical. "One Sunday night, I found your mom crying into a roast. She worries nobody's cooking for you. She worries a lot, Lake, and . . ." Corbin was headed back our way. "So do I. I need this, too. A few uninterrupted hours with you."

Lake shot a glance in Corbin's direction and lowered her voice. "Okay, fine." She shook her head. "I can't believe I'm—it's for my mom, all right? Don't mention it to Corbin."

I guessed maybe her boyfriend wouldn't be too happy about our date tonight. That was fine by me. A weight lifted from my shoulders knowing I'd see her later. I was going to be late for golf, but it was worth it.

Outside, I took my Nokia from my suit pocket so I could call the client once I was in a cab.

"You have a cell phone?" Lake asked.

I gave it to her. I liked watching her turn it over in her hands. I didn't have to ask if she owned one—they were expensive, and I only had it for work.

"It looks like Corbin's," she said with a smirk, handing it back to me. Although I hated hearing his name from her mouth, her sudden attitude was kind of cute. Very cute, actually. I was so engrossed with her that I didn't hear a car pull up.

Lake looked behind me. "You're taking a taxi all the way to Manhasset?" she asked. "How much does my dad pay you?"

I turned around. Corbin had already flagged down a cab. "Thoughtful of him," I uttered. I couldn't be too upset—I'd get Lake all to myself tonight—so I smiled and thanked him.

"No problem," he said. "Hope you have a nice stay. I'll keep trying to get Lake to come home with me for the holidays. Maybe next year."

Lake blew hot air into her fists, and I wondered why she wasn't wearing gloves. "Even if I were welcome," she said, "I wouldn't go."

"You know you are," he said. "Charles just needs some—"

"Corbin," Lake gave him a look that'd shut me right up, "don't."

"All right." He held up a hand to wave at me. "See you around, man."

I hoped not, but in a few hours, Lake would be all mine. "Six o'clock," I mouthed at her before forcing myself into the taxi.

4
LAKE

At five in the evening, I stood on the balls of my feet in front of the bathroom mirror, doing my best to admire my floor-length, strappy black velvet Calvin Klein dress. I'd bought it secondhand under Val's guidance last fall but hadn't yet worn it. My first thought as I'd slipped it over my head was that Tiffany would say it was old and "so over." I didn't own many nice things, though. I'd left most of my clothing in California. Moving across country with two suitcases had been hard to do, but I'd also needed to shed that old life. Start over. Now, I didn't have much. Corbin made good money even though he'd only held a paid position at his company a year, but it didn't feel right when he tried to take me shopping. He always overspent. The two nice dresses I owned were gifts from him he hadn't let me refuse. Tonight, I wanted to wear something I'd bought myself, even if it wasn't new, even if it was a bit too fancy for where Manning and I were headed.

When the front door opened, I poked my head out of the bathroom, half-expecting Manning to have broken in again, but it was Val. My best friend and roommate hurried into the living room, her spiral curls bouncing around her ears in the odd, grow-out stage of a "do-not-mention" haircut. Since *Felicity* had aired on the WB a year earlier, Val had consistently been mistaken for the TV show's star, Keri Russell. But Val needed to be her own person, so in an act of rebellion, she'd chopped off her beautiful, blonde ringlets over the summer. And then Felicity had debuted the same haircut in October. Now, not only did Val look even more like Felicity, but people thought she'd copied the show, which really got Val going.

"I'm on break from a double shift." Val untied the waist apron she wore to wait tables at a chain restaurant in Midtown. She blew by me, unbuttoning her starchy blouse. "Some brat threw a fucking bowl of mac and cheese at me." Pinching the shirt by its collar, she made a face and dumped it into a hamper in the corner. "That shit is hot and yellow and—don't you work tonight?"

Part of me wanted to tell her about my visit from the past, but the other part knew better. "I called in sick," I said as she flurried around me.

"Yeah? Why?" She ran into the bathroom where her back-up uniform hung on the shower curtain bar. "Damn. Of course it's still damp." She pulled it down, slipping it over her shoulders as she went to the mirror. "Are you okay?"

"I'm fine."

Buttoning up the blouse, she glanced at me in the reflection, then turned. "Holy shit. You're wearing the CK dress! You look amazing."

I smoothed my hands over my stomach. "Really?"

"Where are you headed dressed like that? One of Corbin's functions?"

"I'm going to see a show, actually." I left it at that and ducked around her to grab my hairbrush. When she didn't respond, I continued, "I'm overdressed, but who knows when I'll get a chance to wear this again?"

"Are you going with Corbin?" she asked.

"No." I combed my hair, avoiding her eyes.

"Who then?"

Val was the only person who knew the whole truth about Manning and me. She wouldn't like that I was seeing him tonight, but I didn't want to lie to my best friend. After all she'd done for me since we'd moved here, I owed her the truth. "You remember Manning?"

She didn't respond. I didn't have to see Val's face to know her reaction. Warmth crept up my neck as she made me stand there in silence that grew louder and louder.

"Hmm, Manning," she said finally. "I think so. If you're talking about the sorry, cowardly piece of shit who broke your heart . . . then yes, I recall."

I set the hairbrush down. "That was years ago."

"I remember. I was there as you basically fell apart at his wedding—*to your sister.* As you cried yourself to sleep every night for—I don't even know how long. Maybe you still do. I was there when I spent my first Christmas away from my mom so you wouldn't be alone during the holidays."

"I know. I get it." I turned and braced myself against the sink. "It's not what it looks like. He's in town for work, and my mom bought us tickets to—"

She grabbed my shoulders, stunning me into silence. "What are you doing? What the *fuck* are you doing?"

"I'm going to see a Broadway show, it's not a big deal," I shot back, wiggling free from her grip to leave the bathroom.

"How can it not be a big deal? How did this even happen?" She followed me to the bedroom and stopped in the doorway, her shirt cockeyed and exposing her navel because she'd missed a button. "Who does he think he is, calling you out of the blue?"

"He came by this morning."

"And you slammed the door in his face, right?" she asked. "Is that why the lock is fucked up?"

I found my stilettos where I'd dropped them earlier and sat on the edge of the bed to buckle the straps. "It's just dinner and a show. That's it."

"*Dinner?* Are you insane, Lake?"

"Stop yelling at me."

"*No.*"

The sharpness of the word forced me to look up at her. Her red face didn't distract me from the sheen over her eyes. She barely knew Manning, and *she* was the one crying? "How could he do this again?" she asked.

I was tempted to defend Manning, and that was proof Val was right. He'd already begun to get to me. It wasn't fair to myself, or to her, either—she'd been by my side since the night on the beach I'd told her I had feelings for my sister's fiancé. "I know," I said. "I turned him down at first, but then I changed my mind. I already agreed."

"Because he knows you can't say no to him. He knows how badly he hurt you, yet he has the balls to show his face here. He's an asshole and a coward. A felon, a liar, and maybe even a cheat." She put her hands on her hips. "If he shows up here, I'll call Corbin to come take care of this."

"Corbin already knows."

"He knows you're going out with Manning? That you're getting all dolled up for him?"

"No." My face burned hot with embarrassment that I'd gotten caught wanting to look nice for him.

"Corbin knows Manning's in town, and this is normal attire for Broadway—"

"Don't give me that shit. You're dressing up for him because you're still in love with him."

Still in love with him. I hid my shiver by crossing my arms. Neither Val nor I had said Manning's name in months, because it saddened me and upset her, but that didn't mean I was fooling either of us. Hearing her acknowledge my feelings for him for the first time in a while made me realize my love for Manning hadn't lessened even a little. That was why I'd agreed to meet him. That was why I'd taken extra care to look good tonight. But that didn't mean I forgot, even for a second, what he'd done to me. "He's my sister's husband," I said. "That's all. I think he and I can have a simple meal like civilized adults."

"Really?" She stomped across the room toward my dresser.

"What are you doing?" I asked, standing.

"If you don't have feelings for him, you won't mind if I destroy this, right?" she asked, digging her hand into my underwear drawer.

"Wait!" I leaped toward her. "Don't."

She held up the small wooden box I thought nobody knew about. I tried to grab it from her, but she jumped back and showed it to me. "A few minutes in Corbin's fancy fireplace should do the trick," she said.

"Stop it." The box might've been small, but it and its contents were some of the only sentimental things I owned anymore. "I only have it for the earrings, and they're worth a lot."

Val opened it and showed me the inside. There were no earrings, only the mood ring I'd found in Manning's things at the courthouse so many years ago, right after he'd been arrested. "Funny," she said. "Somehow these *earrings* turned into a cheap-ass ring Manning never technically gave you."

"Tiffany didn't even buy those earrings, my dad did, and it was probably out of guilt for how he treated me."

"Didn't you pawn them for rent money?" Val asked.

Ashamed, I stopped trying to fight her, stopped fighting at all, and let the tears flood my eyes. "I don't know what to say, Val. Do I still love him? How could I not? But he's changed, and so have I. I'm smarter now. I'm not going to let him hurt me again. I promise. Please don't ruin the box. Or the ring."

"He chose your *sister*, Lake. He married her." Val shook her head at me. "Four years, completely undone. We've been working through this for *four* years, and he's going to unravel it in a night."

"I won't let that happen. You're blowing an innocent dinner way out of proportion."

"Does Tiffany know about it?"

I went quiet, and that was all the answer Val needed. Of course Tiffany didn't know, because it wasn't innocent. It wasn't simple. Manning and I could never be either of those things, no matter how hard we pretended or how much time had passed. "No," I admitted.

"Of course she doesn't," she said. "They *are* still married, right?"

"He wasn't wearing a ring, so I'm not sure . . ."

"You didn't even ask?" Val tossed the wooden box at me. I jumped into action, catching it so it wouldn't hit the ground.

"I didn't ask because I was scared of the answer," I said, "not because I don't care about hurting her."

Val left the room, and I followed. She gathered up her apron and purse from the coffee table. "You know something, Lake? I've hated him all this time. You were young, and so fucking optimistic, and I hated him for stealing some of that from you. But you're an adult now." Tying on her waist apron, she pinned me with a look. "If you go down this path, you have no one to blame but yourself."

Her words stung. I loved Val, her spirit and her loyalty, but she didn't know Manning like I did. She didn't understand what he and I had been through. "I take full responsibility," I said. "Trust me—I know what I'm doing."

"Do you? You're an idiot if you think he can't ruin you in a night. I've seen him do it. I'm not going to stick around for an encore. And don't worry, I'm not going to waste Corbin's time with this. You're on your own." She walked down the hall, looping her purse strap across her body. "At least this time when Manning crushes you, you'll know it's coming."

I wasn't sure how long I stood there watching the door after she left. Wave after wave of tears hit, but I did my best to breathe through them. It wasn't so much Val's harsh words that stung, but the fact that she was right. I still loved Manning. Still hadn't figured out how to resist him. I'd worn my hair down hoping he'd touch it again. I'd chosen my highest heels to feel closer to him. I'd almost let him kiss me this morning, in this same spot, despite the fact that he was married and had hurt me before.

I shoved aside some *Jane* magazines, knocking over a bottle of tommy girl, and sank onto the coffee table. I had to be stronger than I'd been back then. The jewelry box's corners cut into my palm so I opened my hand. I'd tried so many times to throw this memory away, but I'd dug through trashcans for it. I'd taken it to a pawn shop, only to snatch it back from the man behind the counter before he'd even had a chance to look at it. Not that it or the ring was worth anything. It was just a box.

The morning of the wedding had been the same day I'd met Henry, Manning's best man, more of a father to Manning than his own dad. Henry had come to my hotel room to deliver my maid-of-honor gift from Tiffany—a polished, walnut wood box that had fit in the palm of my hand and had been engraved.

Lake Kaplan
Maid of Honor, 1995

I remembered back to the moment Henry had handed it over to me.

"It's beautiful." My voice broke. "Tell him thank you."

"Him?" Henry asked.

"Manning. He made it, didn't he?"

"He sure did." Henry held out his palm for the box. "May I?"

I gave it to him, and he studied it like I had, his fingers grazing over each corner and ledge, testing the brass hinges on back. "Manning's got talent. I heard he's making some furniture, too." He passed it back. "How'd you know it was from him?"

"We're friends." I looked for any recognition that Manning might've mentioned me, but there was nothing. "We were friends before . . . all this."

"That so? I have a daughter a little younger than you. You'll meet her tonight." He nodded. "I always wished she and Manning were closer in age. He'll make your sister a good husband."

Teeth clenched, I breathed through my nose as the word scraped out whatever was left inside me. Husband.

Henry was looking at me a little funny, so I pushed through the stinging in my chest and replied, "Yes, he will."

"I'm glad to see Manning become part of such a nice family. He's a good kid. A really good kid."

I'd never heard anyone refer to Manning as a kid. I tried to keep the emotion from my voice. "I know he is."

"Well, aren't you going to open it?" Henry asked.

"Open what?"

"The box. That's not the gift, you know. It's inside."

"Oh." I creaked open the lid. Two small diamond earrings winked at me.

I'd worn the earrings during the wedding so as not to upset Tiffany, but they were gone now, replaced by a cheap piece of costume jewelry Manning didn't even know I'd kept.

I sat there, turning the box over in my hands, until I went and set it on my dresser. In the bathroom, I pinned my hair into a quick up-do. I was almost finished when the downstairs buzzer sounded through the apartment. Manning was a half hour early. I didn't move. I had a choice to make. Why had he almost kissed me when he knew perfectly well it'd do nothing but damage? Was Val right that he knew I couldn't say no to him?

Was I even strong enough to send him away?

5

LAKE

Manning stood on my doorstep, hair combed back, cleanly shaven in a pressed suit and cobalt-blue tie. He looked every inch the gentleman—except for a Home Depot bag in his hand, as if he were actually holding on to a piece of his old self. He took my breath away, leaving me no choice but to stare at him.

"Everything okay?" he asked.

"It's just . . ." I didn't like this suit much better than the first one, simply because it wasn't Manning. That didn't mean he didn't fill it out perfectly, though, with his broad shoulders and trim torso. "Hardly anyone dresses up for the theater anymore."

"You do," he said, scanning my gown. His perusal had always had a special power over me, mostly because of how we'd subsist for weeks or months on furtive glances alone. He took me in, from my bare toenails up to my hair. "You look beautiful. Like a grownup."

To anyone else, it might've sounded like an odd compliment, but to me it said everything. Manning had resisted all his urges over the years, afraid he'd corrupt a young, innocent girl. I wasn't that girl anymore, and he saw it. Finally. One of the stupid tears I'd been holding in from my fight with Val slipped out.

"Hey." He reached up. "Don't cry."

I turned my face away, wiping my own cheek. "I'm fine. What's in the bag?"

He looked disappointed by my brushoff, but let me change the subject. "Stuff to fix your door."

"Oh." I stepped back as he came inside. "You don't have to."

"Did you think I'd let you spend a night here with a broken lock? What would you have done?"

I rubbed my nose to get it to stop tingling. "I don't know. Sometimes we stick a chair under the handle."

He looked at me dead on. "Jesus Christ, Lake. Don't tell me that."

"You asked."

He opened the hall closet and squatted to rummage through the cardboard box of tools. "Someone could pop that door right open in the middle of the night," he said.

"Someone meaning . . . you?" I asked.

He stopped inspecting a screwdriver and let his eyes travel up my body. I thought of him breaking all the rules, then the walls we'd built between us, and then the locks in the night to finally get to me. "If it was in my way," he said, "yes."

I suppressed a shiver. We'd flirted before but never when he wasn't trying to hide or stop it. Right there in his gaze was the heat I'd fantasized about, and years apart hadn't dulled it.

While Manning worked, I touched up my makeup where it'd smeared and managed to avoid looking myself in the eye the entire time. I had no idea how I could go through with this. Or exactly how dangerous it was. If I got hurt tonight, it would be my fault. If I hurt someone else, I'd be to blame. I was choosing this. There was still time to stop it, and yet I wouldn't. Val was wrong; one night didn't mean I was willing to forget everything. I'd grown up the past four years—I'd had to.

"Goddamn it," Manning said. "I didn't get the right measurements. You have a fucked-up door."

If I'd had any question about whether Manning still thought of me as a girl, him cursing in front of me was my answer. He'd done it so rarely back then, it still sounded a bit foreign. "Just leave it. There's hardly anything valuable in here." I came out of the bathroom, picked a clutch from my bedroom, and met him in the entryway. Noting the wrinkles between his eyes were unnaturally deep, I told him a little white lie. "I'll get the super to replace it in the morning. Let's go."

He shoved the box into the closet, then selected a black, polyester coat from the rack. "This yours?" he asked, taking it off the hanger as if he did it all the time.

"Yes, but it'll ruin my outfit. I don't own anything nice enough to go with this."

He opened it for me to slip in. "You'll freeze."

I didn't want to wear it, but considering this dress was all straps and open back, he was right. I'd be cold. I took the jacket and reluctantly put it on.

"Almost forgot." He patted the lapel of his suit. From the inside pocket, he took something squishy wrapped in tissue. "There's a holiday market happening in Union Square and I noticed you weren't wearing gloves earlier."

I lifted the taped edges to reveal a pair of brown mittens. The palms had pink leather pads knit to look like cat paws. "These are for me?"

"Well, they're not my taste. I know they don't go with your outfit, but you can take them off when we're inside." He took the wrapping from me, balling it up. "I didn't want you to be cold."

I tried one on, wiggling my fingers. "Manning."

"Don't worry, they're handmade," he added. "Didn't cost much."

I wasn't sure what he saw in my eyes, but I wasn't upset. It was just that I loved them. "Thank you."

He held open the door, ushering me through. "Don't mention it."

Downstairs, Manning stood on the curb to hail us a car.

"We should take the subway," I said as two cabs passed us by. "It's cheaper and faster."

"I'm not taking you underground looking like that," he said with a quick head-to-toe glance.

"The subway is perfectly fine, but if you insist, then this is how you do it." I stepped into oncoming traffic with my hand raised.

Manning grabbed my bicep to pull me back. "Careful—"

A taxi screeched to a stop in front of me. I looked back at Manning and laughed. "See?"

"You're going to give me a goddamn heart attack," he said, opening the car door. Still holding my arm, he urged me inside. "I'm an older man than I was when you knew me, Lake."

"You were always an older man to me," I said as I ducked into the backseat. Was Manning still sensitive about our age difference? As we pulled away from the curb, I checked his expression. Instead of the shame I'd sometimes see, he raised an eyebrow.

I leaned between the seats toward the driver. "Fifty-third and Broadway," I said. "Can you turn on the meter, please?"

"Broken," he said.

"Then pull over and we'll get out," I said.

"It's no problem." He waved me off. "I make you a good flat rate."

"I've got the fare covered," Manning said.

"No, he's going to rip us off," I said. We stopped at a red light, and I opened the door to get out.

"Okay, okay," the cabbie said, pressing the *on* button. "It's good."

I slammed the door and relaxed back into the seat. Manning watched me for so many blocks, I finally asked, "What?"

"Nothing."

"I told you you'd hate it here."

"That's not what I was thinking." He slid his hand across the leather seat toward mine, then froze, as if remembering my hand wasn't his to hold. I wanted to ask about his wedding ring, but how? And what would I do if he said he and Tiffany were ending their marriage? Did that have anything to do with why he was here?

Before I could decide how to ask, he beat me to it, nodding at my hand. "Is that from Corbin?"

I inspected *my* ring, a thin silver band I'd bought for a dollar at a flea market. "No."

"Someone else?" he asked.

"No . . ."

"Did you end up telling him you'd be with me tonight?"

I paused for emphasis before answering, "Corbin knows everything about me."

Even in the dark, I saw a shadow cross Manning's face. "Everything? How about you and me?"

I crossed my legs toward the door. Corbin didn't know about that. Or if he did, he'd turned a blind eye to it for too long for it to ever come up. I let Manning think what he wanted, though. "If you're worried what he thinks of you, you should be satisfied that there's nothing to tell where you and I are concerned. Just like you wanted." The driver honked and swore at the car in front of us. "What would I say?" I continued. "That we kept our hands to ourselves those two years?"

"Do you still wish I hadn't?" Manning asked. "Kept my hands to myself?"

My heart skipped with his unexpected question. Had he really said that, or was this bizarre day messing with my mind? Traffic forced the cab to slow, and I watched people walk along Third Avenue with shopping bags and warm drinks and scarves up to their eyes. I didn't reply to Manning's question. Surely he knew the answer.

"You were young and infatuated," he said. "You would've given me anything I'd asked for. Do you think it would've been right for me to take it?"

"I was young." I kept looking out the window. Maybe I was an idiot to be here like Val had said. "But I wasn't just infatuated."

As we drove in silence, I snuck glances at him. He wasn't as reserved as I would've thought. I couldn't decide if I was glad for it, to have access to him in a way I'd never had, or if it was cruel of him to finally treat me like an adult when it was too late to do anything about it. Wasn't it?

Once in the theater, Manning removed my coat in the crowded lobby, lingering at my back. "I was hoping you'd wear your hair down," he said, his breath near the top of my head. "I like it that way."

"I know you do. That's why I didn't."

He grunted. "Am I bringing out your feisty side tonight? Or is this the new you?"

"I'm not feisty," I said. "I'm hurt. By *you*." I wanted to ignore all of Val's earlier warnings, even if only for tonight—I deserved this time with Manning that'd been taken from me—but how could I let myself forget? I slipped out of the coat completely, leaving it in his hands. "I'm not going to wear my hair down for you, because you aren't *my* husband or boyfriend. You aren't even my friend."

"If you're feisty, if you're hurt, if you're a New Yorker now, fine," he said, his voice as firm as mine. "That doesn't mean I don't know you, Lake. I've always known who you were on the inside, where it counts."

"I'm sure that's one of the lies you've told yourself over the years." I pulled my mittens off by the fingers. "You know best. You know me. You know everything. Well, you don't." Theatergoers milled around us, sipping wine from plastic cups during animated conversations. I hardly noticed them with the way Manning glowered at me. "There are people who know me better than you now," I said.

"Because he orders you hash browns when you're fucking hungover? That doesn't mean shit."

Admittedly, his jealousy over that tiny tidbit of information made my skin tingle with pleasure. Because of the backless dress, I hadn't put on a bra, and my nipples hardened from the cold and Manning's relentless gaze. "You're making more of what you and I were, Manning. We never even kissed." I barely managed to keep my voice steady. If we'd gone this long without being intimate, maybe what we had wasn't as strong as either of us had thought. What two people could be this enamored and stay away from each other as long as we had? It was pathetic, really.

I went to find our seats in the orchestra section. The tickets had undoubtedly cost my mom some money and a good deal of planning. For those reasons, I was glad I'd come tonight. My relationship with my mom had suffered because of my dad, and this must've been important to her. But I couldn't ignore the weight on my shoulders. Manning had shown up on my doorstep that morning, and now we were playing nice. It wasn't fair that he should get what he wanted, always. I'd skip dinner, I decided, and that would be it. I didn't owe him any of this, and he could still tell my mom we'd been to the show. There wasn't much left of my dignity, or my determination, but some could still be salvaged.

Manning sat heavily beside me, way too much man for the creaky seats. "I don't like when you walk away from me," he said.

"What you're not understanding is that it doesn't matter what you like, Manning. You have no say over what I do."

He stared forward, gripping the armrest. Eventually the curtain lifted, but I couldn't concentrate on the performance. I felt like a fool for agreeing to this. If I was honest with myself, it was only partly because of my mom. I'd really wanted an excuse to be here with Manning, but what had I expected to get out of tonight? Nothing, and yet I'd still given in to him. Just to be close to him again, to feel the warmth of his attention after years of winter's indifference. It was as Val had said—Manning could undo me in less than one night, destabilizing a life I'd worked hard to build without him.

I turned to him. "Why aren't you wearing your ring?"

"What?" he whispered.

"Your wedding ring. Are you and Tiffany separated?"

"I don't . . ." He frowned. "I've never really worn one since I work with my hands a lot. But—"

"So you're still with her." Disappointment seared though me. What an idiot I'd been, secretly wondering if there might be more to this night than what it was. "You still love her."

Manning looked from me to the stage. "You really want to talk about this here?"

I didn't let him off the hook. "Do you love her?"

He ran his hand down his face, sighing. "Don't make me answer that, Lake."

I got up, and he reached for my hand. I pulled back just in time, squeezing through the row to get out. I hurried through the lobby to the coat check, but Manning had our claim tickets. Pushing out of the lobby into the chilly night, I tried to simultaneously calm my breathing and warm my shoulders. A line of cabs sat out front, but I waited, knowing Manning would come.

Moments later, my coat fell over my shoulders, and I grabbed the lapels, pulling it close. "You shouldn't be here, in New York," I said.

"Neither should you."

Where would I be now, if not for this city? Maybe things weren't perfect, and maybe I'd done a decent job of convincing myself this was where I had to be, but I couldn't imagine I'd be okay anywhere in the world without Manning. I faced him. "I thought I could do this, but I can't. Even just seeing a show together feels wrong."

"That's because it's not just a show," he said, coming closer. I got the sense by the way he flexed and clenched his hand that he wanted to touch me. He rubbed his temples instead. "*Would* you have given me anything I'd asked for?"

I wrinkled my nose, trying vainly to close the gap in our conversation. "What?"

"Earlier in the taxi, when I said you were young and infatuated and I put distance between us because you would've given me anything I'd asked for—was I right?"

I looked at him. It was out of character for him to push like this when he'd withheld, and forced me to withhold, for so long. "Yes," I said, hoping to shock him back.

"What about now?"

"No."

"Good." When he exhaled, the air between us fogged. "Then I won't feel bad asking."

I breathed a little harder, not sure I understood. Not sure I wanted to understand. "Asking for what?"

"Fuck." He shoved a hand through his black hair, pulling it so it stuck up a little. "Do you know why we've never kissed?"

Was he serious? We'd been over and over it. "Because I was too young."

"Try again."

I nearly scoffed at him. He was going to make me say it out loud? I took a step back, thinking of leaving, but he took two steps forward. "What are you trying to prove?" I asked.

"What's the reason? Why haven't we kissed?"

"You were with my sister," I forced out.

He shook his head. "Those are the reasons we couldn't be together. They were why nobody could know what we had. But you know as well as I do, there were more than a few times I could've had my way with you."

My jaw dropped, his uncharacteristic vulgarity catching me off guard. "What are you doing?" I asked. "Why do you want to make this harder?"

"Because you need to hear this. Maybe back then you thought—so what, a kiss is just a kiss. Why not? But it wasn't, not to me. You think it was easy for me, turning down your ripe fucking strawberry lips?"

My face heated. I wanted to melt into a puddle, half with embarrassment over his words, half because my knees were weakening with need the more his control slipped. "What's your point?" I asked. "What good is it to rehash this?"

"You think I wasn't sure, or I didn't want to, or that she was more important to me than you but none of that is true. Here's the truth."

At that inopportune moment, a passing ambulance forced him to go quiet. With its shrill wail, red and blue lights flashing over Manning's face, his words hanging in the air, my heart rate kicked up. What was Manning trying to tell me? What could he possibly say?

Once the street had stilled again, he said, "I knew the second I put my lips on yours, I'd be in-fucking-capable of letting you go. That was why I could never do it before. Those nights we had . . . in the truck, on the lake, and the kitchen counter . . . once I crossed the line, there was no turning back for me. I could never just wake up the next morning and not have you as mine."

My heart pounded so loudly now, I was sure the entire city could hear it. These were words I'd begged for, cried for, betrayed my sister for, and he was *finally* giving them to me. Of course he was right that one kiss would change everything, but back then, I'd wanted that at any cost—to be his through and through.

He stared me down, challenging me to back off or run or make my own confessions. I'd done enough talking, though. It was his turn to stand there, wait for a response, and be humiliated.

Slowly, he shook his head. "I thought you deserved a better future than I could give you. I never kissed you because I wasn't allowed to have you, and I would've had no choice but to take you anyway."

It didn't excuse anything he'd done, and it didn't lessen the pain of those moments, but I knew exactly what he meant. Manning was *mine*, I knew it in my gut. I always had. "So she got it all instead," I said.

"If it hadn't been her, it would've been someone else. I would've worked my way through a line of women trying to forget you. I married her because I thought I was doing the right thing for all of us. And I thought she was who I deserved."

"And now?" I asked breathlessly.

He came closer, until he stood over me, blocking out the moon, the passersby, the skyscrapers that boxed us in. "I worked so hard to keep you innocent," he said quietly. "You're no longer a kid, though. I always struggled to resist you, but I can't anymore. I don't want to."

Panic rose up my chest. I'd known Manning could get under my skin in a matter of seconds, but I didn't think he'd ever try. He'd always been so careful, but tonight, it was as if something inside him had flipped. "You can't say those things to me," I accused. "Back then, I would've given anything to hear them. Back then, I thought I was invincible. Now I know better. I've seen the damage you can do."

"I don't want to do damage. You should know it's been impossibly hard for me, too."

"For *you*?" I blinked rapidly. "Are you kidding?"

"Just because I put us in this situation doesn't mean I don't suffer. You don't see how I've struggled each day."

"Were you the one who had to watch the love of your life marry someone else?"

"No, and it would've killed me, Lake." He moved in on me, and I retreated to the curb until my back hit the side of a taxi. "Seeing you and Corbin together, knowing he's had all your firsts when I . . . when I could've been the one . . ." His voice wavered with emotion. "I get it."

"You *don't* get it," I said through my teeth. "Not even close. She got everything I'll never have. Not only the firsts, but she'll get the lasts, too, and everything in between. *Everything* else, she gets."

Tears built at the base of my throat. I tried to duck away so he wouldn't see how he affected me, but he put his hands on the roof of the cab, caging me in. "I can't change that. It's done. It's in the past." He dropped his eyes to my lips and my panic grew bigger. I was losing control of this situation. "This morning," he said, "if you had let me, I would've kissed you."

"But you didn't. You never do."

"Because like I just said, if I kiss you, you're mine. If I do it, it changes everything. So I know what my question is now," he said, pausing. "Do you want to change everything?"

He had come for me. He was defying fate. I'd convinced myself the past few years that none of this was possible, so I couldn't seem to puzzle it together, and I definitely couldn't believe it. I stared at him. "What are you asking?"

"Things are fine for me at home, Lake. They're not great, and it's not what I thought it would be, but my marriage is good enough. I was prepared to live with that, because I made the decision, and I didn't think there was anything else out there for me." When he swallowed, I saw every vein and ripple of his strong throat. "But when my parole ended, I had to find a way to get here. Once I booked the trip, seeing you was all I thought about. So many things came into focus."

I clung to his every word, expecting him to take all this away again, even as he said what I'd been aching to hear. "What things?"

"No matter what's going on at home, I can't pretend my feelings for you don't exist. It's not fair to any of us anymore, especially Tiffany. If anything, the agony of being kept from you has strengthened how I feel." He worked his jaw back and forth, dropping his eyes to my mouth. "I had to . . . I needed to come and hear you say you've moved on. You're better off. You're as happy as you could possibly be."

He'd just made this real. He had said her name and along with it, all the things I'd wished to hear for years—except one. And then, he did. He gave me the words that'd been at the crux of all my tortured fantasies.

"I made a mistake."

I'd wanted him to admit it even before he'd married her—Tiffany was a mistake. *I* was the one he really wanted. I inhaled back a wave of anxious tears and looked up at the sky. I'd never seen the Summer Triangle here. In this city, I barely saw constellations at all.

He took my chin and pulled my eyes back to his. "The stars can't help you on this one, Lake."

My eyes watered. "So you made a mistake. Are you going to do something about it? Because I know you, Manning. You've let me down so many times—"

He stepped into me, silencing me just with his nearness. "I saw you stumble out of the cab this morning, I saw your shitty apartment, saw you in a relationship that makes me murderous." He lowered his head and spoke above a whisper. "For so long, you've been perfect to me. Untouchable. Unblemished. Now I want to touch you, Lake. I want to blemish you. I don't want you perfect anymore. I just want you."

My entire body shook with the force of my heartbeats. "Why now?" I asked.

"Because I'm done trying to protect you. If we do this, people are going to get hurt, including us, and you have to be okay with that."

I tried to force myself to push him out of the way. Manning—*this*—was the one thing I desired most in the world, but I knew, even through my haze, how terribly it could go wrong. "How can I be okay with that?"

"If you can't, tell me you're happier without me in your life," he said, almost pleading. "It's the only way I'll be able to walk away from you again. Otherwise, I'm going to take what I wanted from the start. And I'm going to erase him. For good. For-fucking-ever."

"Corbin?" I asked, shocked that he was even on Manning's mind at a time like this.

"You know what it does to me when you say his name like that?" he asked.

I knew, because he'd said her name to me, too. "I hope it hurts."

"It does."

I looked at the ground, guilt creeping in. Not because of Corbin, but because Manning's perception of Corbin and me was wrong. I hadn't corrected it so I could use it to hurt him, but I hadn't realized how he'd latch on to that information, dragging Corbin into this. "You have no right to talk about him after what you've done," I said quietly. "He's been there for me in a way you never were. He's my best friend."

"And that kills me," he said. "Give me a chance to erase both of them for us."

My throat thickened. *If only.* "You can't."

He waited until I looked up to respond. "I will," he said without a hint of doubt. He moved his mouth over mine, inches away. He was finally going to kiss me—but then what? Were his threats real? Would he really be willing to change everything with just one kiss?

"I can't trust you," I said weakly. I wasn't even sure it was true. With all the ways he'd hurt me, nothing should've raged stronger in me than anger and skepticism—but in that moment, I couldn't find any of that. On some level, I recognized all the things he'd done, he truly believed he'd done them to protect me. And I knew—I was in too deep with a man who'd ruined my life without ever touching me. If this went any further, I might not survive it. "How is it possible that I could trust you?"

I asked more out of awe that it was true than anything, but he had an answer for me anyway. "Because back then, I couldn't give you this choice.

You wouldn't have considered the consequences." Manning leaned in and my breath caught, my heart leaping into my throat. But he didn't kiss me. Instead, he opened the door of the cab. "I was looking out for you, and I still am. Always. Go home, Lake."

Disappointment hit me first, and then it filtered into embarrassment. Shame. Anger. He'd made me want it yet again, and again, he was taking it away. "I knew it. I knew you didn't have the guts to do this."

He slammed the door shut. "I have the guts. I'm prepared to destroy everything in our way, but you're going to lose your sister forever and your best friend, too. And once you put this in motion, I'm never going anywhere you aren't. I'm not walking away from you again. So you better know for goddamn sure you want this." The night had gotten quiet around us, but he grew louder. *We* grew louder. "This isn't like that night on the beach, when you begged me to love you knowing I wasn't allowed. I'm allowing myself now, and you know what'll happen if we do this. Not only will people get hurt, but everything you know about me is only going to get worse." He set his jaw. "I've always thought of you as mine, but now you will be for real. If you thought I was overprotective or possessive before, you have no idea how bad it can get. Are you ready for that?"

Every nerve in my body buzzed. Manning made me dizzy, he inspired an ache between my legs, he was the force behind the hammering heart in my chest. I'd spent every day of my adult life wanting him, loving him, willing to give up anything for him. That hadn't changed—I'd only been made to ignore it. I didn't want to get in the car, but I knew I was supposed to. I was supposed to hate him for what he did to me, and that only made everything more confusing. "I don't know if I'm ready."

He opened the door. "Then get in the fucking cab—go home. If you have the smallest doubt about me, go and think and don't come back to me until you know for sure what we're getting into. Or stay away and be satisfied."

Did I have doubts? There was no question I did. My instinct to love him was as strong as my instinct to cower from him. To cover my chest, anticipating the next blow. He'd beaten my heart black and blue, so what right did he have to try and take it back?

I moved to get in the taxi, but to my surprise, he stepped down from the curb and cupped my face in his palm. With dreamlike slowness, he lowered his mouth to my cheek for a chaste, gentle kiss. Between the open door and him, I was caged into a corner, completely blocked from the rest of the world—consumed by his scent, the warmth of his hand, his smooth lips on my skin. "This doesn't mean I don't want to fight for you," he said. "That I don't want you more than anything, even knowing the damage it can do. It just means I need you to be sure this is what you want."

It's what I want, I nearly screamed, but regardless of the fact that Tiffany and I had been as far apart as possible without actually being estranged, she was still my sister. And he was still her husband, still the man who'd hurt me all those years ago. Who'd nearly *destroyed* me. I couldn't be expected to forget that in a day.

"Fuck," he muttered, wetting his lips.

"What?"

"I was wrong. I said kissing you would change everything, but everything has already changed." He closed his eyes for the briefest moment. "It's too late for me. So in case this is the last chance I get . . ."

And then, tucked against a cab, in the middle of a busy city street, under our starless night sky, Manning bent his head and opened my mouth with his. Our tongues met, our lips pressed together, his hand curled into my jaw—and we kissed. I couldn't believe, just like that, it was happening. We felt each other for the first time but fell into the kiss like old lovers. His thumb grazed my cheekbone as I slid my arms around his neck. When my knees buckled, he caught my waist, pulling me against his solid body, his need pressing my stomach—undeniable, hard, begging. The kiss didn't last long, but it was so right, so heady that I had to pull back because I'd forgotten to breathe and was seeing stars. Worried I might pass out, I steadied myself with a hand on his chest.

He held me there a moment, searching my eyes, and then he took my elbow and pushed me into the cab. Without another word, he closed the door behind me and paid the driver through the passenger side window. "Avenue B and Houston," he said and hit the roof.

My heart ached for him. My insides clenched for him. I was ready to be consumed, to sign over my life to him, to hurt anyone who came between us—and I understood then why he'd shoved me in the cab. Why he'd held back all these years, denied me, hurt me, pushed me away. Once we jumped off this cliff, there was no coming back for either of us. We might fly, we might hit the ground, but once it was done, things could never go back to what they were for anyone involved. I fought every urge, every instinct to call for him, to ask him to come with me.

He'd said it was too late for him—I feared it was too late for me, too.

6
LAKE

Alone in my apartment, my Calvin Klein gown draped over the back of my desk chair, heels discarded at the door and makeup washed away, I tossed and turned in the dark. I wanted Manning there, caging me against the mattress the way he had the cab. I needed him to make up for all the years we hadn't been kissing the way we had hours ago.

I kicked off the bedspread and stared at the ceiling, restless, aching, lost. He'd sliced open a wound long bandaged, scarred though not healed, and now it wouldn't stop bleeding.

Midnight became two in the morning, then four. I drifted in and out of sleep. I could have Manning, but he'd come at a price. Was I willing to pay? Corbin wouldn't understand, and maybe Val wouldn't either.

My parents would never forgive me. Tiffany would be devastated. But after years of drifting apart from all of them, would severing those relationships hurt more than saying goodbye to Manning?

I forced myself to remember my sister, the good, the bad, and everything in between. The time, after she'd hit puberty, she'd pushed me out of her room while her friends were over, and I'd almost fallen down the stairs. The summer we were nine and twelve, and she'd carried me half a mile on her back because I'd sprained my ankle during handball. All the nights I'd sat across from her at the dinner table and shared an inside joke or called her *annoying* or let her use me as a scapegoat for whatever trouble she'd gotten into that week. The nights I'd lounged in her bed and watched in the mirror as she'd attempted bigger lips with the aid of liner or modeled clothing out of shopping bags, tags springing off her as she walked a makeshift runway.

I tortured myself with the memories but the instant that afternoon she'd sauntered up to Manning at the construction site came to mind, I lost my heart to my stomach. She'd swiped him right out from under me, and he'd let her. She'd already gotten more of him than she deserved. I could acknowledge the terrible thing I was doing to her, and how painfully I loved him, but I couldn't think of them together so I didn't.

A garbage truck growled and beeped down my street, stirring the peaceful night into a new day.

Regardless of the fact that I'd seen and wanted and loved him first, he *legally* belonged to her. She'd kissed and touched and made love to him first, but he *actually* belonged to me.

I didn't choose *her,* he'd told me. He hadn't chosen me, though. Could I get over that?

Give me a chance to erase both of them for us. Would he ever be able to?

I wasn't sure, but what also echoed in my mind was what he'd said right before he'd finally put his lips on mine. *In case this is the last chance I get . . .*

The last chance. The end of us. Did I say goodbye to him for good? Or had my fate always been to get everything I wanted, just not the way I'd planned?

The excruciating idea that I might send him back to Tiffany, that I'd give her more of the time and love that belonged to me, was too much to handle. Unequivocally, without question or condition, I loved Manning and he was mine, and I didn't want to wait any longer.

I sat up in bed, the room a dreamy white-blue with early dawn. Wrapping the top sheet around myself, I clutched it to my chest and went to the living room to dial 411. There were people I should've called first. Tiffany, to confess everything. Corbin, to prepare him for the blow. Val, to get her to stop me. Instead, I asked for the W in Union Square. When the front desk connected me to Manning Sutter, the line rang and rang until I eventually had to face the fact that he wasn't there at six in the morning.

A pit formed in my stomach. I'd never asked how long his trip was. What if he'd only been here two nights and I'd missed my chance? Worse, what if something had happened between the theater and his hotel? As defensive as I'd been of my city, it was true—this wasn't the safest place. I knew someone who'd been hit by a cab, and I'd read news stories about people falling onto subway tracks. A friend of one of my classmates had been mugged not far from the theater where Manning and I had just been.

I traded my sheet for the first things I found, baggy jeans and a white sweater warm and fuzzy enough to face a wintry day. I grabbed my purse and boots on the way, but I didn't even make it into the hall.

Manning stood at my front door, still in his suit, his hair as disheveled as it'd been after a hot day on the construction site. I didn't need to ask why he was there. By his hungry eyes, I knew the answer. He stepped into my tiny doorway and I flinched, my heart pounding, the silence growing thick between us as he dominated the space.

"I . . ." I choked. Overcome, I tried to tell him I'd been coming to find him. He was so large, so *there*, impatience rolling off him. I knew what he wanted, what I wanted, but faced with the reality of it, I wasn't sure how to ask for it. "I called the hotel . . . I . . ."

"You better find your words, Lake, because I'm going to need to hear you say it before I take a step into this apartment."

My chest rose and fell faster as I tried to catch my breath. The gap between us lessened, growing tenser. Hotter. He was here. He'd come for me. I just had to say it. "I thought about it all night. I thought about you."

"And?"

"I know there'll be consequences, but . . ." I bit my bottom lip. "I want this anyway. I want you."

He kicked the door shut. My breath caught with its slam and before I could even exhale, Manning had my face in his hands, his mouth landing hotly on mine. He walked us backward while I tried to keep up, grabbing his shirt, touching his stubbled cheeks. I reached my arms around his neck, but he was so big—had he always been this tall?—that I stumbled. He caught me by the waist, pressing my back up against a wall.

I lost all sense of where we were in the apartment until he drew back. As he held my face, steps from my bedroom, there was nothing but the heated breath between our parted mouths, and then his thumbs as he grazed each one to the center of my bottom lip.

"Lake." His voice was sweet and thick as syrup, all the intensity of the moment poured into my name. How could it not be that way? There were a million things I wanted to say and do. All that made sense right then was him.

"Manning," I responded.

He touched my hair, gentle and reverential, then fisted the hem of my sweater, pulling it with a ferocity that made my insides tighten. "I've never done this," he said.

My stomach was already flipping, my hands shaking, my thoughts giddy, so his unexpected words provoked a nervous giggle. "Done what?"

"I want to feel every part of you against me." He returned his hands to my cheeks and pecked my forehead, then the tip of my nose. "I want to know all the ways you fit me."

I tilted my head to meet his mouth.

"No," he said. "Hold still."

It was harder than it sounded not to move as he pressed his lips to mine, slow, damp, then kissed his way around my mouth, each contact growing more urgent. When his hips connected with my stomach, we each inhaled a deep breath. Manning was kissing me. The roughened mouth I'd dreamed about was opening me up. His solid, strong, slightly crooked nose pressed against mine. He made love to my mouth—that was the only way to describe it. Maybe he'd really never done this, because this wasn't sex. It was an act of pure love.

His grip tightened and the kiss turned greedy. He became demanding, hard, almost angry. I was willing, soft, almost terrified. If he was as scared as I was, he didn't show it. I tried to take his shirt off, but I couldn't even get a button through its loop. His big body trapped me to the wall, and I felt nothing from the waist down except his erection against my stomach. Things suddenly became real—I was sixteen again and unsure I could keep up with such immensity. "I don't know what I'm doing," I blurted.

"It's me, Lake. Focus on me." He took my trembling hands in his steady ones and moved them around his neck. With a hand under my bottom, he lifted me, and instinctively, I wrapped my legs around his middle. As he ground into me once, a need I'd never felt took over.

"*Manning.*" I didn't know what else to say during the best moment of my life so I just let him kiss me dizzy. Except that wasn't right, because I was kissing back, my own mouth hot and insistent, eager to consume him, to take everything I'd ever wanted. It got ugly, our noses mashed, teeth clinking, lips burning.

Manning held me so tightly, I didn't notice we were moving until my back hit the mattress. With the urgency of his hardness rubbing my most sensitive spots, his hands everywhere all at once—my hair, my face, my hips and legs—my fear fell away like a robe, baring my naked self, flushed with acute longing. I bypassed his buttons, gathering the fabric of his dress shirt in my fists as I tried to get it over his head. He yanked it off by the collar and stood. Watching me from the foot of the bed, he undid his pants. "If only you could see yourself right now," he said. "You are my fantasy come to life, you're so . . ."

As he stripped down, my throat closed. His tender words couldn't distract me. It was not humanly possible that penis would fit inside me. I scooted back on the bed and away from him until I saw it there in his face—he was afraid, too. Here I was, underneath him for the first time, when he'd fought so hard to keep me at a distance. No matter how many years had passed, or how much I'd matured, I couldn't expect Manning to switch gears this fast. I knew him. Part of him would still feel like he was tarnishing something pure.

"Manning?" I said.

"You're scared," he said. "I'll slow down."

Now, the only thing that alarmed me was that he might change his mind. I reached out for him. "I'm not," I said. "Not at all. I'm ready."

"Are you?" he asked, staying where he was. "Nothing'll ever be the same afterward."

Words could not express my need for him. It would take more for me to break through this wall Manning had put between us, this sense that I was too pure for a man like him. So I channeled my inner-Val, since she was the most confident, experienced girl I knew. In the steadiest voice I could manage, I said, "I want you so much, Manning, please—I need you to . . ."

His jaw ticked. "Need me to what?"

My heart raced. I didn't know if I was wet enough for everything standing in front of me, but I'd fooled around before and had definitely never felt this hot or horny or excited. "I need to feel you inside me."

"Lake . . ." I could see his instincts warring. If his guilt won out, I'd die on the spot, either of embarrassment or sexual frustration, I was sure of it.

"It's okay, Manning," I said, a little more timidly than I meant. "You can fuck me."

He closed his eyes, frowning as if the words hurt him, but it only lasted a second. With a flare of his nostrils, he grabbed my ankle and pulled me back down the bed. My sweater rode up to my waist, and he impatiently yanked off my jeans without even bothering with the fly.

He climbed over me, spreading my legs with his knees. "You know what you're asking for, Birdy?"

I didn't. I'd never been fucked. I'd never been made love to, either. But I was afraid if I told Manning the truth, he'd only see that sixteen-year-old girl in front of him and talk himself out of this. I was a virgin, and I was scared, but more than that, I wanted to feel every moment of this, to give us both everything we needed. So I bit my bottom lip and said, "Yes."

I barely had time to appreciate the expanse of his chest before he was fully on top of me, his hands inside my sweater, his length against me, this time with only the thin layer of my underwear between us. I was dying to touch him, to take in everything that was happening, but things moved fast. Where did I put my hands? Did he want me to be loud, quiet, rough, gentle? What did he like?

Reading my hesitation, he said into my mouth. "You can touch me. I'm completely yours."

"Where?"

"Any-fucking-place you want." He cupped the back of my head in one hand and lifted my butt with the other. "Don't you know how crazy you make me? You never understood."

"I did," I said.

"No you didn't. Whatever torment you thought I endured, times that by a hundred. I wanted so bad to just . . ." From behind, he pushed aside my underwear and rubbed between my legs. Only then did I *really* feel how wet I was. His fingers slipped over me and then inside me, and I arched my back with a sudden gasp.

"I want to see you do that every day until I die," he grated out.

Forever. He was completely mine, he'd said, and I was his. Emboldened, I placed my hands on his shoulders and held on as he touched me for the first time. His tenderness surprised me after years of suppressing his desires, but as I looked into his eyes, I read the heat there—the same suppressed fervor I'd seen in the foyer years ago. I didn't want him to hold back anymore. "I'm ready," I said.

"So am I," he murmured. "I could spend the day exploring every inch of you, Lake." He took my panties off all the way. "But before I do, I want to feel you in a way I've denied us for so long."

My heart skipped. I wasn't yet used to this side of him, the one who gave me what I asked for. Manning and I were about to have sex. Manning. Me. Sex. I had wanted it so desperately for so long—*did* I know what I was asking for? "Now?" I asked.

"Yes, now. You want to wait another six years?"

I tried to catch my breath. I needed to relax. This was Manning, not some guy I'd picked up at a bar. That didn't help, though, because this was *Manning*. He could hurt me in so many ways, physically the least of them.

I spread my legs wider as he adjusted his hips and began to enter me. I lost my breath and didn't hear anything he said after that. The pain was real. Everything wonderful about the moment for which I'd waited so long was reduced to the pressure between my legs, the feeling of being stretched wider than I was supposed to.

"Fuck," he breathed, pulling up my top, exposing my bra to kiss my chest. "Are you okay?"

I couldn't speak, so I nodded hard and focused on the weight of what we were doing—and Manning, real and solid on top of me. I dropped a hand onto the feather comforter, satisfied with the way it compressed in my fist. For years, all he'd done was hold back. I wanted him unbridled. I wanted him as hard and as fast as he wanted to give it to me.

"You're so . . . Jesus Christ, you're tight," he said, sounding almost surprised as he slid partway out and pushed back in.

Why, if it hurt, did I want him to do that again? And again and again? His most exquisite agony felt better than any other touch I'd received. "Please, Manning," I said. "Just do it."

"Do what?"

Take my virginity. "I want you all the way in, right now," I said, pulling on his hips.

He looked between us. "You're ready for me, but you're really fucking tight, Lake. I've never felt anything like it. If I thrust, it'll hurt."

After all the times I'd claimed to be a grownup, I couldn't stand the thought that Manning might see me as a child. I looked into his eyes, thumbing the tiny scar on his lip. "I want all of you. Now. I can take it. Haven't I waited long enough?"

"Look at you." He kissed me. "You're so fucking beautiful. So sexy," he breathed into my mouth. "Relax for me and know that you are giving me the world right now."

With his reassurances, I released the tension in my legs, opening wider for him. It wasn't enough to make it feel good, but when he looked me in the face, his brows furrowing with his own pain or ecstasy, my world opened up as well. No matter what, I'd never stopped loving him for a second. "Please," I whispered.

Manning kept his eyes on mine and thrust deep, ripping me open. "Oh my God," I cried as a searing pain burnt a path all the way to my scalp.

"What? What happened?" Manning's voice sounded distant. "*Lake?*"

It took me a moment to realize I was squeezing my eyes shut, one hand tearing at the bedspread while I nearly drew blood from his back with the other. He pulled away, but I scrambled to keep him there. "Wait." I blinked his beautiful face into focus. "I'm sorry," I said. "Keep going."

"You're *sorry?*" he asked, incredulous, his forehead wrinkling. "What was that? You're stiff as a board." He took my chin, forcing my eyes to meet his. "Tell me what . . ."

My heart pounded so hard, there was no way he didn't feel it against his chest. I hung on to him, trying to quell my queasiness. Realization dawned in his expression the same moment I opened my mouth. "I'm . . ." I started. "I've never . . ."

"Shit." He pushed up. "*Shit*, Lake."

"No," I said, trying to bring him back on top of me. "I don't want you to stop."

He got off the bed, going pale as he looked at the sheet and then down at himself. "You're bleeding. You're fucking *bleeding*." He paced the room. "Oh, God."

"I-I'm sorry. I just wanted it to be perfect." Things had moved so fast. I didn't care—I didn't want to slow down. All my friends had lost their virginity in high school. I was the only one who'd held out and for what? At twenty-two, I still felt exposed and childish. I pulled the sheet around myself and sat up. "Please don't go," I said, hiccupping. "I'm sorry I didn't tell you."

"Stay right there," he said, anguish on his face. "Don't move."

He left the room. Mortified, I kicked the stained sheet away, hurrying to put my underwear back on. I pulled my sweater down as far as it would go, afraid he'd return and see the truth—as far as I'd come, in many ways, I was still that same, inexperienced sixteen-year-old girl.

7

LAKE

Manning returned to my bedroom, wiping his hands on a damp cloth before he ran it over his shaft to clean the blood away. "Why are you getting dressed?" he asked, glancing at my underwear.

Hadn't I exposed enough? "Don't leave, Manning."

"Leave?" He kneeled at the foot of the bed, looking up at me. "Lake—I'm not going anywhere. Lie back."

I did as he said, and he gently moved my underwear aside to wipe the blood away. Even if he didn't mean it to, it felt good, the towel tepid and soothing. I moaned softly, and he lingered there, running it over me with a little more pressure. Just as the warmth started to build, he threw the towel aside. "Up."

Cautiously, I rose from the bed, standing before him in just my sweater and panties. He was still hard, still tortured as he looked me in the face. "You're a virgin?"

"This doesn't change anything," I quietly begged him.

To my surprise, he dropped to his knees and pulled me to him by my hips. "Sweet, sweet girl," he said, his eyes intently on me. "It changes everything. Why didn't you tell me?"

Unsure of how to put it, I spun the thin ring on my index finger. "I—I was afraid you'd think I was too innocent and not go through with it."

"But you and Corbin—"

"Were never together," I admitted.

"Yesterday it seemed like . . . and your mom said he was your boyfriend."

"I never told her that. She assumed, and I think Corbin wants her to think so because he . . ." I closed my mouth. This didn't seem like the right moment to upset Manning.

"He still wants you," Manning said. "I know that; it's hardly a secret. But he was all over you yesterday. I thought you were a couple."

"I let you believe that because I wanted to hurt you."

He ran his hands up my backside and under my sweater, squeezing my waist as he dropped his forehead on my stomach. His voice nearly broke when he said, "You waited for me."

"Not waited. Hoped. I didn't think it would ever happen," I said, my heart in my throat, "but I couldn't bring myself to do it with anyone else."

"I don't deserve it."

I touched his hair, inky black softness sprouting through my fingers. "If not you," I said, "then who?"

He turned his face up to mine again. "If I'd known, Lake, I never would've done it like that. I'm so . . . *fuck*, I'm so sorry. I want nothing more in this world than to worship you. To show you how much I love you because words aren't enough."

Immediately, tears filled my eyes. "Love me?"

"Was there ever any question that I do? Even with all the fucked-up things I did, you can't tell me you didn't know, for a moment, that I was in love you."

Hearing the words I already knew to be true was validation for all of it. For the way I'd pushed him so many times over those two years I'd lived at home. My confessions had scattered on the beach the night I'd found out about the wedding—*I'm all wrong without you*, I'd said, and had gotten no response but waves crashing on the shore. This morning, though, he loved me. A tear slid down my cheek. "Show me, Manning, please. Don't make me wait any longer."

With a kiss to my chest, he sat back on his knees. Holding my hips, he brushed his lips down my stomach, then pressed them to the front of my underwear. It was an innocent kiss that felt anything but—and one that made me inhale a shaky breath. He kissed me there again, dampening the white cotton. Despite the gentle way he touched me, I felt the urgency in his movements as his fingertips dug into my skin, then a pull in my stomach so sharp, it almost hurt.

I tugged his hair. "I want this. You don't need to go slow."

"Yes I do. Let me savor this. It'll hurt less if you're wet and ready."

"I am ready." I couldn't breathe fast enough. I only wanted to feel as close as possible to him. "It didn't hurt that bad," I lied.

He stood, tilting my head up by my chin. "Being your first means everything to me. I haven't just dreamed about it, Lake. I've had nightmares about it."

"That's what I was afraid of," I said.

"I've hated myself for how badly I've wanted you." He tucked my hair behind my ear, then slid his hands down my back, pulling me flush against him. "You were always the last person I should be fantasizing about. You were too young, and then you were too pure, and then you were gone. All those times I was tempted, I thought . . ."

He trailed off as he scanned my face. My nipples were already hard in my bra, but as his gaze darkened, they tingled. He had to know he had nothing to hate himself for. I stepped out of his embrace and pulled my sweater over my head. I wanted to press myself against his naked chest. I was nearly bared to him, my panties clinging to my pubic bone with his saliva, but I still didn't know how to act or ask for what I wanted.

"You thought what?" I prompted.

"I thought it'd kill me to say no to you, but I did, and here I am."

Early morning sun glowed through the windows, lightening the white walls. Now that we'd slowed down, I had time to think about what we were doing. The countless times I'd imagined sex with Manning, I never thought I'd be this nervous.

Manning set his dark eyes on me, and there was so much behind them, I couldn't help asking, "Are you having second thoughts?"

"Not even close. I'm just having thoughts."

"Like?"

He stuck his fingers under the straps of my bra and slid them down my shoulders. "Turn."

I faced the bed. He pressed a wet kiss on one shoulder, running his mouth up the line of my neck. My hair stood on end. I closed my eyes to savor the brush of his knuckles over my back as he unhooked the clasp of my bra. I caught it before it fell off.

He put one arm around my stomach and pulled my back to his front. "It's okay," he said, gripping the bra between the cups and taking it from me.

He hummed against my skin and took my breasts in his hands. His long fingers met in the middle as he squeezed me to him harder, rolling his hips into my backside.

"I'm thinking about how I've dreamed . . ." he murmured. "And fantasized . . . of having this. How I've tortured myself over *not* having this."

The fear in his voice calmed me a little. This wasn't just a big deal to me. I put my hands over his, my insides tightening with the way his palms scraped my bare, sensitive skin.

"Let me see you," he said.

I turned hesitantly, my face warming, my eyes on our bare feet. I remembered the night I'd stripped for him in the lake, me and him in the moonlight. I'd been young and foolish around Manning too many times to be that confident now. He stood there staring until he said, "You're shaking."

It wasn't only that winter had seeped into all corners of my room, or that this would change everything for me. I couldn't imagine a life in which I didn't give myself to Manning, and at the same time, I couldn't believe it was really happening. "Have you ever done this before?" I fought against the urge to pull my hair over my shoulders, the only means left to cover myself. "I mean taken someone's virginity. Obviously it's not your first time having sex."

"It might as well be. Nothing's ever mattered to me as much as this."

"Nothing?" I asked. His words made me courageous, so I touched his chest. "Not your wedding day? Or the day your sister was born?"

He moved my hand over his heart. "Nothing. And no," he added. "I haven't done this before."

I wanted to touch him more, but his other hand moved between my legs, stealing my focus. I swallowed up at the ceiling, my lids falling closed as his fingers firmed through the thin material of my underwear. I grabbed onto one of his shoulders, hanging on to him.

When I opened my eyes, he was watching me. "I can't believe I'll be your first," he said. "And your only."

"My only," I repeated, still getting used to the idea. Not that I'd ever thought of anyone else that way, but I doubted any of this would seem real for a while.

The words affected him, too, his expression contorting as if it hurt him. "How many others did you turn down for me?" he asked.

I sucked my lower lip into my mouth. "Besides Corbin? None."

"You don't even realize, do you? How many asked you out? How many wanted to, but couldn't? They never even stood a chance. You don't even know what you do to us."

Focused on his words, I almost missed him slipping a finger under the elastic. With the skin on skin contact, I sighed, wanting more than his feathered touch. "You don't have to hold back," I said. "I can take it."

"I need to go slow, otherwise I'll destroy you, and I'd like if we could do this more than once before I die."

"You were so excited, though. I ruined it."

He chuckled. "Don't worry. I'm still excited."

"But it's not . . ." His finger slid right into me, all the way to the knuckle. I lost my train of thought, gripping his shoulders to keep myself upright. "It should be . . ."

He lowered his mouth to mine and whispered, "Should be what?"

"It was explosive before," I breathed. "Fireworks."

"Maybe you don't feel what I do," he said. "Just because we aren't tearing each other's clothes off doesn't mean there aren't fireworks." With his free hand, he held the back of my head and kissed me. I couldn't even handle *that*, his lips hungry, his tongue searching, his finger moving faster and faster inside me. Still holding my neck, he kissed the underside of my jaw, my throat, my collarbone. I salivated for him. I got wet for him. Nothing mattered but the way he held me in place, his grip strong on my jaw, my body against his. Manning wouldn't have his fireworks any other way but this—burning a slow path through the night sky to an explosion.

"Christ, you're incredibly wet, Lake," he muttered. Was I supposed to be embarrassed by how much his touch excited me? I couldn't tell if he was concerned or aroused until his next comment. "You're going to slide right onto my cock."

I gasped, so shocked that I bucked my hips on his hand. "*Manning.*"

He lifted a corner of his mouth in a half-grin. "What?"

"I've never heard you talk like that. You wouldn't even curse around me."

"There were a lot of things I kept myself from saying around you, but I won't anymore. I'm gonna say them all."

"Say something to me you wouldn't've said before."

"Okay." He took his hand back and stood before me, glorious, naked, huge in every sense of the word, his muscles carved and defined to perfection, as if by my own design. "Get on the bed so I can fuck you, Lake."

My chest stuttered as I exhaled, everything inside me coiling with a fierce need. Biting my lower lip, unable to look away from the heated, almost angry look in his eyes, I staggered back and sat on the mattress. I had no choice but to crawl up the bed as he climbed over me, propping himself up with his arms.

"Say another," I pleaded.

"I want to feel your hands on me."

I ran my nails over his dark stubble, touched the veins in his neck, grazed his chest hair and silently counted his abdominals with my fingers. He let me explore, but after a few moments, he took my hand and lowered it between us. When he placed it over his penis, my throat went bone dry.

He shut his eyes a brief moment, groaning with that one touch. Encouraged by his response, I pushed my palm against the length of him. He twitched in my hand, pink and thick and alive. He was beautiful. All of him.

"God, Lake," he muttered, inhaling through his nose. "Touch me."

I tried not to look as nervous as I felt. I couldn't even wrap my hand all the way around him. I tried to make my fingertips touch, surprised by how hot he was. How had he even gotten it in? Bleeding the first time was normal but he must've torn right through me.

"What're you thinking?" he asked. "I want to hear it all."

"Nothing," I said.

"You have to be a hundred and ten percent honest with me when I'm in your bed," he said. "Do you hear me? Nothing, I mean nothing, is more important than trust when we're like this. That was the last time you'll stay quiet when I'm hurting you."

"What if I want you to hurt me?"

He gritted his teeth. "Then you say it. We talk about it *before* we get in bed. So I'll ask again—what're you thinking?"

"I don't know how you fit inside me earlier," I said simply. "It defies physics."

His eyebrows rose, as if he'd expected any answer but that one. "It's not anything our bodies weren't made to do." He kissed my chest, then slipped a hand under my bowed back, pointing my breasts to the ceiling. He licked his lips, looking torn, then sat back on his calves to remove my underwear. Cupping the undersides of my knees, he slid me to him, holding my legs open, his penis dangerously close. "It's still going to hurt," he said, reading my expression. "No matter how wet I get you, I can't fix that. I'm just going to go slow. At first. Until you get used to me." Holding my leg in one hand, he spread his other over my stomach, maybe to soothe my trembling. "And you're going to get used to me, Birdy."

When he lowered his hand to touch me, I arched my back, but didn't look away from what was about to go inside me. "Manning?"

"Mmm?"

"Even after I turned eighteen, you wouldn't come near me. Did I not turn you on?" I knew how he'd answer, but for all the times he'd shut me out, I wanted to make him squirm. "What's different now?"

He followed my line of sight down to his erection. "Nothing. I've been hard for you before."

Manning didn't squirm at all, but *I* did, wiggling with excitement, biting my bottom lip. "When?"

"That turns you on, huh?" He grunted, lazily exploring me with his hand. "All the times you tortured me just by being close?"

"A little," I admitted.

"A lot." He removed his finger and licked it. "I've barely even touched you and I can taste you on my hand."

My heart beat in my stomach. Manning may have kept quiet about these things in the past, but it definitely wasn't because he was shy. He took me under the knees again, spreading my legs to lie between them. "Wrap them around me."

I locked my feet behind his back.

"Now your arms," he said. "If it gets to be too much, tell me. Or dig your nails into my back and I'll stop."

I circled his neck and tugged on the ends of his hair. "Is hair-pulling allowed?"

He dropped a kiss on my lips. "*You* can do anything you want. Can't hurt me."

With that, he started to push inside me. He paused to adjust himself, working only his head in. I sucked in a breath but it didn't hurt as much this time.

"There was that time on the horse at camp," he said. "You were between my legs and your hair was so soft. You were scared. I felt protective."

I wondered if all the love I felt showed on my face as I looked at him, thinking back to that time when I'd been head over heels for him. It'd affected him, too. Manning got up on his hands and pushed harder into me.

This time when he thrust, it felt good. Slick. My arms loosened, and he grabbed my wrist, putting it back around his neck. "Don't let go, Lake. Please."

I squeezed him more tightly, even as he stayed propped over me. "Then what?" I asked.

"I got hard for you. I was so fucking confused." He started to move, sliding in and out of me. His neck went veiny as he groaned. "And ashamed."

For all the times over the years *I'd* felt confused and ashamed, I didn't want that for him. I knew how hard this was for him, letting himself have the girl he wouldn't even allow himself to want. I gripped the back of his neck. "I'm glad it's you."

"I don't know if I deserve this."

I pulled on him. "You do. Please. Show me how much this means to you."

He bent his head to kiss me, and the moment our lips touched, he let loose. Now I knew what he'd meant. Our bodies were made for this. Each thrust came more slippery, more out of control. I opened for him, taking him deeper, a man who'd never been anything but composed around me. This was a side of Manning I hadn't yet seen, and I couldn't believe I was doing this to him.

"Am I hurting you?" he asked through clenched teeth, even as he seemed completely lost in it. "*Fuck*."

"No," I said, accepting all of him now. "Don't stop."

He kissed me hard on the mouth, sliding one hand over my hip to lift my thigh. He ground into me with more force, driving so relentlessly that the ache deep in my stomach became more of a throb. It was no longer a feeling I wanted him to ease but a place I needed him to fill. He tore his mouth away, keeping his forehead against mine. "How does it feel?"

I was sure I had tears in my eyes when I said, "I can't even answer that."

"I can. You make me so fucking crazy, Lake." With the emotion in his voice, in his face, I started to understand what this was all about—why people confused love and sex. The urgency of his kiss, the sudden build of pleasure, the slapping of skin on skin. If my life were a song, this was the crescendo. I hadn't truly known what it'd meant to love anyone, even Manning, until now. "When I think about you between my legs back then, about all the times I wanted to say *fuck it* and steal you away . . ."

As he took me back years, the present came into focus. The climax building inside me was almost painful, the way everything up until now had been. "It's too much," I panted.

"Then let go," he said. "Let it take over."

Hearing Manning's voice, feeling him on top of me, inside me, his face close to mine, I'd never needed anything more than to take what he wanted to give me. My face burned as I arched my back and gave in to him. He took up a pattern, each hard thrust with a grunt. All I could do was hold on as his back slickened with sweat, as my climax obliterated every thought in my head other than *yes, God, yes*. Every noise but my pained moans. Every feeling but unadulterated pleasure and Manning shuddering over me.

He slammed into me and said, "I can't hold back anymore. You feel too goddamn good." The thought that I weakened him brought me back to earth. Fascinated and sated, I watched his face screw up, his teeth clench. He grabbed one of my hands, lacing our fingers together as he buried himself in me and came hot and fast.

He gave me all his weight, his chest heaving, our bodies stuck together with a film of perspiration. After some time, he lifted his head. His brown eyes had looked upon me with a rainbow of emotions, and not always positive ones. In them I'd seen regret, anger, frustration. Now, they held a depth of love, something I'd gotten glimpses of and had tried to convince myself was all in my head.

Still hanging on to him with five fingers dug into his back, I asked, "Are you okay?"

"Am I?" He grinned. "Birdy, I have never been better."

"You're shaking, too, you know."

"Yeah, no shit. Am I crushing you?" His body covered all of mine, pressing me into the mattress, hiding me from the rest of the world. The apartment's icy air cooled my limbs but wherever our bodies touched, I was warm. "Yes. It feels perfect."

He readjusted his grip on my hand so it no longer felt like he was hanging on for dear life. "I guess I should've warned you the first time would be fast," he said. "I'm not going to pretend I had any control."

"It was fast?" I asked.

He chuckled. "I plan to lose hours of my life learning all the ways to make you come."

I blushed a little. He'd shown me pure bliss, yet that was only part of why I was so at ease. "I feel so close to you right now."

"Me too, Lake." He smoothed a hand over my hairline, and his fingers caught in my tangles. "You've never been more beautiful."

I started to laugh but stopped when I saw that he was serious. I was sweating, and I knew without looking that my face was red. "But I'm a mess," I said.

He shook his head, as if in awe. "I did this," he said, thumbing my warm cheeks, then a mark on my chest. "And this." He kissed me gently on the corner of my mouth. "Pink swollen lips," he whispered. "How can you not be the sexiest thing to me when this mess is because I just had you?"

I moaned involuntarily as he took my earlobe between his teeth, the ache between my legs returning. "Can we do it again?"

"Give a man a minute to recover." He shifted between my legs, still inside me, and I inhaled sharply at the unexpected thrill. But as he reached down to pull out, I noticed the stickiness between my legs and gasped so loudly, he froze.

Oh my God. Oh fuck. We'd had sex without a condom.

It hadn't even occurred to me until this moment. Being with Manning felt so natural. So real. As if anything outside of us didn't exist. Except that wasn't true.

"Manning, we didn't—"

"I know." He stared at me, his expression unreadable.

"What do we do?" I asked. Was he in shock? Angry? "What's wrong? What are you thinking?"

"I'm thinking I'd like to know if you're on birth control."

"I'm not . . . why would I be?"

He dropped his eyes to my chest. I couldn't tell if he was disappointed or upset, but it wasn't like it was my fault. If anyone should've spoken up, it should've been him. I couldn't get pregnant. I was too young. Too broke. I was still in debt because I'd spent the past four years in school to *follow my dreams*. Dreams that didn't include children. As the possibility of a baby hit me, the reality of our situation did, too. It'd been easy enough to ignore before we'd given in, but now that we'd had sex, I almost couldn't wrap my head around what it meant. I'd not only had sex without a condom, but Manning was still someone else's husband.

I began to sweat for real. "I need to get up," I said.

He looked up. "Lake, listen."

"Can you move?"

"Freaking out isn't going to change the situation."

"I need to get up."

"And *I* need a goddamn minute to lie here with you, Lake. Do you have any idea what this meant to me? I've never had this—"

"You're *crushing* me," I cried, avoiding his eyes. He was a married man, and he was unbearably heavy, pinning me, his mistress, to the mattress. And he wasn't just *someone else's* husband. He was Tiffany's. "Get off. I can't breathe."

He rose onto his arms, and I ducked out from underneath him. I pulled the top sheet off the bed, crossing the room as I wrapped myself in it. Maybe it was subconscious guilt, but on my way to the door, my eyes landed on the tiny wooden box on my dresser. The gift Tiffany had given me as her maid of honor. Val had stood in this same spot last night and reminded me of the truth.

He chose your sister, *Lake. He married her.*

Val would be so disappointed by what I'd done. Once again, I'd ignored the consequences like Manning had said I would. I hadn't even cared enough about my own sister, my own future, to protect myself. Manning knew I couldn't say no to him.

Look what you've done, Lake.

Tiffany's accusation the day Manning was arrested was never far from my mind, and this time, there was no doubt it was true. I'd done something awful, and like Val had said, I had nobody to blame but myself. I was an adult now, and using a condom was as much my responsibility as Manning's.

"Lake, come back here." I turned to Manning, who sat on the edge of the bed with his elbows on his knees. "I see your mind spinning."

"We barely even talked about her," I said. "We didn't even . . . we just . . . ."

"I know what we did." He stood and turned away to search the floor. The sight of his naked, tight behind nearly made my heart give out. He was as fit as he'd been that day on the construction site, every muscle visible just beneath the surface. And there, staring back at me, was his subtle, almost invisible tattoo. The thin, black, uneven triangle on the back of his shoulder both warmed and taunted me. I'd always be there, inked onto his skin, but so was that third point. Was it her?

He bent to pick up his boxer-briefs, then pulled them on. "Let's make something to eat, and then we can figure this out."

I couldn't believe I was standing here thinking about his ass after what I'd done. What kind of a person—what kind of a *sister*—did that make me? Tiffany was no angel, but this was another level of betrayal. "Eat?" I asked. "We just had *sex*. How can you think about food now?"

"Well . . ." He turned, a corner of his mouth cocked. "I know it was your first time, but typically—"

"I'm serious, Manning," I said, closing the sheet more tightly around myself. He had a *life* with her. I knew nothing about it, except I could picture them holding hands, kissing, sleeping in the same bed, because it'd all played out in front of me. Every time they'd come up in conversation with my mom, I'd gotten off the phone. I couldn't handle it then, and I certainly couldn't now, naked with Manning's cum dripping down the inside of my thigh. "We shouldn't have done this," I said.

"No?" he asked, wiping the crooked smile off his face. "You look me in the eye and say that, because I'm thinking the exact opposite. That I've been a fucking fool for letting so much time pass without you underneath me."

"You don't even care that you've hurt her," I accused.

"Are you fucking kidding me?" he asked. "Just because I'm not hysterical doesn't mean I don't care. I was trying to shield you from some of the pain, but if you want to have a chat about Tiffany, let's talk." He cracked his knuckles. "You want me to say I feel like shit for hurting the woman who's stood by my side the past four years, then—"

"Stop," I said, covering my ears as I dropped into a squat. "Please stop."

He got down in front of me, taking my elbow. "Lake, calm down. Come sit and we'll talk through this."

"We didn't use protection," I choked out. My stomach churned, and for a moment I worried I'd vomit. I wrenched my arm out of his hand. "What were we thinking? You should've said something. You should've insisted."

"Don't pull away," he said. "I've spent a lifetime trying to stay away from you while you did nothing but make it hard for me. Do not pull away now that I can touch you."

"But it only makes things worse."

He ran his tongue over his bottom teeth, raising two angry eyebrows. "*Worse?*"

I hadn't meant it that way, but the truth was, I'd never been able to think straight or make the right decisions while Manning was around. I was blind around him and always had been. Consequences never mattered until it was too late. I stood and dropped a hand to my side, clutching the sheet closed with the other. "Maybe it's best we take some time to think. Separately."

"Too late for that," he said, taking a firm step toward me. "You can be pissed, or ashamed, or whatever's happening with you, but you're going to do it with me here." He reached for me. "You had your chance to tell me to go, and—"

I stepped back.

"Lake," he warned. "What did I just tell you? I need to be able to touch you right now."

Seeing his frustration, how unraveled he was after we'd only had sex once, excited me. I continued to back away and then spun to bolt from the room. The apartment was so goddamn small, the only private place was the bathroom. I went for it, but Manning was faster, blocking the doorway. I retreated around the living room, my back to the wall as he advanced on me. I dragged a kitchen chair between us and he tossed it aside. The front door was my only exit. I knew I'd never leave the building in a sheet, that I was being irrational, and that he'd catch me before I even got to the door—but I ran anyway, to make him chase me, to make him angry.

He caught up with me in the entryway, picked me up by my waist, and threw me over his shoulder. My stomach dropped with excitement and shame. "We can't do this again," I said, struggling against him.

"We'll be doing it for a lifetime, so you'd better get the fuck over it. I'm not going to chase you down every time."

I had the sensation of falling before my ass hit the kitchen counter. I sucked in a breath, surprised as the sheet fell open, baring me to him. "Manning, I'm serious."

"So am I, goddamn it," he said, yanking me to the edge until he was pressed right between my legs. "I'm dead fucking serious. What'd I tell you outside the theater? Once you're mine, you're mine, and I'm not going to let you run off." He took himself in his hand, gliding his head along my slit. I looked down, fascinated. I hadn't seen us come together before. His tip came back glistening. Was it any surprise that our struggle had left me wet and him hard as granite? Our whole relationship had been push and pull, one long struggle. "You want to know the truth?" he asked. "I've dreamed about it more times than I want to admit—coming inside you and claiming your cunt in the most irreversible fucking way."

My chest tightened, breath sucked right from my lungs with his words. I'd never had the guts to even *fantasize* about hearing him say something so wrong. So dirty. Knowing how hard Manning had worked over the years to keep me pure, his desperation to ruin me only made me hotter. "Do it again," I said. "I want it."

He was poised to enter me, but he didn't. "I want it, too," he said, glancing between us, his knuckles whitening as he gripped himself. "But *fuck*, Lake. I wasn't thinking straight before. We can't take the risk."

Doubt tugged at me—was he not committed, did he not want to stay in New York?—but I knew deep down it wasn't any of that. Manning had promised he was looking out for me. Getting pregnant was the absolute last thing we needed in our situation.

"Put your arms around me," he said. "I miss your warmth already."

I melted a little, pulling myself against his chest. "We've done a terrible thing," I whispered into his neck.

"I know, but you can't punish me by running. I want nothing more than to make everything up to you. Tell me how to make it right." He scraped his cheek against mine. "You want me to end things with her before we do this again?" he murmured. "I'll go straight to the airport, Lake."

He stayed where he was, almost inside me, and I wanted him. Ashamed as I was, I didn't think I could send him home to her now. "I don't want you to go. I've waited so long."

"Then I'll stay right here with you."

"For how long?" I asked.

"I don't know, but I can't end my marriage over the phone. My flight home is scheduled for Friday."

Four days. That was all I'd get for now. "I hate her," I said, trying to picture anything but Tiffany's face. "I hate her for what she's done to me, for so many reasons. But I love her, too."

"I know you do."

"And so do you." The cold counter bit my skin through the sheet. "You've done all this with her."

He pulled back to look me in the face. "My need for you is more than anything else. It's all-consuming."

"That doesn't change the fact that you've been with her, and that you love her."

He took my face in his hands. The warm eyes I'd come to read so well dimmed in a way I'd also, unfortunately, come to understand better than most. My words hurt him. Maybe it wasn't fair to blame him for loving his own wife, but I hated that I hadn't been his first love as he'd been mine. That *she* would always be between us. "Lake." He had a thick but beautiful neck that conveyed his emotions just like his eyes. The veins were pronounced but elegant, his Adam's apple bobbing as he swallowed. "You asked me last night if I love her, and I didn't answer because . . . I'm ashamed that I don't."

I shrank from him. It wasn't the answer I'd expected, and I could see that it pained him to say it. "What?"

"I love her as a friend, and as a person, too—I've come to know her well enough to anticipate and even appreciate her tenacity to be who she is without apology. She and I have been through a lot together. But how can I be in love with anyone when you exist?" He put his forehead to mine. "I'm so in love with you, I have been for so long, that there's no room for anyone else, not even my wife. And it makes me feel like the biggest piece of shit to admit that."

My chest ached. Were the years of disappointment and sadness worth this moment? I couldn't help thinking they were. There was no clear answer. I didn't want to hurt my sister, but I wasn't going to let Manning go now that I had him. "Promise me," I said.

As if he felt my surrender, he pressed a hand to my back and my body arched, my breasts into his chest. I wanted him inside me, whatever the cost. "Anything," he said.

"Promise me you'll leave her."

All I'd done for years was analyze and resist and dream. Now, everything I wanted was right in front of me. Tiffany hadn't hesitated to take it from me.

So I would take it back.

8

MANNING

Sitting on the kitchen counter, Lake clung to me as if I might disappear into thin air. I couldn't really blame her. Even as I stood right between her legs, I could hardly believe where I was.

She'd begun to shake again. I wanted to gorge on her, lose myself in her, forget anything outside this apartment existed, but I worried that if Lake didn't understand the life I was leaving behind, the worse it'd be when she was forced to face it. Tiffany wouldn't lose just a husband, but a home, stability—and a future.

"When I got on the plane here, Lake, I knew what I was getting into," I said. "If I arrived and saw that this was where I needed to be, I knew what I'd be leaving behind. But you don't. You know nothing about my life there."

"Why do I need to? Will it change anything?"

I hesitated. "For me, no. I already know what's at stake." Asking me to end my marriage was fine for Lake, because she hadn't been around for any of it. I was the one who'd surprised Tiffany with a trip to the car dealership after her promotion to assistant buyer. It was me who'd fought with her endlessly over her dirty dishes and the dust I created working in the backyard and each of us forgetting to close the garage door. We were over halfway through a remodel on a home we'd bought together and for which we'd painstakingly chosen granites and paint colors and goddamn cabinet handles and God knew what else— it was always something with the fucking house. If it wasn't the expense and energy of remodeling, it was the guilt I harbored for wearing a suit every day while other men built my home. Tiffany didn't hear me when I told her I hated that not even a drop of my own sweat had gone into putting a roof over our heads. She even bought brand new furniture because what I made didn't come from a store.

None of that occurred to Lake, though, because she lived in fucking la-la land where love was the only thing that mattered. And I loved her for it. I wanted her to stay there, but more than that, I didn't want Lake to wake up one day and resent me or herself for the life she'd pulled out from under her sister. In the past twenty-four hours, I'd seen that Lake could handle herself here in New York, and if she could do that, then she could face the truths I would've kept from her years ago. "I hope it wouldn't change anything for you, either," I said, "but you should still know."

"There's nothing that can make me feel better or worse. Even if it's a bad marriage." She curled a hand against my back. "Is it?"

"In some ways, it's the kind of marriage I thought it would be. We get along most of the time. We have fun. When she pulls shit with me, I call her on it, but I get tired of that." Tiffany hated when I traveled and would go out of her way to make me feel guilty about it. And when I *was* home, she tried to manipulate me into doing things I didn't care about, like shop, or go to rooftop bars with her friends, or sit on my ass at the beach when we had a perfectly good pool at home. I started to pull away from Lake. If we were going to talk about Tiffany, I figured I should get dressed. "I want a partner," I said, "not someone I have to babysit or watch myself around."

"Don't go," Lake said, climbing back onto me. "Don't leave this spot. Don't talk about her." She nuzzled my cheek, then drew back to look me in the face. In a breathy voice, she said, "I just want you to promise me this is it for us."

There were times at home I couldn't picture Lake clearly, she'd been away so long. But I'd never, not one day, forgotten the unusual blue of her eyes. Anything I'd come across in that color had been like a blow to the chest, but not anymore. Now, I wanted to live in that color. "I promise you, Lake, it's you and me now," I said. "I wouldn't be here now if there were another way."

"I need more." She moaned when I pulled her a little too far onto the head of my dick. "You owe me more."

Her hair was tangled from my hands, her cheeks flushed from my cock partway inside her. What *I* needed was to either separate from her or fuck her, to feel the friction of her airtight pussy. In that moment I'd give her whatever she wanted. "I thought the passion my parents had could only turn me bad," I said to her, "but it's going without it that's put me too close to the edge. I need to be able to feel you whenever I want. What do you need?"

She breathed through her mouth, looking about as frustrated as I felt not being inside her. "Leave Orange County and come live here," she said.

Southern California was the only home I'd ever known. I'd fought my way to a living. I had a house, a wife, and a career that was making me richer than I'd ever dreamed I'd be. I knew what Lake would say to that, though, because she'd said it before—those were just details. This, her and me, was what mattered. Back then, I'd told her it wasn't enough. I wasn't going to do that to her again. "Of course I'll come," I said. "I had more than enough time to think it over as I sat outside your door all night. What I'm more worried about is work and supporting us."

"You *cannot* work for my dad anymore. I want nothing to do with them. That's the only way we'll work."

I took a few measured breaths, scanning her face. I couldn't picture myself in a city, but I already knew I wasn't going to be anywhere Lake wasn't. What she was asking for, it was an easy promise to make, because it was exactly what I wanted. "I'll do anything to get you, Lake. If you want me to quit and move, consider it done."

She gripped my shoulders. Her strength, the urgency in her voice, surprised me. "Promise me."

"This'll break your relationship with Tiffany," I warned. "I can't protect you from that."

"It's already broken. I can handle it. Just promise me."

"I promise. The move, the job, the divorce, I promise, now tell me what else you want."

"I want . . ." She avoided my eyes, struggling to get it out, and that had me hanging on her every word. Was there anything I couldn't give her? "I want—I want you inside me."

With that, I lost any sense of what we were talking about. I pulled her nearly off the counter and onto my dick. The sheet fell in a heap at our feet. She slid on easier this time, but it was still the tightest fit I'd ever experienced. To know I was the first man to make her feel this good, to love not just her mind and her heart, but now her body, too, it did things to me. Things that terrified and exhilarated me. I'd kept her at arm's length for a long time because the passion between us, even when it'd been strangled, scared me.

"Why'd you sit outside my door all night?" she whispered hotly. "Why didn't you just come in?"

"You know why. I wanted you to be sure and come to me. I didn't sit there waiting, though. I was worried about the broken lock."

She sucked in a breath as I filled her all the way, until I couldn't get any deeper. "The lock?" she asked.

"Had to make sure you were safe from intruders," I teased, murmuring in her ear. "But believe me when I say, I thought about breaking in. Intruding on you. Why do you think I was standing at the door when you opened it, fighting myself from coming in?"

Her arms clenched around my neck, her eyes squeezing shut as I started to slide in and out of her. "I want you to come in," she said.

I growled a little, watching her take me deeper and deeper. "Look at you," I murmured to her. "You're perfect for me."

"You're too big," she said.

"No I'm not." I never wanted to hurt her, especially her first time, but admittedly, it turned me on to know I *was* breaking her in—that we'd spend a lifetime fitting ourselves together. "I'm not too big and you aren't too small," I repeated, "because my body was made just for yours."

"Erase it for me," she whispered.

It killed me that in that moment, she was thinking about the women—*woman*—who'd come before her. If I thought ending things with Tiffany now instead of later would make this easier, maybe I would've, but I owed Tiffany more than a phone call from her sister's apartment. All I could offer was to make Lake feel good. I wanted to do that above all else. "I can erase it. I can fuck it all right out of you. Just say the word."

She nodded. "Do that."

I twitched inside her just remembering how she'd asked for it earlier to cover up her timidity. Her virginity. Which now belonged to me. It was my own fault she'd waited this long, but I couldn't say I was sorry about it. Once, I'd wanted her to stay that untouched girl. Not anymore. Now, I wanted those words she'd swallowed and saved, as much as I wanted to be the only man to ever get them. "Do what?" I encouraged.

She lowered her eyes. The flush that crept up her chest turned my rock-hard erection to steel. She wasn't the same girl I'd met six years ago, but I hated to admit that her innocence still turned me on as much as anything. So many times I'd restricted my fantasies that it had become a sort of game for me. The things I couldn't have. I'd get so overcome with my need for Lake, that some nights, picturing Lake was the only way I'd get off.

"I can't say it again," she said. "I'm too embarrassed."

"Mmm." I angled to kiss her neck, her collarbone. "I tried so hard not to corrupt you, and now I don't plan to do anything but. You don't have to ask me for anything this morning. We'll get there." Reluctantly, I drew back from her. "But first we need a condom."

Lake chewed her bottom lip. "Maybe we should just . . . I mean, do you really think I'd get pregnant?"

Well, fuck. I hadn't expected her to say that, and it made my erection rage harder. I'd thought a lot about having kids in a big-picture sense but the primal urge to procreate was specific to Lake. In other words, I wanted to put a baby in her *now*. I had no desire to put a layer of anything between us. But one urge of mine trumped all others—protect her.

"Until you and I are here and settled, we gotta use a condom," I said, internally cursing myself. I'd lost control earlier, and as goddamn heavenly as it'd felt, I couldn't put Lake at risk again. "So I better tear myself away and go find a convenience store."

Lake scooted to the edge of the counter and used her foot to open a kitchen drawer. Amidst loose batteries, chopsticks, and a laminated Blockbuster card laid a chain of Trojan packets. "Good thing Val likes to have sex," she said.

"Good fucking thing indeed," I said, picking them out of the junk pile. I was about to tear one off, but instead, I palmed the whole string of them, picked Lake up off the counter, and carried her to the bedroom. I'd had enough of this cold, soulless kitchen.

"Should we leave any for Val?" she asked with a half-smile.

"Nope."

I set her down. I wanted to watch her put the condom on me, but not now. I was too eager. "On the bed," I said.

She slid back on the mattress, watching as I ripped a packet open with my teeth and rolled on the condom. As I secured it, I had to admit I liked the apprehensive yet rapt look on her face.

I crawled over her until she was on her back, noting how her lips were already reddened and roughened from my mouth. I catalogued her freckles as I kissed my way over her right shoulder, down to her elbow. I turned over her forearm, touching the faint crescent scar from a kitten bite, and pressed my mouth to the thin skin of her wrist. Her stomach rose and fell. I inspected the lines of her palm, the downy hair on the backs of her knuckles, the delicate pink of her fingernails. I laced our hands together, turning them over.

"What are you doing?" she asked breathlessly.

"I want to know all the ways you fit me."

"Why?"

I put her right arm back and started on the left. "Does it feel good?" I asked.

"Yes."

"Then let me do it." I was learning her. I'd have the rest of my life to do it, but I was greedy. I wanted to know now. I'd been confined by my imagination all these years. No more. If I touched her and she twitched, or her nipples stood a little taller, or her hips bucked, I'd tuck that information away for later.

I ghosted my mouth between her tits, and her areolas went pink and pebbled. I palmed the bottom of one breast and stretched my fingers to her collarbone. Her nipple grew into the heart of my palm.

"I'm sorry they're small," she said.

"What?" I asked.

"My breasts. They aren't that big."

I looked up at her. If they were small or perky or blemished or gold-tipped, I didn't notice. They seemed just right, and they were hers, and mine, so I wouldn't change a thing. "Are your nipples sensitive?" I asked.

"I think so."

"Does it feel good to have my hand on them?"

Slowly, watching me, she nodded.

"How about my mouth?" I lowered my head, taking half her breast into my mouth, sucking up until I'd reached the tiny pink peak. If I splayed my fingers wide enough, I could squeeze both tits in one hand. I'd sink my cock between them and they wouldn't meet over the top of my shaft. These were things I needed to know. I'd known nothing up until hours ago, and now I'd learn it all.

Lake fisted my hair. I realized I'd been sucking on her nipple hard enough to make her squirm. I tugged it between my teeth, and she urged her pelvis into my chest. Gently, I felt her between the legs. She was wet enough that I knew it was working. However long it took to get her off, I'd do it, but sooner was better so I could start over again.

I slid down farther, to the bottom of her ribcage, her belly button and pubic bone. She was covered in fine light hair that begged to be caressed. It didn't look as if she'd ever shaved, and she was blonde enough that she didn't need to. I would show her how, though. My chest inflated as I thought of designing her most intimate parts to my satisfaction.

I pushed her thighs open, and she tried to close them. "Stop," she said.

She was embarrassed. I planned to inspect every part of her, but I understood if she had a long way to go until she was comfortable with me. "Have you ever looked at yourself?" I asked.

"No."

I thumbed her folds apart and found her pink as candy. I licked my lips as she tried to shove my head away. "Manning."

"It's your first time?"

"Yes."

"Mine too." That was a lie, but as far as Lake was concerned, it was true. She didn't look placated. Maybe she didn't realize what a big deal that was. Eating a girl out was as intimate as kissing her. I'd never cared too much for it. I did it to be fair. But with Lake, I *needed* it, and bad, and in that sense, it was a first for me.

"Maybe we should wait," she said. "I haven't showered since before the show."

"I need you like this," I said. "Not perfect and clean and shiny. I want to eat you when you've been out all day, after you've been fucked and filled by me." I passed just the tip of my tongue over her clit so I wouldn't scare her. "Don't make me wait, Lake."

She didn't answer, but she stopped trying to push me away. Still holding her open, I tasted her. She responded so quickly, squirming under me, that I had to slide my hands around her thighs and hold her in place as I gorged on her. Her tightening grip in my hair and the moans echoing through the room told me it was working. When her pussy was nice and slick, when it got more pliant and metallic-tasting, I pulled my mouth up and continued on my way, kissing down her thigh until she was forced to release my head.

"Why'd you stop?" she asked.

"The first few times I make you come, I want it to happen on my dick. After that, you can come any place you like."

"These aren't the first few times you've made me come," she said. "I've lain in my bed at my parents' house and orgasmed just touching myself while I thought about you."

I groaned with my mouth on the inside of her knee, noting with interest that the closer she was to orgasm, the bolder she grew. I still had plenty of skin to cover—toes, ankles, calves, and more—but my erection was getting painful. Holding the underside of her knee, I stood and hooked her ankle over my shoulder. I ran my hand up one of her legs, along her thigh and then right into heaven itself, pumping two fingers inside her.

I flashed back to my time in solitary confinement when I used to lie on the floor, overcome with guilt and remorse when I couldn't force away the fantasies any longer. Lake on her back for me . . . welcoming me inside . . . begging for me, only me. Young and tight and willing. My heart pounded as I wet my thumb with her own juices and massaged it over her clit. "You have no idea how good this feels for me," I said.

"For *you*?" she asked. Her cheeks and chest were bright red. "Oh, oh. Oh, God."

I watched my knuckles disappear inside her. "There's nothing in this world like your pink pussy, Lake."

With a shocked gasp, she turned her face into the comforter, her expression contorted like she couldn't bear it. "You can't say that."

"I just did, and I don't want you to ever forget that it's true." I rubbed her, bringing her climax on slowly but surely. Just like when I'd made love to her earlier, it was clear that words and memories helped send her over the edge; I could practically *see* her aching from what I'd said. Once I got inside her, I wouldn't last long, so I needed her ready before I fucked her. "Nothing will ever feel this good. Understand me? You and I . . . we're going to do this for the rest of our lives and I can tell you, there's nothing better out there."

Her folds fluttered around me, and she trembled with the quakes. Her hair made intricate art, strands of blonde branching and entwining over the white comforter. I kept her leg pressed to my neck with one hand and angled my sheathed cock against her with the other. When I'd gotten my head in, I flexed my hand over her chest. My fingers, wet from her, left damp spots on her skin. I wanted to cover her, box her in so she felt completely mine. Once I had her back pinned to the mattress and her calf to my neck, I plunged into her.

She cried out, grabbing onto my forearm. I wondered if it still hurt. For all the times I'd kept my hands to myself, I wanted to go fast, hard, have my fill of her and then some. I angled even deeper so she'd feel every ridge, every vein, from her toes to her fingers and know she belonged to this, to me, to us. "I love you, Lake," I said, pounding her. "And I want you to fucking come."

Her chin trembled as she looked up at me. Maybe I was hurting her. Maybe she was scared. Before I could slow down, she said, "I never thought about sex until I met you."

"Yeah? When was that?"

She arched her back, squeezing her eyes shut. "Before the fair, I think?"

"That early on?" The thought of young Lake lusting after me had me thrusting harder into her. I couldn't hold back any longer, but I kept my eyes on hers as my control slipped. "What'd I do to you in your fantasies?"

"You were just so big. You eclipsed everything else. We'd be alone, finally, and that was all it took to . . ."

"But I must've touched you."

"It would be in the truck or on the kitchen counter at your old apartment or at my parents' house. That was the only way I knew how to fantasize—to have you finish what you started."

"I'm going to start and finish every time," I promised her. I wished I had three, four, five hands. I wanted to touch her everywhere. I released her leg, but she kept it where it was as I put fast pressure on her clit. She didn't have to tell me when she was coming. Her pussy suctioned me deeper and that was all I needed. For fuck's sake, I'd been ready to come since I'd last blown my load, so I went hard and climaxed with her, tearing through nirvana for the second time in hours.

My heart pounded, my hairline was damp, but I didn't have time to recover. Lake started to cry. I eased her leg off my shoulder. The heavy, wet way my half-hard cock fell out of her made me feel a little sick. As I peeled and tossed aside the condom, I scanned for blood or any sign I'd hurt her.

"What is it?" I asked. I fell to my knees and tugged her into a sitting position so we were face to face.

Her bottom lip trembled, her eyes crystal blue with tears as her shoulders curled inward. She put her arms around me and burrowed into the crook of my neck. "I . . ." she whispered. "Nothing. Nothing."

She wasn't hurt, just overwhelmed. I pulled her naked torso against mine, comforted by the skin on skin contact, but it wasn't enough. With one arm firmly around her, I looked her in the face. "Shh," I said. "You know what?"

She shook her head.

"I've loved you for a very long time. I have thought of you in every capacity possible. I thought I'd never have you, Lake, you have to understand that. I thought there was no chance. That people like me didn't get a life like this."

"Why shouldn't you?"

"Why should I? What have I done to deserve any of it?"

She kept crying, touching my face, seemingly memorizing the parts of it with her hands like she'd be blind by the end of it. "If you don't deserve to be happy, then I don't, either."

"You deserve everything."

"You are, and always have been, my everything," she said. "If you think I deserve that, why did you take it away?"

I had no simple answer for that, not that I needed one. She knew all of it. I pressed my face to hers. Her wet cheeks cooled the heat in mine. I kissed her slowly, thoroughly, until we were crawling back toward the headboard. I got behind her, pulling her against me. Her smallness sank right into the crook of my body, completely sheltered by me. I pulled a blanket over myself and tented her. I could be her shelter, her shield, her home. Her body nestled into mine like a butterfly in its cocoon. I would happily be an ugly, mottled shell to protect her beauty. Her innocence, on the other hand, I had kept intact long enough. I would strip that from her in its entirety. It couldn't be any other way. If she was finally mine, then I'd need to have her in all ways possible—physically, mentally, and emotionally.

I kissed her all over, drinking salty tears off her face and making up for all the times I'd wanted to feel her skin against mine but couldn't. My dick hardened against the softness of her thigh, but I reached between us and shifted it out of the way. I wanted to go again, but it wasn't the time. I raked her hair away from her face to take her in. Did she believe me when I said I loved her? I only had myself to blame if not. I would have to prove it. Over and over. Day in and day out. Having spent all night vigilant at her door, my eyelids threatened to close, but I forced them to stay open until she'd drifted off. And finally, I got everything I'd ever wanted . . . to have Lake, to feel her from the inside out, to sleep with her in my arms.

9
LAKE

I woke up to the moon coming through the window, lighting my otherwise dark bedroom. The first thing I felt was Manning pressed against my back. The second was a chill on any body part that wasn't tangled with his. I did my best to turn and face him, but I had to go slowly, partly so I wouldn't wake him but mostly because his arm was heavy on top of me, and I had to lift it with both hands in order to move. Once I'd turned over, I burrowed into him, pressing my chest and stomach and crotch to his body. I pushed one of my legs between his, lengthening the other against him. He was hot, and big, and with a little maneuvering, I could almost get every one of my body parts against him. Last was my face, which I rubbed against his neck.

"What're you doing?" he asked, his voice heavy with sleep.

"Getting warm."

"The tip of your nose is cold."

I smiled against his throat. "Any part of me not touching you is cold."

He answered by sliding a big hand down my spine. "What about this?" he asked, pulling me even closer by my rear end. "It's not touching me."

"It got you all day. It's nighttime now."

"Mmm, is it?" He twitched against my stomach.

Nerves and excitement buzzed in me. Sex with Manning was unlike anything I could've ever dreamed up. I was thankful for the few times I'd fooled around with Corbin and had dreaded sex enough to stop. I could see now that while I trusted Corbin, my friend, in every sense of the word, I wasn't able to completely bare myself to him. There were times I'd told myself to just get it over with, and Corbin would've been happy to take my virginity, but I was glad I'd trusted my instincts. I'd saved everything for Manning, and he was worth the wait.

"I'll do my best to warm you." Manning rubbed my back, slipping his hand a little down the length of my thigh until the point where my leg was clamped between both of his. "If any part starts to get cold, tell me and I'll put my hand there."

"I can think of a place."

He chuckled in my ear. "*That* is definitely not cold."

"What's it like?"

"Imagine the warmest, silkiest, tightest place you can be. It is, without a doubt, the best spot in the world."

I held in a giggle. Warm and silky sounded nice, but I wasn't sure about tight. Must've been a guy thing.

"Lake?"

"Hmm?"

"What's that noise?"

I listened. Through the thin walls, my neighbors watched TV. Downstairs, city dwellers headed to and from dinner. There was the occasional siren. And then I heard it, the tiny and unfortunately familiar squeaking coming from inside the apartment. I shivered. "A mouse."

"For fuck's sake." He sighed, and now what I focused on was the rhythmic rise and fall of his chest. "Guess I'll have to add that to my to-do list."

"There's nothing you can do. We get them now and then. Val and I just try to be vigilant about leaving out food and keeping the lid on the trash."

"I'll pick up some mousetraps."

"To kill them?" I sat up, leaning my elbow on his chest. "I don't want that."

"These aren't strays we're talking about." He yawned. "You got off easy with the scar that feral kitten gave you. Mice carry disease."

"Do you know what happens if you trap them? They starve to death—they're *poisoned*. Sometimes they chew off their own legs to get free."

"Then I'll get a top-of-the-line trap," he said. "Death," he sliced his hand across his throat, "in a *snap*."

"That's murder," I screamed.

He laughed. "Murder? I love that you're sensitive and humane, but it's a fucking rodent, Lake. Where there's one, there're others."

I stuck out my bottom lip. "But—"

"Gotta wipe 'em out, Birdy."

I exhaled, tracing a circle over his chest with my fingertip. "If you do, I don't want to know about it. I don't want to *see* or hear about it. I'll cry, I really will."

"Say no more." He moved some of my hair behind my ear. "What time did you say it was?"

"Late. We slept all day." I checked the nightstand. "After seven."

"I missed a meeting." He cleared his throat. "I'll have to reschedule it for tomorrow."

My spirits fell a little. Nothing sounded more perfect than spending every minute of Manning's trip right here in my bed, basking in six years' worth of afterglow. I was supposed to work at the diner tomorrow afternoon, but it was a short shift. I put my face back in the crook of his neck. "Do you have to?"

"I'd skip it, but if I'm leaving my job soon, I need to make as much commission as possible before I go."

Sleepy Manning had turned into Serious Manning, the version of him I was probably most familiar with. I caught the tension in his voice and wondered if money worried him. It didn't need to. I had two jobs and had been taking care of myself for a while, and by the looks of his suit and cell phone and long-distance taxi rides, he did all right for himself.

"But after my meetings, I thought you could show me your New York. Give me something to look forward to. I'm moving from the glorious beach after all."

All my warm and fuzzies returned. I tried to wiggle even closer, but every inch of me was already pressed to him. "My New York?" I asked.

"All I'm getting is that there's a lot of garbage and pushy people. Questionable smells. But if you tell me it's great, then I want to see it through your eyes. Can you show me tomorrow?"

I tried to think of what Manning might like about the city, but I came up short. There were buildings he'd surely appreciate with his eye for structure and carpentry, but was that enough? I loved the energy that coursed through the streets, especially around the theater district and Times Square, but I had to admit I wasn't sure he'd feel the same.

"Lake?" he asked when I didn't answer.

Was it fair to ask him to move here, a place that surely didn't fit him? Wasn't that what was bothering me about his suit and tie, his golf game, the cell phone . . . the fact that Tiffany and my dad were trying to force him in a box? I angled my face from his neck to look up at him, and instantly my skin cooled.

"Nose," I said.

He stopped massaging my back and put his hand over my nose, but his palm was so big that it engulfed my entire face.

I laughed. "I can't see."

"Tell me what's the matter."

"How can I ask you to move? I can't picture you here, but I don't know what the answer is. I want to do stage acting, and Broadway is here, so *I* need to be." I blinked a few times, and my lashes fluttered against his fingers. "If I hadn't just spent four years taking out loans and working overtime trying to graduate, maybe we could talk about somewhere else, but not right now."

He spread his fingers, creating slats so we could see each other. "None of that matters. Isn't that what you tried to tell me that night on the beach?"

I flashed back to standing in front of Manning, pouring my heart out while my friends partied around the bonfire yards away. *"They're just dumb details,"* I'd told him, to which he'd responded, *"They're life, Lake. Relationships, marriage, they don't run on love alone."*

I hadn't understood back then—I hadn't wanted to. That was because I'd never had the real, pressing worry I'd be unable to pay a bill. I'd never sustained myself on dollar noodles four nights in a row or reused takeout cartons as dishes to save money or spent an entire winter day outside waiting for a five-minute audition. After a while of living without familial or financial support, I understood that those details didn't just take care of themselves.

"I don't want to send you back to her," I said, "but I wouldn't feel right making you come here. What if you get home, and . . ." It was too painful to form the words. Even thinking Tiffany's name made my gut smart—both because of all the things he'd shared with her, but also because of how I was about to ruin her life, probably beyond repair. I pushed her out of my thoughts. "Never mind."

He ran his hand down my face to pinch my chin, keeping my eyes tilted to him. "And what?"

"We're having an affair, Manning."

"*I'm* aware of that," he said, "but I'm a little worried you aren't."

"I am." I looked at his chest. "It's just too hard to think about."

"Do you think I'll get home and want to stay? That I won't come back? Because once I get on that plane Friday, I'll be facing a shitstorm, and so will you. I need to know you trust me."

I trusted him—didn't I? I had the first day I'd met him, when I'd turned around and found my gold bracelet pooled in his palm. I'd given and given to him, even when he'd turned me away. Pushed me away. Forced me away. I supposed, though, my trust in him wasn't complete. Not after what we'd been through.

161

"You're quiet," he said.

Manning had to be able to trust me, too, which was why I couldn't tell him what he needed to hear, even though I wanted to. I would once I was certain beyond any doubt that he would come back to me. "I'm sorry."

"I understand," he said. "But there are two things you *can* trust me on, so can we start there?"

I raised my eyes back to his. "What are they?"

"I'm moving to New York. Don't worry about how I'll do it or whether I'll like it. You're going to show me around, and I'll love it because—here's the other thing you have to trust—I love *you*. Nothing matters more to me now than being where you are. I realize I've fucked up huge. I know I made mistakes. If you can tell me you believe that I love you, and if you can understand that nothing will keep me from coming to New York or wherever you are, then I'll work my ass off to earn your trust back. And to be worthy of you, support you, make you happy. I can't expect any of that without working for it, I just need you to understand those two things."

"That you love me, and that you're moving here."

"Yes."

For what felt like the hundredth time in days, I wanted to cry, but I sucked in a breath and focused on his words. Manning loved me. It wasn't a shock to hear it, because I'd known it for so long. Maybe over the years I had doubted it or tried to convince myself otherwise, but I had always known. Certainly he'd known it, too, that he'd loved me, and me him, for a while.

I ignored the feeling that this, being in his arms and hearing these things, was too good to be true. We'd weathered the worst of the storm—now we got to live in the sun. There were hard times ahead, but it wasn't too good to be true because we'd worked for it. We'd suffered and struggled and tried to stay away from each other and if none of that could keep us apart, then nothing ahead of us could, either.

"I understand," I said. "I can't just forgive it all because you're finally here, but . . ."

He slipped his hand under my hair, warming the top of my spine. "I would never ask you to. If the roles were reversed, I don't think I'd ever get over it. Not ever."

If I thought too hard about it, I wasn't sure I'd ever get over it, either. Would that mean I could never forgive him? If the answer was no, would I get out of this bed right now? That was one answer I *did* know. Wild horses couldn't tear me away from him tonight. These few days were about us and it was time we deserved. If I went too far down the path of our past, I'd risk ruining something I had begged, fought, and sweat for, so I pivoted in the opposite direction.

"What will you do when you get here?" I asked.

"I'm not sure. The good thing about construction is you can do it anywhere."

"You won't stay in sales?"

He blew out a sigh. "Depends. I will if it's the first job I find. New York is expensive, and if I'm going to support us—"

"I've supported myself for this long," I pointed out.

"There's no scenario I can dream up in which I'm not working as hard as I can to keep you comfortable. It's what I need as a man, no argument. I know you *can* support yourself. It makes me proud that you do. It's important to me, though."

"Is that why you do sales?" I asked. "Because of the money?"

He seemed to think. In the corner of my eye, the digital clock by the bed changed to eight on the dot. "In jail, and after I got out, I was helpless. I worried my future was nothing more than hard labor. I don't ever want to feel that way again."

"Will it be hard to find work as a felon?"

"Of course, but this job I have now, it'll help. I can show them my salary, my capabilities, and hopefully that'll be enough."

"But in sales, you never create anything. You sell other people's ideas and things." My leg began to sweat between his, but I kept it there. "Don't you still want to help people like you used to?"

"You know I can't."

"I don't mean as a cop. You can help in other ways, like building homes. Homes are important. You spend most of your life in one. I'd trust you to build *my* home."

He narrowed his eyes at me and pinched my bottom. "Well, that's not all that flattering. After this apartment, a clown car would be a step up."

I stuck my tongue out at him. "You'll be surprised how quickly you get used to it."

"Yeah? I thought maybe we'd get our own place when I come."

I shook my head. "I like it here. You can do what you want with your money, but I'll pay my share of the rent, and this is what I can afford."

"Well, then . . . a few repairs are in order. You won't begrudge me that, will you?" As if Manning had planned it himself, my faulty radiator groaned in the next room. "Tiffany and I are remodeling, and I've hardly touched a tool. I'm too busy sitting in an office earning the money to pay for all the nice things we can't seem to live without."

"Manning." I couldn't bear it. I tried to separate his old life from this one, but I couldn't. I hated that it meant I didn't get to know about who he'd become over the past few years, but it was too much. "I don't want that office job for you. I don't care about money. I've lived the past few years without it. Do something you love."

"I love work that gives me the means to make you happy."

"And what would make me happy is to see you building homes or making furniture or whatever it is that satisfies you."

He lifted his head to see me better. "Furniture?"

"You made that coffee table with Gary. The one I saw in the back of your truck? Remember, it was my eighteenth birthday?"

"Your eighteenth birthday," he repeated, laughter in his voice. "Did you throw that in for good measure or what?"

I also smiled. Since the moment I'd met Manning until June ninth 1995, turning eighteen had been front and center of my world. "It was a big day," I said.

"Yeah it was. I'll make something small now and then, but mostly I'm too busy for furniture. Gary, he's doing the same old thing he always was. Except that he got married. Did you know?"

Aside from Henry, Manning's father figure, I guessed Gary was probably Manning's closest friend. As proud as I was that I'd introduced them at that first camp meeting, I couldn't help the way my heart pinched remembering that other life. "I haven't seen Gary since the last day I saw you. The wedding."

Manning put his big, bear hand over my hair and his lips to the top of my head. I let him kiss away the memory because tonight, in his arms, was possibly the best moment of my life and I didn't want to ruin it.

"I did get to make a couple pieces for the house," Manning said, "and I try to refurbish things on weekends, but it can be tough."

"Then you can do it all here. Make furniture or build homes or fix my apartment, whatever," I said. "It'll be a fresh start."

He grunted, thumbing the corner of my lips. "That's my girl. Keep living in the clouds, and I'll take care of the rest. What's cold?"

I was all warmed up, but I wasn't about to pass up an invitation to be touched. "My butt."

He grinned, then took a handful of my backside. "Do you miss the warmth? The beach?"

I tried not to show that I did. I didn't want Manning to think I regretted my decision to leave. I didn't—it was what I'd needed to do at the time. Watching him marry Tiffany, going through the motions of giving a maid of honor speech, receiving congratulations, watching them dance at the reception—it'd been clear there'd been no other choice.

But at times, I did miss Orange County, more than I wanted to admit. My family, my past, my youth, were all there. I couldn't bring myself to admit it, though. "No. I've had an amazing time here, and now that I've graduated, I'll get to devote all my free time to finding work."

"Tell me about the acting. Is it everything you wanted it to be? Do you love it?"

"It's . . ." I chose my words carefully. Again, I didn't want him to think I'd made any mistakes, but if I expected him to be honest about his work, I had to be as well. "I want to be able to tell you, Manning, but you can't get upset or overprotective about it like you did with my job."

He took a deep enough breath that I felt it through my whole body. "That means it's bad."

"No, not bad. It's just so different from what I was used to. From what I thought it would be. It's competitive and you have to have thick skin. Sometimes I'm outside in the cold waiting in line for hours or I'm running on nothing but coffee all day or I'm up until four in the morning memorizing lines. That's just the start since I haven't even been auditioning long." The sad thing was, I enjoyed it. I was living a fantasy I'd started to develop my first year in college, when actors would come to our classes and talk about the struggle of their early days. And since I'd suffered for my craft with others who were in the same boat, I'd become close to my classmates fast. It wasn't like the high school friends I'd had in Orange County. I hadn't spoken to Mona or Vickie in a couple years. These were real friendships, like what I had with Val and Corbin, only my classmates and I shared the same weird, deep desires I did. I wasn't going to feel bad about my career choice just because it worried Manning. "If you come here," I said to him, "you have to be able to let me do my thing without getting upset."

I felt his silence more than anything. When I checked his expression, he was looking at the ceiling. "The graveyard shift really bothers me, Lake. I don't like the idea of you walking home in this city at that time. The rest of it, I don't know, we can work it out.

I can bring you food and blankets while you're waiting. I can run your lines with you."

"You won't always be able to, Manning. Sometimes you'll have to work or sleep or I'll need to run to an audition right when I hear about it, even if we're in the middle of something."

He nodded a little. "I hear you. I'll work on it. If your skin is thicker, I guess mine will have to be as well."

"The city will do it for you."

"Yeah?" he asked. "Is that what it's done to you?"

There were plenty of memories to choose from, but there was no failure like the first. I'd moved here heartbroken, penniless, and lost—I must've ridden the subway to every borough at least once by accident—but the icing on the cake came right before my first semester. "You already know I'd been accepted to NYU. I deferred a semester. But I also had to apply for the drama school and undergo an artistic review. I was denied." In high school, I'd always been so focused on the core classes like science, math, and English. Dad had never allowed me to consider my drama elective as anything more than a hobby. "I took general education courses my first semester and at night, I attended these acting classes in some basement. It was enough to get me in the following semester, but not enough to turn me into an actress."

He frowned. "Why do you say that?"

"We had to do these workshops where we'd learn and practice technique. Well, at the end of my second semester, one of my professors kept me after class to tell me I was getting a 'D'."

"*Excuse* me?" Manning teased. "Lake Kaplan got a 'D'? Have you ever scored a grade lower than a 'B'?"

"No." I smiled. "I was devastated. I could handle the written work and book study, but when it came to theater, I wasn't a natural."

"She who excels at everything," Manning said.

"Apparently not. I'd never had a teacher criticize me, and here the professor had 'firmly suggested' I change majors." I crossed my arms over his chest, resting my chin on them. "Not only that, but nearly everyone around me had been acting since they were children. The closest lessons I'd had were piano. I was the slow one in the class, and that was true up until graduation a few days ago."

"Did you switch classes?"

"I wanted to." I remembered standing in the registrar's office during winter break, ready to give up. Val and Corbin had gone home for the holidays and I was looking at a Christmas and New Year's by myself. I'd been in New York a year, but I'd still acutely felt Manning's absence in my life. I was used to spending Christmas morning opening gifts with my dad and Tiffany while my mom prepared a three-course dinner. I'd had a wonderful life. I'd failed at nothing until I'd failed to win Manning, and after that, things had just fallen apart. Maybe the real me was a failure, and I'd been coddled my whole life, but the alternative was eating crow and majoring in something my dad would've chosen for me, like business. At the last minute, I'd turned away from the office and gone back to my empty apartment. "In the end, I decided not to. All I'd had left at the time was school. So, I repeated the class the following semester."

"And?"

"I got a 'B'. I was hoping for an 'A' second time around, but at least it was enough to move on."

He craned his neck to kiss my forehead, and I felt his smile against my skin. "I still love you if you're a 'B' student." He snickered before I could protest. One single "B" did *not* a "B" student make. "So what changed after that?" he asked. "Or did it?"

"The next teacher I had worked one-on-one with me. She said she could see my pain when I was off stage, but for some reason I was holding back. She coached me to tap into that."

"Into the pain," he murmured, passing his hand over the top of my head.

"It helped. Sometimes I think of you, and her, and all that I've missed out on, and I put it into the craft. I'm still not great, but at least I'm learning not to hold back."

"Lake . . ."

"It's okay," I said to his chest. "I needed something, and I had that."

"Now you have me, too."

I nodded slowly, unsure of when it would start to feel like that was true. Like Manning was mine. With him by my side, I thought I could work in the city's sanitation department with a smile on my face.

"I'd like to meet your friends when I get back from California," he said.

"They're my family." I looked up at him again. *Family.* That was one thing I'd been without for years and wouldn't get back. My dad and I were at the bottom of a mountain neither of us seemed willing to climb.

"Does he ever talk about me?" I asked.

Manning knew exactly who I meant. He moved his hand to cup my face. "He misses you."

"He said that?"

"He doesn't have to. We all know he does."

I guess Manning's hand on my cheek was meant to soften the blow. I'd gone from being constantly under my dad's thumb to not speaking to him once in over four years. Whenever Mom and I were on the phone, Dad was either "swamped with work," "not feeling well," or "on his way out the door." Mom must've told those lies for herself, because the truth was obvious.

"You were the apple of his eye, Lake—of course he misses you. Pride is a fucked-up thing and you hurt his."

"I had to go. I couldn't stay there after that night."

His arm underneath me tensed. "I know it isn't fair to say, but it was hard for me, too," he said.

"It didn't seem that way to me." I fell quiet remembering those moments at the altar, the way Manning had shaken Gary's hand and smiled. "You looked happy."

"That was intentional." He stroked my hair. "I was terrified if you thought I wasn't, or that I had a single doubt, you'd stop the wedding. I felt so sick that I could barely focus on what was happening around me. Even when I wasn't looking at you, all I saw was you . . . and then I did look. You were crying, and I worried I'd made a huge mistake."

Warmth prickled my scalp and finally, I felt not a bit of cold anywhere on my body. I was even sweating a little. "I would've stopped it," I said. "I wish I had. All this could've been avoided."

He shook his head. "I had to go through with it, Lake. I wanted it back then. Wanted a family, and to be accepted, and to do good and be good. I didn't believe there was another way for me. I knew for sure I couldn't be the man for you."

He paused, gauging my reaction. It hurt to hear him say he'd actually *wanted* those things, but there was something to the idea that we wouldn't be here otherwise.

"I figured once I married Tiffany," he continued, "you'd go off to USC, graduate with a great job, meet someone smarter than me, more deserving, someone with the means to give you a great life. Never in my wildest dreams did I think, even for a second, I could be that man for you."

"You were," I said. "You are." I angled up toward his mouth for a kiss, but he didn't give it to me.

"Am I?" he asked against my lips.

"Yes," I whispered. "I have a good life here, one that finally feels like my own. I'm doing what I want and having fun. That's how I know I still need you. Without you, I could have all this and way more, and it still wouldn't be enough."

Finally, he let our lips meet, kissing me softly at first, and then with a little more urgency. Again, the stiffness between us begged for my attention. I went to reach for him, but he caught my hand and kissed my palm. "That can wait. I've been dying to know everything about the last four and a half years. I want to hear all of it."

I understood too well that craving to hear every last thought his mind had held since I'd met him, just as long as it was about me—no one else. I wanted more about him, but so much of his life in California was made up of things I couldn't bear to hear about. I whispered my next question, not even realizing I wanted to know. "Why didn't you come sooner?"

"I couldn't. It took me a year to make this trip happen."

"And before that?"

"Parole. I couldn't leave the state." He looked out the window. "Your dad wasn't able to expunge my record like I'd hoped. I think maybe he thought he could, but in the end, it was all talk."

"And by then it was too late," I said. "He's such an asshole."

He turned back to me. "He has a shitty way of going about things," he agreed, "but he's not a bad guy. Not really. His intentions are usually in line with mine."

My head shot up. "You're defending what he did? He pushed you and Tiffany together because he knew it would keep me away from you. Don't you see that?"

"I saw it right away," he said. "That first time he took me in his study and got me to agree to a summer wedding. I've spent a lot of time with him the past few years, though, Lake. You'll be surprised to hear he and I are pretty close."

I laid my head back down, concealing a scoff. "I'm going to pretend you didn't say any of that."

"It bothers you?" he asked.

"Obviously. I would really rather you cut off all ties with him. Leave that dumb job and all of it behind."

"It's not going to be that easy," he said. "I've gotta sell my half-finished house and hire a lawyer and God knows what else. Fuck." He pulled the sheet off of us, disentangling from me.

"Where are you going?" I asked.

"I need a cigarette." Seated on the edge of the bed, he snatched his suit pants off the ground and

175

dug through the pocket. "This is the longest I've gone without one since I went to jail."

I curled up on my side, watching his back as he hit the top of a pack of cigarettes on the heel of his palm. He picked at the plastic before unwrapping it.

"Don't," I said. I had no handmade bracelet to offer him anymore, just a plea. "Don't smoke."

He glanced back at me, eyebrows drawn, a cigarette dangling from the corner of his mouth like the day we'd met. "I won't be long."

"You're leaving?" As soon as I said it, I realized why. I should've guessed after years of doing this dance with him. "You still won't smoke in front of me. I'm old enough to fuck, but not for secondhand smoke?"

He reached back and slid his hand over the curve of my hip. "*Fuck*, Lake? You think it's safe to say that around me?"

From the heated look that one word got me, I figured there *was* a way I could get him to stay. "Every time you crave nicotine, we can *fuck* instead," I said.

"You wouldn't survive it," he said. "I'm afraid you won't as it is."

I bit my bottom lip. "But—"

"Stay warm." He pulled the sheet up over me, just under my neck. "I'll be ten minutes, max." He stood to get on his pants without even bothering with underwear.

As he started for the door, I stopped him. "Smoke here. You'll freeze downstairs."

"Look, Lake," he said, turning back. "It's not about your age or being too innocent. I don't want to ruin your crystal-clean lungs."

"You did it in front of Tiffany, didn't you?"

"Yeah, so what's that tell you about how I feel? Smoking is a part of me, and so are you. It's not easy keeping the two separate."

I sighed. I could see him getting frustrated, so I dropped it. "Anyway, that wasn't what I meant. I was going to say, use the fire escape."

He looked past the bed, out my window. The metal landing was situated halfway between my room the living room and was big enough for just a couple folding chairs and a stool. "Is Val home?" he asked. "Would we have heard her come in?"

"I doubt she's here. She sleeps at her boyfriend's place almost every night."

Manning rounded the bed, and I turned on my other side to watch him. It could take me up to a minute to work the window open, and I usually had to get Val to help, but Manning pulled it up with ease and climbed outside. He closed it almost all the way, then tilted the chair to dump snow over the edge before he sat. He took up as much space as Val and me put together, his bare feet nudging the metal edge, his head bowed to avoid hitting the frame.

I could hardly believe Manning was sitting half naked on my fire escape. He looked out over the side, frowning down to the street. He smoked faster than I remembered, taking a drag every few seconds. He had a lot on his mind. So did I. And our conversation had barely even scratched the surface. It was as if we were making up for lost time while gliding past the very real, very scary details of our situation. But this apartment felt like a safe haven from all that. I didn't want to think about what was to come. I just wanted to live in here with Manning for as long as possible.

"Lake," he called, ducking his head to see me through the window. He'd lit a second cigarette. "It's fucking freezing. Come warm me up."

I couldn't help the smile that broke over my face. My first ever invitation to be around him while he smoked. I sprung up from the bed, tugged on panties and a t-shirt, and went straight for the window.

"Uh-uh," he said, stopping me. "Put some clothes on."

"I'll be fine. I'm more used to this weather than you are."

"It's not that." Switching his cigarette between hands, he lifted the window with just one. "You look good enough to eat, and I don't want anyone's mouth watering for you but mine. Understand?"

The hair on my legs prickled as my face warmed. I understood. I didn't want anyone else looking at him, either, but after all this time apart, I just wanted to hear him say it. "Explain it to me."

Licking his lips, he looked me up and down. "I've spent years keeping my hands and thoughts to myself. I know what runs through a man's mind when he sees someone like you. I'm going to spend my lifetime making sure anyone who crosses your path knows you're mine. So hurry up, Birdy, I'm fucking shivering out here."

10
LAKE

Wrapped up in a blanket like a human burrito, thrilled to finally be allowed around Manning while he smoked, I maneuvered onto my fire escape. I still didn't trust the structure, even though Val and Corbin had coaxed me onto it plenty of times. It often shook when all three of us were on it, and despite not being a religious person, I'd send a quick prayer up to the heavens.

There was hardly enough room for both of us, but since Manning could practically fit two of me on his lap, that was where I sat. Still shielding myself, I opened the blanket, tucking it between us, trying to get him in it with me. He just watched me, one arm hanging over the side of the chair, the other hand delivering his cigarette to his mouth now and then.

It wasn't perfect, but when I was satisfied, I drew up my knees and curled into a ball against his chest. He never took his eyes from me. "You scared?" he asked.

"Do I look scared?"

"No, but this thing probably doesn't feel any more secure to you than a Ferris wheel or a horse. Don't worry, though. It's strong. I won't let you fall."

I looked over the edge. He was right. It wasn't so much the height that scared me, but the fact that it didn't feel sturdy. "Val and I play TLC albums and drink wine coolers out here in the summer."

"Yeah? Tell me more about that life."

"What you see is all of it. Work, auditions, friends, nights on the fire escape, and until recently, school." Flurries snowed around us, either from the sky or the landing above. "You haven't told me anything about yours."

"You said you don't want to hear about it."

"So tell me something that has nothing to do with her. Just something about you."

"About me?" He squinted out toward some buildings and took a long drag, exhaling with a sigh. "I've been getting into the hard stuff, thanks to your dad."

I widened my eyes. "He's driven you to drink?"

He chuckled. "No. After Sunday dinner, he and I will go in his study and drink expensive liquor. He's teaching me all about it. We talk about guns and work and sometimes even art."

This time, *I* laughed. "You're lying."

"Nah. He likes books and so do I. You know that. Once in a while we'll put on a mob movie, *Goodfellas* or something, while your mom and sister bake dessert."

Tiffany, baking? I couldn't picture it so I didn't. Anyway, I was more annoyed that Manning got along with my father, who hadn't just kept me from Manning—he'd kept Manning from me, too. How could he condone that? "What're you reading now?" I asked, desperate to change the subject.

"You," he said, slipping his free hand under the blanket. "I'm a blind man feeling his way around the story." He tiptoed his fingers up my bare thigh. "Deaf, hearing a melody for the first time. A fool suffering to understand Tolstoy's Russian."

"You are a poet," I said, my mouth dry. I'd trade all the letters I'd longed for from him and never received for the love story he now recited through smoke and snowfall.

"Here's something you don't know about me," he said. "After I said my vows and walked down the aisle, I turned and looked at you, and you were in Corbin's arms, crying."

I didn't know what to say to that. If he was trying to say he was jealous, he probably deserved a punch in the face for it. "You should be grateful someone was there for me," I said. "I don't know what I would've done without him."

"Oh yeah?" Manning said wryly. "Grateful. Let me just think on that."

"Want me to tell you how things looked from my perspective right then?" I asked. He stayed silent so I said, "I didn't think so."

"I still can't get those images out of my head," he said, not looking at me. "You at the altar behind Tiffany. Just standing there sobbing. I was so worried you'd try to stop it. I couldn't let you speak up in front of all those people. It wouldn't have changed anything." He cleared his throat. "That's what I was thinking during the ceremony, start to finish—*don't say anything, Lake. Don't say a word. I love you, I'm sorry, and please stay the fuck quiet.*"

"That's what you were thinking while you were getting married?" I asked. "That you loved me?"

"Yeah. I'm no good, huh?"

If I hadn't been bundled in my blanket, I would've touched his face. For some reason, that seemed like the thing to do when he was being hard on himself. I needed to find some way to bring his eyes back. "Manning?"

It worked. He turned his head to me. "Yeah, Birdy."

"Would you do anything differently?" I asked. "Would you have left my bracelet where you found it?"

"Do you wish I had?"

"Not fair." I shook my head. "I asked first."

He thought on it awhile, and I rose and fell with his chest as he breathed. "I can't answer that. I wouldn't put you through the last few years again. Through all that maid of honor bullshit, and having to leave your family behind, and everything that came after it."

"But then we wouldn't be sitting here."

"No, I suppose not."

"What if I told you I wouldn't change any of it?" It wasn't the easiest thing to admit, but I'd had to see the silver lining a lot since I'd left. Val had done a good job of making sure of that. I wasn't always sure this was the right path for me, but if it ended with Manning, it had to be. My throat was dry from the frosty air and the smoke. I held in a cough so he wouldn't get paranoid about the cigarette. "I never would've had this experience in L.A."

"At the very bottom of it, Lake, I don't think I could take it all back. We had to go through it." He ran his tongue over his teeth. "Ten years from now, we'll remember it as the beginning."

"Ten years?" I asked. "You think that far ahead?"

"Ten, twenty, fifty. I don't know if I can live in a city my whole life, but maybe we move upstate so you can stay close enough to perform."

I blinked in disbelief. "You'd stay here on the east coast?"

"We can travel some of the time. I've always wanted to check out European architecture." He held out his cigarette, drawing an invisible picture in the darkness. "Gaudí has this extravagant temple in Barcelona that would make you smile. It looks almost cartoonish. Then I'll take my little actress to a show at Shakespeare's Globe in London." Dropping his hand, he squeezed my thigh over the blanket. "Then of course we'll have to see the ocean. Maybe South of France or the Amalfi Coast. But no topless beaches. Or those little bikinis they wear. I want you all to myself."

I cozied up to him, basking in the glow of our bright future. "I can just pack a muumuu."

He nuzzled my ear. "Or I can find ways to keep you in the room the whole trip."

I lifted my chin to give him better access to my neck. We were good at hiding away from the world— and from those who cared about us. I realized when Manning left California, he'd be saying goodbye to more than Tiffany. "Will you miss Henry when you move?" I asked.

"Nah. I don't see him a ton as it is. He and I could talk on the phone once a year and it'd work for us."

"What'd you say to him at the wedding?"

"Henry?" Manning sucked on his cigarette. "When?"

"Before the ceremony. I was watching from behind the arches. Henry looked at me from the altar like he knew . . . everything."

"Huh." Manning shook his head slowly. "I didn't say anything to him. He congratulated me and asked how it felt to have found the love of my life. It was weird he'd chosen those words. Forgot about that until now."

"How'd you answer?"

"I didn't. I could never lie to Henry. If he'd asked me if I was happy, I could've said yes. I was. If I couldn't have you, at least I was building a life with someone I cared about. If he'd asked me if I was doing the right thing, yes to that, too, because I thought I was at the time." A flake fell on his nose, and he rubbed it away. "But was I marrying the love of my life? No. So I just stood there, sweating, hoping he'd leave it at that."

"I don't think he believed you. The way he looked at me, it was like he knew."

"Maybe he did. He's a smart guy, but as a cop, he gets responsibility and duty better than anyone. If he knew you were the love of my life, he also knew there was a reason you weren't the one walking toward me."

My heartrate kicked up just hearing Manning say that. "What if I'm not the love of your life?" I asked. "What if I never was? What if we've changed?"

He set his head back against the metal railing and laughed. "Of all the shit we need to worry about, it's not that."

"But how do you know?"

He looked down his nose at me. "Don't you know you're the love of my life?" he asked matter-of-factly. "Are you worried I'm not yours?"

"I wasn't the one who needed six years to figure it out. I knew right away."

"Right away, huh?" He shifted me on his lap, bringing his feet in so his knees cradled me. "I knew, too," he said quietly against my ear, squeezing me to him. "Why do you think I'm here now? Why didn't I just move on with my life? I was fucking confused. You were sixteen and heaven-sent and I just wanted to keep you in my dirty, dusty construction site. I felt like a fucking perv for the things I wanted to do to you."

"What things?" I prompted.

"One day I'll tell you, but I have to pace myself." He nuzzled me with his day-old stubble, sending goosebumps down my arms. "I saw you before you saw me. You stuck out. I couldn't take my eyes off you, because you personified a breath of fresh air. Certain things you did, like grabbing your backpack straps when you got nervous, reminded me of Maddy." He glanced up. The mesh of the fire escape above us blocked most of the sky, but there wasn't much to see anyway. "When I tried to give you your bracelet, you looked terrified. I thought you'd run away, but you didn't. You came back to find me."

I'd been so curious about the big man on the wall in the Pink Floyd shirt. I could still feel the heat of that summer day, but not even the California sun could warm me to the core like sitting under a blanket against Manning's bare chest.

"You didn't judge me the way your family and other people did," he continued. "It wasn't that I saw you and wanted to fuck you . . . it was just that I had this urge to be near you. To be good enough for someone like you. I wanted to be a better man for the first time since Maddy had passed. Since then, I'd just sort of been existing, living in the dark."

He took a drag. Smoke floated over the railing, gray and wispy under the moonlight, gone in an instant. I closed my eyes to hold on to the vibrations of his voice against me. I knew that this moment would end, like they all did with him, but at least time for us would only be finite for a few more days. Then there'd be no rules, no withholding, nothing in the way.

"Those early days I met you," he said, his gaze distant, "it was more like you were the *light* of my life. Maybe you knew right away that you loved me, but I had to resist it, or I would've caused us a lot of problems. The trouble with that, though, is that I fell in love with you anyway." Finally, he met my eyes again. "And because I fought it so hard, that love is deep and unshakeable. That's how I know you're the love of my life. That love is a part of me."

In drama class, that was what we called a monologue, and it was the *best* one I'd ever heard. I could've died right then knowing our love hadn't all been in my head. That Manning had seen me that first day, really seen me. I put my palm on his chest. He was still much warmer than I was. He flicked his cigarette over the fire escape and covered my hand with his. "That love is a part of me, too," I told him. "You were an adult when you met me, but I wasn't. I was still growing up. My heart formed with you already in it." I wanted to tell him I loved him. I had tried, earlier, but the only time I'd actually told him, he'd crushed me. As long as he was legally bound to Tiffany, there was still a chance I could lose him, so I kept it to myself.

And suddenly, just like that, we were kissing. I'd imagined it so many times, the freedom to touch my lips to his, especially curious about the flavor of cigarettes. "You *have* to quit smoking," I murmured.

His chest rumbled underneath me. "Does the taste bother you?"

"It makes me think of all the times I watched you smoke or play with your cigarette. I wanted to know so bad what it would be like to kiss you. Cigarettes always make me think of you. I even let a classmate of mine kiss me at a party because he was a smoker, so I could imagine it was you. That way, I wouldn't have to die wondering what a smoky mouth would be like. So no, it doesn't bother me."

He inhaled through his teeth. "You kissed someone else?"

"Of course I have. Haven't you?"

My sarcasm was lost on him. He released my hand to sneak an arm under the blanket, around my back, tightening his hold on me. "Who else have you kissed?"

A part of me wanted to tell him—and that part was larger than I cared to admit. "I've been on dates. I kissed some of them."

"How many?"

"Over the years? I don't know. I made out with one of Corbin's frat brothers, and Corbin nearly broke his nose."

"What about Corbin?"

"I kiss him all the time," I said. I didn't necessarily want to rub it in Manning's face, but he asked. He probably deserved to visualize me with others the way I had him so many times with Tiffany. "Usually when I'm drunk or when we're having a nice time together. I just haven't been able to take it much further than that."

"But you did take it further."

I bit my bottom lip. It was maybe more than I needed to share. If I knew Manning, his imagination would be torture enough. "A little," I said.

"How little?"

"I'm not going to say. In one day, you've already had more than he ever did. So you should be happy with that."

Happy, he was not. His expression remained passive, but I felt the pull of his muscles, saw the tick in his jaw. "What about the night of the wedding?" he asked. "When you were crying. Did he kiss you then?"

"No."

"He's not going to bother you anymore, is he?" Manning asked. "When I go back to California to sort shit out, he'll stay away? Hearing about you and him, you and anyone, makes me want to put my fist through a wall, Lake. I know it isn't fair, but it's the truth."

It was laughable that Manning should have any say over my love life, but it was also a turn-on to see him get annoyed after so many years of getting nothing from him. "He's my best friend," I said. "He's not going anywhere, but I promise you, I will never, ever kiss him again."

Manning took my chin, lifting my face to his. "Swear to me you will only kiss one person from now on."

"I will only kiss you."

"So do it," he said.

I did. I never wanted to move from his lap, from his possessive hold on me and even more possessive words. His scruff scratched my lips, but more urgently, his erection had been digging into my thigh since we'd woken up. I pulled on the fly of his slacks until it gave. It took some maneuvering, but I managed to squeeze my hand between us, into his pants.

"What're you looking for?" he asked.

The second I wrapped my hand around him, his neck corded. I moved my fist back and forth over his shaft, my eyes glued to his face as I relished how solid he felt against my palm.

"I want to watch you," he said.

Shielding us with the blanket, I scooted over on his lap enough to lower his zipper and pull him out. My fingers seemed even whiter against his bloated purple head.

"Your hand looks so good on me, Lake. Feels fucking amazing."

Emboldened by his praise, I moved a little faster. "Can you show me how you do it?" I asked.

He took my wrist and spit into my palm before lowering my hand back to slide it along the length of him. "Fuck." He let go of me to grasp the metal frame over our heads, shifting underneath me. "The saliva."

The way he groaned from his chest and dropped his head back made me squirm along with him. I wanted to know exactly how it felt. I wanted to always have this kind of power over him. He looked as though he'd give me anything I asked for just then. If I'd done this years ago in the truck, could all our heartache have been avoided?

"More," he said, grit in his throat.

More? I moved faster, but his saliva had already dried. I started to wet my hand again but paused. By *more*, did he mean something else? This was as far as I'd gone with anyone but Manning. When I looked up, he was watching my face, and I had my answer. Manning knew the thoughts running through my mind, and if he wanted me to stop, he'd have told me to. He'd never had any problem telling me no. "Will you let me do more?" I asked.

He bit down on his bottom lip. "I will let you, yes."

I got up and kneeled between his legs. The cold metal stung my kneecaps, but Manning's legs closed around my shoulders, warming me. He drew the blanket over my back and partly up his lap.

I took in the sight of him, my heart skipping with momentary doubt. I never would've thought to call a penis *beautiful*, but that was what it was. It stood tall and vertical, pink and veiny, so rigid I wondered if erections could ever be painful. He still wore his pants, but thick, black hair covered him, trailing up to his navel and smattering the tops of his thighs. I wrapped my hand around it first, still fascinated by how thick it was. I put just his head in my mouth. The slightly briny taste surprised me, and I licked around the ridge. When I pulled back, the tip was darker, his veins more pronounced. I ran my thumb over one, following it down his shaft. When I accidentally grazed him with my nail, he hissed.

I pulled back, realizing I'd been sitting there for a while and hadn't even done anything yet. I glanced up at him for direction, but all I got was a heavy-lidded stare. "Did that hurt?" I asked.

"It felt good."

"You can tell me what I should do," I said.

"I like watching you explore," he responded.

I put my hand back on him. There was a raw masculinity about everything from his waist down, including the way he smelled, and I wanted to commit it to memory. I kissed my way along his shaft, keeping my eyes open. I made my way up again, then sat back. My heart pounded. The thing was, I had thought about this so often, and yet had no experience at all, and this was *Manning*. For a moment, I regretted that I hadn't used all our time apart to practice, kind of like how my classmates and I rehearsed endlessly for our drama productions in school.

I didn't want to hide from him, so I admitted, "I'm a little nervous. Once again, this is a first for me."

"Nervous?" He closed his body over me, bringing us face to face. "I've memorized everything about your mouth. The curves and lines when you're happy or sad, confused, nervous, excited. There's a freckle on your top lip I can only see when I'm close enough. I know the exact spot of your dimples. I could identify your tongue in a lineup. Do you think that *I* think this mouth can do any wrong? Do you think I haven't fantasized about it in every way possible? On *my* mouth, or wrapped around my fingers, or sucking my dick?"

I gripped one of his thighs when he said *dick*, overcome by the violent fluttering in my stomach. "That doesn't help me," I said. "In fact, it only means I have more to live up to."

"Nah. Knowing I'll be the only one ever inside your mouth . . . watching the way you handle me for the first time . . . I'm making an effort *not* to come so I can enjoy this. One day, this mouth will know all the ways to send me to the moon but in this moment, you are everything I need."

I took a fortifying breath, still nervous, but confident enough now to give it a shot. I burrowed a little deeper into him so his long legs encompassed all of me. He kissed the top of my head and pulled the blanket higher. On my first try, I fit as much of him into my mouth as I could, then let my lips glide over the veins and ridges of him, sucking lightly. Manning's fingers found my hair, getting firmer until he was guiding me up and down at a quick pace. My jaw soon ached, and it was getting harder and harder to catch a breath, but the taste of him, the look on his face, the feeling of being both subservient and powerful—I'd never experienced anything like it. I felt, finally, like a woman with a man instead of a virgin fumbling through her first time.

When he stopped me, I was gasping a little. "That's it?" I asked.

"No, not quite. I'm going to come."

"And? What should I do?"

"Swallow it if you think you can."

Everything up until now had been like unwrapping one present to reveal another. If that was what he wanted, I'd do it. I blinked at him a few times, nodding.

"Good girl." He urged my head back down so I could finish him, and swallow I did. Not gracefully, but afterward, he cuddled and kissed and praised me, seeming disproportionally satisfied.

He carried me back inside as one big bundle, through the window and everything. "It was too dark out there," he said, cradling me. "Next time, I want to see you better."

"How?"

"On the bed. And once I've gotten a good look at you, I'll do it to you at the same time."

My eyes surely popped out. "*What?*"

He laughed as I blushed and said, "There's no end to the things we'll do." Flexing his arms around me, he brought me in for a kiss.

"Don't drop me," I said.

"And let you fall?" He sounded incredulous. "No way. You're light as a feather, Birdy."

11
LAKE

I came up from the subway half expecting Manning not to be there. Before he'd left my apartment in the morning to go back to his hotel and change for a sales call, I'd drawn him a map designating where to meet me later. Then I'd called in sick to work because today was important—I was going to show Manning *my* New York. And there he was, outside of the Duane Reade, right under the blue pharmacy sign like we'd planned. He had his hands in his coat pockets and a cigarette between his lips.

Outside the comfort of my apartment, he was real, and he was waiting for me. I couldn't quite shake the feeling of being sixteen and having no say in when I got to see him. That he'd appear and disappear based on forces I couldn't control.

As our eyes met, he made no sign of recognition except for the familiar stare I'd come to expect from him over the years—until I stepped off the curb, and he looked both ways for me.

I walked up to him and took the cigarette from his lips. He looked at it, almost daring me to take a drag. I dropped it in the snow. "I can't believe she hasn't made you quit."

"Nobody makes me do anything, Lake."

"You almost quit once. For me."

"That was a different time." He nodded at me. "Put your coat on."

It hurt that Manning wouldn't stop smoking for me, if not for himself. It wasn't an unreasonable request to want him around as long as possible. "What if I won't kiss you after?" I asked.

"You said you didn't mind the taste."

I hesitated. I liked the taste, actually, because it reminded me of him. That wasn't enough of a reason to risk his health. I didn't want to start a fight, though. I wanted to be in his arms. We weren't at the point where I felt I could reach out and touch him whenever the urge struck me, so I just stepped close enough to break the barrier of politeness.

"What's wrong?" I asked when he stayed where he was.

"You wasted a good cigarette."

I pursed my lips. "Really."

"I've fought a man for the same thing."

"So fight me."

The corner of his mouth twitched. "It's not because of the cigarette."

The cold day started to hit me. I'd taken my coat off on the stuffy subway, but now I was more interested in being warmed by him. "So what's it about?"

"We're in public."

It took me a moment to register his meaning. I was the other woman. Except that I wasn't. I was his, always, from the beginning. Tiffany was the one who'd stolen him away. *She* was the one who should be kept at arm's length on the street. "You're going to hide me away?" I accused.

"It'll take some time for me to acclimate."

"Why?"

"I'm used to checking over my shoulder with you." He removed one hand from his pocket and took the ends of my hair in a loose fist. I thought I could stand up to him, but with that one touch, I wanted to melt. I fought to keep my eyes open. "You never had to be the one to worry about all that," he continued. "I did. I was older than you. Even now, I feel like people are looking."

"Nobody is, Manning. I'm twenty-two."

"I couldn't let my guard down for a second, even after you turned eighteen. Couldn't get caught staring at you."

"I *loved* when you did. Even though most times I looked at you, you looked away."

"I had to. You didn't think about things like that, because nobody cares if a sixteen-year-old stares at someone older. Not true the other way around, though."

Hadn't I worried I'd be found out? Maybe some part of me had wanted to get caught. I didn't think about consequences much in those days. Now? I supposed there was the slightest chance someone might recognize us, considering there were people from Orange County who'd moved here. Corbin, for one. Val would never tell, even if she was angry with me. I tried not to show my disappointment, but I needed him to know I was more mature now and could play by his rules. I shivered. "It's okay. I can wait."

He opened his coat and pulled me into it. "I can't. I'll just have to get over it."

"What if someone sees us?"

"They won't." He rubbed my shoulder, bringing me closer and closer.

I parted my lips, expecting his, but he only stared. "What's wrong now?" I asked.

"I'm remembering your mouth on me last night on the fire escape."

Despite the fact that I could see my breath, I warmed at the memory. After all the ways Manning had fought me over the years, I couldn't believe he'd finally given in. "We can go home and do all that stuff again right now."

"No, don't."

"Don't what?"

"Tempt me, when all I want is to spend a normal day with you. Even being allowed to fantasize about you is a whole new world to me."

I quirked an eyebrow at him. "But you did, right? Even if you weren't *allowed*?"

His expression sobered as he squinted over my head a moment, then took my coat. "Do you have a plan for us?" he asked, opening it for me.

I wasn't sure why he couldn't answer that. After all the things we'd said and done the day before, I didn't believe for a moment he'd never thought about fucking me. Maybe he wouldn't admit it to others, but to me, it was welcome. I turned to put one arm in my coat and then the other. "Not a plan so much as some places to hit," I said.

He turned me around, buttoning up the coat. "Where are we headed?"

"It's no fun if I tell you. Let it be a surprise."

When he'd finished, my collar nearly choked me. He fixed the lapels, his eyebrows wrinkled. "I don't like surprises."

"I'll remember that for the future." I tilted my head up. We were face to face and still hadn't kissed.

"Lead the way," he said.

"Okay." I didn't move.

"Was there something else?"

I rolled my lips together. I had, in my mind, made it very clear what I wanted. To ask for it was a completely different thing than hinting at it. It wasn't some easy thing to just kiss him, considering he towered almost a foot over me. I would have to rise onto the tips of my toes, and I would have to put my heart on the line *again*. No, it wasn't easy at all.

"You can touch or kiss me when you want," he said. "You don't have to wait for me."

I shifted. For the briefest of moments, I thought—*no, I can't. You don't belong to me.* I would be kissing and touching someone else's husband.

Maybe sensing my unrest, Manning put his hands under my jaw, lifting my face to his. I rose onto my tiptoes, and he nuzzled his nose against mine a few slow seconds before Hurricane Manning made landfall. Nothing felt more exhilarating than being whipped into a frenzy by his kiss, but his anxiety about being in public belatedly hit me. It almost felt gratuitous to be intimate outside the privacy of my apartment.

I ended the kiss but smiled. "Let's go while it's still early. Daylight is precious this time of year."

"It's only noon."

"I know. I hope you have comfortable shoes on."

We started in the theater district, zigzagging through streets, alleys, and avenues. We'd been here the other night, but this time I pointed out the plays I'd been to, those I still wanted to see, and the ones I'd give my left leg to score a part in.

"Do you sing and dance?" he asked.

"I've taken lessons for both, and I'm all right on the piano, but I don't typically try out for musicals, which can be limiting. I like speaking parts, dramas mostly. It's thrilling to be up in front of all those people."

He looked up as we passed Carnegie Hall. "Have you done it a lot?"

"We had performances in school. Some of my friends are writers and have cast me in small productions. And then there's auditioning, which is basically baring your soul on a stage so they can judge and reject you."

He brought my hand in his pocket, rubbing his thumb over my knuckles. "What moron would reject you?"

I laughed. According to my more experienced peers, the brutality I'd experienced was simply a preview of what was to come. "You'd be surprised."

"Have you tried out for any of these?" he asked about the flashing billboards around us.

Rejection wasn't the easiest thing to admit when Manning had always known me as a type-A overachiever. "A couple, but I've never gotten a callback."

"What about other kinds of acting, like in front of a camera?"

"Some of my friends are interested in that, but most of us, like me, want the stage." I squeezed closer to Manning to let a dog walker by. I smiled at the fact that his hands and arms were tangled with leashes, yet he seemed in complete control of the five or six pups in his care.

"Should I be jealous of the guy or the dogs?" Manning asked.

I wrinkled my nose at him, and he kissed my forehead. "Dogs," I said. "Always be jealous of the dogs."

I took Manning along Central Park South, by the Plaza Hotel, FAO Schwartz, and down Fifth Avenue to see the holiday displays. The windows were decked with wrapped presents, shiny tinsel, and ornamented Christmas trees. Some featured toy trains and Barbie dolls, and others exquisitely beaded gowns, multi-colored sequined heels, and lush crimson velvet.

Everything behind the glass exuded warmth, even the fake snow. "What will our holidays be like?" I asked Manning as we wandered.

"However you want. We can spend it with your friends, or we can stay home on the couch watching *A Christmas Story*."

I smiled a little. "The one with the boy who pokes his eye out?"

"Well, technically he doesn't, but yeah, that's the one. I used to watch it every Christmas with my family before Madison passed."

My heart deflated. "Then we can watch it, too," I said, squeezing his hand, "or we can start our own traditions. There's lots of New York Christmas movies to choose from. Like *Home Alone*."

He nodded gravely. "A classic in its own right."

"What were your holidays like growing up? With Madison?"

"My parents always made a big deal of them. It wasn't all bad all the time, not at all. We were a pretty normal family for the most part. Lots of presents, at least what they could afford, mostly for Maddy." He surveyed the shops without giving much away. "She cared more about decorating the tree and wrapping presents for us, though. Usually things she'd made, like jewelry for my mom, or found."

I rested my head on his shoulder, hoping to offer even the smallest bit of comfort. Losing a family member wasn't just about their absence. The DNA of his existence had been altered. My sister was still alive, and yet my life had changed dramatically without her in it. It was especially hard around holidays, so I held Manning a little closer. "What was your favorite part?"

"The food, I guess. My mom would cook more than I could eat and that's saying something."

"I'll cook for you." After we walked a few blocks, I asked, "What's Christmas like now?"

He cleared his throat. "Good."

"I mean, I know what it's like at the house. Mom puts on Christmas music twenty-four-seven and it always smells like cookies."

He nodded slowly. "That's right. Tiff and I go over in the morning and spend the day there. It took awhile for things to feel normal after you left."

I was lucky to have made enough friends here that now I always had somewhere to spend the holidays, but that didn't replace the warm, cozy family den where I'd grown up opening metallic-ribboned presents and drinking eggnog with nutmeg. Tiffany's gifts to us were always wrapped sloppily, but she'd bounce up and down while we opened them, unable to contain herself.

"What kinds of things did you buy her?" I asked.

"What's it matter?"

"You wanted me to know about your life," I said.

"The usual. Jewelry, clothes. Things for the house or kitchen."

"The kitchen?" I asked, remembering his comment about dessert after dinner. "Does she cook now?"

"Some nights. And she's not half bad."

I scowled. She couldn't be a good chef. She didn't have a culinary bone in her body, not like me or my mom. But she'd had years of feeding Manning, learning about what he liked or didn't. That was time I'd never get back. My mind automatically drifted to the bedroom, where she'd also had time. "How was it with her?"

He kept his arm around me, his eyes forward as we navigated the crowded sidewalk. For a moment, I understood what he'd meant earlier about feeling as if people were looking at us. We were doing something wrong, and it seemed they could tell. "I didn't mean you should ask about this stuff," he said. "Things that'll make you jealous."

"It's just food," I said.

"You're not asking about cooking anymore, but I know you don't like to hear about that, either. You think I like imagining you feeding another man?"

"I didn't, though . . . not on a regular basis, anyway." My palm began to sweat in his, and I took my hand from his pocket. I could feel myself veering down a dangerously steep hill, but now that I'd started, I couldn't apply the brakes. I'd been thinking—and trying not to think—about this since he'd shown up on my doorstep. "So you can ask me all you want about cooking for other men, and I told you about Corbin, too, so now I want to know what it was like for you and Tiffany, and I don't mean in the kitchen."

He blew out a sigh and shrugged. "It was fine."

"Fine? That's it?"

"I don't know what you want me to say. I can't tell you it was the worst thing in the world unless you want me to lie."

I didn't want him to lie, but I wouldn't have minded hearing it was the worst thing in the world. "What was good about it? Is it because she's experienced?"

"No." He rubbed the bridge of his nose. "Christ, Lake. No, it isn't that. It's sex. When I said you should know about my life, I meant the important things. You know your sister's, well, when she lets her guard down, she's sensitive and kind. She's really great like that, but it never lasts long with her. She lets unimportant things take over her life. She can be materialistic that way. And she's petty—she lets other people get to her, like you or your dad."

"Me?"

"Now that you're out of the picture, she gets to be the golden child. Your dad is more patient with her than he used to be, but it's clear she'll never be what you are to him. And that's hard on her. Even though you're gone, your presence at the house is strong."

Tiffany and Dad were getting along. These were the things I wasn't sure I wanted to know. It only highlighted how much I'd missed. I'd now spent over a fifth of my life without them. "It's better for her that I'm gone. She gets Dad, and she got you."

"She misses you. I know you don't believe it, but she does."

"Will you miss her?"

He looked down at me. "In some ways, sure. How you might miss a close friend or a roommate you've come to rely on."

I tried not to look hurt. He was choosing me in the end, and that was what mattered. "But do you have any doubts about leaving her? Will you miss her so much that you'll think of her when you're with me?"

He rolled his lips together, then stopped in the middle of the sidewalk and took my left hand. He held it up between us and ran his thumbs up the center of my palm. "Imagine if you had to have surgery to remove this hand." He kissed the pads of my fingers. "This beautiful hand that I'll do everything I can to protect, I should add. You'd miss it, wouldn't you? It would be hard. Something important would be gone. It would take time to get used to."

I sighed. To remove a hand was no small thing. Tiffany was Manning's other half and had been for much longer than I'd even spent with him on my own. "It would be really hard," I agreed. "Too hard."

He smiled a little, then pressed my palm against my own chest, right over my heart. "Now imagine the surgery was to remove this. You can live without one, but not the other. Which would you choose?"

My throat got so thick, I had to wait a few seconds to respond, and in that time, my last six heartless years flashed before me. "But you lived just fine without me."

"Just fine, yeah. When I thought I could never have you. Now that you're mine, there's no other way. I'd be a fool to cut out my heart to save my hand."

I curled my fingers into a fist. "I feel the same."

"Do you? Let me hear you say it."

"I . . . I love your hands. I know how hard you worked to keep them to yourself when you didn't want to."

"And your hands made me feel so good last night, Lake. What about my heart?"

I swallowed that pesky lump, trying to rid it so I wouldn't cry. "I love it, too."

"You always believed it was good. That I was good. Even when I tried to convince you otherwise."

I'm no good, he'd said last night. The fact that he was here with me was progress, but I would have to make sure, going forward, he knew what a good man he was. And examining the past probably wasn't the way to go about that. "You know what?" I asked.

"Tell me."

"You'll make a great father one day. The best."

He frowned. "You think about that?"

"I don't need to. I just know. Do you see that in our future?"

"Yes, Birdy. I see it. I see it so clearly. I want—I want to be everything my dad wasn't, everything *your* dad wasn't." He brought my palm to his mouth for a series of kisses that ended at my elbow. Reinserting me in his coat, against his side, we continued walking. "I'll do whatever it takes to make you proud, but I worry," he admitted. "Of course I do. I didn't have the best example."

"You honestly still think you'll become your dad?" I asked.

"Do *you* worry I will?"

"Not for a second."

"I have concerns. Like my temper when it comes to things I care about. So—you. And when we have a baby—our baby."

My jaw could not drop far enough. How was

Manning speaking so freely about things he'd held against his chest for years? He steered us through the crowd. I flattened my hand on his hard stomach. Thumb to pinky, I only took up about a third of the expanse of his torso. "You have a temper where I'm concerned," I agreed, "but why? What are you afraid of?"

"You saw how I reacted on the beach that night. There've only been a few other times I've gotten that upset."

"Tell me about them."

"It mostly has to do with my dad."

"And the time they sent you to solitary confinement."

"And that." He nodded. "If I let my temper get the best of me at any moment, it could change everything for me. I could go back to jail. Worse, I could hurt you."

The hair on the back of my neck stood up. Not because I thought he'd ever get physical with me, but because I could hear in his voice that he believed he could. "You wouldn't," I said.

"You don't know that. I told you how it was with my dad. There was no telling what would set him off. And I'm the same, Lake. That was what landed me in SHU."

"You never told me why you snapped."

"I never told you to protect you from that world."

"But we can't have secrets from each other now,

Manning."

He pulled me close, kissing me on the lips. "Your safety and happiness will always be my priority."

I read between the lines. He would keep from me the things that might hurt me. "I don't want to be in the dark, Manning."

He looked anywhere but at me. "Hmm."

I didn't think I could ever make Manning do anything he didn't want to, which was why it was important he see me as an adult, not the girl on the construction site. "We're going to be partners," I reminded him.

"We already are. We have been. Don't you know, no matter what was happening around us, that you were always in the center of my mind? That I would never do or say anything to let anyone hurt you?"

"Anyone but you. You hurt me most of all." As I said it, I slipped my hand back into his. I wasn't sure why, except that I knew this conversation was hard for him. Still, I couldn't stop from pressing the wound. Maybe it was revenge, or maybe it was that my insecurities needed coddling. I didn't think I'd ever tire of hearing his thoughts.

"I was selfish. I didn't want to be away from you. I wanted to feel like a good man, and that's how your sister made me feel."

"And I didn't?"

"You just made me feel good. So good, I thought it meant I was bad. How could I feel such a connection for someone I shouldn't? Can you see the logic in any of that?"

I twisted my lips. What would have happened if Manning had not come into the house that day at Tiffany's invitation, which later resulted in their first date? I'd been a child then, admittedly more naïve than most. I couldn't have handled such a man as him, not like Tiffany. What if he'd done all the things I'd tried to get him to do, like take off my clothes in a truck while I was away at camp or kiss me on my sister's kitchen counter while she slept in the next room? Would he still be here? If not for Tiffany, would he have left for good to get away from his feelings for me?

We passed more beautiful, glossy stores. Whenever their doors opened, warmth seeped out. "I wish we could spend this Christmas together," I said. "I'd cook you a turkey and you'd fix my heater. We could watch movies under the blankets and maybe fool around a little."

He kissed the top of my head. "Not maybe. Definitely. Next year, Birdy, I promise you."

I was stealing my sister's husband, shattering her world so I could build my own. But my love for Manning was stronger than anything else. If I got to live eighty more years with him, I wasn't sure I'd change anything about the past few that might've prevented that. And I understood why loving me sometimes made him feel like a bad person.

In that instant, it was true for me, too.

12
LAKE

"Have you loved other girls?" I asked.

"I can tell you this much," Manning said, lacing up his skates on a bench. "I've never gone ice skating with another girl."

We'd circled around the city to Rockefeller Center. It'd taken a little bit of convincing on my part to get Manning to do this, but not as much as I had thought. "Why'd you agree?" I asked, standing over him. I'd had my skates on in a third of the time it was taking him.

He glanced up at me, which wasn't saying much. His head came up to my breasts while seated. "When you smile like that, it's hard to say no to you."

"And how come you never skated with any other girls?"

He tightened the lace on one boot and stood up to his full height, causing my head to fall back. With the blades, he must've been over six foot six. "You know why."

"Because you've never been asked?"

"I've been asked."

"Because you don't know how?"

"I've played hockey before. I know how." He took my hand, intertwining our fingers. "It's because I wasn't in love with any of them, Birdy."

"But you've been in love before."

"I've loved, and been loved, but I wouldn't say, after knowing you, that I'd ever been *in love*." His brows sank. "I know that isn't enough. Not by a long shot. But it's something."

We made it about three laps around the rink before I fell. While holding Manning's hand, I'd been watching him, not where I was going, and nearly collided with a child. When I overcorrected, his grip was strong enough to keep me from flying, but I still landed on my butt.

Manning bent over me, lifting me by my armpits. "Are you hurt?"

I beamed up at him. "No."

"I'd better inspect you anyway." He led me over to the rink's low wall and lifted me onto it by my waist. I shivered as I remembered him putting me on a brick wall on a hot, sunny California day years ago. "This hurt?" he asked, feeling around my outer thighs.

"No."

He extended my arm, checking the red spot where I'd hit my elbow. He lowered his head to tenderly kiss the skin. "How about this?"

I giggled. "Of course not." I hooked my skates around the backs of his thighs and pulled him between my legs. "But you should inspect more places."

"Which places?"

"I think I hit my lips on the way down."

He narrowed his eyes at my mouth, then pecked me. "Seems all right to me."

"And also my . . ."

He was completely mine, on the hook, hanging on my words as if we were the only two people in the rink. And his eyes heated as if I were the only female on Earth. "Yes, Birdy?"

"Never mind."

"If you won't tell me where you hurt yourself, I'll have to go ahead and inspect everywhere. But best if we wait until later, when we're alone."

I wrinkled my nose, smiling. "I like that plan. Will you get on the wall with me?"

"How come?"

"So I can pretend we're back at the beginning. Like it's the first day I met you."

He didn't look at me, but upon me, his face full of adoration. "Why would I want to go back there? It was pure torture. I remember it clearly enough."

"Me too. You were as important as the sun."

"The sun blinds you."

"Yes you did." I nodded. "I've seen nothing but you ever since."

"Selfishly, I'm glad for it." He wrapped his arms around me, surprising me with a slow, uninhibited kiss. "If it's all right with you," he whispered into my mouth, "you stay on the wall, and I'll just stay here."

"It *is* easier to kiss like this."

"It's easier to do a lot of things like this. If we weren't in public right now, I'd open a few pesky buttons and zippers and be inside you."

I held onto him as the image of us together hit me hard. Sex was possibly the best thing I'd ever experienced, and we'd barely done it that much. "Can we go somewhere?" I asked.

"Where would you like to go, my love?"

"Anywhere. I have business with a few pesky buttons and zippers."

"Mmm." He kissed my neck, nipped my earlobe. "Yeah. Let's go somewhere."

"Your hotel?" I asked.

"Ah." He pulled back a little. "I'm not sure that's a good idea."

"Why not?"

"Because it's . . ." Hesitating, he rubbed the underside of his jaw. "I'm expensing the stay, obviously, but I put the room on my credit card, and I'll get reimbursed."

"Oh." It took me a few seconds to put it together. "*Your* credit card, which doesn't only belong to you."

"I can bring my things to your place," he said. "I felt bad last night about scratching you up with my stubble."

His five o'clock shadow was the least of what bothered me. I took my arms from around him. "Go then. Get your stuff and we can meet later."

"Hey." He pinched my chin to keep me from turning away. "Do you want to make love in a hotel I paid for with an account I share with your sister? What's the alternative?"

I wiggled to get off the wall and he let me. When my blades hit the ice, they began to slide out from under me, but he caught me by my waist like I was some kind of doll, setting me upright again.

A woman around my mom's age approached us, slowing to a stop with her pre-teen daughter in tow. "We were just saying you two are the most adorable couple we've ever seen," she gushed in a southern accent.

"Mom," the girl said, rolling her eyes before she sped off.

Manning tensed and moved to stand a few inches in front of me. He reached back and took my hand. It felt protective rather than loving, as if something had him worried. For whatever reason, his uneasiness melted my anger.

"Thank you," I said.

"It's awfully sweet," she said. "I'm trying to figure out if you're the high school sweetheart type of couple or if you're in that honeymoon phase. Which is it?"

"We met in college," he said. "So I guess it's the first one."

"Well, you're precious."

"Yes," he said, squeezing my hand. "She is."

"Oh my. He's a keeper." She winked at me, teasing. "Are you married, and if not, when's the wedding?"

Wedding? There was no wedding, and maybe there would never be. At least not anytime soon. And if there was, it would be a pretty lonely affair without my family in attendance.

He's already married.

I almost said it to see her reaction. *Someone* had to stop us, and maybe it was this woman. Things couldn't keep going as well as they had.

"In the summer. That's her favorite time of year." Manning moved his arm around my shoulder. "It'll be intimate, just close friends."

"And family," the woman added.

"No, no family."

I couldn't have my own family at my wedding, but neither could Manning. Realizing that actually made me feel closer to him. I cozied into his side. "Are you sure that's my favorite time of year?" I asked. "I never told you that."

"You're a summer baby." He looked down at me. "Born in June, grew up in the ocean and under the sun. Or has that changed?" He grinned. "Are you an ice queen now?"

I couldn't pick a favorite season. I loved them all for different reasons—although winter was certainly pulling ahead based on today. "Any time of year is fine with me," I said.

"She's an easy bride," he told the woman. "Doesn't need much, and neither do I. Just her."

"Let's see the ring," the lady said.

Manning smiled. "I haven't asked yet."

She gasped, slapping a hand over her mouth. "And I ruined it. Did I ruin it? You're too sweet." She winked at me. "Marry him. Surely you're already beating the women off with a stick. No reason to delay."

Manning's mood visibly lightened. "You hear that? Why delay the inevitable?"

Feeding off their playfulness, I relaxed. "Okay. I guess so."

She clapped her hands. "Oh, you've made my afternoon. My entire trip. I'm going to go home and tell all my girlfriends I witnessed a proposal." She pushed off. "Best of luck to you both!"

"Why'd you lie to her?" I asked as Manning watched her skate away.

"Not a lie so much as a fantasy. Didn't any of that sound good to you?"

"You said we met in college, though."

"I was teasing." He skated back from me, our hands locked between us. "Come on. I've seen enough of your New York for one day. Now I want to go back to heaven."

"And that would be . . .?"

"My *precious* girl," he said, mocking the woman's accent, "in her precious bed."

I pulled on his hand, but he was so solid that all I did was glide toward him. When I collided with his side, I leaned on him for a kiss. No matter how much of my weight I gave him, Manning never budged, not even in skates.

13
MANNING

Lake'd been asleep for ten hours. I'd worn her out, whereas I was just getting started. I'd woken up throughout the night and morning to check on her. My visions of bad-things-happening shouldn't have been as severe as they'd been when she was younger. Back then, she'd been naïve, and she still was in some ways, but she was an adult now. She could care for herself.

Those visions hadn't gone away, though.

When the woman at the ice skating rink had approached us, my heart'd locked in my chest, my instincts turning predatory. I'd felt threatened by a woman in her forties and lied about meeting Lake in college because for the briefest of moments, I'd expected her to say, "Get your hands off that child."

It was ridiculous; nobody would look twice at us now, but it'd seemed as if she'd known, on some level, how old Lake had been when I'd met her. Known all the reasons Lake and I weren't supposed to be standing on that rink, touching and kissing as freely as we'd been.

Lake slept soundly on her stomach. It didn't even look as though she were breathing. I moved some of her fine blonde hair off her neck, soothed by how warm her skin was. I wanted to touch and be touched by her. I wanted to have her now and keep having her until it became too much. I couldn't help the feeling she could be taken away from me at any moment.

There was a lot to figure out, a lot left to say, but I didn't want to go there yet. For two more days, Lake and I were a regular couple in love. We didn't need anything but each other. My stomach grumbled. Each other, and some food.

Lake stirred, smiling before she even opened her eyes. "That feels nice."

I realized I was petting her. "I woke you. I couldn't keep my hands to myself."

"Did you have sex with me?"

"While you slept?" I heard the alarm in my voice. "I generally prefer you to be conscious."

She smiled wider. "I guess it was a dream then."

"So all the sex we had over the past forty-eight hours wasn't enough? You dream about it, too?"

"All signs point to yes."

I was understandably hard. Not only had I just woken up, but she was on her stomach, the sheet light over her shoulder blades. It'd be the perfect moment to have her from behind for the first time.

"Is it late?" she asked.

"Hmm. I'd say around noon."

Her head shot up. "*Noon?*"

"You were out like a light."

"*Shit.*" She turned over, keeping the sheet around her breasts as she sat up. I pulled it down so I could see her, thumbing a bubble-gum pink nipple as I salivated. "I'm supposed to be arriving at work right now."

"Can you call in?"

"I already did yesterday and the night of the show," she said, standing. "Damn it."

I reached for her hand, pulling her back on the bed. "It's not inconceivable that you'd be sick for four days. Tell them you have the flu or something."

She sighed, letting me fit her back against my front. "I already said it was food poisoning."

"Well, you're not a doctor. How could you have known?" I nuzzled her neck. "Besides, I have another job for you."

"Does it pay more than minimum wage?"

"I'm hungry, Lake. I need to be fed."

She twisted in my arms to look back at me and sigh. "I guess it's a good thing I picked up all the ingredients for the Lake Special on our way home last night."

When she'd turned, her crotch had brushed mine, and now I had a dilemma on my hands. I was horny for her. I was also starving.

She wiggled out from under me and grabbed a thin robe off the back of her door.

"Do you need to be clothed to make sandwiches?" I asked.

She smiled as she tied it closed. "What if Val comes in?"

As she left, I got up to take a piss. I guessed it was too much to ask for Lake and me to have a space of our own, but I really fucking hated that we couldn't just relax.

On my way out of the bathroom, I pulled on my underwear and found Lake in the kitchen, peppering the counter with ingredients. "I've been craving the Lake Special since I had it the first time six years ago," I said.

"You had the real Lake Special last night," she teased.

"I did." I came up behind her, pulling some of her hair aside to kiss her neck. "And I'm going to have at least a few more helpings today."

She pointed at a cabinet. "Can you get down the plates?"

"You mean these?" I asked, reaching for a stack of dishes in the door-less cabinet right in front of us.

"No. I have special plates on the top shelf. In case . . ."

"In case?"

"I ever had an important guest."

I raised my eyebrows at her, reaching above her head to the top cabinet. "What do you do when I'm not here to get them down for you?"

"I have a stepstool."

It was so cute, I almost picked her up right there and took her back to bed.

"Also," she added, "you're the only important guest I've had."

I kissed the top of her head. The plates were hard plastic with flowers, nothing special, but to me they indicated she'd been thinking of me when I wasn't around and that was definitely something I'd hold on to while I was away.

"Manning?"

"Hmm?"

"Want to learn how to make the Lake Special?" she asked.

"Won't you always be around to make it for me?"

"Mhm, that's the plan."

As I watched her smile to herself, my lungs constricted. Lake had always been part of me, tangled with my insides in ways I'd often wished she weren't. I held her as close to the chest as Maddy's death or my time in SHU. But in only two and a half days, she'd become my world. And in another two and a half days, I'd be separated from her again. How long would I be gone? I didn't know. I didn't care how to make the damn sandwich, but I would take an excuse to watch and listen to her do anything. "Teach me."

"Wash these." She slid over a cutting board with lettuce and a tomato. I indulged her, sneaking glances at her bare legs when I could. Once I'd cleaned and sliced, I washed my hands and without drying them, slipped them inside her robe, hugging her from behind.

She inhaled a breath. "Your hands are wet."

"Mmm." I ran them over her stomach then held her back to my front as she worked at the counter.

She put out four slices of bread and spread mayonnaise on each of them. "Be generous with the mayo, but don't overdo it or it'll get soggy."

"Uh-huh." I put my nose in her hair. What I would've given over the years to smell her shampoo. Feel her voice vibrate against my body as she spoke. Get a taste of the heaven I'd come close to before I'd been hauled off to prison. "Do you still have that watermelon lip stuff?"

"Huh?"

"That Chapstick you wore a long time ago."

"I could probably find some," she said distractedly.

"Find some."

"Are you listening?" she asked, picking up an avocado.

"I'm trying." I took it from her, cutting into the gnarled skin and slicing it onto both sandwiches.

"The ratio of meat to cheese to condiments is very important."

"Tell me more about that." I kissed her neck. Pinned her to the counter with my hips. Returned my hands under her robe, this time lowering them between her legs.

"Oh," she moaned, squirting barbecue sauce on the counter.

"You're making a mess," I scolded.

"What?"

I caressed her, feeling an undeniable ownership over a body I'd only gotten command of a couple days ago. I wasn't as familiar with her as I wanted to be, though, not by a long shot. I looked forward to learning everything that made her knees give out the way they were now. "How's that feel, Birdy?" I murmured in her ear, holding her upright, rubbing her.

"This isn't sanitary," she whispered back. "For the sandwiches."

"I'm not the one making them. Doesn't matter if my hands get dirty."

She bit her bottom lip while I lazily determined if she was wet enough now or if I should find a way to get her there. I needed to be inside her. Her teeth dug into her lip harder as I fingered her. She gripped the bottle of sauce and failed to keep her little squeaks inside. I urged her onto her toes, lifted her robe, and bent my knees enough to pull down my underwear and slide inside her.

"Don't stop on my account," I said, pushing deeper. She still couldn't take all of me in one go, and easing in was a sweet kind of torture. "I guarantee you we'll be hungry when we're done."

Breathlessly, she slapped ham onto both sandwiches. "The order of the meats matters . . ." She gulped, her fist curling around a deli bag of medium cheddar. "And the cheese, too . . ."

I laughed to myself, wondering how long she'd last, then squeezed my arm between her and the counter. "What next?" I asked as I circled her clit.

"I don't know." She fell forward and her hair parted, exposing the top of her spine to me. "I forget."

I kissed the nape of her neck. Even that was sexy, the light freckles that hid under her blonde hair. I moved in and out of her until she had to grip the counter. I covered her hands with mine, interlacing our fingers as I held on with her and took her faster and faster until I was hanging by a thread, doing everything I could to make her come. She climaxed with her entire body, her shoulder blades jutting out and her hair shimmering like a golden waterfall.

I pulled out not a second too soon and came on the counter, right next to the sandwiches.

"*Manning*," she scolded.

I had to chuckle as I massaged her slender shoulders, blowing on her damp hairline. "It was either there or your pretty robe," I said, still catching my breath. "Come here."

She turned her head, giving me her mouth. Kissing her was such a natural thing, but I'd been unable to do it so long, it felt exceptional. I needed it, and that was a first. I'd been satisfied after sex, but I'd never *needed* to feel close to anyone like Lake, to touch her, to know she was also sated and comfortable. As I kissed her, I realized what I loved about her in this moment wasn't just her vulnerability, but that she'd brought it out in me, too.

When she tried to pull away, I kept her to me with a hand on her throat. "Not done with you yet."

"I really should try to make the second part of my shift," she murmured. "I need the money."

Money. Lake wasn't supposed to want for anything. For someone like her, the basics should be covered so she could be free to do and be what she wanted. That was the vision I'd had for her, the one my stubbornness had ruined.

"I mean, don't *you* have work to do anyway?" she asked, wiping down the counter. She checked to make sure the sandwiches had been spared and resumed making them.

Work was a reality I couldn't ignore. I hadn't missed another meeting since we'd slept the day away, but only because I'd been rescheduling them to make room for her. The truth was, I needed to work while I was here. I was going to lose these clients once I left Ainsley-Bushner, but I couldn't pass up the commission I would need to get me through the next few months. And not only that, but I hadn't mentioned to Lake I was due a sizeable bonus at the new year. Anxious as I was about leaving my job without a replacement, I wasn't sure I could walk away from that, but it would mean not initiating the divorce until after the holidays.

I wiped my brow, tucking myself back in my boxer-briefs, and leaned back against the sink. "Yeah, I actually do need to run to Beth Israel for an appointment, but that's ten minutes from here and I liked the idea of you waiting for me here until I returned."

"It's twenty minutes," she said, "and you can come back here after your meeting. I won't be home until after ten, though."

"After ten?" I tried to get her to look at me, but she focused on slicing the sandwiches down the middle. "Are you fucking kidding me?"

Her head shot up. "What?"

"You were going to work a ten-hour shift? Isn't there a law against that or something?"

She laughed a little, plating the sandwiches. "I haven't been arrested yet."

I thought of Lake on her feet all day, leaving after dark, when the streets were quiet. She wouldn't be doing that alone tonight, but I couldn't always be here to walk her home.

She held out the plate to me, but I kept my eyes on her. Not even a monster sandwich could dislodge the pit in my gut. "I really wish you'd quit," I said.

"Can't. The tips are—well, they aren't great, but they're tips."

"Can't you pick up more hours at the animal shelter?" I asked.

"If I could, I would. They cut back during winter so I'm only there one day a week right now. I don't make tips there anyway."

"Lake." I took the plate and put it on the counter. "You're my girl now. I have big plans for us. I can't go back to California knowing you're working that late at night, that you're living in a place a step down from the shed in my backyard."

"I resent that," she said. "I was doing fine without you, and I'll be fine when you go."

"You'll be fine?" I asked.

"Financially, yes."

I took her waist and brought her close. "And in a non-financial capacity?" I asked, hugging her.

She looked at my chest but thawed a little. "I need this job. Not just for the money, but if I don't keep busy day and night, even when the rest of the city sleeps . . . the minute I stop, I'll think about you there with her."

"I'm coming back for you, Lake."

Our eyes met again. "But when? I won't feel like I have you until all that is finished."

I wanted to lie to her and say it would be quick, that I'd be on a return flight in no time. I worried Lake wasn't facing the truth of our situation, and though I'd bent over backward in the past to protect her from this kind of pain, I was beginning to see how that could ultimately hurt her. "It might be months," I said. "Tiffany and I own a home together. I'm leaving a job with a salary I probably won't be able to command again. I'll do everything in my power to get back to you as soon as possible, but I'm untangling two lives—"

"I get it." She tried to push out of my grasp, avoiding my gaze. "I have to keep waiting. It wasn't enough that I saved myself for you and thought of you every single day we were apart."

"Lake." I held her in place.

"I have to get to work."

"I'll cover your rent while I'm gone. Instead of working the diner, you can focus on auditioning."

This time she pushed hard enough that I let her go. She carried the dishes to a folding table so rickety, I'd flatten it out if I sat on it. "You know I can't accept that," she said, her back to me.

"Why not?"

"Because I'm not some mistress you can stash away."

"Come on—*mistress*?" I asked. "You know that's not what this is. I'm doing my best to fix my mistakes. If I go back and rip the carpet out from under my life without worrying about the details, it's going to hurt all of us even more. Especially Tiffany."

Lake paused. "What makes you think I don't want to hurt her as much as possible?"

"I know you don't. No matter how she's treated you, you've never been vengeful or nasty." I walked up next to her, moving the curtain her hair made away from her face. "It's one of the first things I noticed about you that day on the lot, then at the fair, and it's one of the things I love about you." I kissed her temple. "You're generous and kind and patient."

"No I'm not." She pinched the bridge of her nose as if holding in tears. "I'm ruining her life. If you'd married someone else, I'd feel awful enough about breaking up a marriage, but this is my own sister. I don't know how I can do it."

"You aren't. I am. I'm leaving her for you. I'm coming for you, whether you tell me to or not." I didn't let Lake see that I'd be going home to the person I'd spent the last six years trying to fall in love with. Maybe my heart didn't beat for Tiffany, but I had slept next to her for years in a bed we'd picked out together. I'd gotten to know her tastes inside and out. Tiffany wasn't always easy, but she was my friend, my partner, someone I'd one day assumed I'd have a child with. I knew Lake felt guilty about this— she and Tiffany were blood, after all—but this would undoubtedly be the worst thing I'd ever done. My father had hurt people intentionally and had later had the nerve to ask for forgiveness. While my marriage was no accident, it *was* a mistake, and gutting Tiffany was something I'd always regret. The only comfort I had was understanding for the first time that staying with Tiffany for the wrong reasons would be worse in the long run than leaving her now. Lake was my star in the sky, but Tiffany needed to be the star of the show, and I couldn't give her that.

"I've felt disconnected from her for so long," Lake said. "It felt personal when she took you from me. All of this makes me sick . . . just not enough for me to let you go."

"You can't let me go, Lake." I kept my nose in her hair, inhaling her. "I won't be let go."

14
MANNING

Lake got fired from the restaurant. She'd missed too many days and then when she finally *had* shown up, she was hours late. While she wasn't happy about it, it did mean we got more time together before I left—or so I'd thought.

The day after she'd been let go, she had to work the shelter's front desk, and no amount of sweet talk on my part could convince her to call in. To top it off, the place was in Brooklyn, an area I'd never taken the time to research. Since I couldn't spend the morning with her, I jammed as many appointments into our time apart as I could. I turned on the charm and sold the shit out of Ainsley-Bushner pharmaceuticals. I wanted to leave Lake with money, and return to her with it, so she wouldn't ever have to worry about our situation.

While she was finishing up at the animal shelter, I worked on repairs throughout her apartment—and there were plenty to choose from. Between loose floorboards, a faulty flush valve, mold, and a backed-up shower drain, I'd already been to the hardware store twice.

With half my torso under her kitchen sink, I tried to come to terms with the fact that this time tomorrow, I'd be leaving for the airport. Five days hadn't been enough time. A thousand days wouldn't be. Every minute I spent without her, my body ached. My mind wandered too far away. Was Brooklyn as dangerous as I'd heard? What if leaving her tomorrow would be too hard? What if she was held up at the shelter, and they needed her another hour of the twenty-four I had left with her?

I heard the door and glanced up as Lake came into the kitchen, a spring in her step. "I told my boss all about you, and she let me off a little early," she said, grinning. "What're you doing?"

"Replacing corroded nuts and traps," I said, trying not to sound as relieved to see her as I felt.

She laughed. "Have you been at it all day?"

"I tried to get as much done as I could before I go." I used my sleeve to wipe sweat from my upper lip since my hands were greasy. "And I needed somewhere to take out my sexual frustration. You went for a run this morning and left me all alone in bed."

"I'm sorry." She set her purse on the kitchen table. "It calms me down."

"You're not calm?"

"You're leaving," she said. "And I'm scared. It feels . . ."

She was scared—she didn't know the meaning of the fucking word. I had no idea how I was going to get by once I returned to California. I was already on edge being away from her.

I put down the pliers to slide out from under the sink. "How's it feel, Lake?"

She crossed the kitchen, stepped one foot over my torso and looked down at me. Would've been nice if she were wearing a skirt, but she had jeans on. After seeming to think, she lowered her ass onto my chest. "This is how it feels," she said. "Like I can't breathe, and when I do, it hurts."

She could've crossed her legs and given me all hundred and ten pounds of her, it wouldn't matter. "This doesn't hurt," I said.

"If I sit here long enough it will," she said.

"I don't think so. I think the longer you sit here, the better it will feel."

I didn't want her to waste time being sad. The clock was running down, and I hadn't felt this content since before she'd left me in California. I wasn't ready to let go of it. "Look, if the divorce is going to take awhile," I told her, "I'll fly out to visit. Even if it's for a day or two. How about next time I'm here, we paint this place? Any color you want. I'll build you furniture that matches and install some lighting. You won't even recognize the place when I'm done with it."

She smiled and moved her ass into my lap, right where I wanted it. "What if I want hot-pink walls?" she asked.

"Then you're going about it the right way. But wait until you hear what else I did today."

She raised an eyebrow. "What?"

"Caught two mice, set them free, and sealed all the holes in the walls."

She gasped. "Are you serious? You didn't kill them?"

"Against my better judgement, no."

"Oh my God. You're my hero." She wiggled on my lap—that alone was worth all the extra effort it'd taken me to spare the lives of fucking rodents—and said, "You deserve a reward."

I took her hips as my balls tightened up. "That so?"

"Manning?" she asked, leaning her hands on my chest.

"Yeah, Birdy."

"The other day, when I did that . . ."

"Did what?"

"You know." Slowly, she ran her tongue along the edges of her teeth. Not to be sexy, but to say what she couldn't with words. My cock stirred anyway. "Was it okay? Could I do it better?"

I watched her mouth, remembering the pure ecstasy of having it on me for the first time. It'd be impossible to describe that feeling with words. "You're asking if it felt good when you gave me head? Did you like it when I did it to you?"

She blushed, curling her hands into my t-shirt. "Yes."

"How much did you like it?" I asked.

She thought it over. "I never imagined sex could be that good. It's the happiest I've ever been, having sex with you."

I swallowed painfully, suddenly overcome. I knew it wasn't the sex that made her so happy, but the intimacy of it, because the same was true for me. "Lake, I'd venture a guess that however good it felt for you, it was ten times better for me."

"But isn't it always like that, with all the girls?"

There was something about getting your dick sucked by the one you'd fantasized about for so long—it wasn't the same as any other girl. Technique, capability, experience . . . it all went out the window. "You remember that night in the truck?" I asked.

"Of course."

"How anything, even one touch, would've felt like the world?"

"Yes," she whispered.

"That's how everything feels now. You were perfect. And as we get to know each other, it'll only get better. You'll learn what I like over time."

"I want to learn now."

I pulled her down and kissed her. I was sweaty and greasy, but if I had to take her in the shower, that wasn't a problem for me. Unfortunately, I didn't get the chance. I heard a squeal, and Lake drew back in time for me to see Val whirl around in the doorway.

"Gross," she said, covering her face.

"What are you doing here?" Lake asked.

"I *live* here," she shot back.

Fucking Val. This wasn't how or when I'd wanted to see her again. I just wanted time alone with Lake, who was getting up off my lap when I wanted her to be doing the opposite.

"I meant why aren't you at Julian's?" Lake asked.

Still shielding her eyes, Val put out a hand and felt her way to the kitchen counter. "We broke up. I need vodka. *Now.*"

"Oh no. Again?" Lake asked. "You can open your eyes. We aren't naked or anything."

Val dropped her hand and started fixing herself a drink. "Why were you having sex on the floor?"

"We weren't," Lake said, her voice pitching. "Manning was fixing the sink for us. He did a ton of stuff around the apartment."

"Awesome. Now I don't have to flash the super to get his attention." Val turned on a small radio in the corner of the counter and switched the song from 2Pac. "If only Julian wasn't so precious about his *artist's* hands—"

"Wait, back up," I said, climbing off the floor.

"What? Not a fan of Marcy Playground?" Val glared at me, chin over her shoulder, and raised the volume on "Sex and Candy."

Shutting off 2Pac was an offense in and of itself, but that wasn't what'd snagged my attention. "No— what was that about the super?"

It was the first time she'd looked at me since she'd walked in, and her eyes narrowed. Lake hadn't mentioned any issue there, but by Val's expression, I was pretty sure she knew my history with Lake—and didn't approve. Val turned to face me and tried pushing some of her curls behind her ear, but they kept popping back out. "Why do you think everything in here is broken?" she asked. "The super won't fix shit. I haven't figured out if he's lazy or if he's staring so hard at my tits while I talk that his brain short circuits."

"You didn't seriously flash him, did you?" I asked her. I knew Lake would never do that, but I hated the thought of a perv in the building. For fuck's sake, he probably had a key to their place. My face warmed. "Where does this guy live?"

"We can handle it," Lake started. "We've *been* handling—"

"Lake, sweetheart." I cut her off, cracking my knuckles. "I'll take care of it."

Val raised a freshly made cranberry vodka in my direction. "Apartment 6E. Have at it."

I left the girls and headed upstairs. The super was a gangly old man, short on hair and abundant in beer gut. I was pretty sure Charles would forget his pride if he knew his daughter was relying on this man for anything.

"The building's not up to code, which you know," I told him as he answered the door in a wife-beater. "Let's start with the lock to the building. It needs replacing."

"Who are you?" he asked.

"I'm visiting my girlfriend in 5C, and she needs some repairs."

"Right." He scratched his graying chest hair. "I have her requests. I'll get to 'em when I can."

He started to close the door on me, but I caught it. "I've done a lot of it the past few days, but she needs her radiator replaced among other things. Handle it by next week, or I'll report you to the Attorney General's office right before I bring the fire department by for an inspection."

"Who the hell are you? Do you sign my paychecks?" he asked. "I'll get to it when I get to it."

"It's not an empty threat." I had no problem calling for back-up however I needed to. I'd once wanted to serve the public. There were other men out there like me and I could find them. "I'll get the landlord on the phone right now if we need to bring him into it."

He shook his head. "Fine. Next week. That all?"

I held the door open and added, "That's my girlfriend down there and her roommate. Lake tells me anything I don't want to hear, and I'll come back for a less friendly visit. No firemen. Just you and me."

He raised a hand. "I have no idea what you're getting at, but I got no business with those girls. Only doing my job."

I released the door and went back to Lake's apartment. I didn't like the situation, but I had to trust Lake and Val were smart enough to know what they were doing. They'd lived in New York for years after all, and Val didn't strike me as the type to take shit.

When I walked into the kitchen, the girls were talking about Val's ex, some guy with what sounded like a chick's name. It didn't appear that Lake and I would be getting the alone time I'd planned on. "I'm going to hop in the shower," I said, giving Lake a look that made her stand and follow me into the bathroom.

"She broke up with her boyfriend," Lake said.

I stripped off my shirt and flipped on the water. "I heard. What does that mean for me?"

"She needs me." Lake gave me a reproachful look. "She's sad."

"*I'm* sad." I pulled her into my arms as the mirror steamed over. "I don't want to share you. It's our last night together."

Lake kissed me quickly on the lips. "I just need to listen to her for a bit. Clean up and go wait for me in the bedroom."

"Don't be long," I said, releasing her.

After I showered, I spent the next thirty minutes on Lake's bed, staring at the ceiling and listening to her clock radio as I fantasized about all the things we were supposed to be doing. When she walked in the bedroom, closing the door lightly behind her, I was already hard. I sat up, reaching for her, pulling her onto the mattress. "Come here."

"Shh."

"Why?" I asked.

Her long hair brushed the tops of my forearms. "Val's right out there."

I took off her top, laying her back on the bed. "I don't care."

"I do. I don't want her to hear us."

"Then she should leave." I opened Lake's jeans, running my hands over the smoothness of her stomach. She lifted up to get out of her pants but all I saw was the beg of her hips, welcoming me. When I had her stripped from the waist down, I said, "Turn over."

"Can you be quiet?"

"If I have to be. Can you?"

She reddened, then flipped onto her stomach. With my knees on each side of her, I opened the clasp of her bra to run my hands over her back. My thumbs touched in the middle, over her spine.

"Are you going to give me a massage?" she asked.

"Later, if you want."

She turned her face, resting her cheek on the pillow. "I'd like to give you one."

Alice in Chains came on the radio as the DJ introduced "Nutshell." I gathered Lake's hair in my hands and moved it aside. "How come?"

"I used to look at you on the construction site and think you worked so hard," she said. "I wished I could go to your house and make you feel better after."

"Yeah?" I slid my hands down her sides to grip her waist. I could feel her ribs, and she had a smooth, slight ass. She wasn't eating enough. "Tell me more about that."

"When you get back, if you decide to do construction, I'll give you massages after. I'll light candles in here and you can tell me where you're sore. I'll work on your back until you're healed. I used to think it was so unfair that you worked your body so hard."

I lowered my hands, prying her cheeks apart a little. She shivered. Immediately, I thought about taking her this way, pressing into her from behind. This was why I couldn't be with her that night in the truck. I couldn't be trusted. I might've ruined her that night, and if I hadn't, I would've soon after. One time with her wouldn't have been enough. I'd only been in New York a few days, and my mind was already running with all the sordid ways I could have her.

"Do you miss it?" she asked.

"Miss what?"

"Construction."

"You just finished telling me how unfair you thought it was."

"But it was a better fit than sales."

"I told you, I'll take the first job I find. If it's in sales, then I'll do that. I'll look at construction, too."

"Don't do that," she said softly. "I want you to do something that makes you happy."

"I know you do, but that's a luxury I won't have, at least not when I first get here. Maybe down the line I can concentrate on finding something more fulfilling."

She turned her head to lie on the opposite cheek. "I'll find a new job that pays better."

"I don't want you to worry about that," I said.

"I'm not. Waitressing jobs are a dime a dozen here."

I couldn't talk her out of it, so I went at it from another angle. "Then you'll have no trouble avoiding the graveyard shift."

"I'll avoid the twenty-four-hour job listings," she said, shifting under me, "if you promise not to worry."

"Sure," I said, as if it were a remote possibility, and squeezed the tops of her thighs. Her skin was unnaturally soft all the way down. I ran my knuckle over the backside of her knee. "You have the finest blonde hairs here."

"Sometimes I forget to shave that part."

"At the tops of your thighs, too," I continued. "I saw them when you wore those short shorts at camp."

"I can shave higher."

I shook my head to myself. It wasn't what I meant. "When I was in solitary, I used to think about that, how I'd seen a part of your leg you hadn't meant anyone to, and how it was so close to heaven, and I would get lost . . ."

"Lost how?" she asked, her back expanding with an inhale.

"Turn over again."

She didn't. "Are we going to have sex?"

"Eventually. I want to look at you first."

"Manning?"

"Yeah, Birdy . . ."

"Why do you want to look at me so much? It makes me self-conscious. I don't want to turn over and lie here while you look at me."

She had no idea how touching her, seeing her, was a delicacy I never thought I'd ever be allowed to taste, much less gorge on. I was leaving tomorrow. I needed this to sustain me while I was gone. "Don't be self-conscious. I just like the way you look. Turn over."

With a sigh, she moved onto her back but kept her hands over her breasts. She was uncomfortable, and I didn't want to push her. I was eager to get to the point where she could relax around me, though. "My cell in solitary was about half the size of this room," I said to put her at ease. "Imagine having to stay locked in here for a few months . . . or, in some cases, years."

"Did the guards talk to you?"

"No. They just pushed food through a hole most days. Then, they'd take me to the rec area, which was a slightly bigger room without windows where I could shoot hoops alone for an hour. And they'd watch me shower."

She widened her eyes. "Really?"

I nodded slowly, bringing her ankle to my mouth. "So I wouldn't try to pull anything."

"I thought about you so much while you were gone. Did you think about me?"

"Every day." I inhaled a breath by her calf, watching her face as I ran my stubble along her skin.

She shuddered. "How did you think about me?"

I could tell what she was looking for. It was my own fault. I'd kept her in the dark about these things, because of her age and innocence. She probably felt insecure about that, wondered if I'd thought of her at all. But of course I had, in all manners of ways. With her leg in my hand, shame tightened my chest. It should've turned me off to remember fantasizing about her while she was underage—I'd been unable to stop, even after I'd learned my dad was a pedophile. Instead, my erection raged on. Back then, I hadn't been able to have Lake in any other way but in my mind. Now she was lying in front of me, still young and sweet and wide-eyed at heart, but with the body and mind of a woman.

I found a condom in the nightstand, put it on, and got horizontal on the mattress, lying between her legs so my lower half hung off the bed. I parted the blonde curls over her mound and kissed her once.

Her hands went into my hair, grasping me as I licked her like a peach-flavored ice cream cone that held the sweetest nectar at its core. When she got so worked up that she was trying to push my head out of her legs, I crawled over her and entered her quickly. She covered her mouth to muffle her moans, but I removed her hand and kissed her, swallowing them for her. Having to be quiet irritated me. I cradled the top of her head so she wouldn't hit the wall and spent my frustration by fucking her fast and hard. When she was close, I put my other hand over her mouth so she could scream into it, but we weren't fooling anyone. I looked into her eyes and she didn't turn away, maybe because my hands held her head in place. As she accepted the length of me with each contraction, I came before I was ready.

I scanned her face. Her cheeks were flushed where my fingers pressed into them. I removed my hand, and her labored breaths came hot against my chin. "Damn," I panted. "I wanted to look at you more before we did that. Couldn't help myself."

She spread a hand on my back. "You can try again later."

As my heart rate slowed from hammering to pounding, I released the tension from my muscles, giving her my weight. She was sweating, sweet-smelling but briny. Me? I was far from sated. I'd had her body, now I wanted more. I wanted her to know, every day of her life, that she could tell me all her thoughts and desires and secrets, and I'd never tire of hearing them. And for that kind of intimacy, I had to reciprocate.

"It turns me on thinking about that time I couldn't have you," I admitted.

She nodded lightly. "It's the same for me."

"No it's not. You were underage. Innocent. It was wrong."

She sighed, fluttering her fingers over the back of my head. "But you didn't do anything, Manning, so it's okay."

"I wanted to. Very badly." I lifted my head to see her reaction. "When I was in solitary, I'd jerk myself off thinking about fucking you—and you were *seventeen*, Lake."

She bit her bottom lip. When she moved, I became more aware of my cock softening between her legs. "I'd be upset if you hadn't thought of me that way. You have to forgive yourself."

Should I be forgiven for all the things I planned to do to Lake in order to ensure she was always mine? I wanted to make her feel so good, she could never leave me. "It's more than that," I said. "There's something you should know."

Uncertainty crossed her face. "About?"

"My dad."

The tension in her arms eased, but the wrinkles in her forehead didn't. "What is it?"

I ran a thumb between her eyebrows, smoothing her skin. "He was . . . he *is* . . ." I worried once it was out there, Lake would see everything differently. I wouldn't blame her. I was *inside* her right now. She might shove me off, disgusted with me. I was at my most vulnerable, and that was the reason I both wanted and didn't want to tell her. "He molested Maddy before she died."

Lake's eyes instantly filled with tears. "But she was nine."

I gripped both sides of Lake's face as it screwed up, lowering mine right above hers. "Can you understand why I feel this way? Why being with you made me feel like I was no better than him? I can compartmentalize it better now, but back then, I couldn't. I would think of you and feel like a monster."

She covered her face and began to cry. "No."

"Lake."

She shook her head. "Stop."

My heart pounded. This was exactly what I'd been afraid of. I thought of all the despair and rage I'd felt since learning this about my dad, and now I was passing that onto the one person I wanted to protect. "Do you want me to leave?" I asked.

255

"Leave?" she asked. "You're so . . . why? *Why* do you do this?"

"Do what?"

"I'm so angry with you."

I pulled her hands away, confused. "Angry?"

"How can you think you're anything like that, Manning? How could you spend all those years living with this? I know you're not a monster. *You* know you aren't. Please, Manning, stop doing this to us."

"Doing what?"

"Don't put yourself, or us, in that box. It's not you. You loved me, didn't you? You understood me. You wanted to care for me."

"Yes."

"And you never, not once, touched me." Redness rimmed her eyes. "There's no way you can equate what we had with his actions. How could you? It makes me want to physically hurt you to get you to open your eyes, and your dad, he . . . he—" She couldn't finish her sentence.

"I know. I know. Don't cry." I kissed the tip of her nose, still holding her wrists even though she struggled to cover her face again. "Stop."

"How long have you known this?"

"I got the letter while I was in prison."

"When?"

I looked her full in the face, trying to think of how to explain. She came to the conclusion on her own, though.

"I *knew* there had to be a reason you went to solitary," she said. "Something that sent you over the edge. I knew it."

I kissed her again. I was crushing her, so I let her arms go to lift myself off her, but she immediately hugged me closer. So much for her threats of physical harm. "I went to SHU a few nights after I read the letter," I said. "One of the guards had seen you trying to get in to visit me—"

"He saw *me*?" she asked.

"Yes. He was a piece of shit, always trying to get under my skin. He'd talked shit about Tiffany before, but when he started in on you, and how young you were, and the things he wanted to do to you—"

"Oh, no. Oh, Manning." She dug her fingernails into my back. "Is that why . . .?"

I nodded slowly, my eyes moving between her lips, ears, forehead, eyes. All of her. "I couldn't take it. Not after the letter I'd read from my dad. Suddenly, that guard was a molester who could get to you while I was stuck in there. That guard became my dad. He became me."

Lake's hands shook as she touched my face. Her tears made straight lines down her temples. "I'm sorry. I should've listened. I never should've gone there."

"I'm grateful that you did. At the time, I would've spent more time in SHU if it meant keeping you away from there, but now that so much time has passed . . . I can admit I would've done the same if I

257

were you. And it gives me some peace knowing you never forgot about me."

"I tried. Did you ever read any of my letters?"

"No."

"Where are they?"

"At the house."

"Do you think Tiffany knows about them?"

"They're hidden in the attic, but with her, anything's possible." I thumbed away some of the wetness on Lake's face. She was the first person I'd ever told, and with that information out of my brain, I realized Lake was right. What she and I had wasn't bad or immoral or wrong. She was a part of it, and her goodness always prevailed, and I was not that monster. "You know what?"

She barely even whispered. "What?"

"Instead of continuing to blame myself for something I never had control over, I'm going to make it right, Lake. I'm going to be everything my father wasn't. You and I will have a family one day, and—"

She cried more, and I had to nuzzle her to make sure she heard every word. "And I'll spend a lifetime making up for his mistakes. I will be the best father to our children."

"You can't say that," she said, sobbing into my neck. "It's too early. We're not even official."

"We *are* official," I said, smiling about how juvenile it sounded, and also at the idea of raising a family with her. "If anything, it's late, not early."

I thought I felt her smile against my neck, too. For all I'd dreaded telling Lake the truth about my family, a weight lifted. We'd turned a hard conversation about something ugly into a glimpse of a happy future. Being with Lake had taught me there was such a thing as second chances. I wasn't my past or my father's mistakes. I was just a man becoming the best version of himself for the girl he loved—for his Birdy.

———

I held Lake until she eventually calmed and I could no longer ignore the voices coming from the next room. "What's going on in there?" I asked.

"Val invited some people over," Lake said. "Every time she and Julian break up, she has a party claiming to celebrate. Really, she wants an excuse to get drunk or high."

With a heavy sigh, I dropped my forehead on Lake's chest. "You're fucking kidding me."

"We won't be able to hide in here. They're my friends, too. They'll find us."

"Lake." I implored her. "I want time alone with you. I'm leaving tomorrow."

There was a crash in the next room followed by laughter. Lake shrugged it off. "One of the kitchen chairs has a loose leg. People fall in it all the time."

With a knock on the door came Val's high-pitched voice. "Roger's early," she said. "Come say hi or we're breaking in."

"Roger?" I asked, covering us with the top sheet. "Does your door lock?"

"No." She craned her neck out from under me to call, "Don't come in here. Give us five minutes."

"You have four!" a man yelled from the other side of the door.

Lake tried to get out from under me.

"I'm not done with you," I said. She laughed, but I hadn't meant it to be funny. I was dead serious.

"They'll come in here, Manning. Believe me."

I let her push me off. "Who's Roger?"

She picked a shirt off the ground. "A friend from class."

"What kind of friend?"

"A gay one."

"Ah." Relieved, I watched her dress. "You forgot your bra."

"It's fine."

I sat up, grabbing my own clothes and searching the bed for her undergarments. When I didn't find them, I lifted the frame a little. There was no bra, but I did pull out something familiar, something I hadn't seen in probably six years. "Who do we have here?" I asked.

When she turned and saw the stuffed bird in my hand, she lunged at me. "Oh my God."

I held it over my head, out of her grasp. "It's Birdy," I exclaimed.

"I tried to hide her," Lake said, her cheeks pink.

Unable to contain my grin, I looked up at the blue and white toy I'd won for Lake at the Balboa Fun Zone since I couldn't take her on the Ferris wheel. "Why would you hide her?"

"It's embarrassing." She bit her bottom lip, obviously anxious about the bird. "Did you know Birdy was a blue-footed booby, not a pelican?"

"'Course I did," I said, setting it on her head to resume looking for her bra. "I don't want to go out there and make nice, Lake. I want to be alone with you, talk to you, make love to you, and then sleep with you. Birdy can stay, but they've got to go."

"We should at least say hi. Then we can, I don't know, go for a walk."

"Are you going to tell them who I am?"

She pretended not to hear me, busying herself by fixing her hair in the mirror above her dresser.

"Lake."

She turned to me, still hugging the stuffed animal under one arm. "What am I supposed to say?" The hurt was evident in her voice. "Should I lie like you did to that woman at the ice skating rink? Is that what you're asking me to do?"

"No."

"These are my friends," she said. "I can't hide you from them forever."

"I'm not asking you to. Tell them the truth."

"But some of them know Corbin, and also . . . he's been calling."

"Calling where?" I sat on the edge of her bed. "For what?"

"Nothing. Everything. He's my friend, Manning. We talk all the time. He left messages on the machine, and I've been ignoring him."

I took a deep breath, dropping my eyes to the floor. Val could be annoying, but because she didn't take shit, she was good for Lake. What about Corbin? I hated the idea that once I left, he'd still be here, but I had to face the facts—in four years, she hadn't given in to him. For *six* years, he'd been trying, and evidence would show he'd been respectful about it. And with that realization, I kinda felt bad for the fucker. "Have you considered that ending the friendship would be doing him a favor?"

"Him?" she asked. "Or you?"

"Him. I know what it's like to love you from afar. It isn't easy."

Looking lost in thought, she caressed Birdy's head, then put the toy on her dresser next to something else I recognized—the wooden box I'd made her for the earrings she'd worn as Maid of Honor.

"Do you regret it?" Lake asked.

I tore my eyes from the jewelry holder. "Regret what?"

"Loving me."

"Obviously not, Lake."

"Then maybe he doesn't, either."

"He does, he will, because he won't win you. He'll never have you, and that's why it isn't fair to him." I waited until her eyes returned to mine, and the sadness in them made my gut smart. "I'm sorry," I said. "I know he's your friend, and if you want things to stay that way, I can't stop you. But a part of me can't help but feel bad for him."

She shook her head. "It's not like that. Corbin knows nothing will ever happen between us, and it's still not enough for him to end our friendship. Trust me."

I didn't believe that for a second, but I said, "Okay. And for the record, I didn't lie to that woman to keep our secret. She doesn't know us. I don't want anyone to. You and me, we're you and me. Nobody's earned the right to know our story."

"Our story." She let out a breath then came over and straddled my lap. "I thought you were ashamed of us, and that was why you lied."

"It's going to take me some time to get used to touching you without looking over my shoulder," I admitted. "But rest assured, the decisions I make are with you at the front of my mind." I picked her up, carrying her over to her closet. "Where's your overnight bag?" I asked. "We're leaving."

"Where are we going?" With her legs wrapped around me, she shifted on my crotch to reach behind me. "It's on the top shelf."

I took it down, and a moment later, she feathered her fingers over the back of my bare shoulder. "Summer Triangle," she whispered.

I stood still, letting her trace the three stars, even though the tattoo had brought as much angst outside prison as it had comfort inside. Tiffany didn't understand it, so she didn't like it. "It's for you," I told Lake. "I carry you on my back wherever I go."

"You said the same thing about Madison when we were in the truck."

"She's the third point. My girls."

Lake shuddered in my arms, hugging my neck. "I'm sorry, Manning. I didn't know your sister, but I'm so sorry for her."

"I know." I could've stood still with her all night, but the noises from the next room were getting louder, as if more people were showing up. "I need you to get down or else your friends are gonna walk in here and catch us in the act."

"Oh, okay." I set her down by her waist. "Where are we going?" she repeated.

I didn't answer, just started dressing. She'd figure it out soon enough.

Roger was apparently someone Lake had met in class, and they ran lines together all the time. He made a big thing about me coming out of Lake's room, both of us looking and probably smelling like we'd just fucked. I lasted with Lake's friends about four seconds until excusing myself to the fire escape for a cigarette. I wanted to meet them, but not while I was this agitated over the little bit of time we had left.

Val followed me outside, climbing out the window. "Can I bum one?"

Years earlier, I'd told her no, but I didn't want to be the adult here anymore. We were all equals now. I gave her one.

She lit it quickly, took two furious drags, and finally let it rip. "You have some nerve. You're a fucking asshole. I can't believe you're doing this."

Val had obviously been holding in her feelings about me. Over her shoulder, Lake was watching us. I wasn't sure if she could see me, but I leaned over and closed the window most of the way so she wouldn't hear. "This might surprise you," I told Val, "but I appreciate what you're doing. I'm glad Lake has had someone here looking out for her."

"She's had two someones. Me and Corbin. We picked her up off the ground after you trampled her, and it's been four years of getting her to be human again. Now you come in here and fuck it all up with that smug expression on your face. You got her fired from her job?"

"Not on purpose. She—"

"Fuck you."

I scrubbed my jaw, hoping I didn't look smug at that moment. "I'm not leaving this time."

"Lake probably believes you, too. Well, guess who's going to be cleaning up your mess when you don't come back?"

I smoked down my cigarette, watching her. I was not used to taking this kind of shit. Not at all. If this wasn't Lake's best friend, if it wasn't Val's way of protecting Lake, I'd have walked away already. Instead I said, "I'm coming back, and you and I will have to be in each other's lives."

"I can't even believe I'm having this conversation with you. Poor Tiffany. I don't even like her, but poor fucking Tiffany. You screwed Lake over, now you're going to do the same to her sister."

"Who's better for Lake than me?" I asked, my voice louder than I meant it. "Who's going to take better care of her? Love her more than I do?" I flicked ash over the railing, my face hot. "You don't know the half of it. Lake's all that means anything to me. I can tell you without a doubt in my mind that nobody will love, protect, or care for her like I can. I'm the man for her. The only man."

The night went quiet as we stared at each other. I'd never said anything like that in my life, and it hit me for the first time that it was true. Always in the back of my mind was the fact that I didn't deserve Lake. But nobody was worthy of her virginity, of her love, so why the fuck *not* me? I would appreciate it more than anyone else.

"When are you leaving?" she asked.

"I have to go, but I'll be back."

"When?"

Now, she was the one who wore the smug expression. She had me, or she thought she did, but she didn't know that nothing could keep me away very long. "I fly back tomorrow."

"When will you be back in New York?"

"I'm not sure yet. I—"

"Yeah, thought so. My money's on never." Val stubbed out her half-smoked cigarette, gave me the finger, and stumbled back into the living room.

Lake came over quickly, peering out at me, lit from behind like an angel. "What was that?" she asked.

"Nothing, Birdy."

"What happened? Val looks upset."

I squatted down to Lake's level and took her chin between my thumb and knuckle. "All you need to know is that I'm not going anywhere," I said. "Except to my hotel. Get your bag. We're leaving."

15
LAKE

The mid-December night was alive with holiday cheer. Manning had wanted to take a cab to the hotel, but I'd insisted we walk. I loved to see the bell-ringing Santa Clauses, steam billowing from manholes—and hot chocolate cups—and the lit Christmas trees and menorahs in people's windows. Or maybe I just needed time to come to terms with where we were going. Having Manning in my apartment had felt like a dream, but going to a hotel with him evoked the same uneasiness I'd gotten when he'd offered to help me with my rent, as if I was his mistress.

Manning kept his eyes forward. With our elbows linked, the tension in his body was evident. New York wasn't like Orange County. We passed loud-mouthed street performers, tripped on uneven pavement, and avoided brushing against beady-eyed men. There was something to see everywhere we looked, and though I found it exciting, I wasn't sure Manning did. To him, more things could go wrong here.

Whatever Val had said to him, he'd been brooding ever since. He'd fussed with my scarf and coat outside the apartment before insisting he walk closest to the curb. Admittedly, it hadn't been the best time for Val and Roger to burst in. I thought back to Manning's confession about his dad and squeezed closer to him.

"Cold?" he asked.

"A little."

"We're almost there."

Had I known Manning was trying to reconcile his own desires for me against his father's for Maddy, would I have done anything differently? I couldn't be sure, because I didn't see things the way he did. What Manning's father had done to a nine-year-old girl had nothing to do with love or attraction. Manning and I had never so much as kissed. Just because he'd felt something for me when I was under eighteen didn't mean he was a sexual predator or some kind of innate monster. I saw it clear as day, but Manning had always struggled to see himself as I did.

When I glanced up, I caught Manning half-turned, doing a double take at a church with massive wooden doors decorated with wreathes and bows. "What is it?" I asked. He looked forward again, silent. He'd never struck me as the religious type, so I couldn't fathom what had crossed his mind. "What are you thinking about?"

He took a few moments to respond. "Marriage."

With one night left, that was the last thing I wanted to talk about. His marriage had nothing to do with me. Everybody involved had known going in what Manning and I had, but they'd chosen to pursue the relationship anyway. Manning had made his own decisions, and so had Tiffany.

We were quiet so long, we passed another church. This one had tiny white lights strung along its staircase railings and an enormous stained glass Jesus that looked upon us.

Manning's cell rang, and he took it out of his pocket before silencing it. He hadn't looked at me in blocks. "Who was that?" I asked.

We turned a corner and sidestepped a man shoveling the sidewalk outside a bodega.

Manning stopped. "I need a cigarette before we get to the hotel," he said. "And then I think we should talk about the logistics of what comes next. I know it's unpleasant, but it is what it is."

The clerk placed his shovel against a wall and followed Manning inside. I turned my back on them, on the harsh light streaming from the store onto the sidewalk. I didn't see what there was to talk about. I'd thought the plan was for him to come back as soon as possible. I didn't need to hear the horrible details of how it would happen. We were about to do an awful thing, and if we could stop ourselves, we would, so what was the point in beating the topic to death?

A woman passed me, the toddler attached to her hand pulling the opposite direction, trying to get to the fresh pile of snow the shop clerk had created. The boy managed to wiggle free and jump into the heap with both boots. She picked him up, playfully rolling her eyes at me as she hauled him off. I smiled at them. I hadn't seen snow fall until I'd moved to New York, but in the four and a half years I'd been here, I'd never just played in the snow like that. I'd been forced to grow up fast, to fend for myself. Since Manning had arrived, I'd finally started to feel light again. I wasn't ready to let go of that. Of him.

I felt Manning's eyes on me, a sixth sense I'd developed from being unable to communicate with him any other way when I was younger. I looked back at him leaning between the shovel and a display of poinsettias and miniature Christmas trees. He stuffed a pack of Marlboros in his pocket, watching me as he cupped a hand around his mouth and lit a cigarette. "If this was easy," he said, "we would've done it long ago."

"If what was easy?"

"You and me."

"Can't we talk about it tomorrow before you leave?" I asked, sighing. I wanted to go back to that day at the ice skating rink when we'd done nothing but wander, kiss and touch, eat and make love. "Watch this." I turned to face him completely. With a sly smile, I walked backward a few steps and planed my arms. "Ready?"

"What for?"

I leaned back on my heels until my balance wavered, then fell into the snow with a *crunch*. Winging my arms and legs like jumping jacks, I grinned. "Look," I said. "I'm making a snow angel."

"I see."

I froze right through my cheap coat, the ends of my hair wetted, but I got up on my elbows and smiled at him. "Come make one with me."

"I like watching you do it," he said, pinching the butt of the cigarette, amusement in his eyes.

"If you won't make one, I'll have to think of another way to get you over here." I balled up some snow, packing it tightly while he raised his eyebrows at me—a warning I intended to ignore. When he didn't make a move, I threw the snowball at him, narrowly missing his shoulder.

He didn't even flinch. "Have to work on your aim," he said, winking.

"Fine. You win." I stood, bending at the waist, brushing snow off my pants. I pretended to fix my socks while stealthily forming more ammunition. Peeking to make sure he wasn't looking, I straightened up, much better poised to hit him. I launched the snowball and it smacked against his chest so hard, his cigarette fell from his mouth onto the sidewalk.

I stifled a laugh at the way his nostrils flared. We stared at each other a few tense seconds before we both broke into a run. Halfway down the block, he caught me by the waist and lifted me into the air. Even as I gave in to a fit of laughter, I struggled against him, making it as hard as I could for him to carry me.

Right before the entrance to the W, he tossed me into another pile of snow and fell down beside me. "Just to be clear, this doesn't mean you win," he said, spreading out on his back like he had that night at the pool in Big Bear. I scooted over to make space for his impressive wingspan. Manning made what had to be the largest snow angel in history, then held his hand palm up for me. I took it, letting him pull me over to him.

I rolled onto my stomach, resting my chin on his broad chest. Before Serious Manning could ruin the moment, I asked, "What's your favorite color?"

"That's easy. Blue."

"I should've guessed," I said. "All boys like blue."

"Not the shade I'm thinking of. It's more of a baby blue, or turquoise water—"

"The ocean. Why?" I asked. "Is that your favorite place in the world?"

"Nah."

"Where would you be if you could be anywhere?"

"Where would *you* be?"

My instinct was to say the beach—it was my home, or it had been once. Was I even that girl anymore, though? Wasn't it normal for tastes to change over the years? "Here, I guess."

"Don't sound so sure," he teased, reaching up to brush sleet from my hair. "It's okay if it isn't New York, Lake."

"Why wouldn't it be? My friends are here. I'm building a career. I even have a hairdresser I like." I pursed my lips. "I've made a life here."

"But it's not like you left Southern California because you didn't like it there. If New York felt like the only option . . ."

I wanted to argue just to prove him wrong, but the truth was, I sometimes felt out of place in the city. I'd grown up playing barefoot in sand and salt water, with the sun turning my gold hair white. Not that I didn't love it here, but I sometimes wondered if the city would ever feel like my true home. "What about the mountains?" I asked. "I've never seen you as happy as you were in Big Bear. Is that where you want to be, somewhere with nature?"

"I want to be where you are," he said. "New York can be your dream home, but mine is you."

I shivered beneath a coat of goosebumps. Manning rubbed his hands over my back, but it was his words, not the cold, that got under my skin. I sat up, throwing a leg over his lap to straddle him. "I want to live on a mountain," I said from above him, "just like this. With my great bear."

He grabbed me by the waist with a throaty growl. "So, Goldilocks thinks she can tame a wild animal?" he asked, shifting me on his lap so I could feel how untamed he was. "She should be careful what she wishes for."

"She wishes to try, even if it takes a lifetime."

"Close your eyes," he said. "Picture a time you were happiest."

Maybe it was all the bear talk, but my mind went back in time, right to Young Cubs Camp, sneaking peeks at Manning across the cafeteria, or during counselor hour after the campers had gone to bed, or before breakfast, when we were supposed to have our eyes closed for Reflection. I'd forgotten that the morning Manning had been arrested, he and I had shared a moment right before the cops had shown up. After the night in the truck, our eyes had met during Reflection, electricity buzzing between us as if it were the beginning of something.

"What is it?" he asked. "What's making you smile?"

"Camp," I said. "I loved being around you all week. And riding the horse. That was fun."

"It was." He ran his hands up my thighs. "Is that your happy place? What about memories that don't involve me?"

I traveled back again, this time to playing board games at night during Christmas break, Tiffany screaming when she won, screaming when she lost, and my dad struggling not to lose his temper and ruin

Christmas. One morning when I was seven and Tiffany was ten, we'd woken up and found a Labrador puppy under the tree. We'd named her after Daphne from *Scooby-Doo*, but she'd gotten sick within six months. Seeing how much Tiffany had loved that dog, Dad had shelled out thousands of dollars in vet bills, but it hadn't saved her. Tiffany had been devastated. I opened my eyes and started to get up. "I don't want to play this game anymore."

Manning sat up, watching as I brushed snow off my pants. "It's not a game, Lake."

"I don't know why you're doing this. What's the point of forcing me to look at what I'm giving up? Are you hoping I'll change my mind and tell you not to leave her?"

"No. I just want you to understand what lies ahead. Once I talk to Tiffany, there's no turning back." He held out his hand to me. "Come here."

"No."

"Then help me up."

I took his hand, but after a short-lived battle of strength, I found myself in the snow again, stubbornly holding in a laugh as he feathered his fingers up my waist. "What's your middle name?" he asked. "You never told me that day on the wall, and I've wanted to know ever since."

"You could've asked any member of my family over the years," I pointed out.

"I wanted you to tell me."

"Dolly," I said, "and I hate it."

"Dolly." He kissed my cheek. "Lake Dolly Kaplan."

"Manning Raymond Sutter."

He looked surprised. "How do you know that?"

"I saw it on some of the paperwork for your arrest."

"Come on, Lake Dolly Kaplan. My goldilocks, my little bird." He stood, holding out a hand to pull me up. "Your locks of gold are all wet and your wings, too."

16
LAKE

There wasn't anything special about Manning's hotel room—an oversized, stark white bed that hadn't been slept in for four nights. A luggage stand with his open, organized suitcase next to a closet where he'd hung a garment bag. A desk with a logoed notepad and pen, which sat next to a phone with a flashing red light. "You have messages," I said.

"I know." As if remembering his cell phone, he took it out, wiping it on his pants. "Fucking thing got wet."

He set it on the media console, and it lit up with missed calls from Tiffany. I took off my coat. The melting snow on my pants and in my hair suddenly felt less whimsical and more cold and sticky. "You were right," I said, looking away from the blinking red light. "I don't like it here."

Manning turned me by my shoulders, hugging me to his torso. "I know it's hard, but I need you to be strong, Lake. We can't get through this if we aren't in it a hundred percent."

I glanced up quickly. By the way my stomach dropped thinking Manning might have doubts, there wasn't a percent high enough to convey how badly I wanted this. "I'm in," I promised.

He thumbed the apple of my cheek, then kissed it. "You know why that shade of blue is my favorite? Why I've loved it since a warm summer day in 1993? I don't really have to tell you it's your eyes. My Lake. You are my favorite color."

I hugged him back, but I couldn't help thinking how my eyes were simply a shade darker than my sister's. Mine were a lake, still and shallow, but hers were the color of the endless, manic ocean.

"You're shivering," he said. "Get in the shower. I'll join you after I check the messages."

The red light continued to blink at me. It felt personal, like a judgment—as if Manning listening to his messages before showering was equivalent to choosing Tiffany over me.

I went into the bathroom and turned the water on hot, standing under it with my eyes closed. How many times had Tiffany tried to reach Manning over the past few days? Had they spoken when I wasn't around? He hadn't mentioned it, but I hadn't asked, either. I wasn't sure I wanted to know.

When I turned, Manning was on the other side of the glass, wrestling his wet clothing off. He had dark circles under his eyes like the night I found him at the sink after a nightmare. He slept soundly with me, or so I'd thought. But maybe he didn't sleep at all. All week, I'd been able to ignore the fact that Manning had another life, but had he? Of course not. It would've been impossible for me to expect him not to think of her at all, my sister, the woman with whom he'd spent day in and day out since I'd last seen him.

"Were the messages from Tiffany?" I asked when he opened the door and stepped in.

"Yeah."

I swallowed. For my own sanity, I wanted to keep on ignoring what I was doing to Tiffany, but not only was it unfair to her, it was unfair to Manning, too. "What did they say?"

"You want to know?" He ducked to stand under the shower stream. He was so big that he took all the water, and I just stood there dripping.

"I guess."

"Nothing at all," he said. "She's worried because she hasn't been able to reach me. She wants me to call her."

"When was the last time you spoke to her?"

"When I arrived," he admitted quietly. "But not since."

Tiffany was worried, and she had every right to be. Because of *me*, her own sister. I'd had her husband for days, and I had to face the truth—she probably knew what was happening here. "How can I do this to her?" I asked. "How can I have already done what I have—and still be doing it?"

The hotel's bar of soap looked even more miniature in his big hand as he began washing himself. "It's too late to ask that," he said, moving to let me have the water back. "It's already done."

"Are you going to return her call?"

"I don't know if I can." He shook his head. "She sounded tense. If I call her back, and she asks if you're here, I can't lie to her. But I won't end my marriage over the phone."

I twisted my flea market ring as cold, hard reality wedged itself into what should've been a relaxing, steamy shower. "Do you think she knows?"

"She has to. She's been pouting ever since she found out I might come to New York. She knew years ago that she was hurting you, and she knows now to be worried that I'm here." He lathered his chest. "I know Tiffany better than anyone, and I'm certain she made a deal with herself a long time ago to ignore my attraction to you. Like me, she thought it could stay hidden."

"I tried to tell you it couldn't," I said, my voice thick. I couldn't avoid this anymore. Manning and Tiffany had a life together, and it was because of choices *he* had made. "You spent all those years planning never to be with me. Well, as hard as I tried to move on, to forget you, I *never* did. *I* never planned a life without *you*."

"I didn't forget you, Lake. You think I'd be here if I had?"

"How can your mind change so completely in a few days?"

"It didn't change, and it didn't take a few days. I always wanted you, but I had to live through not having you for things to become clear. To come here after four years and see that what I feel for you hasn't fucking lessened at all, to see that maybe I can actually be *good* for you, I can now admit the truth. You and I *should* be together, and we can, but you have to face the truth about the situation before I get on that plane tomorrow."

The truth was that Manning had wholeheartedly believed he would spend his life with Tiffany. And that hurt more than any of this. "You never would've married her if you'd had any hope for us."

"I had no hope," he confirmed.

I wasn't sure what to say to that. I'd never given up on us. I'd held on to my virginity for him. I'd accepted my diploma with pride, hoping he'd feel the same when he heard. I'd kept the jewelry box he'd made me even though the corners cut into my skin when I clutched it. But the opposite was true for him. He'd given up hope—or maybe he'd never had it at all. "You told me you don't love her," I said. "What else do I need to know? Isn't that enough?"

"Your sister and me—we've had our ups and downs, but I don't think she'll see the divorce coming. She's a pro at turning a blind eye. I'm working overtime to cover the remodel on top of a mortgage, which is fucking ridiculous because I could've done it myself if I'd had the time, but someone has to pay for it. And even though Tiffany *constantly* asks me to, I refused to take any more money from your dad after the wedding."

I forced myself to listen, not because I wanted to know, but because it was clearly important to Manning that I understand what his life was like. "Doesn't she work?"

"She's a buyer for Nordstrom, and she's really great at her job." He stepped under the stream of water to rinse. "She moved up quickly once she got on the right track."

For some reason, that took me right back to being in her shadow. She'd always loved to shop, and now she got paid to do it. Well, after all the ways she'd complained about my relationship with Dad, it sounded like a great life she'd built for herself despite me. "Good for her."

He put the soap down. "She wants a family, though."

"*Tiffany* wants a family?" I asked. "I thought she hated kids."

"People change. She's twenty-six now. Has it in her head she's going to have a little girl she can dress up and pose with for Nordstrom's kids' catalogue."

"So she doesn't actually want a kid. She just wants a way to get more attention."

He massaged his jaw, watching me. "She started talking about it after the honeymoon. So last year, before I knew I was coming on this trip, I told Tiffany once the remodel was paid off in spring of 2000, we'd start trying for a baby."

"That's in a few months." During my darkest moments over the years, I'd imagined the call from my mom that Tiffany was pregnant, but even then, I hadn't been able to picture them having a family in anything more than a vague, abstract sense. I could, and had, vividly imagined getting that call, though. Tears built deep in my throat. "You wanted a family with her?" I asked.

"I wanted a *family*, Lake. When I told her that over a year ago, I knew I'd come to New York when my parole ended. But back then, it never occurred to me that I'd give myself permission to do anything other than check on you."

We stared at each other. In my mind, Tiffany was still the cavalier teen girl I'd grown up with, giving our parents trouble, talking casually about sex, concerned with only one thing—herself. How was I supposed to reconcile that with the woman Manning described? How was I supposed to face that fact that Tiffany wanted to be a mother, and Manning had wanted that, too—and that they'd been planning to start so soon? I was taking that from them. "I get it," I said. "What we're doing is wrong." In the privacy of our shower, where nobody else heard us, knew us, understood what we'd been through, I said, "But it's not enough to change my mind. Have you changed yours?"

"I've stayed away so long," he said. "I need you more than anything. Don't you see how I need you?"

I had eyes; I saw his need plain as day. We were naked in the shower and he'd been hard since he'd stripped down, but I didn't think that was what he meant. I wanted to be angry for the things I couldn't fix, to retreat, for a little bit, into the life I'd had before he'd come to New York. The life where I had permission to resent him and bitterly hope he was unhappy. More than that, though, I wanted his hands on me. I couldn't remember anything ever feeling as good as being touched by him. So I went to him, and as soon as he enveloped me, I cried against his chest. I cried for Tiffany, and for what I was taking from her, and for the fact that even though she and I hadn't been close in a long time, once Manning told her, I'd lose my sister. For good.

"I'm sorry, Birdy," he said. "You don't know how sorry I am. I was blinded by fear, and I made mistakes."

I looked up at his face, blurred by my tears. It was the second time I'd heard him admit it, and by the way it looked painful for him to swallow, I thought maybe it was the hardest thing of all for him to say—that this was his fault. Stripped down to nothing, with nowhere for either of us to hide, we had to admit the terrible things we'd done, and those we were about to do.

"Do you regret marrying her?" I whispered.

"I regret hurting both of you." He smoothed his hand over my hairline. "When you asked me what I was thinking about earlier and I said *marriage*, I was thinking about you, not her. What do you want, Lake?"

Speechless, I stared up at him, the way I had many times since the day I'd met him. He'd towered over me on the street, blocking out everything else, consuming me, captivating me. Tonight was maybe the first time I began to feel like he and I were in this together, like I wasn't a girl trying to keep up with a man.

Manning sat on the bench of the shower, pulling me to him by my hips. "What do you want?" he repeated, his eyes on mine. "What life do you dream about?"

I dreamed only of him. When the one thing I'd ever wanted hadn't been within grasp, the details hadn't mattered. Once I'd left California, I hadn't really fantasized about marrying him or long walks on the beach or candlelight dinners. I'd just missed him and wanted one more touch, one more look, one more of the shared, private moments we'd done so well. I put my hand on his inky wet hair. "I don't know."

"Yes you do."

I wanted *him*, at any cost. I wanted to make his wish come true and turn him into a father. That was the truth, but I couldn't force it out of myself, even though he probably needed to know it with what lay ahead of him. "I don't want to talk about it. Not here in this hotel. Not while you're still with her."

I thought he'd argue, but instead he said, "I understand."

"Will you tell her about us?" I asked. "Or just that you want a divorce?"

"She has to know. They all do. But I don't know how the fuck I'm going to do it. Not only do I have to think about her and your mom and dad, but there's the legal side of things, getting a lawyer when I won't have a job . . ."

He kept talking, but all I needed to hear was "*dad*" for my blood to boil. Much of the situation we were in was his fault. The more time that went by, the more convinced I was that Dad had pushed Manning and Tiffany together to keep me focused on school and away from Manning. "He'll try to get you to stay," I said, cutting him off. "He'll do something."

"Nothing can keep me away, Birdy. I'm coming back to you."

"When?"

"If I could tell you, I would. I have no way of knowing that."

I thought about how it would feel when he was back with Tiffany while I waited here for him. It would be impossibly hard. He'd be with her. He'd be hurting her for me. "Maybe I should come with you."

"I don't think you should."

The soothing steam of the shower, the rhythmic beat of water drops against the tub floor, the utter pleasure just from being held by Manning—none of it could dislodge the pit in my stomach. Could I ask Manning to do this alone? Did Tiffany deserve the chance to look me in the face when I upended her life?

"But she's my sister."

"If you're there, it's a memory that will haunt you, Lake. I can give you the gift of bearing that memory for you."

Manning was always shouldering the burden of us. I hadn't forgotten his words that night on the beach, how he bore things I didn't even know about so they wouldn't fall on me. I touched his cheek. "You shouldn't have to shield me all the time. I'm older now. I don't need to be protected."

"You know I wouldn't have it any other way." He pulled me closer, kissing the space between my breasts. He brushed his lips over my hardened nipples, down my waist. His hands wandered everywhere he could reach, from my lower back down to my ankles. His mouth became hungrier. Redness bloomed wherever his lips touched.

"I can't get enough of you," he said hoarsely. "What'll get me through every night without you is knowing I won't have to hold back when I return. I'll

289

be able to have you over and over until I'm forced to stop because another round can only kill you."

"You can never kill me," I panted. "Not this way."

He kissed my stomach, then flattened both his palms over it. "Lake," he murmured.

I stared at his hands on me as they softened. "Manning."

"You know you could be pregnant already."

I shivered, steadying myself on his shoulders. One time, we'd lost ourselves to the moment—was that enough to change the course of our future? It would be hard. I had no money; he'd have no job. There was a lot of pain ahead of us, and that was no environment for a child. But as all the things that could go wrong filtered through my mind, I realized Manning didn't sound scared, or even surprised. "What if I am?"

"Then a baby will come out in nine months."

"Manning, stop." I tried to push away from him, but he had his hands on my waist now, his scruff scratching the sensitive skin of my tummy. "We can't," I said. "What would we do? I should take the morning-after pill."

"I want the chance to make things right with the universe," he said. "To be the opposite of my father."

"You can have all that, but not now. We can't have a baby, Manning." The statement was so ridiculous, I had to laugh. "There are so many reasons we can't."

"Can't what?"

"Have a baby."

Manning stood suddenly, forcing me to step back. He shut off the shower and got out. His movements were abrupt, his mood darkening. I stepped onto the bathmat, soaking it as he leaned his hands against the bathroom counter and looked at himself in the mirror.

"Are you mad?" I asked.

His jet-black hair dripped water into the sink. He was as aroused as I'd ever seen him, his eyes hot, his knuckles whitened from his grip, his penis purple at the head. He opened an arm to me, and I went to stand in front of the mirror with my back to him, letting him cage me in. He raised to his full height. Barefoot, I barely came up to his chin.

He put his hands on my stomach again. "I know it isn't the right time, but I can't help that I want to put a baby in you. You're the only one who's brought out that primal side of me—protect, provide, mate."

My stomach tightened so painfully, I sucked in a breath. I'd had no idea, until that moment, a sentiment like that could be erotic. "Manning."

He bent his knees and slid himself between my wet thighs without entering me. "It's just my instinct. Fuck you. Own you in all ways possible. Claim you in a way nobody can ever take from us." His voice grated. "Close your legs around me."

Breathing through my nose, I braced myself on the lip of the counter as he held my stomach and pushed back and forth between my thighs. "It's too soon," I murmured, but I couldn't deny the truth. Pregnancy was already a possibility, however small.

He rose up a little, running his shaft through my ass cheeks. I tensed as he passed over my most intimate area, a spot it'd never even occurred to me to let him touch. He looked darkly at me in the mirror as he whispered in my ear, "Another time."

Hair sprung alive on the back of my neck, his words slithering right down my spine. He spread my lips from behind and began to enter me. "I won't come in you," he said. "But I want you on birth control when I get back, at least until we're ready for more."

More. Manning and I would have and be *more*. My grip tightened on the edge as he entered me. I was certain I'd never get used to that initial penetration. It turned me on as much as any other part of sex, maybe more, but for now at least, it also felt like being impaled. "Don't stop," I said.

We watched each other as he worked himself inside me, all the way to the base. Then he took me against the counter, unbridled, without hesitation, like it was the first time again, like we hadn't been doing this over and over since Monday. Manning took great care to make sure I climaxed first, slowing down his thrusts as he worked my clit, all while I watched in the reflection.

He'd unleashed in me a latent desire to be owned and claimed in all the irrevocable ways he'd described.

For us to be, as he'd said, irreversible. Maybe it was the fact that he was leaving or that I was overcome by this new unfamiliar instinct to give him a baby, but I held his gaze in the mirror and said, "Come inside me."

"I can't," he said, but he pulled my elbows behind my back, getting leverage to take me even harder. His mouth was hot in my ear. "How can I do that to you?"

"Because I'm begging for it."

"God, Lake. *Fuck*." He released my arms to grab my hips and hold me in place as he came, growling from his chest. This time I was ready for it, and I felt his heat fill me. I'd never experienced anything like it, and I was owned—his through and through, just like I'd always wanted.

Bent over the sink, I watched as he came down. He held my head, his eyes closed as he whispered things I couldn't understand into the back of my hair, as if in prayer. I knew I should feel guilty about the fact that we hadn't used a condom, but Manning looked about as content as I felt. For the first time, it didn't feel like the end of the week, but the beginning of our lives.

We got back in the shower. He washed my hair and between my legs. I soaped his body, gliding my hands over the planes of his chest, the hard lines of his muscled stomach and the curves of his biceps. I trailed my fingers down the ripple of his veiny forearms until I had him hard and eager in my hand.

"You're ready to go again?" he asked.

I blushed, embarrassed by my hunger. "Aren't you?"

He thrust a little into my fist. "Do you need more evidence?"

"I brought something to show you," I said.

"What's that, Birdy?"

"We have to get out of the shower."

We dried off, and I toweled my hair dry as best I could. We'd had all the difficult conversations, and we were still doing this. Finally, it felt real, like Manning was coming home to me—like Manning was *mine*. I was so excited to show him my surprise that I pushed him out of the bathroom while he was still wrapping a towel around his waist. "Don't look yet," I said, dumping my overnight bag all over the floor, too impatient to rifle through it. When I found the pajamas I hadn't worn in five years, I ran into the bathroom, changed, and came out to find Manning smoking through a small sliver of window.

I stood across the room from him, waiting for his reaction. I wasn't sure if he'd remember. He looked me over, his eyes lingering on the thin straps, the lacy edge of my pajama shorts. He took a drag and blew it right into the room.

"Manning."

"Huh."

"The smoke."

Absentmindedly, he waved his hands, his eyes still on me. When he didn't speak, I glanced down at the pink gingham pajama set I'd bought to wear on prom night. It was the same thin camisole and matching shorts I'd been wearing when Manning had set me on his kitchen counter and almost kissed me while Tiffany had slept in the next room. "It's—"

"I know what it is."

"I sewed the strap."

"What was wrong with the strap?"

"You tore it that night," I said.

A low grumble from his throat. I'd gotten the sense during our time together that Manning liked to be reminded of my younger self. Our gentle interactions from that time in our lives could be changed into the most forbidden kind of sex we could have. I would think of all the times I'd had to restrain myself and imagine acting on them. If we had access to that truck we'd gone out in the night on the lake, I'd fuck him in it.

But, even if it were true that our unspoken roleplay did it for both of us, perhaps there was a line. Now that I knew about Manning's father, and what had driven Manning to such extremes in the past, it was possible he could use this as an opportunity to beat himself up. "Did I go too far?" I asked.

Skyscrapers rose behind him, lit windows dotting the darkness. He didn't make a move, but the look in his eyes said *come*. Barefoot, I crossed the room. "Is it okay?" I asked. "I'll change back."

He took another hit of nicotine, adjusting his towel with one hand.

"Manning?"

"Yeah."

"Are you going to say anything?"

"No."

"Why not?"

He put out his cigarette on the exterior windowsill and stood. With his hands on my shoulders, he walked me backward until the backs of my legs touched the bed.

"What are you doing?" I asked.

He untied the string of my shorts. "I'm making love to you in your sweet pink pajamas, Birdy, that's what I'm doing."

17

MANNING

I woke up with a pink-pajama-clad princess in my arms. After I'd made love to her well into the night, I'd had her put the pjs back on. Even now, as I opened my eyes and took in the outline of her breasts under the thin fabric, the sliver of skin under the hem of the top, my greedy dick twitched. I hadn't been inside her for a few hours, and I wanted more.

Lake's hair was tangled between us since she hadn't brushed it after the shower and I'd had my hands in it all night. It also smelled fucking amazing. I buried my nose in it, and that led to nuzzling her neck, pressing kisses to her cheek. We'd only just gone to bed, but my time with her was limited. I had a flight to catch this afternoon.

I squeezed her close. Months of winter had made

JESSICA HAWKINS

her pale, while my skin was brown and darkened with hair, like some kind of beast. I had a moment of panic that I wasn't supposed to be in this hotel, that I'd actually sleepwalked into her bedroom, unable to help myself any longer, and taken her against her will.

She sighed and snuggled her ass into my crotch. "Manning?"

"Yeah, Birdy."

Her cheeks went a little pink and she shook her head. "No, nothing. I just wanted to tell you how happy I am."

"Hmm." I didn't buy it. There was something behind every sweet little *"Manning?"* and I wasn't letting her get away with it. "You want something, but you have to tell me what," I said. "I can't read your mind."

She was trying not to look giddy. After a moment, she repeated, "Manning?"

My chest rumbled with a chuckle. The sleepy, sated expression on her face made her seem even more adorable. Fuck, the obscene things I had done to her, and still planned to do . . . I really was a beast. "What is it?"

"You remember the other night how you made me, you know, with your mouth and hands?"

I kept laughing. "I remember."

"Can you do that again?"

"I've corrupted you."

"It's just that it felt so good."

"Aren't you sore?" I asked.

"A little. That's why your mouth feels nice."

I'd gone overboard last night. I hadn't meant to take her more times than I could count, but I wasn't able to get enough. I'd come and be hard minutes later. I was so fucking scared of what would happen once I got on that plane. I wanted to stay and not deal with all the shit waiting for me at home.

"I don't care," she added. "I don't know how long it'll be before we're together again."

Panic tightened my chest once more. It wouldn't be any easier here for Lake as she waited for news from me. "We should probably take a break for a little while," I said.

"Oh. Are you sore, too?"

She was too cute this morning, and maybe that was intentional, to torment me for leaving. "No," I said. "I just want to lie here with you for now."

She ran her fingers along my forearm and I fought to keep my eyes open. After last night, after the past few days, I thought I could sleep for a week.

"You know all those things you said last night?" she asked. "Did you mean them?"

I knew what she was referring to, and for better or worse, I meant all of it. Begging for me to claim her pussy, no matter the consequences? "Fuck yes."

Her cheeks rounded, as if she was holding in laughter. "So you're really going to move into my *shitty* apartment? That *dump*?"

"It won't be a dump once I'm through with it."

"What about Val?"

I swung my leg over hers, trapping her against the bed. "What *about* Val, goddamn it?"

"She can stay with us, right?"

I scraped my stubble against a part of her neck that made her howl. "It tickles," she screamed, trying to get away. "Fine, fine. Val can't come!"

I released her. She hopped up and started jumping on the bed. "I can't believe it's finally happening," she said, her top billowing enough for me to get quick glimpses of what was underneath. "You and I are going to *live* together."

I watched her, mesmerized by her golden hair, her sparkling blue eyes. I would've agreed to anything she asked for in that moment. I hadn't seen her this happy since I'd gotten here, as if the dark cloud hanging over our affair was lifting. "Yes we are."

"And buy groceries together. And paint the apartment. And sleep in the same bed. *Every* night."

"You got it."

She jumped so high, she reached up and touched the ceiling. "This is the best day—no, no, no. It's the best *morning* of my life."

"I don't get a full day?" I asked.

"No, because you have to leave."

I couldn't take my eyes off her. I wished I had a cigarette so I could just lie here and drug myself and watch her jump all morning. "You know, now that we're together," I said, "when you do things like this . . "

She was out of breath and smiling as she stopped and looked down at me. "What?"

"You can do them naked."

She hid her face with her hands, but I caught the redness creeping up her neck. "You don't think I'm being childish?"

Maybe she was, but didn't she know I loved her like this? Hadn't I fallen for her before any of this, when she'd been naïve and silly and prudish, as Tiffany had liked to call her? Hadn't I gone overboard again and again trying to protect this side of her? Childishness was allowed. "I love you," I said.

"Then come up here and jump with me."

"The bed would go right through the floor."

She stepped over me with one foot so I could see right up the leg of her shorts. "Enjoying the view?" she asked.

"Very much." I licked my lips, running my hands up her calves. "Take off your top."

We'd been together less than five days, and she was still self-conscious. With hesitation in her eyes, her movements were stilted as she peeled off the tank . . . and dropped it on my face.

I tossed it aside. "Keep jumping."

With a light laugh, she bounced the mattress enough to make her tits jiggle. Jesus, I felt like a fucking king in that moment—a king preparing to devour his only subject. "I never thought," I said, "not in a million years . . ."

She grinned. "That I'd jump on top of you?"

"Did you hear what I said just now? I love you, Lake." I knew she felt the same, but she hadn't said it since I'd arrived. I understood why, but now I was headed into battle, and I needed her to armor me. I slid my hands higher, causing her breath to catch. "Tell me you do, too."

She stood there, her chest rising and falling, her expression turning serious. "You know I do."

"So say it, my beautiful, silly girl. It'll keep me going while we're apart."

Her legs trembled as I massaged her through her shorts. She made me wait, and when she finally said it, her voice was as soft and lovely as the pussy my fingertips were inching toward. "I love you," she said.

I'd heard it before, when she'd told me on the beach, but it felt like the first time. I wanted her as much now as I had that night, as much as I had hours ago when I'd fantasized about impregnating her, as much as the first time, when I'd stood outside her unlocked door, fighting myself. "Good girl," I said. "You are, aren't you? Show me how good you are. I want to see all of you from this angle."

Slowly, she stepped out of her shorts. "Like that?"

"Underwear, too."

She did as I said, and I reached up easily, running my thumbs through the blonde curls covering her mound, parting her sweetly pink pussy for my viewing pleasure. "This image will stay with me until my deathbed," I said matter-of-factly. I touched her with as much restraint as I could manage. "You *are* a good girl," I said, easing a finger into her. "I can fuck you raw and you're still wet for me."

She whimpered, and my lids fell with that little noise. I continued my exploration of her, felt her tense as I approached her asshole. Did I think she was ready for me to play there? Not by a long shot. She didn't yet know the half of what I'd do to her. For now, it was fun to watch the filthy thought occur to her, the horrified look it put on her reddening face.

While I was cooking up what crude thing I wanted to do to her next, the phone rang. I froze, and so did she. I knew without answering who it was—and so did she. It was early here, which meant it must've been dawn in California. I wanted to wait until tonight to talk to Tiffany, until we were face to face, but I owed her at least a quick conversation before I got on the plane.

Later. Now wasn't the time.

We stilled until the ringing stopped. Lake's expression had fallen, and I didn't want the countdown to the flight to start just yet. I dropped my hand to my stomach. "Come sit down and let me do '*that thing*' with my mouth," I said, teasing her.

"If you insist," she said, a smile spreading over her face. She started to step off me, but I grabbed her ankle. "Where are you going?"

"To sit like you said."

"Why over there?" I asked, pulling her down. "My mouth is right here."

303

18
MANNING

It was just after ten in the morning, and I'd already worn Lake out again. She'd fallen asleep on my chest forty-five minutes earlier and had barely stirred. I'd have to start packing for the airport soon, but for now I was content to stay here and run my hand from the base of her spine up to her neck and back. She had the smoothest skin and baby fine hairs, with random freckles that reminded me of the constellations Maddy had taught me when we were kids.

Lake looked so fucking peaceful that when the phone rang, I grabbed it without thinking so it wouldn't disturb her. She woke anyway and now I was pinned under her with what was likely Tiffany on the line.

I cleared my throat and brought the phone to my ear. "Hello?"

"Hello?" Tiffany said. "That's all you have to say? I've been calling and calling. Where have you been?"

Lake furrowed her eyebrows up at me. I smoothed my hand over her hair and said, "Yeah, I'm sorry, Tiff. Hold on a sec."

"Are you kidding?" she asked.

I put my hand over the receiver as Lake got up. "Give us a minute," I whispered.

She nodded, wrapping a blanket around her as she ducked into the bathroom and shut the door. I watched her go, hoping last night was the breakthrough Lake and I needed to be able to talk about this. I'd need to lean on her a lot in the coming months.

I picked up the phone again. "Hey. I'm here."

"I've been worried, Manning. I call late at night and there's no answer. I called you over an hour ago and you weren't there."

"I was here," I said. "Sleeping."

"At nine in the morning? Since when do you sleep in?" Her voice pitched as if she'd already had several cups of coffee. "And that doesn't explain the rest of the week."

I rubbed the inside corners of my eyes. "I know." I didn't have an explanation, and I didn't want to lie to Tiffany so I just said, "I've been busy."

"Busy?" Her voice broke. That jarred me into waking up.

I sat against the headboard, keeping my voice down so Lake wouldn't have to hear this. "What's the matter?"

"I was so excited to talk to you. I called and called, and now I just feel . . . so stupid."

"Stupid why?" I asked.

"You've been unreachable practically all week. Thank God Daddy said you'd been to your meetings or else I would've flown out there."

"You're exaggerating," I said, my hands sweating at just the prospect.

"Am I? Or have you been avoiding me?" She got strangely quiet, and I fucking knew it was coming as she took her next breath. "Is it because you—is she . . ."

Fuck. Now I was wide awake. This was the exact reason I hadn't wanted to pick up her call. If Tiffany chose now to voice her suspicions about Lake, after all the years we'd swept my feelings for her under the rug, we were about to have a brutal conversation over the phone. I swung my legs over the side of the bed, leaning my elbows on my knees. "Tiff, I . . ." I started. "Can we talk about this when I get back?"

"No."

"I don't know what you want me to say."

She paused, the familiar sounds of *Good Morning America* in the background. I could picture her curled up on our eggshell-colored sectional from Robinsons-

May with a cup of coffee before getting ready for work. "I want you to say you're coming home tonight."

I inhaled. "I'm coming home, but—"

"Then never mind. It isn't stupid." The TV went quiet, as if she'd muted it. "I don't want to start things off on a bad foot. Come home, and we'll put all that, we'll put New York, behind us."

I sighed longingly at my jeans, which hung on the back of the desk chair with a pack of smokes sticking out of the pocket. "Start what off, Tiffany? I still have to pack. Can I call you from the airport once I've woken—"

"Manning, babe, listen." She took an audible breath and then squealed the way she had when she'd gotten her promotion and slid down our tile hallway in socks. Stunned, I pulled my ear away from the phone at the same moment she said, "I'm pregnant." The shrieking continued as she teased, "*That's* what I've been calling to tell you, you big dummy."

With the phone a safe distance from my ringing ear, I swore I'd misheard her. All the baby talk last night had gone straight to my head. "You're what?" I asked.

"We're having a *baby*, Manning."

This time, I heard her loud and clear, bolting up so fast, I dropped the receiver and had to chase after it. I nearly tripped over the coiled wire, and as I picked the phone back up she was saying, ". . . believe it? You're going to be a dad, just like you wanted."

What hit me first was a sense of pride—*my* baby, *I* was going to be a dad—but in the next moment came the crushing realization that this wasn't right. Tiffany was on the other end of the line, not my Lake, who was in the bathroom, preparing to jump off a cliff into a future with me. It was a baby I'd once wanted, still wanted, a beautiful blessing, a chance to atone for my father's wrongs—and the one thing that could truly come between Lake and me.

"How . . . how is that possible?" Not only was Tiffany on birth control, but since I'd found out I was coming to New York, we'd hardly been intimate. I lowered my voice as I searched the tangled sheets for my underwear. I couldn't have this conversation naked. "You can't be pregnant."

"I can and I am," she said, her mood dimming. "Birth control's not a hundred percent effective. You know that."

"The fuck it isn't," I said. "We've been together over four years and suddenly it isn't effective?"

She went from joyful to distraught in the flip of a switch. Any other time I would've rolled my eyes, but I could decipher Tiffany's fake crying from the real deal, and this was the latter. "You asshole."

"I'm sorry." I pinched the bridge of my nose, squeezed my eyes shut, and tried to wrap my head around this. All night I'd talked about wanting to have a kid. I didn't want one just because it was around the right time in my marriage for that kind of thing. It'd been ingrained in me to take care of others from the time Maddy was born. She'd been six years younger than me, and I'd grown up protecting her—not just in a general sense, but sometimes literally, keeping my dad away from her. Or so I'd thought.

I couldn't find my underwear, so I pulled on my jeans instead and got my cigarettes from the pocket. "I didn't mean to curse at you," I said into the phone. "I'm just . . . shocked."

"That's not why I'm crying. You're *whispering*," she accused. "Why? Is someone there?"

Shit. Fuck. I took the phone as far as the cord would allow and leaned back against the windowsill, facing the closed bathroom door. All I could think was *fuck fuck fuck*. Tiffany wanted to know if there was someone in my hotel room? Damn right there was. Lake, my beautiful, delicate bird, whose hopes and dreams were pinned on me. The love of my life, who I'd probably never deserved, and whom I definitely didn't now. I was going to be a father. I thought I'd gotten to a place where I could really do that designation justice—but how could I deserve one and not the other? I put the phone between my shoulder and ear and lit my cigarette with an unsteady hand. "Tiff, stop crying."

"I can't. I tell you I'm pregnant and you yell at me."

The more she said *pregnant*, the more real it felt. The less control I had over the situation. "Have you been to a doctor?"

"*Yes*. With my mom. Do you think I'd call if I wasn't sure?"

"Yeah, I do. Six fucking months ago, you were convinced you had skin cancer and let me think that until you admitted you hadn't been to a dermatologist yet. Tell me, Tiffany—did you have cancer?"

"No, but—"

"You told me last year you were getting fired just so I'd come home early from a work trip."

"We've been over this a hundred times," she said. "I honestly thought I was getting fired! But this time, Manning, it's true, and I'm sorry you're so mad—" Her breath hitched. "I'm sorry you find it so awful."

"I don't find it awful." My stomach churned, and I pulled the cig out of my mouth. Might've been the first time in history one made me want to puke. That was a sign. Stop smoking. I'd have to with a baby on the way. I watched it burn down. "Of course I'm not mad. I just don't understand how it happened. We had a plan, and the timing is all off, so tell me—how did this happen?"

"I . . ." She stuttered, her voice breaking again. "I stopped taking birth control. You *said* we could start trying—"

"I didn't say we could start—what I *specifically* said was that—" I took a drag of my cigarette. Even if it was making me ill, smoking was the thing that calmed me quickest, and I needed to get my fucking head right before Lake came out here. "I said *after* the remodel, next year, *spring* at the very absolute earliest." I cursed. "I said we could once we were able to pad our nest egg."

"But then there'd be some other expense or reason not to do it. We're ready now. You know we are. And once it settles in, you'll thank me, Manning. Who cares if it was a year or so early? Five, ten years down the line, you won't care."

It wasn't one or five or ten years from now. There was only this moment, and it had come too early. For Lake, I had come too late. I'd never been able to get the timing right with her. If there was one thing about Lake and me that persisted, it was that— bad timing. It was this. Finding out I was going to be a father—and realizing Lake would never forgive me for it.

I got up and paced, beyond giving a fuck that it was a non-smoking room. Despite the cold coming in from the window, my hairline sweat. I thought about leaning outside and vomiting. The faucet ran in the bathroom. I needed to reverse my life to ten minutes ago, to Lake sleeping on my chest, trusting me. To when my life had finally been about to start. With that thought came a crushing guilt no man should bear. I was having a *kid*. How I could have just fucking wished that away? I grabbed my hair in a fist. "You should've told me you were stopping the birth control," I said. "When was this?"

"I don't know."

"Yes you do. Spit it out."

"A few months ago. September maybe."

"September what?" I pushed. "When in September?"

She knew what I was getting at. With a contrite sigh, she said, "The beginning of the month."

Of course. That was exactly when I'd submitted a formal request with Ainsley-Bushner to come to New York. Tiffany knew, deep down, what Lake meant to me. She'd done this on purpose. "Christ, Tiffany."

"Are you pissed?" she asked.

The tremor in her voice stopped me from accusing her of going behind my back. She knew what she'd done. It was just like Tiffany to feel trapped and lash out however she could, not caring about who got hurt, as long as it wasn't her. Regardless, she was carrying my baby. "I'm a lot of things," I said. "But pissed isn't the right word."

The door opened and Lake poked her head out, quizzing me with her eyebrows as she leaned on the doorjamb. I forgot to breathe, noting how she'd washed her face pink and fresh, how her eyes were no longer puffy from crying last night.

"Get dressed," I quietly choked out. This conversation would strip us both in lots of ways, and I needed her to be covered up. She came out to pick through her clothing, which was all over the place.

"I have to go," I told Tiffany. "I'm getting in tonight, so I'll just get a car. We can . . . I don't know. We'll talk when I get home."

"I really was excited to tell you earlier in the week. I just got so worried when you didn't pick up." Her voice lightened. "Are you sure everything's okay?"

"Yes."

"Are you happy?"

I couldn't speak. I wanted to be a father, just not this way. Saying I wasn't happy about it wouldn't be right, but I couldn't think of anything worse in that moment than breaking the news to Lake. "Yeah."

"Then say it, Manning. I thought you'd be so excited to get this call, I was so certain you wanted this, and now I don't know what to think. I'd feel so much better hearing you say we're having a baby, honey."

I shook my head, looking at the floor, wanting to die on the spot. "I can't."

"*Please.* I need this. You don't know how stressed I've been trying to reach you." She sniffled. "Once you say it aloud, it'll sink in, and you won't be mad anymore—I just know it."

Bullshit. Tiffany knew exactly what she was doing. Lake was still naked from the waist up, twisted to inspect the seat of her jeans before she buttoned them up. Well, what the fuck. I had to tell Lake somehow, and Tiffany wouldn't stop until she got what she wanted. That was a lesson I thought I'd learned long ago, but it was never truer than in this moment.

I took a deep drag on my cigarette and put it out on the ledge, bracing myself to break Lake's heart again. "We're having a baby."

19
LAKE

The back of my jeans was still a bit damp from the snow, but I figured Manning and I were headed to my place anyway. He had to check out from the hotel and his flight wasn't for a few more hours. I wondered if he had any meetings today, but if so, maybe it didn't much matter if he skipped them considering he'd be done with the job as soon as he told Tiffany the truth.

That was what I was thinking as I buttoned up my jeans and heard Manning say, "We're having a baby."

I glanced up to find him staring at me. The darkness in his eyes struck me first, then how he looked physically pained, sick even, when he swallowed.

A baby? I wondered. Whose baby? What was happening?

Ash from his cigarette had fallen onto his thigh. He hadn't put it out completely, and a thin trail of smoke disappeared out the window.

He dropped the phone to his side. Slowly, the truth started to pierce the bubble I'd been subconsciously protecting the past few seconds. He'd been on the phone with Tiffany. She'd been trying to reach him for days. He wheezed as if he'd just been sucker punched. The silence made everything surreal, the air so thick that I put my hand around my throat, as if I were choking. I stood still so long that I got dizzy.

It was Tiffany. It was *their* baby.

The phone started to honk and he hung it up, breaking the stillness in the room. "Lake, listen—"

"Don't." The sharpness in my voice surprised even me. "Don't say it."

"I have to. Come here, Lake."

My head pounded. Heat burned up my chest into my cheeks. I'd never been able to think straight around him. Never. Had no control around him. Not even a little. I held the heels of my palms to my temples. "I can't."

"That was your sister." His pants were still undone, and his stomach flexed as he stood from the windowsill. "She's pregnant."

I died a little inside. That statement killed off any part of me that was hoping I'd misunderstood. I put a hand up. "Don't come over here." I realized that I, too, was topless. I covered my breasts and stepped back, nearly tripping over my duffel bag. My things were strewn on the ground from when I'd dumped them out last night like an impulsive, *stupid* child. That was what I was. Reckless. Childish. So incredibly naïve to think this could ever work. I put on the t-shirt closest to me, and of course it was Manning's and it smelled like him, which choked me up.

I got to my knees, grabbing my stupid pink pajamas to shove them in my bag, even though I'd just as soon leave them behind.

"What are you doing?" Manning asked.

Leave. I wanted him to leave. *I* wanted to leave. I couldn't even form the word, just kept packing whatever was nearest.

"Lake," he said, as if saying my name over and over and *over* would change anything. He came and tried to get the duffel from me. "Stop it."

"*You* stop it." I stood and shoved him away, but didn't move. "Don't touch me or my things."

"I'm as shocked as you are."

I'd lost him. Again. I'd thought I'd had everything—I'd told him I *loved* him, not hours ago. I'd never really had him, though, and deep down, I'd known that. Whose fault was it that I'd let him convince me otherwise? "You made me say it," I said, unable to stop the sobs from breaking through. "You made me tell you I love you." I threw my weight into my next attempt to budge him, but he stayed put, even as I pushed and pushed. "I got fired for you. I introduced you to my friends. I ignored Corbin to make you happy. And Val, she warned me—she *knew* this would happen."

He grabbed my wrists finally, wrestling me against a wall. Locking my forearms over my chest with one hand, he covered my mouth with the other. "Calm down or they'll think I'm hurting you."

He loomed over me, larger than life, blocking out everything but him. I couldn't look at him while he did this to me again. I twisted my head side to side, bucking my entire body to get him off me. "You *are* hurting me," I snapped. "You're *always* hurting me."

"I didn't know," he said, his voice raised. "She stopped birth control without telling me. I didn't know, Lake, I swear."

My eyes landed on the hotel desk phone, remembering the winking red light. It took me back to last night, when I'd seen, with my own eyes, that Tiffany had been trying to reach her husband—and I'd held him tight anyway. Manning hadn't known about the baby. *He* hadn't done this. And I'd known things could fall apart, but I'd pushed forward anyway.

When I stopped squirming, Manning said, "She did it on purpose."

I blinked at him, panting into his palm. The pain in his eyes, the truth, was enough to clear my haze of anger. This had Tiffany written all over it. All the messages she'd left, the calls from her Manning had missed—maybe she'd even wanted me to know, otherwise why wouldn't she wait to tell Manning tonight, in person?

It clicked. This wasn't Manning's fault. I sagged against the wall and batted my lashes, clearing my vision. The past few days had passed quickly, and yet, they'd thoroughly changed me. Manning and I had felt permanent, but Tiffany had one-upped me in the most ultimate way. There was nothing more permanent than a baby.

Manning lowered his hand. "I swear to you, Lake, if I'd thought there was even the slightest chance this could happen, I wouldn't keep that from you. You know I wouldn't."

I wanted to keep being angry, to scream at Manning and make him feel as hurt as I did. And in the same instant, I was angry *for* him. Protective. Tiffany hadn't just taken this from me, but from him, too. "She tricked you."

"Like I told you last night, we were talking about having a family down the line," he said, loosening his grip on my wrists. "She thought in her own twisted way, it would be okay to start now."

"No she didn't. It didn't just occur to her out of the blue," I said, straightening up against the wall. I thought about how I'd feel if I were in Tiffany's shoes. If it'd been my husband coming to see the woman he truly loved. If I'd been faced with losing him to my sister. I had been through that, but not publicly. Nobody but Val had known about Manning and me when he'd married Tiffany, and that had been bad enough. She wouldn't be able to hide the reasons for her divorce forever. "You said she did this on purpose."

He frowned. "We've always had shit timing, you and me," he said, dropping his hands. "But Tiffany . . ."

"Her timing is impeccable," I said, "and never a mistake."

"I put in a request to come here in September. It didn't occur to me that after four years of me hardly breathing a word about you, she'd go to this kind of extreme."

Three months was enough time to stop birth control, get pregnant, and announce it. I closed my eyes, shedding a few silent tears. "Are you sure it's yours?"

"Yes."

"How?"

"She has issues around infidelity."

"*Tiffany*?" I made a face. "Has she brainwashed you into believing she wouldn't cheat if the opportunity presented itself?"

He hesitated. "This is a conversation for another time, but I have no reason to believe it's not mine."

"What if it's a false alarm . . . a faulty pregnancy test?" A chill ran down my spine, and I shuddered. "Something she made up for attention?"

"She's been to the doctor, and if she's lying about that, I'd never forgive it." He grabbed his hair, holding it in a fist. "That'd be grounds for me to leave her, and she knows it."

Everything in me was tight, like I might snap in half. I loosened my fists and dropped my eyes to our bare feet. A sense of relief came over me, as if I'd been anticipating bad news for days. Maybe I deserved this after what I'd done to Tiffany. Manning was right all those years ago when he said he could hurt me just by loving me, but I'd been so sure it was no longer true, even up until ten minutes ago. "You said this was it for us." My chin trembled. "You said you wanted a family with me."

"I do," he said thickly. He brought me to his chest, hugging me with a strength that took my breath away. "I meant everything I said, and I still do."

I couldn't move. I just stood there, limp, staring out the window behind him. The mirrored skyscrapers no longer reflected the morning sun like diamonds catching the light. They just looked cold. Dead. Cabs honked ruthlessly downstairs, and there was nothing magical about the December chill freezing my tears. Was this still my New York? It didn't feel like it.

"You promised." I shook as the words came out, broken and sharp, shards of the future we'd planned. "You promised no matter what."

"I still do. I still promise."

What was he saying? I wasn't sure he even knew. He was in as much shock as I was, I could tell by the lifeless, stilted sound of his voice. I pulled back. "Manning . . ."

"I'm not walking away from you again," he said, and his warmth returned. He wasn't in shock. He wasn't lifeless. His eyes were melted brown sugar, begging me, loving me, wanting me, still, after all this.

It should've changed everything, but in fact, all it did was make things clearer.

We'd been through this before—he'd *chosen* this. "You could've had me so many times, Manning, but you picked her."

"I settled—I didn't pick her. *Now* I choose. I choose you, and I will never make that mistake again." His hand found my face, and he thumbed the hollow of my cheek. "You told me once love was enough. I didn't think so, but *you* made me believe it is."

"But it isn't, Manning." I put my hands on his chest to move him back a safe distance, enough that I wouldn't cave and give him whatever he was trying to ask for—but instead I curled my hands against his bare chest. "I couldn't think past the moment back then. I know better now—life isn't fair."

"I don't care what lies ahead, how bumpy the road is about to get. I made you a promise, and I'm keeping it." The longer we stood there, the more determined he looked. "It took me too long to say it, but now . . ." He moved his forehead against mine. "I can't imagine not telling you every day that I love you so fucking much. I trust in us."

I worried it was too late for that. This wasn't about trust or love anymore. I believed Manning thought we could make this work, but there was one thing Manning cared more about than me, and that was doing the right thing. That was why I'd lost him the first time. And the right thing for him was not letting his child grow up with a bad father the way Manning had—or without a father at all. "This is it. We're over before we even began."

"No, Lake," he said softly, shaking his head. "I . . ." He ran the tip of his nose along mine, his lips brushing my cheek. "I'll find a way. Trust in me, in us." He kissed the corner of my mouth, whispering. "I'll find a way. I will."

I trembled with his loving words, with the sense of hope he'd finally found, even if it was too late. My hands were red, fisted against his chest, but I still couldn't push him back. "There's no way around this, Manning."

"What if *you're* pregnant?" he asked.

At that, I lost my breath and had to look away. A part of Manning could be growing inside me already, something nobody could take from me, not even Tiffany. After this week, I wanted it, but not like this. I had no choice but to live with the pain of losing Manning, but I could never have his child now. And I *did* have a choice there. "I can't be pregnant," I said.

He put his hand against the wall, keeping me where I was. "You don't know that."

"I can't," I repeated, shaking my head. For once, fate *was* on my side. What I'd thought was irreversible, actually wasn't. "I won't. I'll take the morning-after pill, and if that's not enough . . . I wouldn't keep it."

"Don't you fucking say that." His entire body vibrated, but he wasn't angry. He was pleading. I recognized a breaking heart when I saw it. "If you're pregnant, you know I'll tear down the universe to be with you."

I *did* know that, and I refused to get him that way. Maybe that was good enough for Tiffany, but I wanted Manning to have chosen me from the start—not because I'd trapped him into it. Manning, at his core, was a good man. And at my core, I loved him above all else. I could never ask him to leave his child, to not be there with Tiffany every step of the way. "Go home," I told him. "Be with them."

"Lake." He slid his hand under my hair, but I shied away from him and kept my eyes down. He didn't belong to me, and he never had. "Don't pull away now that I can touch you," he murmured. "I don't know how or when, but I'll come back to you. You and I have a life here. I've seen it, and so have you."

On a dark beach over four years ago, Manning had made misguided sacrifices out of love. I hadn't understood it then, but now I had to decide if I'd let Manning put himself through this. If he left Tiffany, she'd do everything in her power to hurt him—and she held all the power now. She had his baby. I could ask him to leave her and he would, but she'd turn him into the bad father he was already terrified of becoming.

He was right. I'd seen a life here with him, but I didn't anymore.

I worked up the courage to look at him, my Manning.

"I love you," he said, tilting my head up by my chin to kiss my forehead, the bridge of my nose, my mouth. "I love your sweet watermelon lips, your unrelenting kindness, even to those who've hurt you, your strength to move here all by yourself." He got to his knees, his head at my breasts. Kneeling before me, Manning took my waist. "I love this body, and the family it will give us. The sky seems dark now, but that's how light shines through. I promise you, Lake, I will make this right."

I didn't stop him. I let him hold me. I let him bury his face in my stomach. I could've stayed there the rest of my life listening to him tell me he loved me. I looked up at the ceiling to stem the tears I didn't want him to see. He might take that as indecision, and it wasn't. When I'd breathed through the urges to cry, I lowered my eyes and put my hands on his cheeks. I could've sworn I felt wetness there. "I love you, too," I said. "But I can't do this to you."

"Yes you can. It's not like it was that night on the beach. I'm older now. Stronger. I know I'm not my father."

"She'll take that baby from you, Manning. Can you live with knowing you'll have no involvement in its life? That you won't get to raise, love, and pick your baby up every morning and put your baby to sleep each night?"

"I'll find a way," he repeated, even though he knew—he *had* to know—this was the only way.

His eyes were red, tired. My heart split down the middle. It was just like Manning to try and carry the burden for us. He hadn't asked for this baby, but if he couldn't do right by it, it would kill him. I shook my head. "You need to be a good father," I said. "And that child needs you. Tiffany hasn't always done the right thing, but she didn't deserve any of what we did to her this week." I opened my mouth to end this, but nothing came. I couldn't send him away. Words bubbled up and fizzled over and over, until I had to accept this wouldn't get any less excruciating. I wavered, but I got it out. "It's okay—I'm giving you permission to go."

"I don't want permission," he said, swallowing. "I want *you*. I love *you*. What about you?"

I didn't know. My heart was being surgically removed in the middle of a hotel room, and I felt each acute incision and snip. But I'd done this before and had come out the other side, so there had to be some way through it. The moment Tiffany had gotten pregnant, I'd lost a little part of Manning. A part she would forever own. I could never compete against a baby, and I shouldn't have to. "I don't want to be second best, and I don't deserve it." My voice broke, and I steadied it. "You know I don't."

"You'll never be second best, Lake. I never loved Tiffany a fraction of the amount I love you."

"I'm talking about the baby."

With that, defeat crossed his face. It hurt me more than it should've. I wanted to be mad, to make him suffer and tear out his heart like he had mine but he'd already suffered. His heart hurt, too. I didn't want that for him. He was having a baby and it should've been the happiest news of his life.

He reached into his pocket and showed me the mood ring. "I found this on your dresser. I was going to give it to you at the airport the way I'd planned to years ago, before I was arrested."

I took the ring and inspected it, though there wasn't much to see. It didn't change colors just by holding the band. "It was in your things from the courthouse," I said. "I thought maybe . . . maybe it was for me."

"Maddy had one growing up. She loved jewelry. I got it off a woman in the bar that night we rode around in the truck."

I dropped my hand to my side. "I'm sorry I took it."

"I bought it for you," he clarified. "I wanted you to have one like Maddy's, since she'd loved it so much."

"Then I kept it safe for you," I said and held it out for him. "But it's not mine, and it never was."

"Keep it while I'm away. It's my promise to you. I'll be back. I'll love you. I'll make your apartment into our home. I'll eat your Christmas dinners. I'll be a father to your children."

I stopped myself from accepting his gift and taking the future I was owed. I wanted to ask him to stay and experience all the colors of the mood ring with me, to light me up when I was dark and live in rainbows when times were good. But I had to let that go, and he needed to let me go, so I said, "If you have a daughter, you can give it to her."

I'd never seen Manning cry, but he'd come close when he'd told me about Maddy in the truck years ago, and I could see he was close now. He hugged my stomach to his chest. "Don't do this, Lake. Remember what you tried to tell me all those years ago? Love is enough."

"I'm sorry," I said quietly and tried to move, but he tightened his grip on me. "Manning, you have to let me go."

"I can't."

"You have to." I pried his fingers off, set the ring on the nightstand, and finished packing my bag while he watched. There wasn't anything left to say.

When I had everything, I put the duffel over my shoulder and faced him. He stood at the foot of the bed with bloodshot eyes, taking up all the space and air in the room. I wasn't sure when I'd see him again. I couldn't envision ever going back home now, not with what I'd have to face, so maybe this was it. My chest felt as if it were being drawn into itself like a corset to which Manning held the strings. I didn't want to say goodbye. I wasn't ready.

He closed the space between us and cupped my chin like he was going to kiss me. I wanted him to, but I didn't think I'd survive it. He wasn't mine to kiss anyway, not that he ever had been.

"Birdy," he said.

For the briefest moment, I was sixteen again, fighting my impulsiveness, choking back words I shouldn't say, hiding my love for him. I looked away, and after a moment, turned and left the room.

In the hallway, I couldn't breathe. My chest constricted so hard, I was sure any moment it'd squeeze my heart right up into my throat. But it didn't. The heart was a muscle, and it could be trained. With every injury, it got stronger. So I put one foot in front of the other and resisted the urge to turn back for the only man I'd ever truly love.

PART 2

1
LAKE, 2003

Stage lights flooded over the cast, and we took a synchronized bow. Despite being nearly blinded, I wanted to hold on to this feeling as long as I could. I wasn't sure when I'd get it next. The audience's applause was louder and longer than usual tonight. Maybe they sensed it, too, whatever was in the air. As a cast, we'd gone the extra mile, our emotions high knowing we only had a few nights until it was curtain for good.

My castmate squeezed my hand. We took another bow, grinned at each other, and that was it.

Backstage, we did the obligatory rounds, meeting fans, signing playbills, and holding conversations with castmates' friends. When I saw two dozen roses headed in my direction, I knew instantly who was behind it.

"What are you doing here?" I asked, grinning.

Corbin peeked around the flowers. "I can't make it to closing night next week since I'll be out of town on business. I didn't want to miss seeing you one last time, though."

I took the bouquet and kissed his cheek. "Thank you."

"You get better every time I see you up there."

"You watched the whole show?" I asked. "How many times is that now? Three?"

He shrugged. "I just can't believe you're actually doing it."

"It's just Off-Broadway, and I'm up there less than half an hour total." I nudged him. "I hope you at least brought a date so you wouldn't get bored."

"Not tonight. I thought maybe you and I could get a celebratory dinner."

"Sounds good. I'm starved. Want to say hi to everyone?"

Sometimes I thought Corbin hung out backstage to meet my pretty castmates, but the truth was, they were usually the dumbstruck ones. Even in a world of trained actors and actresses, his charm shone through. He flustered both my male and female counterparts.

After I'd dropped the flowers off in the dressing room I shared with some others, Corbin and I were listening in on a discussion with the director and some fans.

I looked up just as a man in a suit approached us. "Sorry to interrupt, Carl," he said.

The show's director turned. "Mike Galloway. Nice to see you." They shook hands. "Coming to steal away one of my stars?"

"Can't I just sneak behind the curtain to give praise? Do I need another reason?" He winked at me. "Off-Broadway is the new Broadway, I hear."

Carl snorted. "Right. I'd tell you to leave us alone, but the show's run its course anyway. Who you here for? Gina? Keith?"

"No." The man's eyes were still on me. "Lake, right? Do you have a moment?"

I glanced back at Corbin, mostly out of confusion, but Corbin must've thought I needed help. He put a hand on my shoulder. "Regarding?" he asked.

"Apologies. I should've introduced myself first." He stuck out his hand for me. "I'm Mike Galloway, a casting director from California. Mind if we talk in private?"

My director tilted his head at me. "Well, go on, kid. Don't you know who Mike Galloway is?"

Admittedly, I didn't. The name was familiar, maybe someone Roger or a castmate of mine had mentioned. Despite the fact that the rest of the world was obsessed with Hollywood, I hadn't given it much attention. Here in New York, we performed. This was theater. We didn't hide behind glitz and glam like they did in Los Angeles. Not to mention, Southern California continued to be a sore reminder of what could've been.

I led Mike Galloway and Corbin to the dressing rooms. Mike didn't bother looking around, and I got the feeling he'd been here before. "Have a seat," he said to me, even though it was my room.

Corbin and I exchanged a glance, but we sat. "What's this about?" I asked.

"Lake Kaplan." He smiled, gliding his hand in front of him. "It'd look good in opening credits, wouldn't it?"

"I don't know," I said. "It's just my name."

"Not anymore. Lake, this is the second time I've come to see the show, and I assure you it's not because I think it's any good."

"All the way from L.A.?" I asked. "Do you normally come to the theater looking for . . ." I sat back. "What *are* you looking for?"

"You have a friend working as a PA on the new Marvel movie?" Mike asked.

"Val?" Corbin and I asked at the same time. Val had left New York soon after the Twin Tower terrorist attacks. For one of the strongest, most resilient people I knew, Val had been shaken to the core by 9/11. She'd been wanting to break into Hollywood for some time, and that was the catalyst she'd needed to move. She'd been a production assistant on more than a few film crews but was still struggling to break in. I'd only spoken to her a few days ago, but she hadn't mentioned any of this.

"She gave your name to a colleague of mine who knew I was coming out here in search of talent. But you aren't just talent, Miss Kaplan. You're a star."

"I'm a supporting role, and a small one at that," I deadpanned. "Plus, my vocals don't compare to anyone else's in the show—*yet*—and my footwork needs—"

"That stuff's not important for what I need." He waved a hand. "Your director is notorious for overlooking star quality anyway. He always puts the good ones in the back, and that's where I often find my hidden gems. You, Lake—you have a look that I'm after."

I touched the ends of my hair. "What?"

He scratched his chin. "I'm casting a TV show in California, and I want you to come meet with us. I've shown your headshots to the directors and they're very interested."

My gut reaction was a nervous giggle. Neither Corbin nor Mike laughed, and that made my bubbling laughter more embarrassing. Not only was Hollywood knocking on my door, but they wanted me to pursue a life in Los Angeles, the exact thing I'd run away from years ago? *Why?* I had a lot of work to do on my craft. My castmates had been at this since they could walk. I often felt like I was playing catch up with them. I'd worked hard and come a long way, but acting didn't come naturally to me, and from most angles, I was still an amateur.

"Do you have a business card?" Corbin asked.

Mike took one out of his wallet and handed it to him. "I'm not here to say Lake has the part, but I can assure you, it's promising." He shifted his attention to me. "I've already spoken to your agent. You should have a message, or five, from June. Check your cell."

I just blinked at him. "I can't afford a phone," I said.

"Your pager, then. Surely you've got one of those?"

Between monthly rent and student loan payments, I rarely had much cash left over. My part didn't pay well, and yet I'd devoted time to perfecting it that I probably should've spent making money. "I don't, and actually, flying out to Los Angeles would be financially difficult."

"We'll handle the expenses, and I know this production is coming to an end. We can set up a meeting after closing night."

Corbin leaned his elbows on his knees. "What exactly is the part?"

"Five twenty-somethings in California working in the arts. Think *Friends* meets *Center Stage* sprinkled with the issues of today." He pulled at his chin, looking me over. "The parts I have in mind for you would depend on your demeanor and how you play off the rest of the cast. I need a bitchy blonde babe who's always pulling strings behind the scenes. The other part is America's sweetheart—adorable, sugary girl-next-door that every boy wants to marry."

I couldn't help thinking of Tiffany in that moment. Where I stood in comparison to her was obvious, but I'd never consider myself as anyone's sweetheart. "Are those the only two options?"

"Your friend mentioned you have some family drama? She wouldn't get into specifics, but she said it was worth asking about if you were comfortable."

"What does that have to do with it?" I asked. "I wouldn't let it get in the way of my craft."

He laughed. "No, it's not that. It can help. This is where we're on the verge of something huge." Mike hiked up his pant legs and sat on the coffee table across from me. "Reality television."

I tilted my head. "What?"

"*Survivor. The Bachelor.* You've seen the craze over Paris Hilton and Jessica Simpson. The world wants to see beautiful Californians, and they crave a story—struggle, gossip, drama. This show rolls it all into one." Mike shifted to Corbin. "Are you two dating?"

"Uh." Corbin cleared his throat. "No."

"Doesn't matter. Look at you. You'd be a perfect addition to Lake's story."

"My story?" I asked. "I don't understand. I haven't seen any of those shows."

"You've watched *Real World*, haven't you? MTV?"

"A little."

341

"It's just like that, except it would be a little more—how do I put this . . . *contained*. You aren't running completely wild. We'd give you direction, even though the American people would see it as real life." He opened his hands. "Now that I'm sitting here with you, I'm thinking America's sweetheart. You have a real naïveté about you that would play well on camera."

"But I'm not that—I'm an actress," I said.

"You would still act. Loosely. That's why they hired me, a casting director, to find the right people. I feel very good about this, Miss Kaplan, and I'm rarely wrong. That's why they pay me the big bucks."

Corbin narrowed his eyes. "Would she have to move back?"

"Of course. We'd go through rounds of interviews, background checks, physical exams and whatnot, but if you're hired, you'd be expected to move there. You'd live your life as you normally would—auditioning, going to school, dating, fighting with your family—whatever it is you'd do on a daily basis, just with some input from producers."

"I don't speak to my family," I said.

"Even better. There's opportunity for real, meaningful stuff there, and maybe even a reconciliation at some point. We can work out the specifics," Mike said. "We'd set you up with a roommate, another member of the show, and you'd all be friendly. Filming starts this summer so there's plenty of time to get situated."

Going home? Reconciling? Those were reasons enough not to do it. To me, California wasn't sunshine, palm trees, beaches and killer weather. It was the site of my first heartbreak. It represented the regret of losing what I'd never had, and the division of not just my family, but Manning's, too. "I'm sorry, I really don't want to return to California. I love New York."

"It wouldn't be forever. Plus, if the show gets picked up and it's a hit, maybe they'd follow you wherever you go and set you up along the way. If you want to come back to New York, discuss that as a storyline with the producers."

"What's it pay?" Corbin asked.

"More than she's making here," Mike answered.

"And that would be?"

"For the purpose of the show, we'd want you living like a normal twenty-something. No flashy apartment or car, just business as usual. So, the pay is decent, but it's not a movie star's salary or anything. Let's just say you could get yourself a few cell phones." He winked. "One for each boyfriend."

Hollywood was a far cry from Broadway, but it was hard not to get swept up in Mike's excitement. "I have to think about it," I said. "I went to Tisch to be a performer, and this doesn't sound like what I had in mind."

Mike stood. "Reality television is the wave of the future, Lake. Take my word for it. Not to mention, if this takes off, you'll be famous. Once your contract is up, you can turn that fame into anything you want—movie roles, a clothing line, charity work, or, of course, you can come back to Broadway with an audience directors won't be able to ignore."

I shifted on the couch and felt Corbin's eyes on me. The idea made more sense as a means to an end. It wasn't the most honest way to make my career, but I couldn't imagine any of my peers turning down an opportunity like this. I already knew Roger, who'd been chasing fame since he'd narrowly missed being cast for the *Mickey Mouse Club*, would scream for me to accept. I thought of the animal shelter where I'd worked up until last year when they'd had to shut down due to lack of funding. "Could I draw attention to issues I'm passionate about?" I asked.

Mike checked his watch. "That's a question for the producers, but I think they'd welcome it within reason. Nothing too depressing. Listen, I have a dinner to get to." He shook my hand. "I'll be in touch, and your agent has more details. Plan on flying out soon after the show closes."

He exited stage right, leaving Corbin and me as startled as he'd found us. I turned to Corbin, glad he'd been here for that tornado of information, but also fairly sure he'd say it was a bad idea. "You don't think I should do it, right?" I asked.

"Why do you say that?"

"It's a little insane. Acting for reality? And I'd have to leave you and Roger and New York and the career I've made here."

"Lake, you'll be twenty-six this year. Your life here is in limbo," he said. "You're single, and in a few days, you'll be out of work. Val's gone."

"I've been trying to build a name for myself in theater, though."

"Well, maybe this is just one way to go about it," he pointed out. "Not all paths will be the same."

I studied him a few moments, the way he fidgeted with his hands laced between his knees. "I'm surprised," I said. "I would've thought you'd tell me to stay."

"If I were being selfish, yeah, I would. But the truth is, Lake, sometimes I don't know what keeps you here."

I pulled back a little. I'd wondered the same, but I thought I'd done a pretty good job of being happy considering I was living with a permanent hole in my heart. "What do you mean? I know I haven't found a lot of success like my friends, but that's because I haven't been working at this as long."

"I see them killing themselves every day to get auditions and take dance classes and singing lessons. Roger's on Broadway because he can't *not* be. I know you do those things, too, but your friends have a fire inside them I sometimes think you're . . . missing."

I sat back, trying not to look as hurt as I felt. "Seriously?" I asked. "How can you say that to me, that I don't have fire? You've brought me a pillow because I had to spend half a night on a concrete floor waiting for news about a show. I rehearsed for this play seven days a week, and now that we're in season, I practically live in this theater."

He rubbed his jaw. "Maybe I'm wrong then. It seemed like some of your passion flamed out after graduation."

That hollowed out my chest a bit—which was a normal reaction to thinking about that time in my life. My five days with Manning, and how he'd left New York and taken a very crucial part of my heart with him. Not to mention my ability to trust and love. It was no surprise to me or Val I hadn't had a healthy relationship since.

Since December that year, I'd been in motion. I ran every day, usually between auditions. I worked for a temp agency, picking up administrative work all over the city when I wasn't performing. I put my heart and soul into my nights at the theater. In the beginning, I hadn't been able to stop and think or my mind would spiral back to what my life would've been if I hadn't left after the wedding. What would've happened if I'd graduated USC and gone to grad school.

I'd been on the go so long, chasing an exciting and exhilarating career—those things had been further from my mind than normal lately. I wished the same was true about Manning. I thought of him constantly—what I'd lost that day he'd left New York.

What he'd lost several months later.

All the pain between us seemed too great to overcome. "I don't want to leave New York," I said quietly. "I think I'll say no to the audition."

"Lake." Corbin sat forward and paused, as if he were considering how to phrase what he had to say. "Don't say no out of fear."

"I'm not afraid."

"I don't believe that. You're an adult now, and that puts you just as much in the wrong as them. You have to face your family. It's time."

"I'm not having this conversation again," I said and went to stand.

"Listen to me," he snapped.

Surprised, I sat back down. It was rare for Corbin to raise his voice at me. "Your family misses you. You miss them. I know you do, so don't try to deny it. You've let pride get in the way too long, and that makes you no better than your dad."

"Are you kidding me?" I asked. "I'm his daughter, and he's pretended I don't exist for the better half of a decade."

"He's a jerk, but he's your father, and I know in his own twisted way, he's never wanted anything but the best for you. That's why you leaving has been so hard on him."

I shook my head. There were things Corbin didn't know. If it weren't for my dad's meddling, Manning and I might've had a chance. "You don't understand."

"Whatever beef you have with him, with Tiffany, it's time to put it aside. You're not sixteen anymore, but you're still acting like a child. You never even went to see her in the hospital, your own sister."

I looked at my hands. It wasn't that I didn't care that Tiffany had miscarried—it was the opposite. When I'd found out she was pregnant, I'd wished the baby away. I'd hated Tiffany for how she'd treated Manning and me. But I'd never expected my wish to come true. Despite what we'd all been through, no matter how I felt about any of it, Tiffany hadn't deserved to lose it all. And not just the baby.

Months after the miscarriage, almost a year since New York—she and Manning had divorced.

"Give me one honest answer," Corbin said, "and then we can drop it for good."

I crossed my arms into myself. "Fine."

"Are you staying in New York because you love it, and it runs in your veins, and you can't imagine being anywhere else? Or is it because you don't want to go home?"

I didn't have an immediate answer. I rarely stopped to wonder whether New York was where I wanted to be, because deep down I knew the truth— my roots, my one love, my youth, would always be in California. But going home meant reopening wounds, admitting mistakes, looking my family in the face after all the pain I'd caused them. Because it was true— they might've hurt me over the years, but I'd hurt them, too, in ways I could never take back.

"You haven't talked to your dad in *eight* years," Corbin said.

And I hadn't talked to Manning in over three. Hadn't kissed or made love to or even laid eyes on him in *three* years, and my dad had played a part in that. I'd been proud, but so had he. If Dad still couldn't pick up the phone, then it was better this way, because I had nothing to say to him. "If I go to California, it's not to see them," I said. "It's because I want a change."

Corbin sighed, standing up and holding out his hand for me. "I think that's a mistake—but I think it's also a start."

2

LAKE

I took the job in California. The network had made it hard to say no. I'd been flown out to L.A., put up in a costly hotel, and encouraged by Val, Corbin, and Roger to say yes. When I'd said I'd need time to think about the offer, the producers had sweetened the deal. Of the five principals hired, only two were making more than me, and they were both minor local celebrities.

The world would fall in love with me—according to the producers and crew. Of course, I'd never had it in me to play the villain. They'd set me up with a roommate, a struggling set designer named Bree, who was also on the show. Corbin and Val had been around for some of the filming, but I'd refused to bring my family into it, even though the producers sometimes made me talk about my dad and Tiffany while filming. Cameras followed us around, intrusive and cumbersome, all to marry the slice-of-life reality Mike had promised with plots the writing team molded into stories.

Late summer, a couple months into shooting, Val invited just about everyone I knew in L.A. over to her house for the pilot. When Bree and I showed up, sans cameras but with party platters, the applause began.

Bree bowed, but I only hid my reddening face. I hadn't gotten into acting to be famous. I loved that I could access a different part of my brain and heart and use those to create a world for others. An escape. But I'd gotten more attention over the past few months than I'd ever wanted, and we hadn't even aired yet. With a look, I implored Val to make it stop.

She picked up a bottle of champagne and got on the coffee table. "Who wants alcohol?"

Some of our friends held out their glasses, and others took their places around the TV, which was currently muted on *Charmed*. Not everyone was so easily sidetracked, though.

"They put up a billboard on Sunset Boulevard," Roger said, holding out his glass for champagne. "You're like goddesses gazing upon us mere mortals."

Bree handled the attention better than I did, so I slipped into the crowd as she whipped a disposable camera out of her purse. "I already took a whole roll of photos this afternoon."

I disappeared into the kitchen to prepare the appetizers I'd brought. I was setting the oven as Val floated in. Tonight, she was Bohemian Val, Sienna Miller-meets-Stevie Nicks with heavy bangs and straightened blonde hair. She'd paired an off-the-shoulder floral dress with a wide leather belt and fashion cowboy boots.

"What're those?" she asked over my shoulder as I stood at the island.

"Homemade bagel bites. Just like the frozen kind, except I made these."

"You are such a good mom."

I smiled a little, tossing the foil wrapping into the trash. "I'm doing whatever I can to keep the nerves at bay."

"Well, then I should probably keep what I know to myself," she said, leaning her upper half on the island, "but you know I won't."

I glanced up at her, arranging the food. "Okay . . .? What?"

"Listen." She checked over her shoulder. "Corbin and I fought for an hour about this, but in the end, I couldn't talk him out of it—and I couldn't explain to him the depth of why this was a bad idea without revealing the truth about your history with your sister." She made a face. "Corbin flew in today."

"Wait—really?" I grinned. "All the way from New York? What's that got to do with Tiffany?"

"She *called* him and asked if she could come tonight."

I stopped fussing with the platter and stared at her. "*What?*"

"I guess she wanted to surprise you, because—duh—if she'd asked you, you'd have told her to take a hike."

Would I have? Tiffany and I hadn't spoken since last Christmas, and even then it'd been a cursory, five-minute conversation. She didn't even live in the area. She'd have to drive in from Orange County. "Did she say why?" I asked.

"*I* think it's just because she wants to grab onto your coattails, I mean, could she be more obvious with her timing? You're going to be on TV tonight." Val picked a diced tomato off one of the bagel bites and popped it in her mouth. "*But* Corbin seems to think Tiffany's making an effort and deserves a chance you'd never give her otherwise. He felt bad that Tiffany couldn't even bring herself to call you."

"Well," I said, my posture sagging. "Shit."

"Yeah." Val lifted a shoulder. "I couldn't exactly tell Corbin that there might be a catfight over he-whose-name-makes-me-gag."

I looked out the kitchen window, where palm tree silhouettes painted the dusky, indigo sky. Did I want to see my sister after all these years? No. She wasn't just the cruelest reminder possible of Manning, but she'd intentionally hurt me. I'd done the same to her, though. I wasn't sure I'd ever be ready to face her, but she was making an effort. After going years without hearing from my dad, that spoke volumes. Tiffany and I had kept in touch, but I hadn't seen her since she'd left for her honeymoon. "Thanks for warning me," I said. "Even though I'm twice as nervous now."

"Don't be. You're older and smarter. She can't get to you anymore." Val turned to get a bottle of *Veuve Clicquot* from the fridge before I could protest. "And the show will be fan-fucking-tastic. You're the sweetheart, so you have nothing to worry about. Bree on the other hand . . ." She grimaced before taking a champagne glass from a cupboard. "I'm worried she's the village idiot and doesn't know it."

I laughed. "Or she knows it, and she'll get more screen time because of it—which would make her the shrewdest of all."

"Touché. So how come instead of being excited, you've been moping around all week like you just found out you have chlamydia?"

I shrugged. According to my agent, castmates, and the media, I was the industry's next "sweetheart." I had "something," the "it factor" and "the right look." I was going to be *someone*. But aside from the few low-budget, hardly attended plays I'd been a part of in New York, nobody had seen me act yet. The cameras didn't even follow me into the auditions I attended during filming, just the preparation before, and getting rejected or called back after.

"Val?" I said, sliding the tray into the oven. "You're around actresses all day on set. Do you think I'm any good?"

"You have a certain quality," she said.

"*What* quality?" I asked.

"The one you have. It's indescribable." She waved me off. "Anyone can learn to act, but not anyone can be a star."

I crossed my oven mitt-clad hands under my arms. "So you're saying I suck."

She laughed. "Suck? No. You're just honing your craft. I'd cast you, and I'm not just saying that. You really do steal the show when you're on stage, and I think it'll be the same on screen."

"I honestly don't know why they bother with me," I said. "I didn't get into that much drama. I mostly met people for lunch like the producers wanted, went to auditions, cried about missing my family, or stood around the bar."

"Did you ever think you'd have to get a job to support your current job? It's like they made you work at that place so the group would have a nighttime meeting spot. It's the after-hours Peach Pit of reality TV."

I snickered. "That's exactly why they set me up there. That, and I swear they knew Sean and I would start dating before either of us did."

"It's because they needed a Bad Boy Bartender," Val said. She'd been secretly guiding me all season, helping me understand the inner-workings of the industry so I wouldn't step in too many piles of shit on national television. "He's got tattoos, a motorcycle, and a bad attitude. How's it going with him anyway?"

"Perfect," I said, tossing the mitts on the counter. Sean and I saw each other when we wanted and the crew got footage for the show. He never prodded about my past or asked how I was feeling. He was flighty and shallow, and that was the absolute most I could handle for a love interest. If my life ended up a series of flings, I wasn't sure I'd mind too much. "Off camera, he treats me all right," I said. "Better than it'll look on TV."

"What about that other guy, the boom operator?"

"I like him, too, but ours is a romance for the shadows. He's not supposed to date the cast."

Val's eyes sparkled as she sipped her champagne. "So that means the sex is hot?"

"Very." I turned away to check on the bagel bites, worried Val would read my expression and sigh the way she always did. Sex belonged to Manning first. It was so fucking predictable but true—he'd destroyed me for anyone else. Sex could be a lot of things, including passionate, but no one would ever come close to Manning. "Do you miss New York?" I asked her.

"Kind of." She sounded thoughtful. "Not more than I'd miss working in film, though. I wouldn't exactly complain if Hollywood was relocated to Eighth Avenue. What about you?"

I leaned back against the counter to face her. New York had definitely had its moments. For me, it had been split in half with graduation in the middle. Before Manning, after Manning. We'd constructed a life there together in five days, and I had spent the next few years not living it. "Coming back was the right choice," I said. "I didn't realize I needed a change until it was in motion."

A male voice spoke from just outside the kitchen. "If only you'd had someone there to point that out to you."

I turned around with my most convincing look of surprise. I was an actress, after all. "*Corbin?*"

He sauntered in with his signature ear-to-ear grin and bouquets in both hands. If I could cash in all the flowers he'd given me over the years, I'd be living in a high-rise in downtown New York City like he was. "Evening, superstars."

"What're you doing here?" I asked.

"Oh, I'm not staying, I just wanted to fly in and drop these off in person," he teased, holding out white lilies.

I rolled my eyes, taking them. "Corbin. You did *not* come all the way here for this."

He winked. "Wouldn't miss it," he said, then turned and gave Val a different bouquet.

She just stared at it. "Aren't those for Bree?"

"No, ma'am. One for each of my best girls."

When Val blushed, I almost laughed. It was such a rare sight. She took the medley of mismatched flowers, an assortment of shapes, sizes, and colors, and looked into them with a furrowed brow. "What are these, grocery store leftovers?"

He laughed. "I wanted to buy something I thought you'd like but I couldn't decide. You have a million different interests and opinions." To me, he said out of the side of his mouth, "Not to mention personalities."

Val raised the bouquet like she was going to smack him with it. He waved his hands in surrender. "So I just pulled over and picked a bunch of different shit. If you grew out of the ground, that's basically what you'd look like."

Val and I stared at him. I started to laugh, but she just looked perplexed. "O-*kay*, thanks for the roadside weeds, I guess?" she said, but when she turned her back to look for a vase, I caught the way she stuck her nose in the flowers.

"That's not all I brought," Corbin said, shoulders back as he moved aside. Even though I'd been warned, I almost dropped my flowers. Tiffany stood behind him clutching a Louis Vuitton purse to her hip. The kitchen went silent. In a short denim skirt and Rocket Dogs, she dressed the part of the girl who'd stolen Manning out from under me, but she didn't look the same. Eight years had passed since I'd watched her leave for her honeymoon, and she was a thirty-year-old divorcée now.

She took a few steps into the kitchen, her eyes bouncing from Val and Corbin back to me. She'd never had much trouble handling a roomful of people, but she looked a little out of her element.

I couldn't quite gauge her mood—or my own. It wasn't as if I never wondered about seeing her. In fact, I thought about it often, especially when I was at my most vulnerable. Right before I'd moved here, I'd almost picked up the phone to ask her if it was the right choice, but what answer could she have possibly given? Aside from a few short phone calls over the years, I'd told her next to nothing about my life. After I'd lost Manning, in some of my darkest moments, I'd wished I could escape into her bedroom for a few hours where she'd play Soundgarden too loud and pet me and tell me things would get better once I understood boys. Well, here we were, almost a decade later, and I still didn't understand boys.

"I can't believe you're going to be on TV," she said.

I couldn't say I understood her, either, or most of the things I was supposed to by twenty-six years old. I was an adult now, and I should've known what to say to my own sibling, but I just gaped at her. Maybe that was why she'd come. To see her sister on TV.

"And . . . I can't believe you're standing in front of me," she added.

For all the ups and downs we'd had, she was familiar. She was home. I wanted to hug her. She wore shoes higher than mine, her top showed more cleavage than the ultimate Wonderbra could bless me with, and her beauty—her curled blonde hair and impeccable smoky eyes—outshone anyone else's in the room. And that was exactly what I needed in that moment—to be a kid again, hidden in her older sister's shadow, shielded from the attention the people in the next room were trying to give me. That was the thing nobody but my mom had ever seemed to notice, especially not Tiffany—I hadn't minded being in my sister's shadow all that much, not until Manning had come along.

Corbin took my bouquet and leaned between us. "This is where you hug."

We put our arms around each other. She hugged the same. Smelled the same. But there was no possible way she could be the same after what she'd been through. "I'm sorry about the baby," I whispered into her hair.

She nodded against me. "Me too."

I'd called after the miscarriage, but neither of us had been in a position to have a conversation longer than a few minutes. I'd gripped the receiver in my hand, tears streaming down my face since the moment my mom had called from the hospital. And as Tiffany had taken my condolences, her grief flowing through the phone, I'd felt *him* there in the background. I hadn't asked to speak to Manning. What was there to say?

This was the first time I'd gotten to tell Tiffany in person. Maybe it was overdue, but I pulled back and looked her in the face. "I'm genuinely sorry. I hope you know that," I said, and it was true. But I couldn't offer my regrets that she and Manning hadn't made it. I was sorry for what they'd been through, and that it'd gotten so bad that, according to my mom, the miscarriage had caused their split, but knowing she no longer had him—no, I couldn't be the least bit sorry about that.

"I can't really talk about it." She glanced at the floor but then back up quickly, her eyes glittering. "Were those photographers out front?"

"Paparazzi." My stomach churned with the word. "They've started following some of us the last few weeks."

"Seriously?" Tiffany asked.

"They might try to take your picture," I warned, even though I knew that could cause her to run out front, waving her arms. "I talk about you and Dad a little on the show."

"*What?* That's so freaking awesome."

"It's not, trust me," I said. "If I so much as stumble, they catch it. If the film crew doesn't, then the paparazzi will."

"Oh, how utterly mortifying." She shifted feet. "Is there anything to drink?"

"If I know Val, there's a roomful of rosé on the other side of that wall," Corbin said. "Come on."

Val nodded solemnly. "You know me."

There were probably things I needed to say to Tiffany, but I didn't even know where to start. And anyway, it wasn't the time. For tonight, maybe it was best we let the alcohol do the talking.

Five minutes before the show, we were all at least a glass-of-something deep. I was too nervous to do anything other than sit on the edge of the couch and sip wine. The first time I appeared on screen after the opening credits, it became immediately clear to me I didn't want to see any more. A pit formed in my stomach as I watched Bree and myself at our kitchen table drinking coffee and browsing the classifieds. A title popped up with my name and "aspiring actress" underneath. How many people in America were tuning in at that moment? Learning that I took my coffee with sugar and cream? It was completely innocuous, boring, and, as Tiffany had eloquently put it—*utterly mortifying.*

My movements on screen were stiff while the rest of the cast looked at ease. They'd taken to having cameras in their face much better than I had. Two had scored forgettable on-screen roles before this, and the others were natural extroverts. Everyone in the living room had their eyes glued to the screen, but I had to look away.

What would Manning think? I hated that he came to mind first, but that'd always been my habit— what was Manning doing, how was he, and did he still think of me? Having Tiffany in the room didn't change that. If anything, his absence was stronger.

The longer the show went on, the worse it got. Corbin had already made an appearance. Across the living room, he and I kept exchanging uncomfortable looks.

During the last commercial break, Val jumped on the couch. "A toast," she said, "to sexy Bree, and to Lake, America's next sweetheart."

I flinched. I didn't want to be called that. Not only was it untrue, but was that what America wanted? I hadn't done anything but sit there. "Please," I said, "it's not a big deal."

Val groaned. "Stop saying that."

"It's a huge deal," Tiffany said. I glanced at her, but she was looking at the bottom of her empty champagne glass. As Val bent over to refill it, my new BlackBerry rang. Only a few people had the number, so I wasn't surprised to see the name *June McPherson* lit up on the screen.

"I'm so sorry to interrupt the toast," I said, "but I have to take this. It's my agent."

"Everyone shut up," Val called. "Answer it, Lake."

While my friends watched, I picked up. "Listen," June said straight off. She'd been my agent for over a year now and never seemed to run out of energy. "Are you listening?" she asked.

"Yes."

"Where are you?"

"With Bree and some friends at a viewing party."

"Put me on speakerphone."

It took me a moment to figure out how, but once I did, I held up the cell for everyone. "Do you guys fucking love the show or what?" June asked.

They cheered. Corbin winked at me, even as I rolled my eyes.

"So do we," she said. "I'm almost positive we have a smash hit on our hands."

Val jumped up and down on the couch as everyone else hooted and hollered.

I took June off speaker, and she laughed. "I'll call you tomorrow," she yelled over the noise. "Have fun tonight."

Everyone clinked glasses as I hung up, while Tiffany downed her champagne in one go. She raised her glass to no one in particular, got up, and left the room. I was sixteen again, watching Tiffany's light go out while mine shone on. My face was front and center of a hit TV show while my outgoing, full-of-life older sister spent her life—where? I didn't even know if she had a desk, a cubicle, or an office, just that she'd recently accepted an associate buyer position at PacSun.

She'd married young and to the wrong man, and had since lost a baby and gotten divorced. I'd betrayed her in the worst kind of way—just by existing. By being the one our dad had pinned his hopes on. By rising to stardom when she'd never secured another modeling job. By being her husband's true love. And yet she had to sit there and toast me. I had the urge to tell her the truth—I wasn't all that great of an actress, I was definitely a bad sister, and most of all, I was unhappy. I was on my way to a life most only dreamed about. One *Tiffany* had dreamed about. And yet I would never have what she'd had. No matter how much money I made, no matter who I met or became, I didn't have Manning then or now, and I wasn't sure how to move past that.

3
LAKE

I left the TV room while the show was still on and found Tiffany out back. She sat at Val's rusted mesh patio table with a fresh glass of wine, staring out at the pool. I couldn't watch the show a minute longer. What I'd signed up for wasn't acting. I'd known that going in, and this wasn't the end goal by any means, but I wondered if this would be everything Mike Galloway had dangled in front of me. Was it a silver bullet to the career I wanted? The cameras had been around while I'd volunteered, but was it the right kind of attention for the animal shelter I went to?

Tiffany fumbled with a pack of cigarettes. As she lit one, my first thought was Manning—the smoky, mint-on-nicotine taste of him. He'd finally let me around his cigarettes after years of wanting to be part of it and anything that involved him. But Tiffany, she'd been in it all along, and now that I stood there watching her inhale deeply with satisfaction, I couldn't help but see things from Manning's point of view. Finally. He'd exposed us both to it, but he'd protected me and not Tiffany. "Do you smoke a lot?" I asked, closing the sliding glass door behind me.

"I quit during the pregnancy if that's what you're asking."

"I didn't mean that." I could tell that being here was hard for her, I just wasn't sure why she'd made the effort. "Did you see how awful the show was?" I asked, hoping to break the ice. There was no better way to bring Tiffany out of her shell than to give her the chance to make fun of me. "Everyone keeps saying it's a hit, but it's so bad. *I'm* so bad."

"You're, like, adorably awkward. Naïve but not in an annoying way. People like that stuff."

"I guess." I pulled out the seat across her, steel scraping over concrete, and sat. "How's Mom?"

"She's excited, even though she can barely get through a conversation about you without crying." She shrugged. "And Dad . . . well, you know how he is."

"He probably thinks this whole reality thing is silly."

"Pretty much."

I touched the thin gold bracelet Dad had given me as a teen. I'd started wearing it again for filming. Even though I was angry at my father, when the cameras were in my face, the bracelet made me feel close to my parents—and Manning, since it was the reason we'd met. No matter how old I got, how successful I might become, my dad's rejection would never not sting.

Tiffany blew smoke from the side of her mouth. "But I guarantee he's watching tonight."

"What about you?" I asked. "How are you?"

"Good." She sat back, crossing an ankle over her knee. "I got a used bike on the Internet for only twenty bucks. I mean, I'm not starring in a TV show or anything, but it's something."

I rolled my eyes at her. "Look, I know this is weird, but you don't have to make it worse."

"I thought I could do this," she said, stubbing out her half-smoked cigarette on the cement. "I thought enough time had passed that I could come here and be happy for you, but I just . . . it all seems so unfair."

I digested her words a few moments. For as long as I could remember, Tiffany had taken offense to my success and happiness. "What part, exactly, is unfair?"

"You have everything handed to you," she said, "and you just shrug, take it or leave it, like it's nothing. You throw away your relationship with Dad. Your acceptance to USC. You ignore us for years to run around New York City calling yourself an *actress*. And then someone shows up at your door and hands you fame and fortune and now you're not even sure you want it."

"That's not how it happened," I said. "I spent years struggling with nothing, trying to make a life for myself without any of your support. I lived in a tiny apartment with a broken heater—" *A broken lock and a broken heart*, I thought, my chest squeezing. "The point is, you're wrong. The only injustice is that you can't ever be happy for me unless you have a leg up."

"I came all the way here to support you, even though you never congratulated me on *my* promotion. When I call you, you're too busy to talk." She crossed her legs and fixed the twisted strap of her shoe. "How can you blame us for not being there for you when you made it impossible to be?"

I got quiet as I thought of the myriad excuses I'd invented over the years to get off the line with her or my mom. "Okay," I said, "but it's not as if any of you, not even Mom, were beating down my door, trying to get me to come home."

"Well, that's not entirely true, is it?" she asked. "Someone *did* beat down your door." She pulled another cigarette from her pack. "He was never the same after New York, you know."

After years of pretending not to notice Manning and me, the veiled accusation had me leaning in, wondering if I'd misheard. "What?"

"Actually, I take that back." Tiffany flicked her lighter a few times before it finally caught. "He was never the same after *he found out he was going to* New York. I can remember the exact moment he came home from work after having been approved for an

East Coast trip to see his 'clients.' He could hardly hide the spring in his step."

I stared at my sister, noting the new wrinkles around her eyes, the veins in her hands, the slight yellowish hue of her once flawless white teeth. I'd buried the memory of my last few moments with Manning as deeply as I could—it wasn't how I liked to remember us, pain rolling off him while he'd relayed what should've been the best news of his life. "I've bit my tongue a lot of times around you," I said to her, "but what you did to him was so messed up. You got pregnant because you were scared you'd lose him."

"You're right, I was scared—that my *sister* would steal my *husband*. Is there anything more messed up than that?"

"If I could've helped how I felt about him, I would've. Trust me." I shifted in the metal chair to ease my stiffness. When I talked about Manning, everything ached, even my elbows and knees. "It's been nothing but heartbreak for me."

"Boo-fucking-hoo." She pointed her orange-tipped cigarette at me. "That didn't give you the right to screw around with him."

I jerked back, shocked equally by the venom and the conviction in her voice. Had Manning confessed everything? "You make it sound cheap, but you knew what he meant to me." I took a breath so my voice wouldn't break. This was a conversation I'd never wanted to have. Despite what Tiffany might've thought, I didn't want to hurt her, but I couldn't forgive what she'd done to us. "You knew what you were doing from day one."

"I thought it was a stupid crush," she muttered to the table. "Do you know how many crushes I had at that age? I could barely keep track. I thought you'd get over it."

"It wasn't a crush. It was more." I leaned forward, waiting until she lifted her head to meet my eyes. "I loved him, Tiffany. I didn't care about anything else. Do you have any idea how it felt to watch him walk down the aisle with you?"

She stood, flicking the butt of her cigarette so ashes landed inches from my feet. "Do *you* have any idea how it felt to walk down the aisle knowing he was thinking about you?"

"No, I don't, because he didn't choose me," I said. "He chose you."

"If you think that, you're even more naïve than I thought." She stared at me, her jaw clenched as she shook her head. "How can you still not see the truth? He chose you. In the end, he chose *you*, and that's what matters."

"Do you see him here with me?" I asked.

"He chose you so many goddamn times. He kept me at arm's length our entire marriage because I wasn't you. After the m-miscarriage," she stuttered, "things got worse, but you know Manning. I figured he'd just keep punishing himself." She scuffed the ground with the bottom of her platform shoe, looking torn about whether to leave or stay. "He didn't. Somehow, he finally found the guts to walk away from me." She sat back down, her posture wilting. "But everything he is now, everything he's done—it's for you. He chose you, and you know it, and why wouldn't he? Why wouldn't he want the perfect girl who gets everything she doesn't even ask for?"

Where was he now? What had he done? I didn't know, because he wasn't mine. Considering what he'd lost, it'd never felt right to call him, and once he'd left Tiffany's, I didn't know where to reach him. Not that I would've tried. What could I say that hadn't already been said? He knew I loved him. He knew I'd give up anything to be with him. He hadn't come for me, and so I'd had no choice but to accept the truth—it wasn't our time, and might not ever be.

"I haven't spoken to him since New York," I informed her.

"Well, then maybe you got what you deserved. Maybe we all did. You're alone. He's probably alone. My baby is gone."

"How can you say that?" I asked. "Nobody deserves that kind of loss."

"What do you know about loss? You never *lose* anything. You *get* everything."

"And you never try to see anything from my point of view. What makes you think I've got it all figured out?" I asked.

"Because I've had to stand by and watch it my whole life. That's the result of living in your shadow."

"In *my* shadow?" I asked. That was the last straw. How could she possibly think that was true when it'd been the other way around? I nearly vibrated with anger. "Growing up, you were constantly talking over me, getting everyone's attention any way you could manage, even when I wasn't fighting you for it. I let you have the spotlight and you pushed me out of it anyway."

"Exactly. You didn't even have to try." She gripped the arm of her chair. "Unless I was talking loudest, Dad ignored me. And the older you got, the worse it was."

"That's only because of college," I said. "Once I wasn't going to USC, he was done with me. Why do you still care what he thinks anyway? He's always been a jerk to both of us, especially you."

She held her cigarette deep in the "V" between her pointer and middle finger. After a drag, she squinted at me as if thinking. "You know," she said, "you're more like him than you realize."

I pulled my shoulders back. Maybe once that'd been a compliment, when I'd bent over backward to impress my father. Now, there was perhaps no greater insult. "I'm nothing like him."

"Neither of you will make the first move because you're too proud. You're both book smart but you lack compassion. That's what my therapist says." She coughed into a fist. "But you know what makes you the most like Dad? You're a cheater. Manning wouldn't tell me exactly what happened between you two while he was in New York, but I know enough."

A cheater? I'd never heard myself described so callously. That was more the kind of adjective to describe someone like Tiffany or, yes, my dad. Except he wasn't a cheater. Why would she say he was? "I don't understand."

"Never mind." She flipped her hair over her shoulder. "Forget it."

"No," I said, sensing she was trying to cover something up. "What do you know?"

Sighing through her nose, she ran her nail along the butt of the cigarette. "I guess you're old enough now. Remember Dad's secretary with the orange hair? It wasn't quite blonde or even red . . ."

The sister I'd barely spoken to in years was suddenly talking, but I didn't know how to register what she was saying. My dad had a funny way of showing love, even to my mom, but he'd always taken care of us. He'd always been loyal. But then again, everyone liked to say how naïve I was, and maybe in this case, it was true. The patio's overhead light got eerily yellow as I put two and two together. "Dad had an affair?" I asked. "When?"

The lines in Tiffany's face eased a little and she turned her face away, as if she were the guilty one. "When we were kids, I walked in on it at his office."

My dad's secretaries had come and gone over the years. I vaguely recalled who Tiffany was talking about because of her hair color and the amount of makeup she'd worn. At the time, she'd seemed older to me, maybe even sophisticated. Trying to picture her again, I only saw a girl younger than I was now. "She was, like, early twenties, wasn't she?"

"Young, old, pretty, ugly. Whatever, who cares?" She rubbed her eyebrow. "Maybe there were others, too."

"Does Mom know?"

"Yep." She bobbed her head. "I was really confused about what I saw, so I told her. She brushed it under the rug and got some nice outfits out of it."

The cigarette smoke was getting to me. First, it'd been just another frustrating reminder of Manning, but now it seemed to have filled my lungs, thickening into a mass in my chest. "How come you never told me?"

She picked at the table's rubber edge. "I just . . . didn't think you needed to know. It was kind of weird growing up with that information. And you looked up to Dad."

"But it would've changed how I saw him, and didn't you want that?"

"I don't know. Not enough to traumatize you, I guess."

It was weird to think Tiffany had protected me in her own way when it'd rarely felt that way as a kid. "I'm sorry," I said. "You could've told me."

She looked out at the pool. "I wonder if it would've changed anything."

With Manning was the part she left off. Would I have stayed away from him in New York if I'd grown up knowing my dad as an adulterer? I didn't think so, and I doubted Tiffany did, either. "You think I'm like that?" I asked. "Like what he did?"

"Are you going to tell me you aren't? That you didn't?" She trained her eyes on me. "That innocent Lake kept her hands to herself the whole week Manning was there?"

It was my turn to look away, wiping my upper lip with the heel of my palm. I couldn't lie to Tiffany and say I'd behaved, so I just sat there sweating under the yellow light like I was being interrogated until the sliding glass door opened.

"There you are," Sean said, fisting a beer and a joint as he came over to kiss my cheek. I realized belatedly that I'd heard his motorcycle out front a few minutes before.

I gestured across the table. "Sean, this is my sister."

"Oh, hey." He sat and gave her his signature sexy—and somewhat hollow—smile. "What's up?"

Tiffany eyed the tattoos peeking out from under his sleeves. "Hey."

"Are you an actress too?" he asked, relaxing back in the chair.

She crossed her legs in his direction. "No," she said. "I used to do some modeling, though."

"I could see that," he said, nodding. "Your family's got good genes, Lakey. Either of you have a light?"

I gagged on the inside. *Lakey* not only sounded gross, but it was like combining Birdy and Lake, and I didn't want my memories of Manning anywhere near Sean. "I've asked you so many times not to call me that," I said, but they were ignoring me.

"Just don't steal it," Tiffany said, leaning forward to hand him her BIC. "These things are expensive."

"I know, right?" He lit the blunt. "I'm always losing mine."

I looked up at a movement in the doorway. Corbin leaned outside. "You forgot to shut the door, man. You're getting smoke in the house."

"Sorry." Sean waved in front of his face as if that'd help. "It's just pot. Won't smell."

Corbin came out with a red plastic cup and took the last seat at the table. He lowered his voice as Tiffany asked Sean about the show. "Did you two have a good talk?" Corbin asked.

"I don't know. It was an honest one at least."

"You missed the end of the show."

"I know. It feels super weird to see myself up there, though. I don't think I like it . . . like *at all*."

"I know what you mean." He stretched his long legs, leaning back. "They edited the promos to make it look like Sean and I were fighting over you during one of my visits. Guess that's why they always mic me when he's around."

"I'm sorry," I said. "I warned you, though. You didn't have to participate."

"I know. I think it's funny." He sipped his drink. "You know when I do come around, I'm just looking out for you, right?"

That was Corbin's gentlemanly way of making sure I knew he wasn't trying to be any more than a friend to me. He and I hadn't hooked up since before Manning's trip to New York, but Corbin and I had never really talked about his feelings. "I know. I just wish you were here more."

"I might be, Kaplan." He winked. "I just might be."

I narrowed my eyes at him. "Don't tease me."

"I'm not. I told you I've been thinking about starting my own consulting firm, and I could do that out here if I want."

"Really?" I asked, grateful for some good news. "You'd move back?"

"Maybe. I could set my own hours, work with clients I actually respect, and then there's the whole settling down thing we're supposed to start thinking about. Raising a family in New York, it's not the same. I kinda miss Cali."

"No way." I smiled. "I never thought I'd hear you say that. Did you meet someone and you're trying to play it off like this was the plan all along?"

He chuckled. "No, but I want to."

"Well, you tell me who you want, and I'll make it happen. The girls on my show all love you. Whatever I can do to sway you, I will. Val and I want you here."

His mouth crooked in one corner as he squinted into the backyard. "I was thinking maybe a waterfront place in Malibu. Open all the windows, live right on the beach. New York has been good to me, but nothing like going downstairs and hopping in the water with my board and my girl. Sounds all right."

Better than all right. New York had been a once-in-a-lifetime experience, but California was in my blood. I wasn't so sure about the reality TV thing, but there could still be some opportunities for me in Hollywood, so this felt like where I needed to be right now. The thing I still lacked was what Corbin described—a home. Val's house and my little bungalow in Santa Monica with Bree had been good substitutes, always filled with friends and food and sometimes pets since we dog-sat a lot. Still, as my sister flirted with my current fling, I knew my life would never go back to what it'd been before I'd left. The rift between my dad and me was too big, and especially now that I knew he'd cheated on my mom, I wasn't willing to cross it. Nor could Tiffany and I ever just be sisters again.

A lump formed in my throat with the biggest truth of all—without Manning, I didn't know that I even wanted to try and make a home anywhere else. I thought I could float through cities and decades if I were never anchored to him. Did I even want that anymore? It'd gotten so hard to even think of Manning. Sean and everyone I'd dated since had been easy, and that seemed like the way to go in the future.

"It sounds like you got it all figured out," I said to Corbin. "I'm jealous."

"Of me? You're the one killing it out here. See all the people who showed up to watch your ascent into stardom? And how many of our friends, all those people you worked with who are barely getting by, watched you on TV in New York tonight?"

He always knew how to make me smile in spite of myself. I took his hand and squeezed it. "As long as you and Val aren't going anywhere, then that's all I need."

I realized Tiffany and Sean had stopped talking and were both looking at me. Sean pinched his joint and stood. "Well, I'm in no shape to ride. It's cool if I stay the night with you, Lakey?"

"Sure," I said. "We can leave in a bit."

"Dope." He winked at me. "I'm going to get another drink."

When he'd gone inside, the look on Corbin's face sent me into a fit of giggles. "Did he say *Lakey?*" Corbin asked.

It took me a minute to catch my breath. I just hoped the nickname didn't catch on nationwide.

Tiffany fidgeted with her pack of cigarettes as if she wanted to light another. It annoyed me how Manning, and now she, too, couldn't get a grip on such a life-threatening habit. She shifted in her seat and joked, "Third wheel."

"Hardly," Corbin said.

"Why is that, though?" she asked. "How come you two never got together? Or did you and nobody knew?"

"We're too good of friends," Corbin said, and I wondered with the swiftness of his answer, how many times he'd given it before.

I was grateful, though—that he'd saved me from having to answer, and that he recognized it was true. What Corbin and I had was special. Maybe if we'd ever slept together or decided to date, we wouldn't be friends now, and that would be the real tragedy. "I figure there's some saintly woman out there who deserves him," I added. "It's not me."

"No, I guess not," Tiffany said. "Not very saintly to sleep with a married man."

Maybe I deserved that, but my cheeks flamed nonetheless. I hated that she'd said it in front of Corbin. Since he was quick to defend me in any situation, his silence confirmed that he agreed. He still didn't bring up Manning's name in any other context than as Tiffany's ex-husband, but that didn't mean Corbin was in the dark about anything.

But it was out there now, and once my shame wore off a bit, I was actually a little relieved. I'd lived in this secret world with Manning so long, I was exhausted from hiding our attraction to each other. So, in the interest of honesty, I finally stopped trying to protect everyone. "Did you ever really love Manning?" I asked. "Or did you just marry him to spite me?"

Tiffany's blue eyes flashed over me before she glanced at the ashtray. She went to pick up her pack again, but I snatched it and threw it in the pool. "*Hey*," she said.

"Just stop already. You and—" I stopped myself from saying *Manning*. "You're better than those cigarettes. It's not an emotional crutch—it's a filthy habit that *will* kill you."

"What Lake's trying to say is that she cares what happens to you." Corbin gave me a reproachful look. "And she's right. Smoking like a chimney isn't going to make anything better."

Tiffany slumped down in her seat, biting her cuticle. "Fine. You want the truth? Until Manning came along, I had *one thing* you didn't—men wanted me. You had the grades and Dad's attention and USC, but I could flirt the pants off a gay man." Her gaze darted from me to Corbin and back. "Then when I saw how Manning looked at you, suddenly everything changed. Guys started noticing you, too. Including Corbin, but he'd wanted me first, didn't you, Corbin?"

Corbin stilled, only his eyes moving as he looked between us. "Oh, I . . . uh." He shifted in his seat. "Yeah, I guess. When you were dating Cane, you were like *the* girl. It was hard not to, like, like you."

He looked so uncomfortable that I brought the conversation back to myself. "I was sixteen," I said to Tiffany. "I got boobs and grew into my limbs that summer. It wasn't Manning's fault."

"But Manning . . . he was the one thing you wanted," she said. "It was so painfully obvious you had this little-girl crush on him that first day he came over for a sandwich."

"So that's why you went out with him?" I asked. "To rub it in my face?"

"It wasn't that conniving. It bothered Dad and it annoyed you, so it was kind of fun. Manning just felt like some rare thing I could have and you couldn't." She looked longingly at the pack of smokes bobbing in the pool. "I mean, I didn't *plan* it like that. When I say it now, it sounds calculated but it just happened. I never meant for things to go so far, you know. Manning was too old for me and not that much fun. He was so serious all the time."

Nobody understood that better than me. "All the time," I agreed.

Her shoulders rose with a deep inhale. "But it turned out, that was what I needed. Dad had given up on me early. Manning didn't. He talked *to* me, not at me. He listened and cared about what I was thinking. At camp, he treated me so well, I let myself believe he was falling for me, too. Then that last night at campfire, when you snuck off with him—"

"You did?" Corbin pursed his lips at me and sat back. "Fuck."

I did my best to look contrite, knowing Corbin wouldn't like hearing something so out of character for me.

"It was like . . ." Tiffany continued. "Like I was starting to really like him and once again, you were getting *every*thing."

"So you married him," I said.

"It's probably easier for you to believe I didn't love him," she said quietly, "but I did. He was the only person who saw me, who treated me with any respect, even in my own family."

"That's not true," I said. "I looked up to you, Tiffany. I tried to step in with Dad when I could. I feel like I lost a sister the day of your wedding."

Crickets filled the next few moments of silence. Even the party inside seemed to quiet as Tiffany and I avoided each other's gaze. "Then I guess that means I lost a sister, too," she said.

Having Corbin there was less comforting than it normally would've been—and a whole lot embarrassing. When it came to Manning, he and I never went there, but I guess now he knew enough.

Finally, Tiffany got up. "I should get home. I have to work in the morning and it's a long drive back."

"You can stay here," I offered.

"It's fine. Congrats again on all this stuff." She sounded tired. "I'll be watching the show. It's actually really good."

There wasn't anything I could say to take back what I'd done. I didn't exactly want to jump to forgiveness, either. Tiffany had made mistakes, too. If she'd reacted maturely to anything, ever, we wouldn't be in this situation. That didn't mean I wanted her out of my life, though. She'd intentionally hurt me, but I wasn't lacking in compassion like she thought. I understood her actions were less out of malice than fear. "You should come by the set some time."

"I . . . would seriously love that," she said.

I knew she would. Tiffany lived for that kind of stuff, and I was pretty sure the possibility of that was a small part of why she'd come tonight. It didn't matter why, though. I was glad she'd made the effort.

As she picked up her bag, I stood. I went to hug her, but she wasn't expecting it, and we did a back-and-forth maneuver while Corbin chuckled. I hugged her more tightly than I meant to.

"I still need time and distance," she said, "but I . . . you haven't, like, *lost* me. Not forever."

I swallowed. Maybe I hadn't been fair just now. Maybe Tiffany really had come to see me—and not just on TV. "Same here."

Once she'd returned inside and Corbin and I were alone, I said, "I'm sorry you had to hear all that."

He just shrugged, leaning on his knees as he laced his fingers together. "Yeah."

"But I feel like she's gotten more empathetic. Maybe it was going through the miscarriage. Or I guess I just haven't seen her in a while, and we've both matured."

He nodded at the ground. "Yeah."

A moth fluttered around the overhead light. I was rambling. Corbin and I had talked about most things under the sun, but we rarely discussed love. Anything to do with Manning, or Corbin's feelings for me, we pretended didn't exist. The longer we sat that way, though, the harder it became to ignore the ebb of Corbin's normally sunny disposition. "Is something wrong?" I asked.

He looked through the sliding glass door at Sean, who was checking out Tiffany's ass as she walked away. "That guy, Lake? Really? In his crusty leather jacket, not understanding half of what's going on around him?"

"It's nothing," I said. "Easy. Sean and I—we're just having fun."

It took a little bit for him to respond, but for Corbin I had time. I waited until eventually, his blue eyes found their way to mine. I started to smile but stopped, sensing this wasn't a happy moment. "Why not me?" he asked.

I flinched, surprised only that he'd asked, not by the question itself. Even though I'd wondered the same thing many times, I only had one answer—the truth—and I wasn't sure Corbin wanted to hear it. "Corbin . . ."

"That guy's a loser. So are most of the guys you date. Why didn't you ever give me a shot?"

Corbin and I had been on countless dinner dates and attended myriad events and parties together. We'd kissed, we'd fooled around, we'd slept in each other's arms. He'd asked me out and he'd tried for more, but that was a long time ago. We'd become so much more since then. He knew it would never work between us. "You know why," I said.

"Manning." He stuck his tongue in his cheek and got a look like the ones Manning used to get over Corbin. "I never understood it. What was Tiffany talking about, sneaking out at camp? You were so, I don't know, gullible back then. I knew you had a crush on him, but if I'd realized he was taking advantage of you—"

"Nothing happened while I was under eighteen," I said. "New York was the first time."

"*After* he was married to Tiffany." He opened his hands, shaking his head. "Explain it to me, Lake. What do you see in him?"

I'd been wrong just now. It wasn't jealousy I was seeing like I'd thought. Corbin just didn't trust Manning, and I couldn't fault him that. "I can't put it into words," I said.

He opened an arm toward the door. "So that guy in there, hitting on your sister—he's the next best thing?"

"Not at all. He's just nothing. We have a good time, he makes me laugh, and he leaves me alone."

"I don't get it. I really don't. You could have anyone."

Anyone? I wanted to say. *Don't you know I don't want anyone? I want Manning.* I pushed the thoughts away and scooted my chair closer to Corbin's. "You asked why it wasn't you?" I said. "Of course I thought about you and me a lot, especially after September eleventh."

"Yeah," he said. I didn't need to explain what I meant—he'd lost not just colleagues but friends in the terrorist attacks, and it was an unspoken truth that it'd changed many of us.

But because I always wanted Corbin to know how much I cared about him, I *did* explain, even though I'd told him the story many times. "I remember every detail of that morning," I said, taking Corbin's hand. "I was seeing that guy Brandon from Chicago, and we'd been out late, so we were still sleeping when we got the call."

"Your mom."

I hesitated. I didn't want to keep anything from Corbin anymore now that we'd started talking honestly about this area of our lives. "Actually no. I never told you, but someone else called first."

"Who?" He glanced at my face, and then said, "Oh."

Brandon had answered the phone, and a man on the other end of the line had asked for me. I'd picked up with a cheery "hello?"—none the wiser about what'd happened downtown.

"Lake," was Manning's response. Simple. One word. But my name from his mouth—it'd always had a certain kind of power over me.

"What's wrong?" I'd asked him.

"I just needed to hear . . ." He'd paused and said, "You should call home."

I'd held the receiver long after he'd gotten off the line, but the moment I'd hung up, the line had rung again. That time it was my mom and she'd been hysterical, ordering me to turn on the TV.

"For a split second," I said to Corbin, "I couldn't remember where you were." My eyes filled up, and I blinked the tears away. "Panic completely wiped my brain. I started screaming for Val, and she ran into the bedroom. She hadn't heard yet so when I asked her where you were, she thought I was going crazy. 'He left for San Francisco three days ago, you loon,' she'd said. 'You took him out to breakfast before the flight.' When I told Val, she completely lost it, Corbin. I basically had to stop falling apart because *she* was freaking out so bad. She was inconsolable."

Corbin rubbed his face. He'd heard this story, but not all of it.

I told him the part I'd been keeping to myself. "After the fear and panic and grief I felt that morning, I thought, maybe I *do* love Corbin. Maybe he's the one."

He sat back. "But?"

"I did love you. And I was attracted to you. That was never the issue. You know the truth deep down—you would've always been second best, Corbin. Always. The only person I love more than you is Manning. My feelings for him are immoveable—I know it in my gut. Nobody will ever replace him."

He searched my eyes with his endless blue ones. They were rarely sad like now, and I couldn't help noticing how beautiful they were despite that. Or maybe because of it. "Back then, I would've been fine with second best."

"I love you too much to do that to you. You need a girl who looks at you, and . . . you're her *world*, Corbin." *Her universe, her sky, her stars. Her Ursa Major.* "She wasn't me."

He scrubbed his hands through his golden hair. "Yeah. I guess now you're going to tell me you did me a favor rejecting me all those times."

I couldn't help laughing a little. "I'll save that piece of wisdom for when you meet 'the one.'"

"And what about you?" he asked.

I smiled sadly. "I already met him."

"Your sister's been divorced for like, over three years or something." He picked up his cup from the table. "Have you seen him?"

I lifted my hair off my neck, warm under the patio light. "No," I said, mustering as much nonchalance as I could. "It's dumb. I thought, back then, you know, that Manning was . . . that we were . . ." *Destined.* I couldn't even get through the sentence without my throat thickening. What was wrong with me? It'd been years and years of heartbreak and bad timing. How many times did the universe have to tell us this wasn't right? "And I don't know anymore. I don't know if he and I were ever . . ."

"Ah, fuck," Corbin said, wrinkling his eyebrows. I must've looked about to burst into tears, because he started to fidget. "This might be out of my league. I didn't mean to make you cry."

I inhaled back the urge, shaking my head. "You didn't."

"It's not dumb, Lake." He put his ankle over his knee, resting his drink on his sneaker. "But would you take some advice from a reformed love-sick puppy?"

I failed to suppress a smile. "Sure."

"Move on. I know it sounds obvious, but if you're still pining for him years later, you're not going to magically get over it. No matter how much you accomplish, a small part of you is holding back, don't you think?"

I thought of what Corbin had said earlier this year about losing some of my fire after graduation. It was only now becoming clear to me that instead of accessing my pain over Manning as my professor had coached me to do, I'd buried it, and that'd hurt my ability to tune into my emotions. Maybe reality TV really *was* the best I could do, because Manning hadn't just taken part of me with him when he'd left New York—he'd changed my DNA. He'd changed the dynamic of the city for me. His destruction had seeped into my career, my home, my heart, and even my innocence he'd been so hell-bent on preserving. I'd had to take the morning-after pill the same day he'd left. Flushing myself of him was a distinct kind of heartache I'd never forget.

"It's like you're waiting for him until you can be happy," Corbin said. "But what're you waiting for? It's been years. Get closure if you need to, but then move yourself on."

Move on. My hope for Manning and me had been holding strong for a decade, through the worst of it. What about his hope? Had he ever had it? If he hadn't come for me by now, then maybe not. "I don't think I wanted to get over him," I said. "I really thought one day . . ."

"I know the feeling. It's like—how could it not happen? But for most of us, it doesn't." He sipped his drink, then wiped his mouth with his sleeve. "I don't believe he's the only person who can make you happy. You can fall in love with someone else if you're willing to try."

Corbin was right—my love for Manning wasn't dumb, but since the day I'd met him, it'd been getting in the way of everything else. It was time to give up and move myself on. I hated to cry in front of Corbin because he was so protective, but I never thought I'd have to admit I'd been wrong about Manning. I never thought I'd lose hope.

"I guess this is why you and I don't talk about girl stuff." Corbin reached out to thumb away some tears. "Hey, Val," he yelled, beckoning for her through the kitchen window.

Val had held me through too many nights of crying over Manning, so for her sake, I pulled myself together. When she poked her head out a minute later, I practiced moving on, like Corbin had told me, and forced a smile with all my might. "We miss you," I said.

She came onto the patio with a bottle of wine and some stacked plastic Solo cups. "I'm not going to toast you again," she said to me. "I know you wanted to strangle me for it."

"Completely true," I teased.

"I thought I was helping you out when I recommended you for this project," she said, separating the cups. "It seemed like a good opportunity. Was I wrong?"

"I don't know," I admitted. "I have a lot of thinking to do about . . ." I glanced at Corbin. "Everything."

Val nodded and filled up three drinks, placing one in front of each of us. When she took the chair Tiffany had vacated, I crossed my feet in her lap.

We sat that way, just the three of us, talking until the party died down.

Every once in a while, I'd catch myself looking up. The moon was full, but I wondered how long until I'd take in the night sky and feel anything other than empty.

4

MANNING, 2004

"Inquiring minds want to know," I heard from behind me as I approached the end of aisle nine. "What *does* a mysterious man like Manning Sutter put in his shopping basket?"

I didn't need to turn to see whose mind was inquiring. "A poor attempt at dinner," I responded.

Martina Klausen was the town's blonde beauty, recently divorced and swimming in money. Because of her straightforward German sensibility and appreciation for a good, strong piece of furniture, I'd indulged her flirting in the beginning. She was the only woman I knew here who didn't beat around the bush too much or need her hand held, and for that reason, she made for a decent distraction from my thoughts.

She caught up with me, craning her neck to inspect the contents of my basket. "Meat, potatoes . . . and lots of beer. Could you be any more of a man? Are you going home to watch the fight or what?"

"I might be if I had a TV."

"But how do you keep entertained in the evenings?" She winked, pushing her cart alongside me. "How about I come make you dinner?"

With my basket in one hand, I took a pack of cigarettes from the pocket of my shirt and shook one free. I slid it out with my lips. "Not tonight," I muttered.

"You need vegetables. I can make 'em just right so they don't even taste healthy."

I stuck the cigarette behind my ear until I could light it on the drive home. That simple gesture reminded me of Lake, how I used to wait to smoke until she was out of breathing distance. That wasn't anything new. Lots reminded me of Lake, especially around Big Bear. Some days, all I felt was the sting of loss and of those memories.

Tiffany and I had gotten divorced almost four years ago and even though Charles had offered to keep me on at Ainsley-Bushner, I'd left my job and moved to Big Bear as soon as I was able. It'd been the last place I'd felt at peace. Up here, there was tons of space for a workshop, and when I shut down the house at night, I could see the stars, every one of them, just miles and miles of endless universe and me.

I fell back to Earth when I recognized Pearl Jam on the grocery store's loudspeakers. The song wasn't "Black," which made me think of Lake every time, but the opening line of "Last Kiss" reminded me of her nonetheless. Was there no escaping her?

Grumbling to myself, I got in line at the cashier while Martina followed, talking about the benefits of cutting out carbs, the latest fad. I likely would've missed the glossy tabloid covers if I hadn't been trying to avoid Martina, but as soon as my eyes hit *Us Weekly*, I felt like I'd been sucker punched. In the lower left-hand corner, the picture was small, but there was no mistaking it—Lake, smiling at something in the distance with a man's arm around her shoulders. A circle with a question mark blocked his face, but I knew the answer. It was Corbin. The headline underneath just rubbed salt in the wound.

Who will win Lake's heart? Our predictions on pg. 28

I'd followed Lake's career enough to know she was on a hit reality show. I hadn't seen it. Once the commercials had started to air, and it became clear Corbin would be a regular in Lake's love life, I'd gotten rid of my TV. It was hard enough that so much in this town reminded me of her, but now there she was, beaming at me in checkout lane three. Like old times, my neck and chest heated with Corbin's possessive embrace on her. What did Corbin have to do with this anyway? He was a big shot in New York last I'd heard, and had no business in Hollywood.

Martina touched my elbow. "Manning?"

I startled. "What?"

"Are you okay?" she asked as the cashier snapped her gum at me.

I unpacked my groceries onto the conveyor belt, glancing at the rag. At Lake. Her smile leapt off the page. She looked happy and that was the thing that both soothed and killed me. She was in a better place like I'd wanted. Maybe all along, she could've been happy with Corbin.

"Last chance to sit back and relax while I whip you up something tasty," Martina said as I paid for the groceries.

I jammed my wallet in my back pocket and the cigarette in my mouth. With another glance at the magazine, I said around the butt, "Fine, yeah. I'll meet you at the house."

Truth was, unless it was grilling, I didn't like to cook. The few times Martina had come for dinner, the food had been all right, and the sex, too. She never overstayed her welcome, and that was exactly what I needed.

Fifteen minutes later, I turned into my long, winding driveway. The house was private, just how I liked it. It looked as if it belonged in the woods, an extension of the forest rather than an obstruction. My closest neighbor was about a quarter mile away. No grumbly trucks would be pulling up in the middle of the night like the one I'd driven around a nearby neighborhood. No young and dumb twenty-three-year-old would hop my fence with the girl of his dreams. No cops would come knocking on my front door without their tires on the gravel warning me first.

I turned on the porch light as Martina parked behind my truck. She walked up the steps cradling two paper grocery bags. "I know how hard you work," she said. "Doesn't hurt to let someone come over and take care of you once in a while."

I took the bags from her and carried them inside. "You know *once in a while* is all that works for me, Martina."

"Oh, believe me, darling—that's as much as I can handle, too."

I sat at the kitchen table, smoking while she started prepping the food. "What's that mean, all you can handle?"

"Just that you're one of those guys. How do you say . . . 'emotionally unavailable.'" She rifled through a bag and pulled out seasoning for the steak. "I went through that with my ex-husband and I'd rather be alone than do it again. No offense."

"Why do you come over then?" I asked, genuinely curious. Not that Martina had been beating down my door, but I sort of figured all women were secretly hoping for something more permanent, and that was something I couldn't give.

"Because you're impossibly handsome, and you're a decent man, even if you try to hide it. Doesn't hurt that you have the most beautiful kitchen

I've ever seen." She looked over her shoulder and winked. "Plus, you're a good lay."

I took a drag. "Just good?"

"You could be the best sex I ever had," she said, "but it wouldn't matter. Your heart's not in it, and that makes a difference for a woman. How about you?" she asked, setting a pot of water on the stove to boil. "When do you think you'll settle down?"

I looked around my state-of-the-art kitchen. I'd picked the best of the best, installed each appliance with my bare hands, sanded down every cabinet door, chosen high-end finishes to complete the look. I put out my cigarette. "What makes you think I will?"

"A castle like this, just for a lonesome king?" she asked, gesturing around the room. "I don't think so. You must be planning for a queen."

Planning for a queen. I didn't want to think too hard about what that meant. There was only one queen, and to have built all this for her, without knowing if or when I'd see her again? I couldn't face that. And anyway, it was hardly a castle. I still had tons of work to do on the back of the house, not to mention the attic and the yard, and—

"I bought you a present. Keep you entertained since you don't have a TV and all." Martina looked into a grocery bag, then tossed *Us Weekly* in front of me.

"What is this?" I asked, playing dumb.

"You stared at it for a full minute at the store. I figured you were just too embarrassed to buy it. Doesn't go with your steak-and-potatoes image."

I ran my thumb over Lake's face. I'd done a good job of ignoring her sudden fame, but sometimes it found me anyway. I opened the magazine. Page twenty-eight asked, "Who will she choose?"

Lake had an entire panel along the length of the page. The top image showed her on the street walking some dogs in a t-shirt from a Los Angeles rescue shelter. Below were three different photos of her with three different men. The title read, "Fresh on the scene, reality star Lake Kaplan has her pick of the pack."

My heart beat painfully in my chest as I forced myself to look at each photo. A guy with tattoos and a leather jacket kissed Lake's temple. Another stood with his arm around her waist on the red carpet. The last, the image from the cover, was Corbin, "A wealthy hedge fund manager who's moved across the country in hopes of getting Lake to settle down."

There it was—the nightmare I'd fought so hard to construct for myself. Was it finally enough to see her happy with other men? Was getting what I deserved enough to absolve me for the sins of my father and myself? Of the ways I'd disappointed Maddy, Tiffany, Lake, and the child I'd lost?

So Corbin was back on the west coast with Lake. He'd gone after her like I'd known he would. Maybe Lake had her pick of the mutts but Corbin wasn't just another dog sniffing around. He'd been there for all of it, all the milestones I'd missed, all the tears I'd caused, and a love I'd barely touched before it was taken from me.

"Any good Hollywood gossip?" she asked.

"No," I said. "I know her."

Martina leaned over to glance at the spread. "Oh, my. Beautiful girl."

"Beautiful, yes. Because she looks happy," I muttered to myself. It should've elated me to see that. It was the one thing I'd always wanted for her. *Soar, Birdy.* After the miscarriage, I'd been in no shape to be a good partner to anyone, but eventually, I'd pulled myself together. For all the times over the years I'd pushed Lake to be the best version of herself, she deserved to have the best version of me, too. She'd wanted me to follow my passions, and once I'd had nothing left to lose, that was the only thing that'd made sense. I'd started making furniture and running a business that was now off the ground. I'd built this house from the ground up, and it would be finished by the end of this year. I earned a decent living and had saved a lot over the years—I had a good life to offer her. But as I stared at the magazine, I had to admit I hadn't accounted for the fact that Lake might've found a way to be sincerely happy without me.

"You never know with these celebrities," Martina said, picking up the magazine to see better. "It's their job to put on a performance, after all."

I glanced up at her. "What do you mean?"

"She does look happy." Martina's eyes sparkled, as if she could read every last thought in my head. "But what if she's not?"

I looked at the ground, shuffling my feet. I'd put Lake through so much heartache already. If she'd found a way to move on, would trying to pull her back in be the right thing to do? But if Martina was right, and Lake *wasn't* happy—then I had no choice. I'd have to put my own insecurities aside. If I could give Lake everything she wanted and deserved, I had to. It would be the most important thing I'd ever do.

Martina held out the magazine for me, but I shook my head, my palms sweaty. I'd seen enough of Corbin's ugly mug for a lifetime. "You can toss it."

Martina raised an eyebrow at me, but she just put it in a drawer.

I had a beer, and then another one with my dinner, and then I had Martina. After she left, I moved on to whiskey, and when I was sufficiently intoxicated, I went into my office closet and took down a shoebox of important papers. I stuck my cigarette in the corner of my mouth and sat at my desk.

On top was a folder with my divorce papers. The last year of my marriage had been the worst by far. Pregnancy should've been a happy time, but Tiffany had resented me for what she suspected happened in New York and took it out on me any chance she got, threatening to leave once the baby was born. I took it without protest, guilty over my inability to stop thinking of Lake and how I'd wanted it to be her. It was unfair to my unborn child and to Tiffany, but Lake had made too strong an imprint on me in the week we'd spent together. When Tiffany lost the baby at nineteen weeks, we stopped speaking. I drank more than I ever had, trying to drown the *what-ifs* that hammered me on a daily basis. What if it'd been Lake who'd carried and lost my child? What if I'd been a better husband, and Tiffany hadn't been so stressed the entire pregnancy? What if I had just kissed Lake that night on the pool deck and never stopped?

After we'd lost the baby, and Tiffany had withdrawn from everything and everyone except her mom, she'd started spending nights at her parents' house. At the end of it, there was no other path but separation. Even Charles had shaken my hand, told me I'd been good to Tiffany, and supported the divorce.

I shuffled aside the past in front of me. Underneath the papers were the stacks of letters Lake had sent me in prison. Some of them were open, not by me, but by Tiffany. I'd only read a couple, while she'd read many. It was one of the last things we'd fought about. The letters were harmless, but that was exactly the issue. According to Tiffany they were stupid and childish and boring, and if I'd kept Lake's nonsense all these years, what did that mean?

I picked up a random one and read about a day in her life back then. It'd all been so simple—calculus, running, report cards, friends, animals, the start and end of summer. The letter was upbeat, and I realized in retrospect, she'd hidden her suffering to make my time inside a little easier. One part caught my attention.

Whenever I mess something up, I think about what you said at camp when I didn't want to ride the horse. I asked what would happen if I fell, and you said I'd get up and dust myself off. After you and I rode together, I felt like I could do it on my own. Not that I wanted to, but that I could. I think one day when I have kids, I'll take them horseback riding and teach them the same thing. I know it's cliché and there's already a saying about getting back on the horse when you fall off, but it's so true, isn't it? It's a good lesson.

I gritted my teeth and drank more. Lake had been so lovely, so naïve. Had I sucked it all out of her, just by loving her? After all these letters with no response, after watching me marry her sister, after probably taking a pill to make sure she'd never have my baby, was she still hopeful? Did she let herself love Corbin as completely as she'd loved me?

An ache radiated through my chest. Surely words written on a page could not cause this kind of pain. I must've been having a heart attack. I sat forward and put my head in my hands. This was why I couldn't read the letters in prison. My mind spun out wherever Lake was involved. I knew I should never read another word. If there was any chance Lake had moved on and left me behind, I needed to turn these letters into kindling instead of keeping them to torture myself.

Against my better judgement, I kept reading, consuming all her thoughts and desires and hopes and dreams. But as I did, I realized that I already knew the truth. It was as plain and simple in these letters as it had been the first day I'd talked to Lake. She'd never asked for much. Unlike her sister, Lake didn't need expensive things or the best home in the neighborhood or a new car to mark every big accomplishment.

Lake would've been happy just to have me.

Despite everything, hope still burned in me for us. Lake deserved that much from me.

5
MANNING

A couple months after I'd read Lake's letters, I had visitors. Henry was the most dependable man I knew. By having my back during my sister's death, when my parents had tried pinning everything on me, he'd saved me, a helpless teenager, from what could've been a shit life. And with all the tragedy he'd encountered as a police officer, it would've been easy for him to send me on my way afterward. Instead, he continued to check in on me, making sure I finished high school despite my situation.

The furniture business was booming, and I didn't trust many people to help me out, but I had a particularly important rush order and needed a hand.

Having retired, Henry had been able to come up and stay at the house for a few weeks to help me get the workload under control.

This was his last night in Big Bear, so I picked up some barbeque for the occasion. Since it was the same week Young Cubs Sleepaway Camp was in session up the hill, and Gary was still the director, I invited him and his wife Lydia over for dinner.

Even though it was August, the nights in Big Bear could get chilly. I built a fire in the pit in the front yard and welcomed the closest friends I had with a cooler of beer on ice.

"You're in a good mood," Gary said, walking up the drive to shake my hand.

I nodded at Henry, who was prepping the grill. "Henry and I have been working around the clock the past couple weeks. Feels good to do nothing but build furniture day in and day out, but I'm also glad this project is done."

"So business is good?" he asked.

"Too good. Any time this week you need a break from the chaos up there at camp, I can put you to work."

Lydia hobbled up the gravel in heels, holding her purse strap to one shoulder and balancing a paper grocery bag in the other. Just like Tiffany, the woman was always wearing something akin to stilts. Always had her brown hair styled, her makeup done. No wonder they'd gotten along so well. "Do you have a website?" she asked, frowning when I shook my head. "You need one. Everyone has them these days."

"For what?" I asked, handing Gary a Bud. "I already have more business than I can keep up with."

"You still need one." When she got to the grass, she gave up and set the groceries down to remove her shoes. "I know a girl who can make you one. Get you some more sales, and then you can hire yourself employees."

Hire more people—that was what Mr. Kaplan had said when I'd spoken to him on the phone last month and told him I was barely keeping up with orders. I didn't see how it could work, though. I built furniture because it was my passion. I used my hands to bring my visions to life, and when I finished each piece, it was no longer mine. It saw my customers through good times and bad—births, weddings, funerals, or just plain dinner each night. Not that I was exactly happy to have missed out on being a cop like I'd planned, but I could see now that it hadn't been my path—my passion was being strong and capable enough to help people, to bring goodness to their lives, and Lake had taught me that there were lots of ways to go about that.

"I like things how they are," I said to Lydia. "Don't need too much else."

An outdoor picnic table was one of the things I had yet to finish for my place. Truth was, four years on and I was still building my own house and the things in it. In the beginning, I worked mostly to push through the guilt and shame I harbored over Lake, Tiffany, and the baby. But then one night, I'd started on cupboards and remembered how Lake had designated a place in her New York kitchen just for guest dishes. She wanted people to feel special in her home. So as I'd made myself a cabinet just for nice china, it hit me just how often Lake had been on mind as I'd laid planks, carved wood, and sanded and varnished surfaces over the years. While my body labored, my mind escaped, often into Lake's warmth. The things she'd wanted, the pieces she'd be proud to have in her home. That was why this house had taken me so fucking long.

I set up fabric folding chairs around the fire while Henry served us burgers and hot dogs. He and Gary caught up for the first time since the wedding. Once the conversation stalled, I nodded at Lydia.

"How's Tiffany?" I asked. Gary and I had introduced the girls, but she and Tiff had remained close since the divorce.

"She's fine. Mostly dating and working. How are *you*?"

"Also fine," I said. "Working."

"Dating?"

I took a swig of my beer. "Nah."

"Because that girl I mentioned is very pretty—"

"Who?" I asked.

"The one who makes websites. She's lovely and sweet and *hates* drama." Lydia curled her toes in the grass, her smile warm. "I love Tiffany, you know I do, but after her, you need someone who'll go easy on you."

"I appreciate it, but no," I said. Lovely and sweet and drama-free all sounded fine, but not better than Lake. "I'm good with the way things are."

"You keep saying that," Lydia replied, "but we don't believe you."

"*We?*" Gary asked. "Don't drag me into this. Although, I will agree, Heather *is* pretty. And I'm not just saying that to get you to meet her. She's nice, and she'd be good for you, Manning."

Henry and I exchanged a look. He was a simple man, who'd lived a simple life. He didn't know about Lake, but he'd seen that I was doing work I loved, and that was good enough for now. "Sounds like you're dragging *yourself* into it, Gary," I said.

"Heather needs a good, solid man," Lydia said. "Do it for her."

"Wish I could," I said. "But I just can't."

Henry cleared his throat. "Anyone need another beer?"

"Me," Lydia said.

"I'll take one," Gary added.

I put my plate on the ground. "I'll get them."

I reloaded the cooler and carried it out, setting it down in the middle of the group—which had gone suspiciously quiet.

"What?" I asked, tossing Henry a beer.

He caught it and held up his hands as if to surrender.

I went to hand Gary one as well but took it back as he went to grab it. "Why do you all look guilty?"

Gary glanced between the Bud and my face, and said, "We were talking about you and Tiff. God knows we've heard her side of the story, but in four years, we've never heard yours."

"That's intentional. It's nobody's business but ours."

"Tiffany made it our business," Lydia said. "But we want you to talk to us about it. It's not healthy that you're up here all alone, taking your emotions out on helpless pieces of wood."

"That's not what I do."

"She's right, son," Henry said.

I sat down, schooled. A couple beers weren't enough to get me talking about my private life, even if Tiffany felt the need to. These people were my family, though. Henry had been there for me as a teen in a way nobody else had. He didn't pester me about these things, but that didn't mean he didn't care. And Gary'd been like a brother to me. "You know the story," I said. "She got pregnant, we lost the baby, and things just fell apart. We had problems before all that, and we just weren't strong enough to take on that kind of heartbreak." That was only part of the truth. After my time in New York, I didn't want any woman but Lake, and I couldn't fake it. I went back to Tiffany out of duty, but without the baby, I'd had no reason to stay.

"You make the divorce sound like it was mutual," Gary said.

"It was, even if she won't admit it. She wasn't happy." Tiffany had wanted the beautiful Newport Beach package—cute kids, shiny marriage, big house. She wanted what her parents had on the outside, even if we'd been worse off than them on the inside. Even if it meant she and I weren't truly happy. By the end, she'd known my feelings for Lake had run deep, and though she got her barbs in, she still hadn't been willing to confront me head on about it.

My friends knew me well, and they left it at that. At some point, night fell, but we barely noticed for all our talking and drinking. A few six-packs in, Lydia was giggling, Gary was smoking a blunt, and Henry just got more stoic, watching and listening to us. Or me, mostly. I had a feeling he had things on his mind, but he was a private man and wouldn't want to talk about them in front of the others.

"Let's have s'mores," Lydia said.

I squinted at her over the top of the fire. "I don't have the ingredients for that."

"We brought some," she said. "Except we need something to put the marshmallows on. Do you have any long, sterile pieces of wood, Carpenter Man?"

Living in the woods with a fire pit in my front yard, this wasn't my first encounter with s'mores. "I think there are some in one of the drawers by the stove," I said.

While Lydia was inside, Gary leaned toward me, nearly toppling out of his chair. "Tiffany must've been a tiger in the sack for you to put up with her for so long."

I glanced at Henry, but he'd fallen asleep. I'd had Tiffany in every way imaginable except one. I had never made love to her the way I had Lake. Afterward, I'd never had the urge to demand every thought in her head, to feel her heart beat against my chest, to touch every inch of her to know she was real. I'd wanted kids, even if it was with Tiffany, but I'd never felt the deep-seated instinct to get her pregnant the way I'd wanted to with Lake. "You know me well enough that I'm not going to answer that," I told Gary.

"Damn. I was hoping you were drunk enough."

"Almost," I joked. "Not quite."

Lydia nearly skipped out of the kitchen with metal skewers in one hand, waving the *Us Weekly* Martina had brought over months ago in the other. "It seems our Manning has a secret indulgence."

Lydia fisted the magazine, sending a crinkle right through Lake and Corbin. I had a secret all right, but an indulgence? I hadn't indulged in Lake in years, not the way I wanted to. What I wouldn't give to run her silky strands through my fingers again, to tug her hair hard enough to make her bite her plump, watermelon-flavored lip.

"Hollywood gossip, man?" Gary asked. "Really?"

"Not that." Lydia showed him the cover and pointed to Lake.

"Aww." Gary squinted at her photo. "Look at our girl, all famous and shit. Is that Corbin she's with? They look happy."

I looked into my beer bottle and repeated to myself the question that'd been running through my mind since Martina had asked it. *What if she's not?*

"Have you seen the show?" Lydia asked.

It took me a moment to realize she was talking to me. "No," I said.

"Why not?"

I'd tried once more since getting rid of my TV. I'd been at a bar in town and the fucking show had been on in the background, ten o'clock at night. Watching her on screen was like taking a screwdriver to my chest. I'd made it half an episode. When she'd gone on a date with some guy with tattoos and a bike—fine, fuck, it wasn't some guy, his name was Sean and I'd never forget it—I'd paid my tab and high-tailed it out of there. I had no idea if he was still in the picture or if it was just Corbin. "I don't have a TV," I said.

Lydia flipped through the magazine. "There's something about Lake, don't you think, Manning?"

Gary rolled his eyes. "Lydia."

She sat down, piling all the s'mores paraphernalia in her lap as she showed us the tribute to Lake's dating life. "Look at those guys. They're crazy about her. I hope she's dating them all."

The beer bottle slipped a little under my grip. *All?* Corbin was enough to deal with. I hadn't considered she might be seeing more than one of them at a time. What right did I have to be jealous? I'd married her sister. I'd fucked women after being intimate with Lake. I thought of kneeling before Lake that first time, dawn breaking outside the window as I'd explored her. Did she remember my confessions about wanting her in the truck? Did she remember how I'd cleaned her between the legs just to fill her with myself? Did she still feel my hands around her waist after we'd fought and I'd thrown her over my shoulder?

"Say something to me you wouldn't've said before."

"Okay. On the bed so I can fuck you, Lake."

"Say another," she pleaded.

"I want to feel your hands on me."

"That right there." Lydia pointed at me, turning her head to her husband while keeping her eyes on me. "What did I tell you, Gare?"

My collar got a little tight, and I felt like I was back at camp again, the police calling me away in front of all those kids. "What?" I asked.

"You get this look when Lake's name comes up. You always have." Lydia held the magazine to her chest. "A look you never get about anything else in your life. Or anyone."

I chugged the rest of my beer and tossed the empty bottle with the rest of the garbage. It didn't surprise me that I got a look. I knew that about myself. Charles had noticed it. Tiffany, too. I was pretty sure Lake's mom also knew.

"I always had this theory," Lydia said. "I think you have a teeny tiny thing for Lake."

Years ago, I would've taken my secret to the grave, but tonight, amongst friends, as an older and wiser man, I just shrugged. "What do you want me to say?"

"Ah-*ha*! So it's true!" When she puffed up, she had to catch the bag of marshmallows before it slid off her lap. "I have a nose for these things."

Gary looked the definition of perplexed, his eyebrows knitting as he whipped his head between Lydia and me. "How teeny is tiny?" Gary asked.

"I'm not talking about this," I grumbled.

"Is this . . . for *real*?" Gary asked, drawing out the question. He was high enough to look fucked up, but I knew that wouldn't get me out of this. I'd seen him hold his own during a political debate after smoking way more than he had tonight.

"No," I said. "It's not that simple . . ." I sat forward as Lydia passed me a stick with a marshmallow. I fumbled, nearly dropping it in the fire. "There's no crush."

"Who said anything about a crush?" Lydia asked.

I stuck the marshmallow in the fire. "You know what I meant."

"Dude." Gary shook his head. "You're so flustered right now."

"I'm not flustered."

"Your marshmallow is in flames," he pointed out, laughing too loudly.

I blew it out, but the thing was nearly black.

"Was it like that at camp? Did you have a thing for her then?" Gary asked. "You dirty bastard. Flirting with one of the counselors."

I was sweating. The beer made my thoughts hazy. I ran a hand through my hair and checked to make sure Henry was still asleep. Luckily he was, because he didn't need to hear this. He was a cop, and a good family man. "It's not like that," I said. "I wasn't . . . I didn't . . ." Except I *was*, and I *did*. I couldn't deny it, because I couldn't lie to them. I'd gotten way too close to the line with Lake when I was supposed to be the adult.

"Dude, relax," Gary said. "She was a sixteen-year-old hot blonde. You think I never flirted with one of the junior counselors?"

I expected Lydia to smack him, but she just rolled her eyes. "You creepy old man."

"What?" Gary said. "I'm just human. You have any idea what I was up to at sixteen?"

"Spare us," I said.

"I would've put my dick in anyone that let me, but nobody did. Lydia, on the other hand, slept with a college professor."

I raised my eyebrows at her and teased, "Did he at least give you an 'A'?"

"She was in high school!" Gary added.

"I told you that in confidence." Lydia threw a marshmallow at him, then looked at me. "My girlfriends and I had fake IDs and daddy issues. It was bound to happen."

"You weren't eighteen?" I asked.

"Seventeen. He was late-twenties." She stuck her tongue out at Gary. "To this day, it was the best screw of my life."

Gary grabbed the arm of her chair and pulled her over in the grass. "Lies."

She wrinkled her nose, then leaned in for a kiss. "Okay, fine. Maybe second best."

I didn't know what to think. Lydia didn't seem fucked up. In fact, her easy intimacy with Gary was making me even more nostalgic than usual. Sometimes I'd sit out here alone and remember those nights at camp. Watching Lake across the campfire. Teaching her the constellations. Walking around the grounds with her in the kind of silence you could only find in the mountains.

The truck, the lake, the stars.

I missed holding Lake in my arms as much as I missed being inside her and kissing her. It occurred to me that *I* was Lake's college professor. Someone else would tease her about me the way Gary did about Lydia's shameful secret.

"You ever see the officers who arrested you out here?" Henry asked.

I hadn't noticed him wake up, and I wondered how long he'd been listening. I knew Lydia and

419

Gary's PDA would make him uncomfortable, so I shifted over to answer him. "I've spotted one while I was in town," I said. "But it's old news. I doubt he'd even recognize me."

"He might," Lydia said. "You're not a forgettable man."

"When it comes to that whole thing, I wish I were."

"Remember how you thought Bucky was involved?" Gary said. "He got fired for going through campers' stuff, so maybe you were right."

"Who's Bucky?" Henry asked.

"Camp chef who had it out for Manning for no reason," Gary said. "Weird guy."

"He had a thing for Tiffany," I said. "*That* was the reason."

"You think?" Gary asked.

"I know." I stretched my legs out in front of me. When it came to my dad or Maddy or Lake, I had a problem moving on from the past, but that wasn't the case with Tiffany. When our marriage ended, that'd been it. I didn't rehash what went wrong or how badly either of us had fucked up. Neither of us had known our last fight would be just that, but it'd been bad enough that I wouldn't forget it. Tiffany had wanted to hurt me, and if I was honest, I'd encouraged her. I'd already checked out of the marriage, and I'd needed her to realize it was over, so I'd taken all her anger in stride.

"Bucky hit on Tiffany several times that week we were up here. She told me."

"I doubt he was the only one," Gary said. "I mean, she's not *my* type, but those kids and their hormones . . ."

"Bucky wasn't a kid," I reminded him. "He was just a thirty-something creep batting outside his league. Maybe the lack of oxygen up here got to him or something, but Tiff told me he tried to kiss her the same night I was arrested."

"How?" Gary asked. "Bucky was with us. We were all drinking around the fire long after Tiffany and the underage counselors had gone to bed."

"She came looking for me right as I was leaving on the alcohol run but she ran into Bucky instead. He tried to kiss her, and when she shot him down, he told her I'd gone out to the bars to meet women."

"She never mentioned that," Lydia said.

That was because what Bucky had *actually* told Tiffany was that he'd seen her sister, Lake, getting into the truck in a skimpy outfit. Tiffany had confessed to me that she'd been more worried than angry until she'd realized that skimpy outfit had come from *her* suitcase. It'd clicked for Tiffany in that moment—Lake didn't just have a harmless crush. She'd been actively trying to seduce me away from Tiffany.

Henry scratched under his nose, looking tired. I figured it was definitely past his bedtime, but he was a detective at heart and instantly read between the lines.

"Those two got something to do with your arrest?" he asked.

"Not really." That last fight, Tiffany had needed to be pushed. On top of everything else we were dealing with, as soon as she'd admitted her involvement, she'd known we were over. "You know how Tiffany is. She was hurt that I'd left, but instead of dealing with it like a normal person, she lashed out. Bucky took her to the dining hall and they called the station to report a drunk driver on the highway. They gave him the description of Vern's truck."

Tiffany had wanted both me and Lake to get caught red-handed, but she'd never stopped to consider the kind of trouble we'd get in. For all she knew, Lake and I were having sex, which would've been a noble thing to put a stop to—if I didn't know Tiffany's reasons weren't exactly selfless.

"You passed the sobriety test, though," Henry pointed out.

"Yeah, but that cop was looking for me. If he hadn't found me on the side of the road and called it in, the police might've believed I'd gone right back to camp from the bar. Instead, they were able to place me at the bar, then driving around the neighborhood, and then nothing until almost two hours later, when I was pulled over." All this was making me crave another beer, but I was already buzzed, and I had to be up early to make a big delivery in Los Angeles. I rubbed my jaw. "Nobody knew where I was from around eleven to one in the morning. Plenty of time for a robbery."

"If not for Tiffany's phone call, your chances of getting off would've been better," Lydia said. "It's almost like she set things in motion."

If only Lydia understood how true that was. All of our actions over the years had changed the courses of our lives, but it was no more true than with Tiffany and me.

When the beer was gone and the moon was high, we stood and stumbled into the house. Gary and Lydia hadn't planned to spend the night, but I had plenty of space, so I set them up in a guest room.

Once I left them, I found Henry in the kitchen, picking up. "Leave it," I told him. "I'll get it in the morning."

He wiped his hands on a dishrag and looked around the kitchen. "I could use a cigar. You?"

I was exhausted from the beer, a long day in my workshop, and the time of night, but Henry definitely had something on his mind. He only spoke when he had something to say, so I'd listen. "Sure."

Henry didn't smoke, but since he'd been here, we'd taken to having a cigar out front some nights. I sat on a crate on the porch while Henry stood with his back against the railing and clipped two cigars. He nodded at the porch swing. "That's new since I was last here."

"It's not much. Only took me a couple days."

Some of the pieces, I hadn't planned to make. The bench had been the result of a custom order. I'd made a crib and rocking chair for a young couple expecting their first child. The night I'd finished, I'd sat and stared at the pieces in a rare moment of pride. A woman would feed her baby in that rocking chair, put him to sleep in a crib I'd made. Not a day went by that I didn't wonder about the child Tiffany had miscarried. She'd gone in for a doctor's appointment, and they'd been unable to detect a heartbeat. Apparently, the baby had died weeks earlier, but it'd felt sudden. One day we were having a baby, and the next we'd lost a boy.

The same night I'd finished my customer's nursery furniture, I'd kept building, and the result was the porch swing.

"You really put a lot of work into this place," Henry said, passing me the lighter. "Ever consider selling it?"

"You think I should *sell*?" I asked.

"Not right for such a nice place to sit here empty. Unless, of course, you had other plans for it."

I toasted the cigar, looking around the house. It meant everything to me, this place, and Henry knew it. I'd built all this with my bare hands. I'd labored over every detail from laying the foundation to installing the toilets. I'd chosen Big Bear for the space, the privacy, and if I was honest, because there was no better place to see the stars each night. "You know my plans," I said. "You've spent the last three weeks here."

"I'm not talking about your business. I see all the detail in the woodwork you've done," Henry said. "I see how painstakingly you've built this home, throwing out anything that wasn't perfect. It's true what they said about Lake."

I looked up at him, thinking I'd misheard, until it hit me that he hadn't been asleep earlier after all. "You were awake for all that," I said.

"Yeah, but it wasn't news to me." He exhaled a satisfying cloud of white smoke. "That crush, it ain't teeny tiny, is it? I saw the way you looked at her at your wedding. You wanted it to be her."

I let his words sink in. Lake had asked me what Henry was thinking at the altar, and now I understood better. Nobody who knew either Lake or myself had been able to ignore the connection between us, not even a man who'd been in our presence for a day. "Yeah," I said. "Yeah, I did want that."

"You've built a house for a family you don't have, because you only want it with her. You built this house for Lake."

I pinched my cigar with all fingers. It wasn't a shocking realization, really, but I hadn't had the guts to put it to myself that bluntly. Though Lake had been physically far away for a while, I'd kept her close during all of this. There was insurmountable evidence, though. It was an ugly but unsurprising truth—I'd spent my days building my bird a nest without knowing if she'd ever give me a chance to show it to her. And it wasn't just for Lake—it was for us.

"Guess I don't have to ask if you still love her as much now as you did back then," Henry said.

"More." I had to laugh at how sad it was. "So much more."

"So why hasn't she seen it?"

"It's not that simple," I said. "There's a history there. No way to explain it, really."

"Try." When I just looked at him, he said, "Go on, kid. Explain it to me."

"Where do I start? I've hurt her. More than once." I opened my hands. "The last time was four years ago. She and I decided to give it a shot the same week Tiffany found out she was pregnant. Then after the miscarriage and divorce, I needed time to feel like a man again. When I go back to her, it has to be as the best possible version of myself, ready to give her the best possible life."

Henry squinted in the direction of the dying campfire, then around the property. "So what's left?"

He was asking what else needed to be done before I offered Lake everything we both deserved? Would it ever be enough? I scratched my jaw, my beard growing in. I'd been so busy lately, I'd hardly had time to shave. "You've got eyes," I said. "Part of the house is still under construction. The attic needs to be completely reorganized, not to mention I haven't really furnished the smaller rooms the way I want to. Plus, I want to build that stable in the backyard—"

"What for? You don't ride."

"That's because I don't have anywhere to put horses," I said, which was a ridiculous lie. Really, I just wanted an excuse to have Lake between my legs again—if that was what Lake wanted, too—and there was plenty of space here for horseback riding. I had enough acreage for all kinds of animals, and wasn't that part of what had drawn me to Big Bear? The openness, nature, the opposite of an eight-by-six cell? The ease with which I could read the constellations each night like a good book?

Only one person could grasp why those things were important. The one who hadn't been able to see the stars at all in New York, and who might need them to light her way sometimes. The woman who deserved all the bells and whistles of a fancy kitchen just to make killer sandwiches. So, for fuck's sake, yeah, maybe all this was for Lake, and that was all the more reason it had to be perfect before I brought her here.

"It'll get there," I said to Henry. "As a man, as a builder, I will get everything as it should be. These pieces take time because they're meant to survive a lifetime."

"Son, I know that. Who do you think you're talking to? But a good amount of time's passed since the divorce." He chuckled a little. "Probably not enough. I doubt there's an appropriate amount of time to wait to move in on your ex-wife's sister. But what happens if you wait too long?"

Henry was most likely referring to someone else swooping in, but that wasn't where my mind went first. I thought back to the morning of the terrorist attacks in New York, waking up to see the Twin Towers on fire—and the gut-bursting feeling that Lake was thousands of miles away from me. Logically, I knew she had no reason to be anywhere near the Financial District, but having just moved to wide-open Big Bear, I'd felt helpless. I was dialing Lake's number before I'd even gotten a grasp on the morning news. I'd been too panicked to worry about the fact that someone else had picked up her phone, but it had set in quickly. Lake and I had spent five beautiful days in her New York, and now, at nine in the morning, another man was waking her up to hand her the phone. As soon as I'd heard she was safe, I'd hung up.

"I hear you," I said. I wasn't sure how I'd bring myself to go to Lake after all I'd put her through, but there wasn't any other way. I couldn't build her a home and never tell her. I couldn't not love her. "The day the house is finished, I'll go to her," I said. "That day, I'll bring her home."

"Huh." Henry nodded to himself. "I was wondering about that career choice of hers, thought maybe it didn't seem right, but guess I was wrong. Maybe she needs all that extravagance to be happy, just like her sister."

"She doesn't," I said quickly. Lake only needed me, the way I needed her, too.

"Then quit wasting fucking time, Manning. I'm willing to bet Lake would rather be here now, helping you turn this into a home, instead of losing another few years until you finally decide it's good enough. Isn't it good enough for her now?"

I shuffled my feet on the porch. Lake had never made me feel like what I could offer her wasn't enough. All that had come from inside me, I knew that. "I don't know," I said honestly. "I don't know if it's enough."

"You're afraid. I get it. Love my wife, and I get scared sometimes, too. Something might happen to her, or she'll wake up one day and realize she can do better." He shrugged. "Hasn't happened yet, though, and we've had a pretty good life together."

Was I afraid? There was no question. I'd better have a damn good reason to ask Lake for another chance after her trust in me had splintered over the years. If I showed her all this, and she didn't want it, I needed to know I'd done everything I could. This was my last shot. Fucking it up wasn't an option. "I've run out of chances," I said. "Our timing is shit. I can't try to get her back and fail again—everything has to be *right*. I need to get this right."

"You run out of chances when you're in the ground, understand? There some reason you wouldn't fight for her until the end?"

I looked over the top of the railing at the fire pit, where embers glowed orange. No reason I could think of. I'd tried to make it work with someone I hadn't loved, with someone who hadn't inspired in me the kind of passion that scared me, and I'd failed miserably. It was Lake or nobody. "No."

"You're a grown man, son. Fear's not a good enough excuse anymore."

Was the house enough as it was? Was *I*? Henry thought so. Lake thought so. I could give Lake what she'd been asking for since the beginning—us. Not knowing if she still wanted that made everything in my body hurt, but I couldn't let that stop me if she did want it. "Yeah," was all I said.

"Yeah," Henry agreed.

When we'd smoked down our cigars and gone back inside, I started to turn out the lights in the kitchen.

Henry stopped and turned around in the doorway. "You never really had a fair shot at the family thing," he said. "Everything that happened with Madison and your parents messing you over, it's tragic, Manning. Really unfortunate. And then the miscarriage. It really breaks my heart."

My throat got dry enough to make me cough into my fist. Henry had lived all that with me. He didn't need to acknowledge it, but hearing it from him struck something deep in me. I could comprehend now, as an older man, that a lot of that stuff had happened *to* me—not because I'd done something wrong. If I'd lost a son years ago when I'd constantly blamed myself for things out of my control, I wasn't sure I'd have recovered. "I know."

"You deserve a family, and you shouldn't have to wait anymore."

I couldn't answer him for the lump in my throat. My last contact with my dad had been the letters I'd received in jail a decade earlier. Henry was the only person looking out for me. I didn't have to tell him he was my family, so I just nodded.

"I want to see you as a husband and a father as much as I want my own kid's happiness. Stop punishing yourself, and stop punishing Lake. You go be the man she needs, you hear?"

Between Lake's age and my marriage and prison and losing a son and Corbin—there'd been a lot in our way, but Henry was right; it'd stolen the spotlight for too long. Our timing had never been right, so why *not* now? I looked up at the roof I'd built to put over Lake's head, at the dining chairs I'd constructed out of reclaimed wood from this very forest where I'd fallen in love with her, and at the countertop I'd sanded and smoothed until it was just the perfect height for Lake to sit and have me stand between her legs. And I finally made the decision.

I wouldn't wait any longer to find Lake and bring her home.

6
LAKE

My agent did her best to chase me down the studio lot. June McPherson was a powerhouse, barely five-foot-four in her highest heels, but she couldn't compete with my trusty old Converse. I slowed to let her catch up.

"You're making a mistake," she panted, doubled over to catch her breath. "Just like running in these shoes was."

I looked down at her. "I told you my plan before we entered the meeting."

"And I told *you* the producers would throw more money at you. I thought once we got in there, you'd cave, not turn it down." She squinted up at me, hand on her side, then rose to her full height. "The salary wasn't life changing, I admit, but you can still do lots with it. And the real money comes later." She dug around in her purse and pulled out her compact as she added, "You'd be able to find homes for all those scrappy dogs and cats you're always talking about."

Thinking I could raise awareness was partly how I'd gotten into this mess. I'd been able to work the animal shelter into my "storyline" on the reality show, and get photographed there by the press, but that wasn't enough of a reason to stay beyond my contractual obligation. "I'll find other ways to help," I said.

"You're sure?" She checked that no strands had come loose from her sleek ponytail, then snapped the mirror shut. "You're really going to let something like job satisfaction get in the way of fame?"

She was teasing, but I knew this wasn't easy for her to joke about. I was becoming one of her most sought-after clients, and I was about to flush it down the toilet. Or I already had. "I'm sorry, June. I'm just not cut out for reality TV."

She nodded a little. "Then I'll find you something else. Something better. You've got a special quality, Lake. You deserve a movie deal, today's hottest director, top billing . . ."

I stopped listening, because I'd heard all this from her before, and it still didn't excite me. Being on stage back in New York was the closest I'd come to feeling like a true actress. From auditioning to improv classes to mounds of rejection, I'd been forced to come out of my shell, grow up, and start making decisions for myself. And my decision was that I needed more than the network had to offer—and maybe even Hollywood in general. I hadn't felt as if I'd done anything meaningful since I'd left New York. Even in high school, I'd belonged to clubs and extracurricular activities that'd given me a sense of purpose. I wasn't sure if I was done with acting forever, but as far as Hollywood was concerned, once my contract with the show was up, I'd be grounding a career that hadn't even launched.

I started for the parking lot again. "I'm going to take a step back from all of it," I told June. "Not just the show."

Her Jimmy Choos clacked along the faux cobblestones of a movie set modeled after New York. "Good. Go up to Napa Valley for a few weeks—take some time for yourself. I don't want you to get overwhelmed. You saw what happened with Sean. Thank God you're no longer associated with him."

Sean and I had broken up months ago, right before he'd gotten caught wasted on camera leaving a club on his motorcycle. The American public had not taken kindly to his drinking and riding, and he'd been shipped off to Arizona for rehab.

Celebrity gossip had become an industry unto itself. Paparazzi was expected at movie premieres and outside of the clubs we frequented, but extravagant cameras had been popping up during my morning run or while doing mundane things like getting coffee. I didn't understand the fascination but some magazines, and even a few websites, were solely dedicated to celebrity culture.

As June and I neared the edge of New York and headed toward what looked like a set for a Louisiana swamp, I looked across the lot and just like that, there he was—Manning unloading furniture from the back of a truck. He was so familiar yet so out of place that I stumbled and June had to steady me.

"What's wrong?" she asked, stopping as I did.

Manning lifted what looked like a blanketed loveseat from the bed, carried it onto a soundstage, and returned with two other men, who helped him with a long wooden table.

"Lake?" June asked, craning her neck to see what I was looking at.

The morning sun shone through the buildings, creating hard lines of shade and light, a relatively cool day for mid-August. Frozen to the spot, I was unsure of what to do. Did he want to see me? Did I want to see him? My reflex was to answer *yes*, but the question was wrong. I needed to be asking if I *should* see him.

Five years after New York, eleven since I'd met him on an entirely different lot, and here we were all over again. After my conversation with Corbin on Val's patio almost a year earlier, I'd been forced to accept that Manning and I wouldn't happen. Since then, it'd become clear that having hope all these years had hurt rather than helped me. I'd considered him in decisions I should've made only for myself. He'd been on my mind as I'd boarded an airplane out of New York for good, when I'd debuted on TV, and even when I'd turned down my contract just now. He'd sat in on all my first dates, and the last ones, too, and I was exhausted. Manning was always in the way, no matter where I was or what I was doing.

I'd finally given up on destiny, on the stubborn stars, and on the idea of *us*, but by the way my heart raced, it was clear I still hadn't been able to let go of Manning—not completely. Back then, I would've seen this random meeting as fate bringing us together. Now, all I could wonder was . . .

Did I walk toward him or away?

Manning took a bandana from his back pocket. As he wiped his temples, he paused, turned, and looked right at me. Of course he'd felt me staring, and he stared right back. June continued to try and get my attention, the men moved dining chairs around Manning, and an American flag flapped overhead, but we just stood there, neither of us making a move. Was this it, what it'd all come down to? Passing each other by, keeping a safe distance, so nobody would get hurt again?

Apparently, Manning had the same hesitation about me that I had about him. Maybe he was also trying to get his life back on track. Or had he moved on long ago? Maybe those were selfish questions considering he'd been through a miscarriage and a divorce since I'd last seen him. They were the reasons

I'd never reached out, but why hadn't he? It was possible I was nothing more to him now than a painful reminder of the past.

But then he shoved the bandana in his back pocket and without another moment of hesitation, he started in my direction. I was sixteen, eighteen, twenty-two again, unable to move or think or do anything but watch him come toward me.

My palms sweat. He commanded eyes as he crossed the lot, but his stayed trained on me and mine on him. He was older, darker, and determined. I was different. I'd lived on another planet the past year and a half, where people expected great things from me that I hadn't been sure I could deliver. I wasn't his immaculate, bright-eyed girl anymore. And to me, he was no longer my Manning, just the man I'd loved and lost.

By the time he reached me, I still hadn't thought of a coherent thing to say. "Lake," he said.

My name from his mouth calmed me. This *was* my Manning—in some ways, he always would be. With him, I didn't have to be anyone other than myself. "What are you doing?" I asked. Unable to imagine any scenario in which Manning would be at a Hollywood studio, I dumbly added, "Are you here for me?"

He laughed. "No. Well, not yet. I didn't plan on seeing you, I mean."

My agent shoved her way between us. "June McPherson."

He wiped his palm on his jeans and took her outstretched hand. "Manning . . . Sutter."

"I'm not familiar," she said. "Who are you with?"

"With?" he asked.

"He's not an actor," I said, smiling at Manning's obvious discomfort. "Can you give us a minute, June?"

"Sure, but just one. We've got a photo shoot across town at noon." She took out a business card and forced it into Manning's palm. "You have something. A special quality. Call me if you're looking for representation."

I frowned at her. Of course, *I* thought Manning had a special something, but she'd told me the same thing not ten minutes ago. How many people had that supposedly elusive *quality*?

As Manning watched June walk away, I had a moment to take him in. He hadn't shaven recently, and his hair was a tad longer than he normally wore it—at least, when I'd known him. Conversely, my hair was a little shorter. The producers wouldn't let me wear it any other way than long and blonde, but I'd chopped a couple inches and added a few rebellious lowlights.

With a light breeze, his hair rustled, and a few of my strands blew into my face. He looked back at me as I pulled them from my lip gloss. "I'm delivering furniture," he said to my mouth. He reached in his shirt pocket, but rubbed his chest instead, returning his eyes to mine. "What about you?"

"I'm on a TV show," I said.

A smile spread over his face. "I know that, Lake. I meant why are you *here*, at the studio? This isn't reality TV."

"Oh." My face heated. I wasn't sure if I was glad or embarrassed that he'd been following my career. This wasn't the life I'd described to Manning way back when. To everyone else, the center of a Hollywood tornado was a coveted spot, but he'd probably already figured out the truth—the attention stifled me. "I had a meeting with the producers about my contract."

"Yeah?" He leaned in. "What about it?"

I didn't want to talk about it. My life had been splashed across the small screen the last year, and it made me uncomfortable that Manning might've been watching. He'd have seen all the fabricated drama between Corbin, Sean, and me. My audition for a commercial for which I'd been passed over. My genuine tears one night when I'd hugged Birdy, missing Manning more than usual, lying to Bree that I was upset over Sean's latest antics. "It's nothing. Did you build the furniture you're delivering?" I asked hopefully.

"Yeah. A midcentury dining set for some show that takes place in the fifties." He scratched the back of his neck. "It's what I do now. For a living."

My heart squeezed with pride. It felt like a personal victory, hearing he was pursuing what he loved, and I hoped I'd had something to do with it. "No more suits?" I asked.

"No more suits."

"Is it just movie sets?" I wanted to know everything. "Do you have a store?"

"Nah. Usually just custom furniture for people's homes. I have a workshop and deliver the pieces myself, but this was a special project. Henry helped some . . ." He cracked his knuckles. "It's funny to see you, actually. Weird. Because we were talking about you just last night."

"You and Henry?"

"And Gary and Lydia—"

"Oh, yeah, cool." Trying to cover up my shock at hearing another woman's name, words caught in my throat, and I coughed. Why should I be surprised? Four years was a long time to be single. For a man like Manning, who surely had women fawning over him, it was an eternity. What if he'd found someone he loved more than me? Someone more compatible, less complicated? Did I want that for him if it was what I needed to finally find a way forward without him?

With a heavy heart, I asked, "Is Lydia your . . ."

He raised his eyebrows. "Gary's wife. You've met Lydia."

"Oh." I should've been relieved, but the thought of him with someone else had already lodged itself in my brain. In my heart. Another reminder of just how large Manning still stood on my horizon, blocking everything else out. I just nodded. "Right."

"They were all at the house last night."

"The house?" I asked.

He inhaled through his nose, squinting over my head. I got the feeling he was going to say he had somewhere to be . . . as if this, us, was no longer important to him. Maybe it wasn't. Corbin had moved on. Why wouldn't Manning, too? That's what I'd been trying to do.

"I built a house," he said finally.

Perfect. That was how it felt to hear him say that, as if it'd been his destiny all along. For Manning, no regular house would do. He needed to be the one to create it. As happy as it made me to hear that, a small part of me couldn't help the regret seeping in—for all the things I'd missed, for the home I didn't have, and the one I'd once wanted with him. "I'd like to see that one day," I said.

"Yeah," he said, nodding, and then he shook his head, as if he'd changed his mind. "Today. Come see it today."

My answering laugh was nervous, and I worried he could read the tension in my body. I hated feeling stiff around him, one of the few people who expected nothing of me but for me to be myself. "Sure," I said.

"Lake?" he said, rubbing his scruffy jaw. "I'm serious. Come by the house tonight."

I should've known he wasn't kidding. Manning was nothing if not *serious*. He was a man of few words, and he didn't say what he didn't mean. I was definitely curious about the house, but if anything, that was a reason not to see it. Even now, my wounds were still a little too open. "I don't know if I can," I said.

"Why not?"

Did I have to say the reason out loud? I couldn't go see Manning's house because it would kill me a little inside. Because he'd broken my heart. Because we had a past we couldn't ignore. Now that I was *moving myself on*, fate chose to intervene by bringing us together on a replica of a New York street in the middle of Los Angeles. Well, wasn't that just like fate to be too late? "Because I have somewhere to be," I said.

"So go be there, and then come over for dinner. For all the times you fed me, let me return the favor."

My breath hitched. We'd been hungry together, and we'd fed each other—at what point would we have our fill? When did I get to be whole again? "I really shouldn't."

"Why not? I need a real reason, Lake. We can eat late if—"

"I'm over you."

Oh, God. I couldn't believe I'd said that, to him of all people. And my voice hadn't even wavered, although I realized I was fidgeting with my purse strap.

Slowly, he raised his eyebrows. "You are?"

"Yes." That time, my voice did falter a little, so I cleared my throat.

He cocked his head, looking almost . . . amused? Maybe I shouldn't have assumed there was anything to this but dinner. "How do you know if you haven't seen me in years?" he asked.

"Because I had no choice." I glanced at the ground, but forced myself to look him in the eye. "I've worked really hard to move on, Manning."

"How?" Again, he sounded more interested than upset.

"I got rid of the box you gave me, and Birdy, too," I said. It was only partially true—they were packed away in storage, but that was a definite step forward.

"Those are things," he said.

"All right." Since he asked, I told him. There was no point in pretending everything was fine, not with him. I released my purse strap, crossing my arms into myself. "I don't look for Summer Triangle anymore, and if you want the truth, I could never really find it."

"They're just three regular stars, Lake, nothing much to see." He patted the back of his shoulder. "If you need them, you can always find them here."

"Always?" The hair on the back of my neck prickled. Instead of dwelling, I'd forced Manning out of my mind frequently the past year. Ironically, I hadn't opened my eyes this morning as I had many times before and thought—*maybe today Manning will come for me.* "Because I *did* need them," I said, "and they weren't there."

"No you didn't," he said. "You did just fine on your own. Look at you. You even moved on." I bit my bottom lip just as he added, "But I didn't. And I think I know why. You and I never got any closure."

I let my mouth part. I'd thought the exact same thing. Though Manning and I had said goodbye in a hotel room almost five years earlier, I hadn't ever been able to shake the feeling that he was mine. And part of me had still hoped after the divorce, he'd come back for me. "I agree."

"So let's have it," he said. "Dinner, drinks, and closure."

Closure. The end. The idea of it seared through me. It brought to the surface all the pain and heartache and love I associated with Manning. Suffering that I wanted to stop—for good. I needed to snip that last thread of hope, the invisible tether between us, and maybe Manning had the scissors at his house.

"You got a pen?" he asked.

I looked over my shoulder. June was getting restless, tapping her foot and then her watch when she saw me looking. I rummaged through my purse, hardly able to believe Manning and I were just going to sit and have a civilized meal, no buffer, no obstacles between us. I gave him a pen I'd taken from the producers' office. He glanced over the network's logo before scribbling directions and an address on the back of June's card.

"That contract thing," he said, "did you already sign it?"

"No."

"Ah." He handed me the card. "Can you read that?"

"I think so. Take the two-ten freeway about an hour and a—wait." I drew back, squinting at his handwriting. "Where do you live?"

"Big Bear."

I looked up at the uncharacteristic cheerfulness in his voice. "*Big Bear*?" I asked. The same place we'd both been hurt? Where he'd been taken away by the cops while I'd stood by, helpless? Where I'd watched my sister leave for a special dinner with him? He'd made me fall in love with him in Big Bear, and he'd broken me over and over since then. "Why would you buy a house there?"

"Not buy. Build." He glanced behind me. "I'll tell you all about it over dinner. So just follow those directions until you see my mailbox. It's white. Well, so is everyone else's, but I don't have a neighbor for a quarter mile, but come to think of it, my address isn't posted anywhere, so I'll paint a red stripe on it. Just in case. That's how you'll know."

I didn't know what to say. I hadn't realized I was agreeing to an entire evening in the equally terrifying and peaceful mountains, away from everyone else, just us. "You don't need to paint your mailbox for me."

He paused and then laughed. Actually laughed, as if I'd made some kind of joke. Shaking his head, he backed away. "You have no idea what you're in for, Birdy. See you tonight."

My stomach fluttered. Maybe that's where my wings had been hiding all these years? "Wait. Manning?"

"Don't try to get out of it, Lake." He arched an eyebrow. "If you don't show, there'll be no closure, and then I'll have no choice but to come looking for you."

As much as I wanted to believe that, I didn't anymore. I just sighed. "I was going to ask what time."

"Whenever," he said. "As soon as you're ready, come to me."

7
LAKE

Manning had gone and painted his mailbox for me—just so I wouldn't get lost. Only it wasn't a stripe like he'd said, but a wobbly red triangle. In the middle of August, the Summer Triangle had found *me* instead of the other way around. All during the drive, I'd wondered what kind of home he'd built for himself here. If I knew Manning, it'd be a sturdy, no-frills house. Remembering the few pieces of furniture of his I'd seen, and my cherished jewelry box, I hoped there was a lot of wood involved. Manning's hands could turn raw wood to perfection—and me to mush.

Manning had found his calling, while I had just found—what? Was a sense of acceptance the best I could hope for? I wanted for myself the same peace he'd seemed to have this morning, but I'd gotten lost along the way. Up until I'd made the decision to turn down the contract, I couldn't help feeling I'd been biding time, waiting for Manning until I could start my life. I'd fallen for him, run to and from him, longed and mourned for him, and where had *I* been during all that?

Leaving the show was the first difficult step I'd made toward happiness in a while. Tonight would be the second. It would hurt, but I'd finally let go of Manning to allow for a life that'd always centered around him. Maybe that had always been Manning's purpose, and the sum of our experiences over the years—he'd helped shape me into my own woman instead of someone else's.

I slowed the car and turned when I reached the mailbox. Manning was right that he had lots of space and no immediate neighbors. A thicket of trees lined the driveway. I'd rolled down the window once I'd entered the mountains, and the air smelled of pine and dirt and 1993.

When the house came into view, I held in a gasp. It was just how I'd imagined except bigger, a kind of rustic yet modern resort glowing with amber light. The honey-colored cabin had a sprawling wraparound porch, large glass windows, and a stone chimney. Big, dark, and comforting, it pulled me in, both exhilarating and calming me. It was impossible to look away from, raw and rough on the outside while exuding warmth. This home was all Manning in every way.

I parked along a patch of grass and turned off the engine. There were stacks of wood off to one side by what looked like an unfinished picnic table. Camping chairs surrounded a fire pit out front. He'd parked his truck in front of the garage and beyond that was a warehouse-looking space that appeared to be closed up for the night.

I got the acute sense that this should've been my life. And wasn't that why I'd come, to stop this persistent feeling of incompleteness? A half-finished love sat heavy in my chest. I hadn't even seen Manning yet, and already, I ached. How could I spend an evening here and leave it all at the end? That question might've been enough to get me to turn the car around, except that I'd already walked away twice before, and I still hadn't been able to reclaim my life. I needed to tell him we were done. I needed to see with my own eyes that whatever we'd once had was gone so I could walk forward on the path he'd been blocking for over a decade.

Manning came through the screen door, walked over to the car, and leaned his hands on the hood to look through the open window. "Well, here's a sight I never thought I'd see. Finally got your license."

I laughed. There wasn't anything funny about it, but I was nervous. "You have to have one in L.A."

He glanced around. "Too bad it's an automatic. You know how to drive a stick?"

"What do you think?"

"'Course you don't." He winked. "Probably never dated a man who could handle a manual transmission."

I relaxed back in my seat with his teasing, staring up at him. I was sure I wore that old look on my face that always betrayed my feelings for him. I never seemed to be able to help that around him. "Did I get here too early?"

"Just a few months," he said, "but I guess that's life."

"Months?" I asked. "You mean minutes. If dinner's not ready, I can help."

He opened the car door and checked me out. "Come on and help then, cowgirl."

I couldn't help blushing. I'd borrowed Val's Steve Madden cowboy boots to pair with a denim skirt and light sweater. I took the keys from the ignition, got my purse, and slid out. "The house is beautiful."

"Thing is, it's not completely done yet," he said as we walked up the drive. "I thought I'd have more time before you saw it. There's a lot more I want to do."

What he was saying didn't quite make sense, but maybe he was just as edgy as I was. He'd never been all that great at small talk.

"Oh, wait," I said, stopping. "I left the window down. I should lock up the car."

"Nothing to worry about out here." He placed a hand on my upper back, urging me along. "Well," he added, squeezing my shoulder, "except maybe wildlife. I know you get a little nervous about those bears."

Goosebumps slid down my spine, hardening my nipples. Manning's hand on me had been many things over the years—restrained, curious, soothing, hungry. But it always elicited a reaction, no matter what.

Because he was looking at me, he almost stumbled on the first step to the porch. I reached out to steady him, smiling, and decided to just break the ice for us both. "Maybe the bear's the one who's nervous."

He laughed a little, wiping his palms on his jeans. "Maybe I am."

Now that I was closer to him, I smelled the soap and aftershave, the freshness of his laundry detergent. Even his hair looked trimmed since this morning. He'd gotten ready for me, and if I was honest, I'd known my cowgirl outfit wouldn't go without comment from him.

We climbed the stairs to the porch, and by the door was a swing for two. "Did you make that?" I asked.

"Yep."

It was charming and unexpected—and it could've probably used a cushion, but I kept that to myself and followed him inside. The entryway's wood floors creaked under my boots. He hung my purse on a hook over a credenza.

"That's the dining room," he said, pointing into a large open space off the entry. A solid oak table with a live edge centered the room, while the iron chandelier overhead lit the swirl of the grain, the marbling of light and dark wood. Large windows showcased the front yard. Each piece looked perfectly placed, exhibiting an attention to detail Manning only gave the things he cared about. At the same time, the table wasn't set, and between the bare walls and floor, he was missing a rug or some art to warm up the area.

I stepped in for a better look, but he called me away. "In here's the kitchen," he said, leading us in the opposite direction and bypassing the entrance to a hall.

I stopped in the doorway—I had to in order to take it all in. The kitchen had high ceilings, a sprawling center island, restaurant-style ranges flanked by prep and clean-up stations, and a farmhouse sink. Amber wood cabinets puzzled together, different shapes and sizes, as if they'd been crafted for certain things. I supposed maybe they had, since Manning had built this kitchen himself.

"Wow," I said. "You really went all out."

"I asked for the best."

"But you don't even cook." Next to a French-door, stainless steel refrigerator was a small cooler just for wine. "And you don't drink wine," I added as my eyes landed on some steaks marinating in a dish on the counter. Then again, I didn't know as much about him as I used to. "Do you?"

"No."

"Then why all this?" I asked, opening the refrigerator. He'd stocked it with all kinds of things— most notably, a telling combination of deli meats, sauces, and cheeses. "Oh, Manning. You're so busted."

"Am I?" he asked, and I turned at the hopefulness in his voice. "Bust me, Lake."

"You've been making the Lake Special."

"Ah. Right." He glanced away, scratching under his chin. "Don't worry, I wouldn't. Not without you."

I closed the refrigerator. "Why are there four steaks?" I asked. Maybe this kitchen wasn't for him, because someone else had made her stamp here. Maybe *she'd* done the food shopping, made his sandwiches, picked out place settings. Was that who he'd installed the wine cooler for? And why he seemed nervous, because he had to tell me about her? "Is someone else coming tonight?"

"Someone else?" he asked. "Are you fucking kidding? It's just you and me, Lake. I wanted to make sure we had enough to eat and steak is the only dinner I really know how to make all that well."

I smiled to myself. I should've known. Always overly cautious. Always thinking of me. Well, I'd thought of him, too. "I brought a bottle of this really nice bourbon. I forget the name. It's a housewarming gift, but I left it in the car."

"I've got a fully stocked bar in the next room." He went to a pantry and took out a bottle of red. "What've I told you? Don't worry about me, Lake. Tonight is about you." He passed me the wine. "The woman at the market said you might like Cabernet Sauvignon with the meal, but I bought others in case you don't."

I held the wine like a trophy. It was a stupid thing to get teary-eyed over, so I pretended to read the label. He'd bought me wine. Why should I be surprised? I'd brought him something special, too, after all. And I realized what he'd meant when he'd said tonight was about me. This was, in a way, a celebration of who we'd become. I was twenty-seven now, but it wasn't just about numbers. Manning had clearly made a wonderful life for himself, and I was on my own path to the same. Tomorrow we'd go back to our lives, but tonight was about me, and him, too.

"Don't cry, Birdy," he said. "It's just wine."

I inhaled back the threat of tears, took a deep breath, and was about to ask for a corkscrew when my stomach grumbled. I put a hand over it. "Sorry. Is it too early to eat?"

"Depends on if you're trying to rush things." He took back the bottle. "I still have to give you the tour, but we can do that after dinner . . . long as you're not planning to dine and dash on me."

"You heard my stomach just now," I said. "Let's do the tour after."

456

He got an opener from a drawer and worked the cork out while I tried not to stare at his flexing biceps. Eleven years after I'd met him, at thirty-four years old, Manning was stronger and more at ease with himself than I'd ever seen him. He'd obviously shaved for tonight, but this morning, he'd had enough scruff to make me wonder if he ever grew out his beard, which then made me wonder if he went and chopped the wood for his furniture himself. I could see my bear in the woods, an axe over his shoulder.

"Lake?" he said.

"Hmm?"

"I asked why you're so hungry." He got a wineglass from a cupboard. "You're not a starving artist anymore, I wouldn't think."

"No, but I do have to watch my figure."

He laughed, then looked over his shoulder at me. "That was a joke . . . wasn't it?"

"I'm on TV, Manning. I don't starve myself or anything, I just can't pig out whenever I want."

He turned to face me. "How would you feel if I said that?" he asked. "That I didn't eat whenever I was hungry?"

Manning knew right where my mind would go with that question. He loved to eat. I loved to watch him eat. The times we'd been unable to communicate with words, it was one of the only ways I could satisfy him. Feed him. Fill him. Love him. I looked at my hands. "I didn't say that. Believe me, I'm better about my diet than other actresses I know—I eat three meals a day."

He looked as though he wanted to say more, but he just picked up the plate of meat. "You want to make a salad while I fire up the grill?"

"Coming right up," I said, grateful for the chance to help. I chose ingredients from the refrigerator. Manning had thought of everything; it was like shopping in a mini supermarket. I took my time making a salad that wasn't too dry, something flavorful he'd like that would complement the steak. I sipped what turned out to be very good wine and poked around the kitchen, opening drawers and cabinets. Left to his own devices, what kind of things did Manning buy for himself? His dishes were white, but like his silverware, some mismatched pieces had snuck in and he had an odd number of drinking glasses. That didn't surprise me too much. I had a hard time picturing him shopping around Target or Bed Bath and Beyond. Everything had its place. He only had what he needed; nothing had been crammed in. In one corner stood a beautiful, shoulder-high, standalone cabinet, but even that sat empty.

In the last drawer I opened, I found an *Us Weekly* with my picture on it. It opened directly to a page about my love life, as if Manning had read it more than once. He probably had—if our roles were reversed, those pages would be crinkled with dried tears.

I took the salad bowl and a Heineken out to the grill. He'd dragged the half-finished picnic table over, so I set everything down next to some dishes and silverware and handed him the beer. He popped the top on the corner of the barbeque.

"Can I help with anything else?" I asked.

"Yeah. Sit and drink your wine. It'll help me relax. But careful for splinters," he added quickly, avoiding my eyes. "Haven't sealed that table yet and you've got on that . . . skirt."

Suppressing a smile at his sudden bashfulness, I sat facing the wrong way on the bench so I could watch him cook. "This Cab is really good," I said.

"Oh yeah? Don't you celebrities get the best of the best, though?"

Knowing Manning had picked this out just for me made it the best. "I saw the *Us Weekly* in your kitchen," I said.

"Someone gave it to me." He shrugged, a beer in one hand, tongs in the other. "Not my favorite thing in the world, reading all that stuff about you, but I can't seem to trash it. Were those your, ah, dogs?"

"*My* dogs? No. I wish." I swirled my wine. "They were from the shelter."

"Mutts," he muttered.

I realized maybe he wasn't asking about the dogs but the "pack," as the press had idiotically labeled my suitors since I was often photographed around the shelter. "I can't have pets. Some days I'm out of the house twelve hours, and I also have to be able to travel on short notice."

"Sounds tiring," he said.

"It is. L.A. exhausts me."

"More than New York?"

"New York was tiring in a different way. Here in Los Angeles, I have to be 'on' all the time. I have to act. It's so shiny and perfect, not at all like New York."

"Not everywhere in L.A.'s like that," he said. "Just what you've grown accustomed to. You showed me your New York, maybe sometime I'll show you my L.A."

I hadn't forgotten that Manning had grown up in Pasadena. Sometimes at night, I'd try to convince myself he'd moved back there, close to me, except that he'd told me before he'd never go back. "But you hate it there."

He flipped the steaks. "There are a lot of different parts to the city. I don't hate all of it. But the truth is, I'd like to take you to Pasadena. Show you where I grew up . . . where Maddy and I grew up."

I stared at his back, unsure how to respond. Returning to his childhood home wasn't something I'd ever pictured him doing, let alone with me. "When's the last time you were there?"

"My parents' house? Fifteen." He plated the meat and brought it to the table. "Enough about me. Tell me about you."

I turned on the bench as he sat across from me. "What about me?"

He cut into the steak. "Just tell me about your life. Good and bad."

I knew what he wanted to hear. Over a decade ago we'd sat at my parents' kitchen table eating steak. All I'd wanted then was him, and all he'd wanted was for me to soar. I had the urge to tell Manning I was doing just that. Not to spite him, but because he wanted it so badly for me. It was almost as if some weight would be lifted from him if I'd just tell him that I was happy.

"I don't even know where to start," I said. "It's a lot to cover in one night."

Head cocked, he'd been about to finish off his beer. He seemed to think a moment before he said, "Start with your family."

"I saw Tiffany last year, and it went okay. Not great, but she came to my job recently."

He swigged the last of his drink and set the bottle down. "The reality show?"

"No. On the show, I have a job at a bar, so she came for a drink. She'll probably be on an episode."

He half-rolled his eyes. "She must be thrilled."

"Yup." I put my elbows on the table. "My mom and I talk, but there's a still a distance between us that'll always exist as long as I'm not speaking to Dad."

"I saw you're wearing your bracelet again. Does that mean you're thinking of reconciling?"

Not that I wanted to make up with my father, but I did wish it could be another way. There was just too much anger and pride between us. "No," I said. "Did you know about his affair?"

"Yeah," he said. "Should I have told you in New York?"

If he had or hadn't, I couldn't imagine things would've turned out differently. It bothered me that Tiffany had compared me to our father, but knowing about my dad's cheating would've only made me feel guiltier during my time with Manning. I scratched under my nose. "It wouldn't have changed anything."

"Didn't think so." He nodded to my plate. "Eat, Lake."

"Oh." I picked up my fork and knife and finally took a juicy, flavorful bite. "I thought you said you couldn't cook."

"Doesn't mean I can't grill." He grinned. "How about work?"

I set down my silverware and took a moment to appreciate the taste of steak prepared just for me. Manning sat across from me, so real. If I was honest, this was one of the happiest moments I'd had in a really long time. Manning made me happy, but he'd made me unhappy more. "I quit," I said.

"You quit the show?" he asked.

"Well, I still have a year left on my contract, but that's what my meeting was about this morning. I don't want to commit to a third season."

He leaned on the table, eyeing me. "Why not?"

"I think back to that time you came to visit in New York. I was struggling and auditioning and bitching to my friends about the unfairness of the industry, but back then, when I got a part, it meant something. I miss that, even though I know, I *know* it sounds stupid."

"You have to give me more credit," he said. "You know that not once in my life have your thoughts ever sounded stupid to me."

I did know that. It felt good to admit to him I'd taken some wrong turns over the years without worrying he'd blame himself or feel compelled to fix my problems. I'd already begun to fix them myself. I was more concerned about what it meant that he'd stopped eating halfway through a meal. "Your steak is getting cold," I pointed out.

He picked up his fork again. "And how do you feel now, on the show?" he asked.

"A little like a wind-up doll. They point me in whatever direction they want and tell me to *go*."

"Well." He chewed and swallowed his steak. "That won't do."

"So many people told me it was the opportunity of a lifetime, but when I saw myself on TV, I didn't feel good about it. I wasn't proud."

"So you can be now. It takes a lot of guts to walk away from something like that."

I nodded. "As soon as I left the meeting it felt as though a weight had been lifted."

"Then it was the right decision."

I released a breath, relieved, as if I'd been waiting to hear what Manning would make of the situation. It was a good thing I'd already turned down the contract, because I would've hated for his last impression of me to be that I was doing something I didn't care about. "Yes, it was."

"So what'll you do now?"

I stuck my chin in my hand. Val and I had been talking about a trip to Europe once she had some time off. "I have some money saved. I think I might travel a little."

With his last bite, he slid his plate away. "You should. We both should."

We could go together, I wanted to say. *Remember architecture in Barcelona? Playhouses in London?* Instead, I patted my mouth with my napkin. "We'll see. I've actually made other plans that might interfere."

"Yeah?" He took a few uneven breaths. "What . . . plans?"

It was hard to believe after all this time, Manning and I were just having dinner and conversation. We were the same people but different, in a place that was the same but different. Physically and emotionally. I was saying things I'd only just begun to discover about myself. "I wonder a lot about what it would've been like if I'd gone to USC. I think at the end, before I left, I'd convinced myself that being a doctor or lawyer or businesswoman was what *Dad* wanted, not me. But I actually didn't know. I ran away to get back at all of you. I would've made a good doctor. Or lawyer. Or businesswoman."

"I agree," he said. "But you're great at whatever you set your mind to."

Manning truly believed that, and I thought the same of him. "I've been giving all that a lot of thought, and I think I decided what's next." I took another bite and smiled. "Are you ready for this?"

"All my life." He narrowed his eyes playfully. "Tell me what you're meant to do."

"I'm going back to school." My heart rate kicked up a notch anticipating his reaction. "To be a veterinarian."

He laughed. "Well, well. Lake Dolly Kaplan."

I scowled hearing my full name, but I couldn't help the grin that broke through. "What? Why are you looking at me like that?"

"Like what? This is my unsurprised face."

"You knew all along?"

"No," he said, "but hearing you say it, it feels good. Feels right."

"I thought the same thing when you told me about the furniture." I smiled, sticking my hands between my knees. "I don't know where I'll go to school yet, but at least it's a start."

As he grew quiet, and I finished my wine, I sensed a shift in him. He'd just laughed, and that was kind of rare, so most likely, he was transitioning into Serious Manning now to overcompensate. After a few moments, he asked, "You wouldn't stay here for school?"

"I don't know. I can go anywhere." I looked over at the palace Manning had built. "I don't have anything like this. It's just me."

"Do you want all this?" he asked. "Would it make you happy? When you close your eyes like we did that night we made snow angels, where's home?"

I inhaled deeply through my nose, shut my eyes, and waited for home to reveal itself. But only the afterimage of the lit-up house glowed yellow behind my lids. I saw Manning's home, and then I saw Manning.

Manning was all I saw.

All I'd ever seen.

I kept it to myself. We weren't in that place anymore. I'd learned a lot of things over the years, and one was that it wasn't always fair to tell him how I felt. Another was that none of us were guaranteed anything in this life—especially true happiness. Why should I have it? Why had I thought, all those years ago, I deserved it? And at the expense of those who loved me? I opened my eyes.

Manning, as always, was watching me closely. "You all right?" he asked.

"That last day, in the hotel . . ." I said, turning the wineglass on the table. "Did I do the right thing, telling you to go back to her?"

Poor Manning looked completely caught off guard by the question. He sat back on the bench. "I . .

. yeah, Lake. Yeah, you did. I mean, I understood why."

"I'm so sorry about what happened, the . . ." I took a deep breath. Manning had to have been devastated over losing a baby, but it hadn't been my time to be there for him. "The miscarriage."

He dropped his eyes to my hand, watching as I fidgeted with my drink. "I know you are."

"I wish I'd told you sooner, I just couldn't. I couldn't face you after we'd planned a life together that never happened. You'd been through so much heartache, and then the divorce—I didn't know where I stood, or if you still believed we could work."

After a few moments, he reached across the table, covered my hand, and looked up at me. "You know what I believe?"

I fought the urge to flip my palm up and braid our fingers together in such a way that it'd be impossible to undo before the night was over. "What?"

"No matter how things had gone, you and I would still be sitting here tonight."

"Really?" I asked, my throat thick. "You think this is a kind of twisted destiny for us?"

"I don't know about all that," he said, "but it's what I believe. It's what I know. We were *both* kids, Lake. We made mistakes, and choices, and it took us a while, but I think all paths lead to here."

Where was here? A fork in the road where we separated for good? A last goodbye? "You seem happy," I said to him.

He looked at his plate. "How so?"

"You just have this calmness about you," I said. "Not like in New York."

"You think I wasn't happy in New York?" He ran his thumb over the clasp of my bracelet. "Those were the best days of my life."

My eyes watered remembering how he'd stood across a snowy street in the East Village, waiting for me to show up at my apartment. It'd been a whirlwind few days. Looking back, I could admit the red flags I'd willfully ignored along with Val's warnings. Maybe Manning and I had each subconsciously known it wouldn't last, and that had made us feverish. "This is different. It's like you have it all figured out. I guess maybe it's the business and the house."

"You like it?" he asked, and I detected a hint of uncertainty in his voice.

"I *love* it. Everything about it. It's a—" I wanted to say *home*, but it wasn't that for me, and that made acknowledging it too hard. "It's you. Masculine but comfortable. But, well, I think it could use a woman's touch."

"It has a woman's touch. You just can't see it."

It did? Whose? Reluctantly, I slipped my hand from his warmth and touched my napkin to the corner of my mouth, trying not to look as crushed as

I felt that there might be someone in Manning's life. Then again, maybe *that* was why fate had brought me here tonight, to make the final snip I needed to cut myself free of him. I stood.

"Where are you going?" he asked.

"I'll help you clean up." I stacked our dishes to carry them back inside. "Then I should probably get home. It's a long drive, and it's getting dark."

In the kitchen, I turned on the faucet and plugged the sink, watching it fill with soapy water, as if it were just another night after dinner. I couldn't remember a recent time I'd been this comfortable somewhere. Not since New York. I didn't want to leave. I'd just arrived. What *was* closure, anyway? How exactly did one get it? Had it been enough to come and see that he was happy, that he'd moved on?

Once I'd started on the dishes, I felt Manning enter the room. "You don't need to do that," he said.

"I don't mind."

"Lake." He came up behind me, put his arms around mine, and sunk his hands in the water, lacing our fingers together. "I used to think about doing this when we had Sunday dinners," he said softly into my ear. "Holding your hand underwater for a few seconds, where no one could see."

My breathing shallowed as I stared at the fizzing suds. "Why didn't you?"

"I might've, if I'd thought either of us could handle it."

I inhaled, my back against his chest, our hands hidden by the foam. He massaged my palms, knuckles, wrists. "What are you doing?" I asked, suddenly aware of his breath on the back of my hair.

"You promised me you wouldn't bolt after dinner."

"What good would it do to stay? This . . . it's too hard, Manning. Being around you will always be too hard."

"I know it is, Birdy. I wanted to ease us into this. I thought you could come here for a nice, simple dinner and tell me all about your life. But it really never was easy with us, was it?"

Nobody could say we hadn't tried. We'd been pushed, and we'd pushed back. We'd wanted love to be enough, but it wasn't. I shook my head and whispered, "No."

"Nevertheless, I keep coming back to you. I can't give you up."

As good as it felt to hear that, I knew the truth— it wasn't that simple. If it had been, we'd have figured this out long ago. I took my hands from the water and turned to face him. "What about closure?"

"Don't want it," he said, stepping back. "Don't need it. Not even sure what it is."

Water dripped from our hands to our feet. I frowned. "But you said . . ."

"I had to get you here, Lake." He passed me a dishtowel. "I don't know what that bullshit was earlier about being over me, but I'm not over you. No fucking way—not now, not ever."

My throat closed. I couldn't breathe. He'd given me no warning, and now I was either going to choke or keel over, and all this would've been a waste. "It wasn't bullshit," I said, drying my hands. "I've been *stuck* in this place for over ten years. I've tried to be happy, to find myself, but I can't while you're in my way."

"Me?" His eyebrows wrinkled. "What are you talking about?"

The backs of my eyes burned with hot tears. "I know you didn't want this for me. All this pain. You wanted me to soar, and I can't—because of you. I have to let go. I have to let *you* go."

"And what did I tell you all those years ago? I won't be let go, Lake."

"It's too hard, Manning. I thought we were meant to be, but maybe we've been fighting against fate, not alongside it."

"I never believed in fate," he said. "You did. I want to fight, I'm ready, so let *me* do the fighting. I've made all of this for us."

I inhaled back a sob. "It's time for us to face the truth."

He shook his head in disbelief. "What truth?"

"That maybe you and I . . . we were never meant to be. There's no twisted destiny or fate or inevitable . . ." The next wave of tears was so painful to keep inside, I had to stop talking. I could hardly get the words out, but it had to be said if I had any shot at a satisfying life without him. "It's written up there in the sky," I said. "Our stars are permanently separated. There're no birds to carry us across the Milky Way to each other. I'm sorry you ever told me that story."

"So am I. It's a fantasy, but we're a reality. Don't you have any faith in me, Birdy? I don't need anyone to carry you to me. You must've always known, when I was ready, I would come for you."

"Then why *haven't* you?" I asked.

"I'm here now, Lake. I'm here for you because I still love you. Always."

"It's too late," I said. "I couldn't see a way to ever be happy without you, so I made the decision to move on."

"I don't believe you." He made two fists as he crossed his arms. "You may love *him*, I get that, it's my own fault, but he will never be what I am to you. You know that."

This was the Manning I remembered from New York. I didn't correct him. What was the point? If it wasn't Corbin, it would be someone else. "You can fall in love with someone else if you're willing to try," I told him. It was the same thing Corbin had said to me on the patio. "We both can."

"Nah, I can't," he said simply. "You're it for me."

My face warmed with all the hurt of the past few years. Was he not even going to try to let me go? Did he think this was easy for me? That I hadn't suffered enough? "You're it for me, too," I said angrily, "but I don't want to hurt anymore. I can't handle the possibility of losing you again."

"I'm not going anywhere, Lake. Do you really think I can ever move on from you? That if you give me your love, I won't fight every day to keep it?"

"What about the last four years? I asked. "You didn't fight for me then."

"Look around you. Look at what I've built. Who do you think this is for?"

My eyes went to the wine cooler, the state-of-the-art range, the painstakingly customized cabinetry. And back to Manning, where they stayed. "What do you mean?"

"I've spent the last few years away from you to become everything you needed me to be. I wasn't going to fuck this up again. You wanted me to follow my passion, so I did. To show you I had faith in us. To create a life that makes me happy, to provide not just for you, but for others."

My heart beat in my stomach as I continued to fight my tears. He had faith? Since when? "But I always had hope in us," I said. "I may have lost it, but you never had it."

"Look at this house and tell me I never had hope. I knew you might never see this—might not ever give me another chance—but I built it anyway." He pushed his hair back and released it, imploring me with his eyes. "I know you can learn to love someone else, but I've tried that, and I can tell you it'll never be what we've got. So I'm asking you to choose me. This, what you see around you, is our home. All I've done, and all I am is for this—for you."

Manning had built this for me? A house—a home? What scared me most about that was how much I wanted it to be true. I stood in the middle of a life I didn't want to leave behind, and he was telling me I didn't have to. I stood before the only man I'd ever loved and left and tried to forget as he offered me everything I'd ever wanted.

I wanted to take it, and I could see how things were different now, but how could I not be afraid? I couldn't fight my urge to cry anymore. I let the pain and fear and heartache of the past leak onto my cheeks.

"I know it's a lot to take in," Manning said quietly. "I don't want to scare you off, but I can't let you leave without knowing how I feel. Give me one thing tonight. Believe in me long enough to see the house I built on faith, for a family I might never have."

I covered my mouth and sobbed into my hand. Manning might've broken my heart and made mistakes, but he was too good of a man not to be a father and husband. "Don't say that."

"I might not get those things, Lake." He backed away from me. "There's only one person I'm meant to have a family with. If I can't, I won't."

He deserved a family more than anyone I knew, so I let that tether between us pull me along with him.

As he left the kitchen, I followed—past empty bedrooms, through the darkened house, until we were at the end of a hallway.

He opened a door for me, and I looked up at him as I walked into a room with walls painted midnight blue—or maybe it was the color of the ocean floor, or a starless New York night. By the enormous, honeyed-wood bedframe with matching nightstands, I could tell Manning had put thought into the master bedroom, just as he had the kitchen.

I walked closer to the footboard, which had been carved with a large bear on all fours in a forest, looking over his shoulder at the trees. My great bear. I didn't see much more than that because my vision blurred with more tears. If I could go back to that night where he'd shown me the constellations and then told me *no* when I'd tried to kiss him, would I change any of it? Would I have left it at that? I wasn't sure. There'd been so much heartbreak and only just enough love to keep me going. Could I do it all again? Was he asking me to?

I turned back to him. "It's been so long," I said, and I wasn't sure if I meant his absence or the time that'd passed since this had all started. "Things are different for each of us. Do we even know each other anymore?"

He came to me and wrapped an arm around my middle. My body locked up as he pulled me against him, but as I looked into his familiar, warm brown eyes, I thawed. It was like snapping together with my matching puzzle piece.

"Do we?" he asked as he cupped my jaw. "Does *this* part feel different?"

Ever since I'd left Manning's hotel room in New York, nothing had been quite right. I'd accomplished a great deal since then, and there was more on my horizon, but still, Manning's absence persisted in me. Even being here with him tonight had been so confusing—until now. I was no longer out of place. I was no longer just me. I was Manning's. His arms around me brought everything into focus. This was still, after all these years, all that mattered. I wondered if he'd known that since he'd seen me on the studio lot, and that was why he seemed so calm tonight.

"It's the same, isn't it?" he asked, running his hand up my back.

"Yes, but is that a good thing?"

"This was never the problem. It was that we had to grow up. You were right. I'm not the same person I was, and neither are you. I'm a better man. And you . . ." He dropped his forehead against mine, inhaling deeply. "I can make you happy. It kills me to hear that you think letting me go is the only way, but it isn't. I promise you. I can be the support you need to soar." He squeezed me closer. "I know you, I always have. That part remains the same—how *much* I love you. How you deserve that love. How I deserve you. How I'm . . ." He paused, sounding strangled. "Good enough to accept it. At least, I will fight to be, every day."

I reached up and traced my fingertip over the scar on his lip. So much hurt, so many wounds and bandages. In his own way, Manning had been looking out for me through all of it. "You've always been good in my eyes. I've waited so long for you to see it, too."

"I see it. My love for you is strong enough to make me good enough." As he said it, his lips got closer and closer, as if he couldn't help himself. It wasn't like Manning to be so vulnerable. He moved my hand over his heart. "I told you I can't go on without this. Since the day you left, I've been nothing but lonely."

"You're lonely?" I whispered.

"Every hour of every day. I miss the girl who meticulously makes monster sandwiches and who's afraid of Ferris wheels and horses but not of moving across the country by herself. I miss not being able to touch and kiss you as I please, the way I did for five . . . . fucking . . . *days* of my life. It was the best time I ever had, and if I die tomorrow, at least I had that time with you." Manning moved his thumb over my quivering chin. "Don't cry, Birdy."

I put my arms around his neck to meet his mouth and kiss him. I'd been lonely, too. I'd had the world within reach, but strangely, in the middle of nowhere, in a town that held some of my worst and most cherished memories, I was finally home.

8
LAKE

Night fell around us. I didn't want to leave Big Bear. I was a little tipsy from the wine, heady from Manning, and after years of meaningless human contact, I just wanted to be held. "Was it always your plan to end the tour in the bedroom?" I teased.

"It's not over yet." He smiled down at me. "You didn't say anything about the bed. Did you see?"

"My great bear."

He turned me back to the footboard, then switched on the overhead light. "Look closer."

Because the carvings were subtle in the warm wood, it took me a moment of squinting to notice the tiny bird perched on the bear's back. He wasn't looking over his shoulder at a tree. He was always watching, always protective of his . . . "Birdy."

"And where's she looking?" he asked.

"Up," I said. "At the stars."

I tilted my head back, half-expecting to see the universe right there on his ceiling the color of blueberries, but there was nothing.

"It's on the headboard," he said.

I wrinkled my nose at him, then went around the bed and moved one pillow. And then another and another. What I saw took my breath away—the night sky carved into his headboard. The constellations, the Summer Triangle, and both Ursas, Major and Minor—the great and little bears.

I'd been wrong earlier. The house wasn't Manning in every way. It was us.

I put my face in my hands and released a torrent of tears.

"Lake."

I shook my head. It was too much. "I can't."

"Is it too much?" he asked, reading my thoughts. "You know how I feel about you, don't you?" I continued shaking my head. "If you don't like Big Bear," he said, "we can go somewhere else. We can go back to New York. You said you wanted to travel—we can do that, too."

No, no, no. I wanted to be here. Right here. Home. For good. I couldn't say it, though. It was too good to be true.

"Lake?"

When Manning got no response, he sighed and picked me up, lifting me into his arms like a new bride. "What would I do with top-of-the-line appliances?" he asked, carrying me through the house. At least I assumed that's what we were doing—I couldn't see for all my crying. "I thought for sure you'd figure it out as soon as you walked in the kitchen," he added. "Did you see that cabinet in the corner? It's for your special guest dishes. We can leave it there or put it in the dining area. That's just one thing we can decorate and fill together."

I'd never felt so overwhelmed, not even when I'd received my acceptance packet to USC, and even then, part of my tears were the doubts I couldn't express with words. Tonight, I had no more doubts. Everything felt huge, but with Manning by my side again, and a career change in order, things also seemed as they should be.

I peeked through my fingers and wet lashes. Outside now, we headed for the small warehouse I'd noticed earlier. My cowboy boots swung as he carried me, and his heart beat near my cheek as I rested on his chest. There wasn't much to the backyard, just a clearing before the forest, the pine trees making dark triangles in the moonlight. "What . . . what goes back here?" I asked.

"You tell me, Dr. Dolittle," he said.

Finally, a smile broke through. "Animals?"

"If that's what you call those rescue mutts." He winked before he set me down to open the shed's sliding barn door. "Here's where I kept my sanity all these years."

Manning's workshop could've housed a small army. I stepped onto an unfinished concrete floor, sawdust under my boots. From sanders to circular saws to vises, the equipment alone intimidated me. Between the work benches, lumber, and planks and slabs piled in corners and against walls, it smelled woodsier inside than the forest behind it. "Where's all the furniture?" I asked.

"I sold it." He pointed to a few half-finished pieces, clustered in the center. "These are my current commissions, due next month."

I turned in a circle. These were his things. His tool belt and goggles and red bandana, knotted and hung on a nail. His sketches on the walls, his sweat in the air.

"I know it doesn't look like much," he said, grouping pencils on a work table, dusting off the surface with his palm. "But it's what I have. In here, I create things I hope my clients will love. It's my escape from everything else."

"Like what?" I asked, facing him again.

"My family, my past. My time in solitary." He picked up a hardhat to hang it on the wall. "But not you. Try as I did, I couldn't help that you were on my mind enough that I had to make pieces for you, too."

"Why?" I asked. I looked around, but there was so much, I couldn't even see it all. The love and sweat and tears and hope he'd given and lost, fought against and for. "Why'd you do all this?"

"I haven't always been good with words. This was one way to show my love for you, and my commitment to our future."

I'd carried hope for us in my heart so long. I thought I'd lost it, but he'd picked it up and put it on his shoulders until the finish line. The evidence was all around me. I walked through Manning's escape, awed by the beauty of his work. The care and love that obviously went into what he'd created. He'd made his bed in here, under the warm lights, out in the middle of nowhere. *Our* bed.

Manning came and took my hand, sliding it over the uneven surface of an armoire. "I haven't sanded it yet," he said. "Feel that?"

I had a moment of déjà vu, some time when he'd asked me that before and it'd been more than a simple question. Did I feel it, the coarseness on my palm, the electricity of his skin on mine? Did I feel him?

"I feel it."

He led me out behind the shed to an area hidden from the house. A motion sensor light flickered on above the door, revealing a small but sturdy-looking dinghy. "You're building a *boat*?" I asked.

"I'm trying. It's my first attempt." He walked around the perimeter. It was the first time since dinner he took his eyes off me for more than a few seconds. "One of my favorite projects yet. I only get to work on it on the weekends."

"Does it work?" I asked.

"Work?" He climbed in to sit on the bench closest to the stern, running his hands along the inside edges. "What do you mean?"

"I don't know." I blushed a little, and he grinned ear to ear. Even though he was sitting, we were almost eyelevel. I hadn't seen a smile like that from him in so long. Maybe ever. He lit up the night, while I just tried to focus on a coherent thought. "Does it, like, float, I guess?"

He laughed. "I sure hope it will when I'm done. Not looking for a repeat of our night on the lake. It nearly killed me."

"I remember it differently."

"Yeah?" His expression sobered. "How do you remember it?"

Since he'd asked, I took a breath and told him the truth for all the times I'd had to keep it to myself. "I remember stripping down for you in the moonlight. Feeling turned on by every last thing, from the water against my skin to knowing your eyes were on me to the mud between my toes when I curled them. I wanted nothing more in the world than for you to touch me. I wanted you so bad, Manning. I would've given anything."

He took my forearm, tugging me closer to the side of the boat. "You asked why I did all this, Lake? I did it for you. I made this boat to take you on the water."

My heart was in my throat. I wasn't sure I'd ever get used to Manning admitting he wanted me, and it was clear to me why he never could before. Once he'd let himself love me, he did it with a ferocity that would've changed me as a girl. That would've worried my family and friends, and changed the course of my future. At some point, Manning had decided I was the only one for him, so he'd built an empire for a queen he didn't have. "You're going to make me cry again," I whispered.

"Don't. I can't stand it. Come in here so I can kiss all those tears off your cheeks for good."

That night in the truck was still clear as day to me. How I'd ached for him and his sister, how scared I'd been when the policeman had pulled us over, how I'd desired Manning enough to tempt him from the moral ground where he'd dug in his heels. "Will you kiss me other places?" I asked.

He wet his lips. "Like I said, I built this to *take you* on the lake . . . the way I probably should've years ago."

His large hand both warmed me and sent goosebumps down to my ankles. "You mean when I was sixteen?" I teased. "God, I'd give anything to go back to that moment just to tell your twenty-three-year-old self what you're saying eleven years later."

"I was a fool." With a grunt, he pulled me hard enough that I had to decide if I was getting in with

485

him or staying on dry land, where it was safe. "That side of the boat's called the starboard," he said. "Now climb over the starboard side and into my lap."

"Manning . . ."

"This is it, Lake. I'm offering you everything I have. And I'm taking what I've always wanted."

That was enough to get me in the boat. I held the front of my skirt and climbed in to stand between his legs.

Looking up at me, he said, "You know this sweater you've got on is see-through?"

"I had no idea," I lied.

"Right. Spin around for me."

I turned away from him to face the bow. He sat me on his lap and ran both hands up the inside of my sweater, lifting it until I pulled it over my head.

"Lake," he murmured, discarding my bra, moving my hair over one shoulder. He smoothed his callused palms down my shoulder blades, my spine, massaging my back, my upper arms. "You're shaking again," he said. "Always shaking the first time."

"Just with you," I said. The light above the barn door clicked off. "It's been so long."

"I needed a woman's touch. And you, you need a man's touch, don't you, Birdy?"

I shuddered, cold and turned on. He slid his warm hands around to my front and held my breasts. "I just need you," I said.

"Is it over with him?"

"Who?"

"Whoever he is. Whoever has you right now. Corbin or someone else, doesn't matter."

I stood, the light came on, and I turned to straddle him. "Don't you see, Manning? You're the only one who's ever had me. I tried. I dated, I had sex, I had boyfriends. I even had a marriage proposal. But you're the only one who's ever had *me*."

"Christ, Lake. Give a guy some warning before you say that shit. Someone *proposed?*"

"I dated a guy from a hit TV show for six weeks, and he tried to whisk me off to Vegas." I put my hands on his shoulders and lowered my voice. "I'll tell you a secret. The more famous people get, the weirder they are."

Manning gripped me under the ass, pulling me onto him until my skirt was around my waist. "I hate that you were around all those fucking weirdos without me."

"At least I didn't become one of them." I smiled. "I don't think."

"You scared me earlier when you said you had a meeting about your contract. All day I was thinking you'd be tied to L.A. a few more years or that you'd get stuck in something you didn't want. But I should've known you'd figure it out." He wrapped his arms around me, holding me tightly to him as he looked me in the eye. "What do you want, Lake? I'll give it to you."

"Just to be here," I said.

"If *I* proposed, would you say yes?"

Again, it was too much. I pushed at his chest, overwhelmed, but he kept me fastened to him. His heart beat strongly against my palms. Or maybe it was my own heart that was racing, vibrating us both.

"Would you?" he repeated. "I know you have obligations and work and travel and now school, but when it's time, will you come here and be my wife?"

I couldn't help that with those words, my mind went to his past. "Did you ever have anything close to this with anyone else?" I whispered.

"Never. You're my first, Lake. If I had loved a hundred girls before you, you'd still be the first. I don't know how else to describe it. You make me unafraid to face not just my mistakes, but my childhood home. I don't know how to be a father after what I've lost, after the example I've had, but *you* make me want to try." He squeezed my ribcage, dropping his forehead to my naked chest. "Because you never stopped loving me, I can forgive myself. I want you to be my wife, but I can wait, and I will, as long as it takes."

He shifted me on his lap. I could no longer ignore the hardness straining against me, and my stomach tightened. I reached between us to open his belt. "You know it's only ever been you."

"Is that a yes?"

"When did you get so impatient?" I pushed his pants down and took him in my hand. "You wouldn't touch me for six years, and now you can't wait five minutes for an answer?"

"I've waited much longer, Birdy. You know that. A lifetime, it feels like."

"Whose fault is that?" I licked my palm and closed my hand over his head to stroke the length of him.

He closed his eyes. "You know everything I built, I imagined fucking you in or on. Our bed. This boat. Every surface in the house I made to fit us." He glanced down, and I watched him as he watched my hand around him. "Put me inside you."

I lifted up, not bothering to remove my skirt. He pushed my underwear aside, and I took my time sinking onto him. I had to go slow. He filled me inch by inch, the stretch so exquisite that I could only drop my head back and beg the stars for mercy.

But mercy wasn't theirs to give. Manning took my waist to guide me up and then back down. I removed his hands to see if he'd let me take charge. "Sit back," I said.

He relaxed against the stern, stretching his arms along the sides. Slowly, feeling every sensation, *I* made love to *him* for the first time. He took off his shirt and I leaned on him to swivel my hips faster, my hands looking a doll's, small and pale against his sprawling, tan torso.

"Fuck, Lake. Let me touch you. This is torture."

Though I didn't mind torturing him all that much, I consented. "All right, Great Bear. You can put your paws on me."

I could've sworn he growled as he stood in one swift motion. With my legs wrapped around him, he stepped out of the boat and lay me on a workbench that seemed to be made for us, only wide enough for me and just tall enough for him. The wood's roughened surface scraped against my back. After Manning's restraint all these years, I welcomed the desperate way he grabbed my hips, his strangled groans. Manning fucked me like I hadn't been fucked since New York, a mix of love and anger, adoration and profanity. He bent over me and took my mouth the same way, his fingers between my legs sending me to the moon.

"Tell me what you're thinking," he breathed.

I squeezed my arms around his neck as he rubbed my clit faster, with more pressure. "*Now?*"

His gaze burned. "I have always, from the day I saw you, wanted to know all your thoughts."

I was exposed underneath him, flayed by his hand so many times over the years. "I think you feel so good . . ." I whisper-panted, "and so right . . . that I . . . can't . . . stand it."

I writhed under him as I climaxed. He held me to him with a hand around the back of my neck, breathing into my mouth. I felt the lock and release of his muscles as he came, too, the brokenness of his thrusts, and then the slippery way he filled me.

I ran my fingers through the sides of his hair as he hovered over me, staring while he labored for breath, looking almost pained. "Manning?" I asked, concerned.

"I love you, Lake," he choked out.

Although it wasn't the first time he'd said it, it felt that way all over again. I smoothed the droplets of sweat from his hairline, holding his stare. "I know."

"Thank God. You had me for a minute there." He kissed my forehead and eased out of me. Rounding the workbench, he sat me up to run a hand over my sensitive back. "You're all red."

"I'm perfect," I said.

He hugged me from behind with one arm and urged my legs open to touch me. "What are you doing?" I asked, fascinated by the gentle way he massaged me.

After a few seconds, I felt a surge of wetness. His fingers came back slick. "You don't know what this does to me. I could have you again right now just knowing you're filled with me."

My heart skipped a beat hearing the possessiveness in his voice. *Protect, provide, mate.* I hadn't forgotten. "I feel the same."

"But I keep forgetting to ask before I do that . . . are you on birth control?"

I relaxed against his back. "This time I am, yes."

"Figures." He nipped the shell of my ear. "We'll have to do something about that."

I rolled my eyes. "*Manning.*"

He laughed in my ear. "Too soon?"

I dropped the back of my head against his chest to look at him. "For a baby? I think so."

He kissed the top of my hair. "It doesn't have to be now. When we're ready."

He said it with such confidence, it was almost as if it were already true. Manning and I would be a family.

"Well, fuck." He came back around the bench, buckling his belt. "I didn't plan for all this. I thought I'd bring you here and convince you to give me a second chance. Now we've gone and had sex in a boat."

I smiled, watching as he picked up my bra and clothing. "What was that you said earlier? All paths lead to here."

He came and stood between my legs, tilting my head up by my chin. "Let's go inside so I can make love to you properly, over and over until either the bed breaks or we do."

"I don't want to break the bed. I love it and plan to sleep in it for many years to come."

He raised his eyebrows. "So you're saying . . ." He dug his hand into his pocket, then got down on a knee and showed me the mood ring. Not only had he kept it all these years, but he'd had it in his pocket during our whole conversation. Just like that last morning at camp. "Lake Dolly Kaplan . . ." He took my left hand and slid the ring onto my fourth finger.

"Wait," I said, incredulous. "I didn't even answer."

He laughed. "It's just temporary, until I can find you the perfect ring."

I bent over the bench, holding his face. "It is perfect," I said softly. "Everything you give me is perfect."

"So is that a yes?"

I sighed happily. "It's not a no." I looked him in the eyes, stripping away the playfulness between us so he'd understand I was serious. My great bear, my one true love, the rock I'd clung to in the angry ocean that'd brought us here, the one I feared wasn't finished with us yet. "I love you."

"Then come to bed with me."

"I will. I just need a minute to myself."

"Whatever you need, Birdy." He kissed my forehead and took my things inside.

I looked at the ring on my hand as it fell over, top heavy. It was still a little too big, too clunky and inconvenient, just like my love for Manning. It was also a deep purple I'd never seen, and though I didn't know for sure, I guessed that must be the color of happiness.

My legs swung under the bench as I listened to crickets chirp and frogs burp and owls hoot all around the woods until the shed light shut off again, plunging me into the dark. I wondered how far the lake was, and if Manning and I would spend summer days there, soaking in the sun, and each other, until night fell. Until the black lake water stilled and let the moon shimmer on its glassy surface.

I hopped off the bench and walked back toward the house, stopping where it was darkest—where the stars shone brightest. Wherever Manning went, I'd follow. If he wanted to live amongst the constellations, I'd move with him around an immovable universe, guided by starlight, and when we got separated, fate would light the path back to each other. Because you couldn't move the stars—Manning and I were inevitable—and as I stood in awe of the infinite night sky, I thanked the heavens for that.

The Beginning

BOOK FOUR IN THE
SOMETHING IN THE WAY SERIES:

LAKE + MANNING

LEARN MORE AT
WWW.JESSICAHAWKINS.NET/SOMETHINGINTHEWAY

ACKNOWLEDGMENTS

Thank you to the best team a girl could ask for. For *Move the Stars* in particular, top billing is reserved for my editor, Elizabeth London, who guided me through some very murky waters (and somehow managed not to toss me overboard). Elizabeth, there's no fate to acknowledge here—you pushed me until the last deliberate word (or *The Beginning*, thank you for that), and that's why everything is as it should be.

At some point, my eyes crossed, and I passed the baton to Katie of Underline This Editing and Becca of Evident Ink, who helped me mold and fine-tune the end of this trilogy into what *Move the Stars* is now. Then, the award for acute attention to detail goes to Tamara Mataya Editing for proofreading. Thank you, ladies, for showing me the light in so many places!

Cover love goes directly to Letitia of R.B.A. Designs, Lauren of Perrywinkle Photography, and models Miranda McWhorter and Chase Williams. Throughout the series, you've all brought my Lake and Manning to life in a way I can only hope to do with pen and paper. That can also be said of the talented audiobook narrators Andi Arndt and Zachary Webber, who held nothing back and embraced these characters so listeners could live this story start to finish.

Special mention must be made of Serena McDonald: you've kept my head on straight (or, at a manageable angle) during the release of each book and in between. Thank you for *manning* the ship when I couldn't, specifically the discussion groups along with Bethany Castañeda, with whom I share a 4-year friend-iversary the same month of the *Move the Stars* release!

And to the ladies of the SITW, SES, and MTS spoiler rooms— you might not have seen it firsthand, but your excitement and devotion to these characters and their tumultuous love drove me on a daily basis—not to just finish, but to make the story better in every sense. As Manning ached to be good enough for his Lake, I strove to deliver a story worthy of you all! In that same vein, it has been nothing but great times in my reader group, The Penthouse, and I'll say what I've said before—it's my author happy place.

Of course, the thank-you list is endless. To everyone who had a hand in this, including bloggers and their enthusiastic promotion and the authors who took time from their busy schedules to read and honor me with a blurb—cheers to you!

TITLES BY
JESSICA HAWKINS
LEARN MORE AT JESSICAHAWKINS.NET

SLIP OF THE TONGUE
THE FIRST TASTE
YOURS TO BARE

SOMETHING IN THE WAY SERIES
SOMETHING IN THE WAY
SOMEBODY ELSE'S SKY
MOVE THE STARS
LAKE + MANNING

THE CITYSCAPE SERIES
COME UNDONE
COME ALIVE
COME TOGETHER

EXPLICITLY YOURS SERIES
POSSESSION
DOMINATION
PROVOCATION
OBSESSION

ABOUT THE AUTHOR

JESSICA HAWKINS is a *USA Today* bestselling author known for her "emotionally gripping" and "off-the-charts hot" romance. Dubbed "queen of angst" by both peers and readers for her smart and provocative work, she's garnered a cult-like following of fans who love to be torn apart...and put back together.

She writes romance both at home in New York and around the world, a coffee shop traveler who bounces from café to café with just a laptop, headphones, and a coffee cup. She loves to keep in close touch with her readers, mostly via Facebook, Instagram, and her mailing list.

CONNECT WITH JESSICA

Stay updated & join the
JESSICA HAWKINS Mailing List
www.JESSICAHAWKINS.net/mailing-list

www.amazon.com/author/jessicahawkins
www.facebook.com/jessicahawkinsauthor
twitter: @jess_hawk